MY WORLD
IS NOT
OF THIS KINGDOM

JOÃO DE MELO

TRANSLATED BY GREGORY RABASSA

For Maria João and António Lobo Antunes:
Friends of yesterday and forever more

JOÃO DE MELO

MY WORLD IS NOT
OF THIS KINGDOM

INTRODUCTION BY KATHERINE VAZ

TRANSLATED FROM THE PORTUGUESE
BY GREGORY RABASSA

ALIFORM PUBLISHING
MINNEAPOLIS

ALIFORM PUBLISHING
is part of The Aliform Group
117 Warwick Street SE/Minneapolis, MN USA 55414
information@aliformgroup.com   www.aliformgroup.com

First published in the United States of America by
Aliform Publishing, 2003
by arrangement with Dr. Ray-Güde Mertin, Literarische Agentur
Bad Homburg, Germany

Chapters 1 & 2 of this translation were first published in the
April 2000 *MARGIN: Exploring Modern Magical Realism*

Library of Congress Control Number
2003107430

ISBN 0-9707652-3-1

Set in Times New Roman
Cover art by Marco Lamoyi, *Primer sueño de Nabucodonosor* (detail)
Cover design by C.Fox Design

CONTENTS

this howling

You are holding a book that Gregory Rabassa translated because it was the most astonishing novel he had read since *One Hundred Years of Solitude*. He undertook this huge artistic task at his own insistence, before (long before, as it happens) a publisher in the United States could be found.

The voyage to our shores of *My World Is Not of This Kingdom* is over a decade in the making; in terms of stretched hopes and pure duration, this is not unlike the journey that my relatives once mustered from the Azores to America or bestirred your families from their own origins. I am reminded of one of my father's jokes: When someone asked why his sense of direction was so terrible, since the Portuguese were famous for navigational prowess, he replied, "Navigation is just wandering forever lost until you run up against something you like."

And so *My World Is Not of This Kingdom* is home at last, brimming with sea air, profoundly welcomed.

João de Melo (the "j" in Portuguese is pronounced like the American "j," not the aspirated "h" in Spanish) is the prize-winning author of *Gente Feliz com Lágrimas* (a splendidly dual meaning: *People Happy with Tears*, or *Happy People with Tears*), in its nineteenth edition now in Portugal, and translated into six foreign translations (but not English); it's been a theater piece, television mini-series, and internationally distributed film.

ii

But *My World Is Not of This Kingdom* is his masterpiece. It garnered most of his nation's literary awards immediately upon its release (including the Grand Prize of the Association of Portuguese Authors, the City of Lisbon Prize, and the Fernando Namora Prize). The author himself felt it lodged him in the literature of his country.

This is a boiling, shocking story; it roars over the interstices of the sentences into a baroque impasto, rather like the volcanic creation of the Azores themselves. Language here is applied with a palette knife, not a thin brush. I cannot name another novel in which a howl is more ferociously unleashed; you may never read a fiercer depiction of soul-crushing, body-mutating poverty.

Though it would be a mistake to classify the novel as merely Azorean, some details about the islands might help, since they exist to most Americans only as mid-Atlantic flecks on a map.

The geography alone embodies isolation—and then the isolation delves farther into a bag of tricks. It surprises people that the nine islands (São Miguel, Terceira, Pico, Faial, São Jorge, Graciosa, Santa Maria, Flores, Corvo) are not exactly cheek by jowl; nowadays a plane ride best spans the archipelago's fog-obscured, broken spine. Inter- and intra-island rivalries seem inherent, along with such a legacy of emigration that there are many times the number of Azorean-Americans (or Luso-Americans, "Lusitania" being the old Roman term for Portugal) as there are resident Azoreans in what shimmers like a wonderland: Whelk and limpet shells form village signs, and azaleas wheeze out perfume. I know of a gazebo where words whispered into a far end of the dome enter, loudly, after a time lapse, the ear of someone on the opposite side. At night, children are wished "pink dreams."

The hydrangeas are a bracing purple (girls wear them as shoulder puffs during parades), the fields offer a meld of jade or primavera green, the water glows like heated sapphires, and sky-blue tiles accent white-washed walls, but sudden upheaval and violence loom—rumble in—via storm, tidal wave, volcanic eruption.

And kept in a confined space, humans seethe entrenched, disappointment metastasizes, and beauty refuses to save us.

(João de Melo, a longtime resident of Lisbon but a native of São Miguel, offers a soaring antidote to this at the novel's end.) I recall Russell Banks' portrayal, in *Affliction*, of New Hampshire: "…in spite of its loveliness, there is an overabundance of madness and despair…So much deprivation and so much natural beauty combine in a life to make it sad and angry beyond belief to an outsider." When *My World*'s José-Maria returns from his travels, he can't imagine a place more beautiful than the Azores, even in its solitude, "and at the same time so many people suffering on it for all their lives when this could have been the paradise of our first parents in the Bible."

Even the wells derive from "clay kneaded with blood," and God is sensed as a "seaquake." Ailments are often psychological and emotional: Island fever, for instance, is wholly misunderstood by Americans; we think it's a sort of wanderlust, a craving for expansion. The true definition is that it's a contraction, a fever of *turning inward*, an almost molecular expansion of only the readily apparent. This is why, in the opening pages, we meet children who took "years to go down and come to know the sea. They would contemplate it from afar, a bluish ribbon." The clerical stoles may be embroidered with marine animals, and Azoreans to this day are reputed to be the best whalers and fishermen ever born, but in massive numbers they turned their backs to the ocean and became dairymen and farmers. Certainly the majority of those who settled in California, where I'm from, were of this island-cooked temperament. And California was their self-same dream made vast.

A crucial historical reason for much of the exodus is that back when sailing ships rounded the Cape of Good Hope loaded with treasure—and, more valuably, treasure-locating maps—the winds blew them to the Azores. After a stop for repairs or trade or rest, sailors would ride longitudinal gusts back to Europe. This made for a virtual turkey-shoot for pirates; the remnants of lookout posts still dot the beaches. *My World* therefore cites the intrusive prophecies of João-Lázaro as inciting a rebellion similar to one "against the corsairs and invaders and plunderers who had threatened the parish in other times."

Then all hail the steamship, and no need for a stopping-over. There followed an advent of redoubled solitude, and death of industry, and emigration.

Though many Americans appreciate that Church and State are the twin lock and bolt of many cultures, it's nearly impossible to convey the rusted-in-place vise they create. João de Melo lets fly his most torrential rage at priests, "that fraternity of owls," especially the syphilitic Father Governo, "the ugliest animal in creation…(with) the ugliness of a skull squashed by the hoof of a buffalo that had wandered off from the herd." Why not ignore the priests, seek other avenues? It's said that Americans don't solve their problems as much as flee from them—but what if there's nowhere to run? What if, instead, you're in a tiny, water-sealed colony where first the criminals got shipped in to till the land, and then priests arrived to yoke the louts (and carve the scratched land into parishes), and then the government calmly swept in to assume its share? My dictionary defines the Azores as a Portuguese possession since the fifteenth century "but with partial autonomy." What half-buried struggles writhe in that neither-fish-nor-fowl description!

The book's dramatic thread almost of necessity deals with land usurpation. (When my great-aunt was on her deathbed in Terceira, a priest convinced her to sign over some of her holdings to the church. Once upon a time, this anecdote was endemic.) João-Maria de Medeiros emerges as the remarkable hero of *My World*, along with his wife Sara and two sons, José-Maria and Jorge-Maria, because he quietly, simply, but definitely protests when Mayor Guilherme José Bento begins to demand land deeds as a tithe throughout the village of Rozário in the parish of Achadinha. João-Maria is aware that his protests will doom him to shape-shifting ruin.

If Father Governo is the first head of Cerberus, then the Mayor is the second. Also known as Goraz "because of his bulging eyes and heavy elephant-fish body," he dreams up new decrees while fornicating, a pastime he churns into violence; he prefers sex when his wife is menstruating because he's excited by blood—the novel is fleshy and direct. His lust eventually kills her, just as his fury reduces João-

Maria de Medeiros into such a gnawing beast of hunger that one meaning of the title blooms like a sinister lichen: The destitute receive the scolding—sad slobs, they have to be reminded of their own religion!—that poverty is a glorious gift, because it insures that their kingdom will be in heaven.

My impulse is to go on at length about the over-the-top, spellbinding imagery and the chain of events that lay out in print some of the most riveting, passionate evocations of a descent into penury and degradation and a thirst for revenge ever fit into the confines of words. Here is the book's spewing center, its stunning emotional core. When Sara digs up a dead dog to feed her family, when the soused João-Maria turns into a rat, it behooves us not to seek comfort by limiting these scenes to metaphor. When grief pours in (I'll let the reader discover the tragedy that causes João-Maria to hurtle back into a patchy semblance of life), when haunting and sexual torment overflow the cauldron, just when we expect the lava to engulf all enemies...a strange, ingenious cooling fixes the story into quite a different artifact, as sweet in its way as toys and kitchenware uncovered in the ashes of Pompeii: We're reminded that João-Maria's original courage was based upon a wish to rise above the earth's notorious clamp and rules, a desire for flight as light-drenched as that of the islands' hovering seabirds called the *açores* (the Luso word for the Azores, "*açor*" being the singular form). Can war and revenge be viewed—thereby defeated—from the heavens?

It would lessen the drive of the book, though, to be satisfied with a simple airy summation. Love that lifts us from the mire is indeed as close as we can come to a cure: But it must be of a potent stripe, practical, down-to-earth, and adamant about justice. When João-Maria's son, José-Maria, falls in love with Maria Água, they share a communion of exotic food, "wheat bread and honey...mulberry jam, fried bacon...carob beans and almonds." One must not only stanch hunger, but elevate satiety into beauty. In contrast to the sick fucking of Goraz, one must funnel love into a redemption that rolls up its sleeves. José-Maria cleans and restores the actual house of his father, and seeks to awaken his brother, Jorge-Maria, whose arrested growth has him fucking...no, I won't unveil this delectably horrific bestiality…surely (I hope) a *sui generis* scream of loneliness.

Because love doesn't merely float, removed: It heals, it polishes the floor, it rescues starving bodies. A portion of scorn is reserved for the poet and dentist Francisco Heitor—a minor character, a bit of mange on Cerberus's fur—for being smug and lofty about his epigrams against the government. He's a dispenser of "torture and poetry." But he does nothing to equal João-Maria or José-Maria's *activated* courage.

The playing out of that courage demands both a going out into the world and a touching back. When José-Maria returns to Rozário from his travels with Maria Água, he's seen that mortality and atrocities of power are everywhere, but he's also been able to defeat island fever. He proclaims to his spirit-throttled father that "death wasn't darkness; it was never having been able to see a little farther in the distance."

Cadete the Healer is thereby revealed as the surprising third head of Cerberus. Despite his dedicated years of study, he's accused of being, along with the priest and mayor, one of the "three fatal diseases" thanks to his superstitions and isolation. When the revelation comes that there already exists a thing out there called chemotherapy, his well-meaning but picayune medical musings, his life's monastic focus, collapse into dust.

The father, João-Maria, insists that he no longer has any enemies, but the son calmly insists that those responsible for wounding the family must pay. Is this a valiant call for justice, instead of resigning one's self to finding it after death? Or is it a warning that the cycles of struggle will never creak to a halt?

Probably both. We are told that the father dissolves wearily into eternity with "no pain…no jubilation, not even the shadow of any use." If love is a form of thinking expansively, then the imagination might also be required to achieve a type of world-love. (A curious distinction exists between the American view of the imaginary, that it's "something made up," and the Latin one, that it's a route for uncovering the truth, that imagination should lead any concrete inquiry into concealed facts.)

A further connection between love and imagination might be detected in the title. "My world" is neither the lofty plateau of fools like poet-dentist Francisco Heitor, nor the preached heaven and political domain of oppressors; it's a bird-realm in which the unrestrained can fly away or alight or hover where the white sun, salt, and dissolved bones mix into a blank page. The birds are in the kingdoms of air and land, and their flight-paths draw lines in the blankness.

Rozário, according to the author, is a mytho-poetic invention, his own microcosm like Gabriel García Márquez's Macondo, a Petri dish that breeds a universal cosmography, but this novel is entirely his own. Though set in the Azores, João de Melo's particular vision is for us all. He's fascinated by how the Azores might expand into Portugal, then Europe, then the Globe; he's also captivated by the idea of America. "America is always present in my books, either directly or indirectly," he told me, "because it's a constant destination for the Portuguese, for Azoreans. And the USA exerts not only a literary and cultural influence, but a reality and presence that can alter or subvert the world order."

The plane that crashes in *My World*—outside dominions slamming into the Azores—is American. The Bosch-like hell of the landscape offers evidence of America's thunderous and devastating force, but the accident is primarily a test of tenderness toward the dead, a call against segregated nationalism: "*Oh my God, my sweet God…*an old couple had held hands and squeezed their fingers together to the point they were melded. Their names most certainly must have been Jim and Debbie, judging from the oval shape still showing on their lips….a (dead) girl was sitting on a log…a girl like that must have had a blue name like that of the angels who come down from the leaves of fig trees and fly inside the Earth."

As for João de Melo, I first met him a dozen years ago at a conference on Lusophone literature in California. I already knew his reputation not only as a writer's writer, but as someone of enormous popular appeal: He's composed essays, short stories, poems, and travel books in addition to novels, joining his generation in forging a sensibility emergent from the Vietnam-like quagmire of the African wars and the collapse of

viii

Salazar's fascism. João's service as an army nurse in Africa is at root of what he considers his most terrifying and pungent book, *Autópsia de Um Mar de Ruínas* (Autopsy of a Sea of Ruins).

I soon discovered that he's that rarity—a successful author of depth and affection; ours is an abiding friendship. Whenever I visited Lisbon, he or his wife, Tita, were there to pick me up at the glass-walled airport. Once we ate lunch at the last residence of the poet Fernando Pessoa, now a museum and restaurant, and with bemusement shared *Bacalhau Espíritual*—Spiritual Codfish!—a creamed fish-and-potatoes dish with carrot shards for a thready bloom of sun color.

I first included an excerpt from *My World Is Not of This Kingdom* in a survey on contemporary Portuguese authors several years ago in *The Iowa Review*, but it's taken Aliform Publishing, with its specialty in Latin American prose, to let sail home to us this dazzling trophy of global literature. I'm grateful that they've expanded its availability to an English-speaking audience, and to Gregory Rabassa for his artistry. In this book a "perfect moment" is coined as "a divine madness that's never repeated." And divinely, madly filled—heavenly, earthly—this by rights would have to be called a perfect book.

Katherine Vaz
New York City, June 2003

(*Katherine Vaz is the author of the novels* Saudade *and* Mariana *and the collection of short stories* Fado & Other Stories. *A Briggs-Copeland Lecturer at Harvard University, she has been an NEA Fellow and was a member of the U.S. Presidential Delegation that inaugurated the American exhibition at the World's Fair/Expo 98 in Lisbon.*)

LA MORT DES PAUVRES
C'est un Ange qui tient dans ses doigts magnétiques
Le sommeil et le don des rêves extatiques,
Et qui refait le lit des gens pauvres et nus;

C'est la gloire des Dieux, c'est le grenier mystique,
C'est la bourse du pauvre et sa patrie antique,
C'est le portique ouvert sur les Cieux inconnus!
                    Charles Baudelaire, from *Les Fleurs du Mal*

Nenhum robinson crusoé povoa a minha ilha
A terra é pequena e não é grande a gente
Desde o tormento metafísico de antero
até aos dies irae destes dias
em que mãos desabrocha algum possível portugal?
          Ruy Belo

And here is death,
the widespread, tiny, and afflicted death of a people
with its mice and spiders;
its proof in the vast weeping of animals and the white sea
of Cadete the Healer;
the ironic syphilis of his holiness Father Governo,
on through the tale of Sara the Saint, and all
of them—up to the events of the life and death and
resurrection of João-Lázaro, the first beggar and
in time a Biblical prophet of the Azores.

1

AT THAT TIME THE PARISH OF OUR LADY OF THE
ROSARY OF ACHANDINHA WAS NOTHING BUT A FLY
SPECK, AS IF A FINGER HAD TOUCHED THE ALMOST
ALWAYS GREENISH BACK OF THE ATLANTIC AND
the memory of the Founders still trickled down across the
basalt pavement and the marine moss. The grimy seaside
houses, with their thatched roofs and adobe walls made of a
cement in every way like clay kneaded with blood, descended
in three rows to the bottom of the valley. There they mingled
along twisting paths where the passage of a team of oxen
hitched to the traces of a cart would have been a miracle. The
first mules had been domesticated by force, some through
restraint, others by inexorable castration, and now they bore
on their bony backs the scarce stones for grinding fava beans
and corn for the watermills of Achada and Salga. They had
the soft, afflicted eyes of all nature that is condemned to the
servitude of men. Their damp, heroic animal sadness would
not be long in sticking to the wall of things as well. And
clinging to the wall of things it continued in its dampness,
even passing through the respiration of the stones, and
began to devour the landscape. The landscape had been
largely devoured when the sadness also reached the mouths
of people and immediately released the white smell of saliva
into their breath. Women began to read the Bible then, as quick
in their movements as bees around the last orange blossom.
The hour of the destruction of the world was approaching,
according to them, because the pale sweat of the Apocalypse

3

was already flowing from their cold-colored hands. And someone observing their bellies trembling with affliction could not have helped but suspect that the women had inherited in their flesh not only the feat of dying very soon, but the volcanic fate of the earth itself. They'd received it, furthermore, at the first moment of the world's creation, when the water of the earth forever entered the days of their despair.

You don't know what Despair is? It's

WIDESPREAD DEATH

the tiny, timeless and widespread death without a body; the warm, wandering, and immense voice of death, absent and announced, that returns in us to places remote and without origin. It awakens, it flies about dispersed and widespread and is inside others, and only exists in them. That was how I came to know despair:

It was at the time when stones had the shape of dinosaur eggs. The skeletons of small animals, which had disappeared until then, were disinterred from inside seashells and fossil rocks. All of that had the remote and perpetual look of water, because the volcanic craters themselves, peopled with the nests of brown mice and salamanders, showed ridges worn smooth by the period of the great rains, all of them dating back to the time of the patriarch Noah. The cuts, the escarpments, the cliffs along the seacoast and the crags without memory were inscribed on the bones and body of that land-Island as if someone had long ago shaped its uncertain and discontinuous surface on a lathe. As for its denizens and things, they lay forgotten within the uterus of insomnia, for they were creatures watched over even in their cadaverous and cold nudity.

More than a century had passed since the peopling of that region when the great volcanic crater received the first nomads from the sea, arriving ahead of storms and tempests and threading inland with their gullets dry from all the helpless shouting. When they arrived there they were a famished and bedraggled people who quickly lost the memory of their previous and nameless places, quite prepared to be grateful for that newfound land of salvation. One day, under the proud command of their captain, Diogo Deniz Faria de Paes, a man quite wisely sent by the King and the Royal Princes in search of the distant whereabouts of God and his bishops, they set foot on the stones of Pesqueiro, the fishing grounds, settled down in tents and caves, forming a barrier against the sea winds, and there they founded the parish.

It is supposed, however, that the fate of such people was to be written down in everlasting form on the basalt itself, since the memory of stone outlasts the time the stone endures. The shape of the boulders, beaten by the sea and the winds, and the humps of the earth, with their promontories, crags and a few mortal wounds, even the sonatina of the waves gave the impression of a certain distant voice that held the secret inside a conch shell—and the mountain had been so stripped of its flesh that its twisted profile acquired the whimsical shape of a giant whose face was fastened to the stone with a wrathful, frightening grimace. There was a god inside it. A dark and secret mountain god who sometimes vomited out incandescent stones and sand and roared so fearsomely that the very countryside, before being devoured by despair, trembled in panic before the imminence of its destruction. The sagacious men of navigation, endowed with abundant days and well-tempered prudence, ordered palisades and watch-towers to be erected, crude things when seen from a distance, so they could stand guard over the four corners of the encampment. Sentries with visors armed with long, sturdy sabers stayed there at night, remembering the great achievements of our people, and so keeping awake and sleepless. They were afraid of the mountain god and waited for an attack by barbarians, if there were such in those parts. But as there were no barbarians whatsoever, or any other earthly people, they only spent their time listening to the silences, the signals and the cold, damp dawns of the countryside gradually being devoured. With that in mind, the proud captain of the sea explored the woods and shoreline there about, always with the firm belief that he would find other lost men and animals on the other side of the silence. He went off and came back with despair in his voice. The mist took him away, the mist brought him back, but with it news of the things he was searching for in vain never came back. In the places he passed through he found beech trees, cedars and hardwoods, great dinosaur-egg stones that lay among the burdocks, ferns and heather; he wandered through underbrush and patches of wild yams, from one end of the Island to the other, eating hillwort and fennel, washing away his sweat with greedy woodland waters, and, finally, he began to die. On the seventh day he invented yellow death. Then he told his men to leave him and go back to those awaiting news of some discovery or sign of people. They carried him on a stretcher, his face covered by a thick beard and his spine in great pain from the death overcoming him. He no longer sought repose from such exhaustion. Hastily gathering his poor people about him, from whom he heard nothing but moaning and lamentation, he spoke, saying that he was dying by the will of Our Lord God, Lord of the Seas, and in His Service—and he left these words written down for the proper understanding of whoever might someday read them:

...so then the captaine marveled much on sighting that lande of such great beautie, losing his eyes for a great longue tyme in the halles and vallies with greate pleasure for himself. And right there he commanded that the regione bear the name Achadinha, foundling, for being a thinge found at that sad tyme when then they reached there. They had great desires of salvatione from the treacherous seas, so much so that the captaine and with him the men and women took care to praye to God for such a great mercie. And as they had not suffered great damages from the mad voyages and their faithe in earthlie things had not lessened, they all agreed to stay right there till Heaven's Providence shoulde give them other means of return to the Homeland. And since the ships were wrecked and others must be constructed with samesuch skill, this they would do with such care and imagination, if this were still to be the will of the people who were with him. Then the women pled for them and their children that this might be in his un-derstanding of things as they had lost some children in the disasters at sea and they did not wish for their part to go off in search of other strange lands where they had all been sent,

that he the captaine take pitie on the greefe they were suffer-
ing and settle there finally in a new home—and that was how
they alle agreed and set about doing what was for their weal
to do.

Just as larvae take leave of their now ripened eggs, so they
slowly opened up their animal caves and came to form a circle
around the fire so they could begin to ponder things. First
they buried the body of Diogo Paes, proud captain of the seas,
in whose memory they carved an epitaph on a basalt slab:

HERE LIES ONE WHOSE ONLY
FEAR IN LIFE WAS
GOD!
THE SAME WHOSE ONLY LOVE
SERVED WAS
COUNTRY!

After that they went to bathe in the gloomy water of the
craters, they observed from which side the sun, the stars and
the rain came up and they retrieved time, beginning with crude
hourglasses made from earthen pots. Then they felled trees
and cut the wood with axes made from sharp pieces of lava.
Opening clearings, they guided water into the first garden
patches, and that was how they spent the six days of the creation of the world. On the seventh, just as God had done, they
washed off the sweat of those first days, ate unleavened bread
with bluefish and fruit from fig trees, and went in search of
the trembling bodies of all the women. And as they drank the
warm nectar of that night they ate the apple of paradise, loved
the eyeless serpent, received the bite of its saliva, and never
again would they know that its venom was also the wine of
the dead. They were certain only that they were once more
the children of men, capable of increasing and multiplying
like the days.

The roads at that time were the strange paths made by a
few of the bravest muleteers to cross the mountains, cutting
through the forest toward the half-deserted settlements on the
shore. At harvest time, pulling on their harnesses, many mules

and donkeys would arrive and their trotting made the foundations and wattle walls of the houses shake. The muleteers' cries, made hoarse by the dust of the road, offered objects that seemed then fantastic in exchange for products of the land, and they had cowbells and rattles sometimes, and cleavers, and water mirrors, and sandals, and cloth; there was clay pottery that gleamed when breathed upon and infusions of liqueur and cheap liquor with galleons anchored in coral, and rope, and single-tined hoes, and sometimes they would read royal texts written on sheepskin that contained obscure expressions or orders in the form of a decree; at other times they sang of facts and feats filled with love and death, generally anonymous misfortunes with seas and ships in the poem, and their voices became so loaded down with salt and sand that they would palpitate, bringing news from the other side of the Island and from all parts of the world that remained beyond the seas and winds and all wandering masts. In exchange for the ever so infinite use of their objects, for their laughter and their sea chanteys, they got news of the land and later left loaded down with errands and orders. A man, for example, would come and say Bring me two oxen worth a bit of money, with a brindle and a five-pointed star on their foreheads, and another man came and said I want a net for catching morays and sea snakes and a flat-bottomed boat to roll through the waters with jack fish and albacores, and then a woman, very ugly and vaguely smelling of lye, a substance not yet invented, asked for three measures of petroleum, two boxes of ointments for buboes, a can of snuff, and a pan for roasting beans and squash. So when the strangers returned on the next trip they now had their mules harnessed to carts and the donkeys loaded down with large sacks of indecipherable merchandise. On the day that the calves, the oxen, the horses and the goats arrived all in a herd the whole parish came out to the road and waited for the muleteers like at some great celebration. All kinds of sounds arose then. There was wine with sweetmeats at every door for those men weary from lack of sleep, from never having slept in a bed warmed by a woman whose body smelled of grass and mountain mud and whose voice would still be in the memory of people who had surely been waiting for her since the beginning of the world. The women washed their feet with cedar water and gave them hillwort tea and passion fruit brandy to drink while the men received the livestock and wept with emotion, thinking that the best thing in life was receiving something from those outsiders and seeing that some women already loved them just as strongly as they themselves wept with joy over the new animals.

At the start of the following winter they inexplicably stopped receiving the visits of the muleteers and the parish went back to being isolated from the rest of the world. They were never able to find out the reason for the disappearance of the outsiders, who were certainly the most desired men in that land. Coinciding with that new isolation, however, the greatest tempest in the memory of the Island's history befell them. The sea began to rise from the first hours of daylight and it wasn't long in becoming all white and boiling, as if its belly had been ignited with gunpowder. In the middle of the morning it was already devouring the land. Teeth of water, those prodigious teeth of water that destroy everything, were dragging off mounds of gravel the height of mountains and floating those chunks of land out to sea until they sank far off. Afterwards came the wind and the rain. For seven days the wind and the rain foretold the flood, and someone got the idea of rebuilding Noah's immemorial Ark. An old man, how-ever, making use of the infinite wisdom that the age of the world already possessed, immediately convinced them of that operation's futility:

"You have to understand the Bible through its symbols."

And, having aimed his foggy vision through the mist, he asked them to consider the distant aspect of the great moun-tain that topped the Island:

"There's an ancient god inside that huge mountain," he stated then with all the unforgettable conviction that old people have. "It's the mountain god, the wise god of the land, who's been there for centuries with no destruction. As long as he exists, we'll be secure in our security."

As a matter of fact, the rain stopped completely a day later and the sea began to return, hour by hour, to its original place.

Instead of the storm of the previous day, an oily calm was slowly coming on, lighting up the day and soon making it so hot that it began to threaten with fire everything that had previously been in imminent danger of being destroyed by water. Ever thoughtful in his drooping muteness, the old man finally admitted that despite everything there was something in that land whose understanding was completely beyond his wisdom.

"Listen to the silence!" he advised, with a shout of hatred.

Bothered by the way in which the muleteers had disappeared, a few men decided to attempt some form of contact with the population on the other side of the Island. They filled a cart drawn by three horses with products of the land and sent it with five volunteers who got midway along the mountain range and became forever lost there. On the searches undertaken afterwards all that was recovered were the cart and one of the horses. When he examined it, the old man was filled with great mortal terror and said:

"They all died: the water in the animal's eyes is cloudy."
And the women began to wail.

At that same moment the old man became covered with sweat and began imagining death. Turning toward the mountain god again, he stood observing it for a time the way one deciphers an enigma, and his face was visibly filling with the suffering of the children, the women, and even the animals. He shouted again, "Listen to the silence!" All those around him did just that. And all quite suddenly. When everyone had looked at the god of the mountain and felt the strict silence all about, they saw that he was moving slowly and even seemed to be floating. He was soon running between masses of clouds, or the clouds were running past him, in great thick rolls, blending his body with that of the moving mountain. The old man, thinking that the people were about to scream in terror, said once more, "Listen to the silence!" A break in the silence actually opened because the people could hear the canebrakes whistling. It was an underground wail, similar to the sound of the awakened dead, the sound of their mortal footsteps as they wandered across the earth carrying the nest of death on their backs. When a steely breath passed by, brushing the *pica-rato* hedges, the gardens, the branches of the fig trees asleep in their own shadow, a moaning of distant birds broke out, like the cry of a submerged whale—like the death cry of an old submerged whale. One dog yelped before all the other dogs in the land. "Listen to the silence!" the old man repeated, impatient now and with the tone of someone who'd warned them. Right after the howling of the dog the cows lowed in their mangers, blind hens flew against invisible walls. Bats were aroused and mice emerged from the depths of the earth. They were tiny, innumerable, and they gleamed like steel in the darkness of the houses. The sound they made as they fled was immediately joined by the wall of the whole earth as it opened up in its ferment. The wailing of the sea was added to that of the people and all the animals. And the wail of the sea grew and came so close to Rozário that for a moment the parish seemed partially afloat within the volume of its waters. There were snakes and razors and pale horses in that sea whose gods, traveling with tridents in their hands, were turning it belly-up, galloping along in the direction of the wind. The old man kept on saying, "Listen to the silence!" but there was no one to hear him now as the collapse of the world had begun. Moments later the sea split in two. The land, the powerful and perpetual land of the Island, began to tremble in a tiny volcanic convulsion until it broke completely, inside and on the surface.

Then the first houses collapsed. They twisted in the air like mouths paralyzed by panic and they kept on shuddering on the ground until dead, because all other living things—oxen, goats, dogs and mice—were going about freely, bearing off someplace a joyless, furious madness. But the houses were dying. They were dying as they twisted in the air, and the wise old man, having looked for the last time at the mountain god, who was still moving about the clouds, stretched out his arms but didn't embrace the ruins of his house; he embraced death.

The following day, as they gathered up the dead to give them burial, they noticed his mouth was still open and without saliva, because tarantulas and crabs were devouring the gums. Since there was no cemetery, they buried the dead at the edge of the forest in the shade of the same trees where all the souls in this world without a resting place built their nests. And since there was no priest on that side of the Island, the people prayed in a group and paid homage to each dead person with his favorite phrase.

"This one here," someone said, referring to the old man, "heard everything in the dark. It's said that he listened to the silence."

2

MANY, MANY YEARS LATER,
VIEWED FROM HIGH UP ON THE OLD PIKE,
ACHADINHA HAD BY THEN BEEN TRANSFORMED
INTO A BUZZING HUMAN HIVE WITH FIVE STREETS,
A BRANCH LINE, AND A DISTRICT UNDER THE TIGHT
and nervous control of the old priest. His name was Manuel
Governo and he'd been posted there by the Diocese of Angra
do Heroísmo with a mission to restore not only the lost knowledge, but above all the terror of the eternal hopes of heaven.
He'd arrived in the flower of youth, wearing leggings and a
patched hooded coat, and he was accompanied by a half-blind,
almost cadaverous donkey. Two suitcases made of wooden
slats held in place by twisted cords overwhelmed his trembling animal with a weave of knots and bindings. One of the
suitcases carried his holy books, underdrawers and cassock,
the other his liturgical implements and vestments.

At the time, Father Governo was only a poor fellow,
although temporarily poor, and he still had the afflicted look
of a seminarian resigned to that poverty. But they set him up
in the best house in Rozário, flanking the church or what was
left of it, and they received him with some degree of excitement. He spent two days receiving visits and giving thanks
for the infinite care of the older women, who fought among
themselves for an opportunity to serve, in the person of the
priest, the spirit of Christ himself. They scrubbed the wooden

floors with soap and oil, gave his clothes and vestments a good cleaning, and fed him a pot of baked beans and some slices of winter squash. In addition, moved by the inglorious poverty, timidity and callow smile of that silent and frustrated seminarian whose ugliness frightened children while still calming them down, the women fashioned some new pairs of shorts for him and promised to take up a collection to get a few yards of cloth for a new cassock.

"You, Father, are among rather poor people," they said, "but people who are proud of their scrubbed faces and their patches."

"Now, now, my dear sisters," he replied, blushing with embarrassment, "didn't Christ teach us that our religion belongs to the poor, just as the poor belong to Him? Because that's the way it is."

The women even convinced their husbands to work in the evening in order to get the house back into a proper state compatible with the presence of one of God's guests. Carpenters tightened the joints of its enormous pine bed, austere chairs, and other cracked or loosened articles of furniture, and masons came to cement the fireplace and the kitchen and replace the washbasins. So while as a group the women swept the cobwebs and mouse droppings and scrubbed the walls and windows, the men got rid of all the shadows in a house so long deserted. As they placed crucifixes in each room they even imagined that at the same time they were driving off the spirits of Lucifer, the black angels and the witches whose nests had darkened the inside of the house. It finally gave off a smell of water and the breath of the wall had lost its musty human mold when Father Governo decided to take a walk through the parish and went from door to door visiting the sick, distributing sweets among the children, and listening to the counsel of the wise and distant old men from that side of the Island. They spoke to him, those old men, about their way of celebrating the liturgy of the earth, about their little mountain and sea gods, and they advised him to bless the house with cedar water boiled over a fire of incense in order to drive out the evils of the night because once, they said, one of them had gone there looking for beams and had come face to face with a big fat woman, a mallow-colored lady with the feet of a goat; another time the people in the houses closest to it had heard shouting and went to find the house was flooded with blood because the Demon had been carrying out the circumcision of black angels there. And one old man said There's a hive of souls from the other world there, Father Governo, and another added They buzz just like bees in rut. And seeing the incredulous look of the priest open up into a smile, the first old man stated that it wasn't a question of some fable, these were proven facts.

"You, Father, probably know how to drive the Devil out of the bodies of possessed people, but don't ever fail to back up your Latin with a good dose of ammonia. It can even disinfect the soul of a fallen-away Christian."

So Father Governo was quick to conclude that he hadn't been sent to a parish there but into the bosom of the most primitive people on Earth. So primitive that even things proven true had been twisted away from the truth.

Furthermore, no one could remember anymore who his predecessor was or what he'd done there. And as for the age-old church, it lay forgotten and useless in the midst of overgrown vines and with its walls tumbling down from the dampness. His first act was to gain the confidence and dedication of those people. A sense of prudence, however, made him approach the matter with the greatest caution, first with simple suggestions, then by making use of the argument that a people without a church worthy of the name can't dream of having any kind of progress or civilization. It was necessary, in short, my dear brothers and sisters, to restore the church and hasten the return of God and Our Lady of the Rosary to Achadinha. In order to end the hesitation he threw out the idea of collecting alms to gather funds. Needless to say, he was counting on the people's hard work for that. As for the rest, they would soon see.

"But it's always necessary to get the best materials, from ebony wood to white cement, and then the stonework and stained glass windows. Not forgetting, of course, plaster models for friezes and vessels. And we need money for all that, brothers and sisters," he concluded forthrightly.

Month after month of work and sweat were needed for them to clean out the weeds, get rid of the mice, and seal up all the human damage. Verdigris had in fact flooded over the plaster and devoured the stone itself, while the ugly tiles on the saints' shrines and altars, almost all their corners chipped, were falling to pieces, as if some strange animal leprosy had been chewing them away. When the brown rats had been hunted down and their infinite nests hidden in crevices destroyed, the work turned to replacing the wood on the floor and in the rotting pews. Decrepit altars received temporary braces so they wouldn't fall apart; the pulpit was propped up and the woodwork had to be scraped in order to get rid of the verdigris that stuck to the fingers, the church was in such a state of disrepair. Father Governo was able to feel some satisfaction one day when he went nosing about the naves and main supports of God's new dwelling place: the rotten smell had disappeared and in its place now spread an odor of green wood and raw linen. All that was missing, he commented, was choosing an acolyte and beginning his religious work immediately.

"You've got Calheta the Bayman, he's got the smell of a sexton," advised the men to whom the priest timidly put forth his idea. "There was a time when he was plumb crazy about priests and he certainly won't refuse being an altar boy for you."

The first mass took place during the month of April on a rainy Sunday, a day when the people of the parish were suddenly awakened by the ringing of church bells. Opening their windows, they realized they were not only hearing that festive ringing but were breathing it in deeply, convinced there was always a second time hidden within time. Everything was set for the reconciliation of men. After so many years of quarrels and absurd hatred they looked at and greeted one another. Then, when the priest came out of the vestry bedecked in his vestments, followed closely by Calheta with his red surplice falling down to his feet, and went to the altar, tears welled up in many eyes and the commotion was so serious that many women couldn't help fainting. They'd sewn the priest's threadbare vestments with a degree of passion and as they breathed in the smell of moth balls they felt they were inhaling the seaquake presence of God. Since they'd forgotten the secrets of the holy office completely, people went in a group to ask the priest to refresh their memories of the mass before starting the celebration of the sacrifice. And then the first of a series of unexplainable phenomena that would occur in that part of the Island happened. While the priest was officiating, the people began to respond with one voice, without any hesitation, and with perfectly babbled phrases, notwithstanding the fact that the language was Latin:

In nomine Patris, et Filii et Spiritus Sancti. Amen. Introibo ad altare Dei.

Ad Deum qui laetificat juventutem meam.

The people looked at each other in wonder, because they couldn't explain the reasons for such a mystery. They could only attribute it to divine inspiration, for with all the many years gone by of forgetting those rites and that discourse, it was quite obvious that it all had been removed from their memory. The sexton himself, an illiterate with the irretrievable fame of a simpleton when it came to any kind of function, didn't make a single mistake in his handling of the holy articles, and he went right along in Latin as if he'd been a scholar in the language. There was even something of the sage in his grave and solemn way of pronouncing *Kyrie eléison! Christe eléison!* His voice had the fervent heat of lyric poets and even the austere wisdom of patriarchs. For that reason he accepted the grave handshake of Rozário's important men, while the women whispered to each other:

"So it's true that sad excuse for a man always had the makings of a great priest!"

The second surprise came from the children as soon as catechism classes began. They couldn't say who had taught them the proofs of God's existence or the commandments of His Law, but Father Governo, astounded and open-mouthed, listened to them go on as if these had always been the object of his teachings. An almost demoniacal smile came over his mouth, because euphoria like that either came from some hidden miracle illuminating their minds or else it was the art of the dark angel who still hadn't been driven out of the unbaptized children.

After a long time, into his eighty-eighth year now, he recalled that day and made a final accounting of his days on earth. None of that had been repeated. As he prepared himself for death, however, he only asked that God remember to keep him in His final peace, inasmuch as he was leaving behind works made up of some teaching and a bit of progress. As proof that those works were his, one had only to look at his two-story house with windows and balconies all around and holdings estimated at more than fifty acres of Rozário's best land, which he willed to some unknown nephews in Lisbon. Nevertheless, when the dawn of his death came upon him, the old people from his time didn't know much about their parish priest. He was lying with his mouth wide open, his belly puffed up like a circus balloon, and his deaf ears, always so avid for the sounds of the world, however, had grown as large as a donkey's at the same time his corpse presented such an ugly aspect that nobody had the courage to enshroud it. Death had been ripening for a long time in that body and from the stench it gave off one might have thought his face had begun to crumble at the very moment his breath ceased.

"He died before death came because he was already rotting away in life," João-Lázaro said with hatred after his own resurrection on the day when, at the head of the powerful tillers of the soil, he arrived in the churchyard and proclaimed a revolution in the parish.

Life still went on between the cultivation of the lands occupied ever since the settlement and the clearing of the woods roundabout. The upper reaches of the Island gave poor people their first notion of ownerless property. It was the only vacant land in Rozário for which no one dared put forth any claim of ownership. So every year, starting in the month of March, men would go up to the People's Woods with their livestock and drive them off with their arms, leaving them free of Winter's tethers and mangers. They would come back from up there with a strange feeling of lightness in their legs weary from climbing the mountain. Peace reigned without anyone noticing. Before the first storms in September, they would go back up the mountain in search of the scattered animals and notice with surprise that the creatures, despite the time gone by, hadn't lost any recognition of their owners' voices, because they answered the calls from far off until they were located. It was precisely an encounter with joy, because the men would weep with emotion and the cattle would run toward them showing great affection. The animals would sniff their hands and then start running about them kicking up their heels, and their voices would ring out from the top of the mountains as if they were announcing the end of their loneliness to all the world. They always presented the solid girth and gleaming hides that had the healthy form brought on by limitless abundance. Sometimes the bulls would cover the females with their powerful virility and then immediately receive the fate of the slaughterhouse after being inventoried. At other times they were gelded, like mules and horses, by the terrible hands of Cadete, who would crush their blood-colored testicles and then leave them bound up for months with a burlap tie. For Cadete's dark arts were not only diverse, but he was especially adept in the way he undertook the most sinister tasks: he trimmed horses' hooves with a chisel and shoed them with hammer blows; he bled and gutted pigs during the days of swine fever that assailed the region; he unraveled the enigmatic deliveries of mares and heifers with a nail-studded stick, and he had thorough possession of the new and infinite knowledge of a person who concealed his own alien surprise in silence. The unusual success of his dealings with animals would eventually bring him to curing people, starting on the day he arrived at the conclusion it was possible to use the experience gathered in the animal kingdom on humans.

"It's only a matter of abstracting the genus and the species," he philosophized one day, "because the human body is made of the same material and feeds on the same conflicts and illnesses of the flesh."

He shut down his blacksmith's shop at the start of the new road and set up a crude doctor's office there after swapping two barren mules for Bárbaro the Pilgrim's perpetual ball. Bárbaro said he'd got the ball in question straight from the hands of a Tibetan hermit, Friar Apanaguião. When the deal was closed, Cadete began to receive in his house cases of rheumatism, hemoptysis, lumbago, acid stomach, fractures, sprains and ankylosis, and all the other imaginable illnesses that a village can absorb. Experimentation with herbs and poultices proved quite decisive, because it not only produced successful cures but also the secret of eliminating pain. So they soon began to bring him other obscure ways of dying, too, such as the unknown maladies of women and children, epilepsy and juvenile tuberculosis, and an endless list of other ailments, evil arts, melancholies, pestilence, and plague. Those who wanted children began to seek him out and those burdened with them who sought a halt to their procreation, and, later on, even those possessed by the Devil and all those who although not possessed by him still suspected the influence of his hidden and malignant powers in themselves. From that point on it wasn't long before they recognized the illumination and miracles of the angels of God in Cadete the Healer.

Cadete was bested in the efficiency of his practices once, however, as he undertook the castration of the wildest horse to ever trod that land—the dark sorrel belonging to the Maias of Burguete. Maddened by the pain, the animal at first began to moan, then frothed with rage and immediately, in the last blast of despair, kicked so hard that he knocked off that armor made of tourniquets and invisible clamps, looped ropes, monstrous poles and frames that was part of his torture, and whose unbelievably solid structure couldn't withstand the animal's fury in spite of everything. Then he went after the man with his teeth and lifted him up by the nape of the neck, only releasing his bloodied body when João Maia aimed a whip at his long head, putting out one of his eyes. Then the horse ran around in a circle, giving kick after kick and wildly cutting gleaming circles through the air. Suddenly he stopped trembling and they saw him chewing the demon's hair noisily, and they thought:

"He's devouring the worst part of his enemy, he's devouring the man's hair."

As for Cadete, he was left without half his hairy scalp and was wiggling on the ground like a poisoned worm, and for three days he hovered between life and death, but in a state of metamorphosis. He administered a medicine of syrupy and bitter herbs to himself, tested the one and only sponge of bull bile, endured poultices of *água-moura*, leeches, and mustard plasters, drank the deadly mixtures of essences of the liver, and went about yellow and green for some time from sweating bile. And after so many experiments he convinced people of the merits of his recipes and considered himself happy at having been able to exhibit the living proof of his body. The scalp removed by the teeth had been transformed now into an encrusted surface from which the healer kept pulling off gelatinous sheets that aroused disgust in some and a tear of pity in those who would never forget his cures. They all noticed, in spite of everything, that his prolonged convalescence was proving beneficial, for it brought on a double revolution, in his soul and in his body. Never more than a skinny, fleshless bird, he was beginning to exhibit a rounded shape from which the belly of a proboscidian stuck out. Without noticing, he'd acquired the status of a fat man, with lazy, bored ways that went with the sweaty flesh and porcine face from which peeped out two eyes that were quite lively and at the same time as icy as death. And for many years, on their long, patient and repeated waits for a cure at the door of his office they would say that his flesh, greenish until then, had become considerably blue, as if some discreet phosphorescence were lighting it up now. That vaguely luminous and dim aspect, with a metallic, almost incandescent gleam, ended up conferring a supernatural appearance upon him, which also came to be of help in the growing glory of his medicine. From all parts of the island, coming from the city, from villages, or from the most remote places to the north and south, people flooded in, having decided to confide their disillusionment with druggists, healers, wizards, doctors, and other worthies to him. They came on foot, along byways, like pilgrims, tied to stretchers or laid out in wagons; they lined up by the door of his office, waiting for the mercy of his hands or his look. When they were carried into his presence their spirits trembled, for Cadete's solemnity would have inspired fear and respect in God himself. From the rear he was death, because the shriveled back of his neck looked like a folio of deathly parchment, and from the front his metallic blue face held two frozen bird's eyes that had the habit of looking past things. On the day he was proclaimed a saint of wisdom, it was said that Cadete had already long begun his long-distance curing, because someone who couldn't be helped at all in his presence would invoke his holy name—never in vain—and receive from him the grace that healed everything and comforted everybody in his or her soul. When he made his revolutionary proclamation to all the Island, João-Lázaro was able to illuminate the secret of his death with a languid and even euphemistic phrase, but sufficiently stony in the way it defined his passage through this dreary world:

"As for Cadete the Healer, he never overcame the contradictions of his ideological dialectic. He made a mess of his life and even messed up his death. He died a perfect hero: hanging himself from a beam."

Well, in those days Achadinha was nothing but a biblical place where death fulfilled some of its main prophecies. First, a wave of red locusts, traveling from the west toward Europe, devoured crops and fruit and burned the landscape all along the coast.

"They're fearsome creatures, like fire," Father Governo said in his sermon the following Sunday in an attempt to console the poor people. "Voracious creatures with mouths of the Apocalypse and greedy, insatiable stomachs, like those Christians in whom hidden sin devours them and others until the complete destruction of the world."

For three days the people went through the fields driving off the plague with wet stalks of lupine in their hands, the women on one side, their faces covered with the shawls of their imaginary widowhood, the field workers on the other, all going at it continually, bending their backs and bathed in sweat. But despite the prodigious efforts by the workers and the women, the locusts left the countryside devoured and devoid of life. Many people went back into poverty then, into the sinful, rough poverty of the fields of the world. Their heretical voices soon rose up from the ground, looking around; they were long-suffering voices from among the seeds of hate and the sound of revolt, voices the color of the earth, speaking thus:

"This could only have come from the Americans, because

they say the Americans are a kind of animal that devours countries from a distance."

Father Governo said no, quite the contrary, they should resign themselves and be humble in their faith, their hearts, and their courage, and he exhorted them to praise God for the fact that the strange creatures, in their fatal hunger, had spared the cane fields, the tree trunks, and the stones themselves. Some agreed with him, others began to spread a blasphemy against the priest and, indirectly, against God and against all the priests in the world:

"If this is why the bishop sent him, he could have saved himself the trouble. Poor people don't need a religion like that. People soft in the head, there are a few of them in the parish…"

After the locusts came the cycles of famine, the Lenten earthquakes, and the epidemics among the animals. Every time the rats came pouring out of their holes and lay down dead on the ground or attacked people like wild beasts, all Rozário was terrified because the rats were foretelling sickness and death. They were red and yellow, some small in size and movement, others, looking more like great famished hares, had feet flattened by the weight of their bodies and sometimes with a shape as sharp as the claw of a kite or some other equally bloodthirsty bird, and they had an anguished stare. Once more the priest took advantage of Sunday to attack the heretical temptations of his parishioners in a preventive way:

"There you have before you the civilization of rats. It's your civilization of rats. How is it that you haven't taken the time to behold the warnings? Make haste, my brothers and sisters, look to your eternal salvation if you remember the tests of fire, of earth, of water, and of animals inflamed by rage. If not, what other proofs can God send for you to place your faith in Him?"

He was no longer the timid seminarian with a faint smile; he had finally assumed the physical form and the manner of any warm and ruddy prelate, and his neck had grown full of folds like the dewlap of an ox. In addition, hair appeared in his ears, in his nostrils and on his knuckles, a sign that his body had bitterly overcome the impulses of puberty. Seeing his appearance, listening to his opinions, the division of the people had become sharpened, even though the priest always found any number of ways to act upon those who were lukewarm. So with every new misfortune he would gather much fruit, because he would always instruct the people in the necessity of appeasing the wrath of Heaven. How? By evangelical merit, he would say; by gathering and receiving in their breasts the philosophy of eternal bliss, because the poor were poor, but theirs would be the kingdom that is not of this world. In the face of such a tendentious form of acceptance, inoffensive men without religion became annoyed, however, and they immediately went on to become his foremost enemies.

Countless times, in that way, the winds went along destroying the corn, as the frost and the blight had already burned the gardens and the apple orchards—and so many other times the men turned their faces toward the north. That was what courage was like, they thought. For every bit of earth broken into lumps by the rain, they would say, The earth is an abandoned child, we have to pick it up around our neck and give it lots of loving with our hands. The following Winter the tillers left the ground fallow. They took refuge in the cowsheds inventing crafts and crude carpentry tools, tanning, and building stone and concrete structures. The industry of leather harnesses, the making of plowshares, grape presses, and gears, Cadete's blacksmith bellows, finely crafted wicker and the precise rims of coopers were all born then, recent discoveries that came to join other instruments of work that had also been invented out of nothing to fulfill the needs of the day. It even happened that one of the tillers, Feliciano, went on to dedicate all his time to inventions. Simple things at first like wooden latches and reinforced bolts for doors; then a double safety catch and spring; then a sliding window, a trapdoor for attics, and a trough for pigs and chickens. After that he conceived of a muzzle for nursing calves and harnesses for draft animals. As a craftsman he built from memory the first mahogany axle, a kind of horizontal tower with imitation shaft and head—and he took timid apprentices into his service, clumsy, silent boys. When he began to be overwhelmed with crazy orders, he became convinced of his genius and his despair in the same measure and told them to get away from his doors with worthless things like that, because he'd decided to start limiting himself to the invention of movable machines for agriculture. That was how he arrived at the building of a synchronic cart, pulled by an animal and provided with a set of alternate blades, which could serve simultaneously to spread manure and sow beets and corn as well as clear weeds and woods and even *conteiras* and wild ferns. All that was necessary was to replace the perforated little boxes through which manure and seeds ran out with a complex arrangement of boards that spun horizontally and were as sharp as blades. Feliciano then felt the fame of his discoveries. Like all creative geniuses, however, he was soon filled with despair, even though he hadn't changed any of his working habits. He shut himself up in a garret to put together vague cardboard images and ponder the function of his little pieces of wood, because he didn't invent things starting with practical facts: he created inventions in the abstract and then found a use for them.

He was planning to dazzle the world with his *Louriela* when despair began to gnaw at his guts. You don't know what a Louriela is? A very simple thing. A kind of whale's insides twisted around like rope. Not a stomach for that dubious daily use of hunger, but an instrument so far removed from progress that up until then another like it hadn't existed on that side of the Island. Well, the Louriela was a grand machine: it was made up of two rolls of cenosoul the color of a plum and a fox and two more rolls of followshalf that moved dizzily about an axle of piocacic oxalin. When they asked him what such a fearsome machine was used for, Feliciano slowly shook his dreadful brow and replied:

"For nothing."

For nothing, how was that? Was he inventing machines for nothing now after so much effort and so many hours in that garret without eating or sleeping?

"Yes, that's how it is. I'm inventing now machines that are good for nothing," he stated.

Then the news went from mouth to mouth that Feliciano had isolated himself from the world and was lost to it, because he was going about inventing machines that were good for nothing. When that reached Father Governo's ears he became upset and admitted that maybe the Devil had returned to Rozário:

"Machines for nothing. Are they inventing machines without any function now or has that man gone out of his mind?" he reacted in a surge of rage because he'd been taking his siesta.

He went out immediately to pay him a visit. He found him completely absorbed in his work, however, and experimenting with that cetacean stomach in all of its elastic capacity, rolling and unrolling it, and in that movement of a solar pendulum, balanced by dinosaur eggs, something rigorous but incomprehensible resided, because Feliciano manipulated it with his fingers and adjusted the apparatus with an absolute sense of precision.

"What are you doing there nights and days on end with that look of a crow caught in a cobweb?" the priest finally asked from behind after watching him work.

Feliciano sensed a somewhat absurd and temperamental irritation in his voice, cautious in the way it revealed itself. The parish had opened all of its paths and they all led to the priest's house. In a short time he'd taken over people's intimacy step by step, coming to rule over them without any great effort. There apparently existed in the blood of the people a greater disposition toward obedience than toward rule or even toward a simple presumption of victory.

"You will have to knock next time, Father. It's rude to walk into a house where someone's working. This is called the *Louriela,* the machine that does nothing." Feliciano was speaking into empty space and not to the priest, because all that time he'd never taken his eyes off what he was doing and not the smallest part of his body moved. "Would your wisdom give me your blessing, then, and leave without any further delay?"

"It must have some use, doesn't it? Nobody carves wood or stone like you without any purpose unless he's got an empty head or a worn-out soul."

Feliciano understood then he should get up from his bench and turn around toward the priest. His forbidding eyebrows quivered with rage and Father Governo prudently backed away, quickly digging out some snuff to fill his nostrils and inhaling it. He gave a strong sniff and immediately felt a kind of terrified courage, because Feliciano's eyebrows were still quivering and his eyes were staring into his while he said nothing.

"I've made machines for everything and I can also make a machine for nothing. I don't believe that you, Father, have come on a religious mission. You will have to leave, you know I don't like to be disturbed while I'm working."

"Of course, of course. That's how it is. But, my good man, people are praying for you, they're worried about your genius as an inventor, and they've finally come to tell me that you're creating a machine..."

"For nothing."

"For nothing, that's right, that has no use. For nothing, for nothing at all."

"Not one that has no use. For nothing."

"That's it, just like that. Are you sick, Feliciano?"

"Just like the world," he answered without sarcasm. "Dead like the world, Father, and with an urge to grab onto your wisdom and toss it out the window into the street."

People say that from that day on Father Governo took to grinding his teeth and biting his tongue, never failing to do so as a sign of anger. When they came upon Feliciano's corpse hanging from his whale's insides and came to tell the priest the news, he refused to give him burial, alleging there could be no divine salvation for a soul with a death like that. That same day he sat down at his desk and began to write a letter to the bishop asking for a transfer. As the diocesan prelate never took the time to answer such letters or to take his reasons under consideration, however, Father Governo got used to the idea that maybe the letter had gone astray...

During the year of typhus, the land was cleared and the cemetery established on a barren tract of land where a box-wood and two rows of cypresses had arranged themselves with such spontaneity that it made one believe in the prophecy of plants. For with trees like that in such a place, it was natural to have been predestined to receive the dead. And it wasn't just the trees: mysterious black birds already roosted in them, restless birds with liquid, hungry eyes who fed on their own corpses and had the distant faces of philosophers and poets permanently remorseful over this ephemeral life. So when Father Governo lanced forth the idea of establishing a cemetery, everybody agreed it should be placed there and nowhere else. Wasn't it true that poets had already written about death in that place? They only had to wall it in and build a basalt catafalque facing east where candles and lamps would burn perpetually. It had the holy presence of Christian death, they said, and the certainty of new rites, and it was agreed once and for all that the dead would no longer be buried haphazardly at the edge of the woods, because it harmed the growth of the roots of the trees. It wasn't practical, and it didn't jibe with religious dogma. Late on Father Governo called for a regiment of hoes and handbarrows, ordered more cement and shiny gravestones, polished gravestones illuminated by the breath of God, it was said, and he showed them how to make tiles and how to carve crosses in the stone, directing the work in person, the lowly scaffolding and the work of the craftsmen—and his almost demoniacal and never-flagging energy also led him to accept orders for several mausoleums in order to confer upon the abode of the dead the proper and respectable look that the worthies of the world deserved. As for his own mortal remains, he destined them for a beautiful marble sarcophagus purchased in the city, for which some people sought to attribute the gift of prescience to him as well as for the rigorous prescription of his human contingency. His tomb was such a monumental structure, with four lateral columns with cornices and capitals and a poplar tree to give it shade, that many of the good people of Rozário expressed a desire to own a house like that—not for death, needless to say, but to live in it the sad life of the huts and haylofts where they dwelt. From that time on, too, the parishioners became aware of human differences and the diverse origins of man. What separated individuals at birth wasn't just the future quality of their days, it was above all the ceremonial death that awaited them after the gangrene of this human condition that awaits everyone. Many years later, under the age-old voice of the three bells and facing the cortege of cassocks, surplices, stoles and mourning banners, the Rozarians perceived that death meant a continuation of being not-alive, as the whole council of the Northeast took leave of the old priest amidst the tolling bells. And for ten consecutive days only the voice of the bells kept the idea of mourning all around. Widows wept for their hairy husbands once again, despairing mothers went mad again over the memory of their infants, their lost angels—and Father Governo's corpse gathered unto itself not the approaching death, but the absent one, the absolute and familiar death of the parish and its people.

While women's wombs broke the isolation of Winter nights, the tilling cultivated barren patches of land and mangers opened up to receive new herds, because demographic growth brought an increase in livestock and cultivated land. Disputed inch by inch, the fields quickly became the object of all the quarrels and discord between families and generations, and their ownership went on to be the work of simple occupation and not registries and written deeds in notaries' offices. So all that was necessary was to turn the livestock loose to wander or to drive them in the direction of the woods and other places sheltered from the wind, or to have a proclamation made in the churchyard or even to fence in some arable surface temporarily, cut the reeds, clear the brambles and the rocks or simply to plow the ground and sow it with lupine or corn—and it was then considered that a certain determined place came to have a title and an owner. Afterward children were stationed to guard against wild doves, kites and blackbirds and huts were built to protect them from the rain. From sunup to sunset their voices could be heard crying in the wilderness at the plague of greedy creatures:

"Hey, get away! Get away, blackbirds! Get away, bunny rabbits!"

The need to have children arose, naturally, not just to populate the world, but because finches were stubborn birds and mice persisted in their devastation. The school at Eira Velha, the old threshing ground, began to function therefore to help the already overburdened school established in Ramal and later on they even had to start one in Caminho Fundo, so certain was the seminal strength in the women's wombs.

Soon afterward stores and taverns came, in crannies on every street, on every square where the public water tap stood, and shelves were put up in abandoned houses, gas lamps were lit, card games were invented, and the urban market soon flooded the parish with a web of manufactured goods:

packages of biscuits, crates of salt and sugar, bicarbonate of soda, soap, brandy, fragrant wine, aromatic liqueurs, butter, salted seeds, saltpeter, paprika and cinnamon, dried pepper, ingredients and concentrates for pickling, an infinity of household matches and lighters, ounces of island tobacco, unknown domestic implements, the indecipherable supply of gadgetry for the house, knives, earthen bowls, pruning shears, and lastly the dazzling world of aluminum and other metals. One day, when Amaral Peixoto's shop displayed the first radio, a new delirium shook all Rozário. It was a monotonous box of noises, furnished with six knobs and an always trembling needle, and it had the singular capacity of capturing nasal voices that spoke with difficulty of battles and storms and mingled noisy waves with intermittent musical chords. It furthered the conviction that between Achadinha and the world a reciprocal advance had come to exist and indicated where it was coming from. Many years later that conviction ended and was surpassed with the coming of the first automobile, seen as a natural and even necessary act. The people gathered in a crowd and went to wait for the machine, running up and crowding around the Redondo curve. The boys galloped behind the explosions and carbonic smoke or hung onto the automobile and brought it gloriously down to the center of the parish, where it was blessed by Father Governo. Then its owner set about explaining for two hours how it functioned and he did so with such understanding that immediately thereafter many people came away referring to couplings and carburetors as if they were completely familiar instruments. The few who already knew the city assured people, furthermore, that they had seen other kinds of machines like that and they took on the airs of well-traveled people. But the rest had never gone beyond a league outside the parish. That's why they were dazzled when they heard about the machines being invented in that world outside. Only a long time later, when an old bus linked the Northeast with Ponta Delgada, did a few more come to believe in the world, in the light of whose phenomena the episode of the automobile deserved nothing but a passing glance.

An identical euphoria touched the village fatefully when Mrs. Idália, the wife of the automobile's owner, ordered her iron sewing machine from overseas. A grave gentleman dressed in black with heavy insomniac eyes arrived from the city to instruct her in its operation and the women avidly lined up to see and touch such a miracle, which in a matter of minutes sewed and darned to perfection work that took a week with needle and thimble. All the women were struck with a feeling of revelation and soon concluded that owning an example of that technical wonder was indispensable. They besieged their husbands, first giving them a taste of their fiery humanity and loving them to the point of torturing their insides, making them half-dead with fatigue, and afterwards they fought to give the gentleman in black the first orders. After four weeks a wagon with six mules loaded with crates went ceremoniously down the Rua Direita and unloaded as many machines as had been requested—and the gentleman in black decided to stay for a week to instruct his customers in the working of his beloved merchandise. He ended up settling down in Rozário and became an esteemed person because of his infinite mechanical ability in the repair and maintenance of the machines, to which he quickly added the art of noble and cultivated manners to the ladies' great pleasure. He set up a small store alongside the barbershop where the poet and dentist Francisco Heitor would come to philosophize about the world, and he went to work transforming his sad cave into an airy place where in every corner the objects, invariably coming from the city on his mule wagon, grew in number and quality. As well, in that advanced phase of prosperity the parish learned his name. He was called simply José, but since he was the product of such elegant manners, the ladies came to bestow a more loving designation on him: Mr. José Wheels and Levers—and that's what he came to be called.

3

TIMES

WERE REMOTE THEN, WHEN IT TOOK CHILDREN
YEARS TO GO DOWN AND COME TO KNOW THE SEA.
THEY WOULD CONTEMPLATE IT FROM AFAR, A BLU-
ISH RIBBON THAT RAN AROUND THE ISLAND, AND
its surface was so convex that it looked like a huge skullcap
set on top of the black stones of Calhau, the stony place.
Cadete guaranteed in a kind of sophistry of his compli-
cated mind that the sea of the Azores was white, but the
children maintained that no color in this world could define
the eternity of the water inasmuch its continuous convulsion
was close in appearance not to the saliva of snakes and their
nests, but to the colorless dampness of all reptiles. It was a
sea of dishrags, an asthmatic sea of lye on a threadbare cloth
with no design, and its thin water, rocky and salty, gave off to
the earth the breathing of a sleep that had no eyelids—and yet
the eyelashes of its death burned with a fire of tiny animals
loose inside that fat, mortal, white sea. With ships passing so
close by there, always at the edge of the rocks, the children's
vision would transform a ship into a small spindle-shaped
city that moved aimlessly along the surly waters, a city in
whose wake rolls of swirling froth burst forth like flashing
knives and serpents on the move. Then, if they asked their
elders to take them to see the sea from up close, they would
invariably receive this negative answer:

"There ain't no sea or nothing like it! You'll get to go there
when you're bigger. Now just shut your mouth and don't
bother me."

These people, it is said, had never freed themselves from the memory of the first shipwrecks. They carry the curse in their blood; the death of the sea; the death that their ancestors cast forth as a blessing at the dubious movement of all tides. These people sleep with the water in their ears, they've got salt on their gums, and their breast rests in the lap of the maternal sands. People like that have algae in their veins and moss in their hair, they always listen to the sea that kills, hear its death. For that very reason the practice of fishing never reached Rozário: wouldn't those people think they were fishing for their own mineralized death? The jurels, salted for Winter, would arrive in carts from Ribeira Quente, called warm shore, and it made them think of warm communion bread. They would arrive on silky October mornings in the month of absinthe, the month of honey, with such a bellowing of *fresh jurel! fresh jurel!* that the whole parish would come to the call, plate in hand searching out the one who was selling the cheapest, a peck of yellow corn for a dozen of those selfsame fish, blue like fingernails in Winter, half a peck of kidney beans, a quart of fava beans, half a bushel of corn for some three hundredweights of heads of the smallest for salting, at other times sardines with their insides hanging out so they wouldn't rot in the jar, others still a loin of albacore or assorted horse mackerels or a tuna as green as mildew. Winter was nothing but the salt of that anthill poverty with roasted seeds, slices of squash or pumpkin, and that weather-beaten, grim life indoors without the strong joy and pleasure of seeing children born. Where can joy be if not in the sea, children of the Island, the furious, unique and final joy of being alive after going there to the bottom of the cliffs to know the sea? The few who went down there to gather limpets, conches and crabs, all to be traded for corn and beans, had the reputation of being loonies, people without much gray matter upstairs, because they'd take on the most unheard of chores so as not to join the ranks of tillers of the soil. Generally, the consumers of mollusks belched up cheap liquor in stores, went through a ritual worthy of chicken thieves and robbers of orchards and granaries, of people awake in what was nighttime for normal beings of this world, so that was

how the sea was to children in school, sometimes in the form
of a song:

With so much sea, death's bite is bitter,
and salt's no better, it's bitter, bitter.

According to what the children thought, however, it was
an annoyance for generations with no morals, because the sea
wasn't so: it had all the fascination of nights with a white
moon, lights sparkled on its convex surface and a smell of
fishing rose up the slopes and shouted out in the voice of
shearwaters; later on it was daybreak and the heroes from the
lighted ships spoke of their journeys to the ends of the earth,
they were men, vaguely blue, who knew nothing of the
despair of unemployed tillers and said that the salvation of
the world could only come along the lanes of the sea. For
some the feeling of encirclement was there on the Island's
barren land, while for the children it wasn't so; there was the
sea and there was more world beyond the sea. That's why it
was necessary to know it and love it, its space was like
maternal space, like the womb, like everything that's repeated
in the blood.

One day the ships passed even closer to the shore and someone spread the news of the end of the world throughout the
parish. The children had heard Father Governo say that the
death of the world was written in the prophecies of the Bible.
First, there would be exploding stars and a burning sky, then
the waters of the sea would invade the Island, no stone would
remain intact nor would any living creature be left upon the
earth. They began to connect it all with the fact that the ships
had stopped sailing far off. Now they were coming along so
close you could make out the shapes of the condemned heads
on deck. The flags at half-staff and the sad brackishness of
the holds were ever so many more indications of the close-
ness of the death of the sea. Furthermore, the very whistles of
the ship reminded one of sick voices as they crawled along
out there tasting the heavy rains, a sure sign death was
already taking a voyage but one without a destination.
Immediately afterwards the great hecatomb of the world drew
in whales and cachalots, because in the short space of a week
ten of those cetaceans beached themselves and soon engulfed

the parish in such a cloak of pestilence and stench that people again recalled the plague.

"What's death?" the children asked them.

"How should we know, my darling little Jesus? Death is dying, that's all."

"Does it hurt a lot, Papa?"

"Well, no dead man was ever able to complain that death hurt him."

"And is it dark in death?"

"God lights things up in the eyes of the dead. Darkness only exists in this misbegotten world of sin and shadow."

Suddenly the sea took on an almost demoniacal fierceness. Mice were seen coming out of their holes and oxen could be heard lowing in despair. The earth tremors started up again. Father Governo immediately began a novena of confessions and became empathic but quite evasive regarding heaven and the punishments of hell, and he went from door to door warning sinners, absolving the sick, spreading the word that it was their last chance to repent. He heard their confessions from morning until night and even afterwards, and he warned the faithful against a hypocritical confession:

"A poor repentant sinner will enter the kingdom of heaven much quicker than a person who judges himself free from malediction!"

That was how things were when they heard, coming from no one knew where, a subterranean shout, a shout from the earth, smothered in gravel, and the shout kept echoing endlessly in the air through the chaotic space of silence and became mingled with the poisonous smell of the dead whales:

"Death is on the way!"

DEATH IS ON THE WAY! DEATH IS ON THE WAY!
DEATH IS ON THE WAY!"

Because, they say, someone had seen death strolling along the edge of the woods at the place where they had originally buried their dead, and it had the look of a woman with the feet of a goat, the perfect symbiosis of the Devil and a female. Death fed on raw yams and beet greens and its breath was so sulfurous that it struck from a distance and even burned the air. Seeing that people were getting ready to flee to the top of the mountain, Father Governo went into action and appeared before the fugitives, all pale and sweaty, pleading with them not to do such a thing:

"There's a much safer place than the top of the Island: our church. Nothing can penetrate it, not even the Devil. Take refuge in its naves and pray."

Then they worked from sunup to sundown hunting the sea birds that were slowly devouring the dead whales. They dragged the enormous carcasses beyond the rocks and cleaned up the bones, teeth, and tons of rotting flesh with oil and fire. Then they buried the ashes in a crater dug out among the boulders. From then on it was known that death had been put off, but temporarily, until the signal for the destruction of the universe came. It was necessary to believe in God. When they asked the priest if he really believed in the end of the world, he stammered out some comments about divine designs and limited himself to repeating the scriptures, the part where they prophesize the possibility of a second flood. So panic suddenly opened like a sort of dead flower in every look, then in people's arms, then in all the muscles of their bodies, and looking at the sea, they thought they could see it growing up to the still uncovered heights. The water would cover nearby surfaces, reach the main body of the cliffs, and its fearsome bosom would begin to submerge all low-lying parts of the Island, not vertically, like the leap of a spring, but something like the way concentric rings turn mills. Professor Calafate, until then quite withdrawn into his everyday life without a history, shaded his eyes with his hand and climbed up onto a crag to get a better look at the phenomenon. In his opinion everything that was happening couldn't be understood by a faith in God but rather by the science of men. He had the frames of his glasses cushioned with little rolls of cotton so they wouldn't hurt his ears. They were, without a doubt, a pair of sad, absent-minded glasses, and he was so softened by the solitude of wisdom that when seen close up like that he seemed a strange being, one almost unknown to the inhabitants of Rozário. Normally he went about lost in the midst of the children. His appearance improved a little with distance, even his rash and rapid movements. When he was close to adults, as at that moment, he was left with the look of some grandfather and seemed to carry a sad, unbarking dog within himself.

"According to the theory of Nostradamus," he said, "maritime motion is circular and always spins in the direction of strangulation. That's precisely what's happening now."

And the men, running toward the mountains, drove their herds of oxen before them with the hope that God might save the animals at least. They believed, also, that the strangulation didn't have the strength to let it crush the earth's deep bones. That was absurd, because in all catastrophes in the world boulders had always been spared, ending up finding new lands.

A great June afternoon was burning bright when the Sun rolled toward the lightless star and produced an eclipse. Those two yellow bodies, if they touched, would start spurting tears of fire like skyrockets at a festival and when they bumped flanks they would ignite the World on fire. Professor Calafate, however, raised some arguments against those and other suppositions, because according to what he said sages had written long ago that the Moon was not incandescent. It was an arid star, covered with dust as fine as flour and, therefore, it possessed a non-combustible body, lost over the centuries in cosmic space. Out of simple prudence, the Rozarians had gathered in grottoes and hollow places and began to believe that there they would be protected from lunar avalanches. In their opinion, Calafate may have known geography and arithmetic, but as far as the stars were concerned he was as ignorant as they. Thus, in a short time they'd been able to verify that the dark face of the Moon had become so pinkish that the Sun seemed about to devour it. The man in the middle of it with a bundle of brambles on his back stumbled and fell upside-down with his skullcap at an angle, and a cone of light illuminated his head, then the brambles, and finally his big boots. Immediately thereafter the Moon went back to its original position of an innocent fetus with its pale, chubby cheek inside a metal sphere.

"Is that what an eclipse is, then? This world of ours is quite a jackass, praise be to God!"

Part of those who'd run off in flight immediately undertook their return to the parish and their homes. After all, they'd been hoodwinked as much by the priest as by all the proclaimers of death. Father Governo had used it as a pretext to confess all the sinners and he may have thought that his conscience had become reconciled with God, but it still wasn't with men. Rozário was welcoming them with a festive ringing of bells, as if they were conquering warriors returning from a skirmish defending the survival of the community. Except that the enemy was a being as imaginary as a phantom. They immediately began to laugh and get drunk. Some ridiculed and mocked Professor Calafate's solitary, wise and quite mad voice of a sad, unbarking dog: *According to the theory of Nostradamus, maritime motion is circular and always spins in the direction of strangulation…* " Oh, if somebody would only give a good swat to those glasses! Others sought him out again, in hopes of new explanations, while the rest prayed, dedicating their salvation to God. Only when the euphoria of the wine of the living and the dead, together in the same places after centuries and centuries of co-existence, had passed did they begin to hear about strange episodes during the hours of anguish the parish had lived through during that time. There's not enough memory to recount them here, but I, narrator of these misfortunes, took some notice of them and I know there's also an agonizing dog in my voice. An agonizing dog because I heard tell that Josefa Luísa was a person with scant activity in the head. The woman of many men on Winter nights, going to them drunk, smelling of cheap liquor and snuff, and with the great genius and talent of Fernão Mendes Pinto, her ancestor, she would devour them as if they were her enemies. She'd sworn not to step foot out of her house, not even when the hour of her departure for the other side of death was announced. She would die, yes, but with a full belly, consoled down to the depths of her soul, she guaranteed. She gathered the neighbors in her yard, where she dragged out bowls of cracklings and pickles, and she set about distributing such great portions of food to those present that indigestion wasn't long in coming. In short, Josefa Luísa had decided that her death, much more than her life, would remain forever in the memory of her survivors. It was even said that she'd probably aspired to the fullness of a perfect moment. You don't know what a perfect moment is? It's not up to me, narrator of these misfortunes, to say, but it's always been supposed that a moment like that would have to be some kind of divine madness that's never repeated in this world. She'd searched through forgotten drawers and cupboards for her last store of liquor and put all her clay cups to use, serving the guests herself. If I were a priest, I would inveigh right here against the ugly sin of gluttony, the most monumental gluttony ever practiced up till now in Achadinha, because I'd never had an opportunity to observe such fury. I am, however, more like the dog of my sadness, and I prefer to bark a little at the shadow of the suffering of those who charged me one day with the narration of their misfortune. New guests kept arriving with the same desperate air of death and Josefa went on welcoming them all merrily with those ways of a mortal witch, eyelashes drooping with fatigue, telling them to sit down and eat. Then I saw hunger many centuries old and I thought of barking furiously at the sea. I was there with my dog of sadness and maybe I could invent some way of biting from a distance and devouring the sea from far away. A very old hunger, with no other like it now except on the Island, that was how I was spawned there, ever so slowly, growing up barefoot in its bosom, and then I learned that life was like all that, barking at hunger the way dogs do sniffing iodine, the way frightened dogs do sniffing the iodine of our imagination.

The effects of the brandy and the wine soon produced a devastating euphoria. But it wasn't euphoria, it was the ominous effect of the wine, the poison of the dead, of its saliva, which is acid and as quick as a bite, and then came the song of challenge for the now drunken women, because the women had sat down on the ground and opened up their legs and were laughing like drunken mares in heat. Josefa was even lying down on her stomach and loosening her hair freely over her back, mysteriously guffawing and guffawing for no reason. Then, staggering around her, eyes foggy from the agitation, the men sensed that her body was quivering in heat. Josefa's voluminous buttocks could have been a nest full of small animals hatching from an egg. When one of the men lifted up her skirt and gave a big tug on her salmon-colored drawers, all the others forgot their desperation about death and thought of fornication without quarter. Each one began to undress his woman, and there were behinds and nothing but behinds, all of them quite alike. If they were patted, those behinds would quiver endlessly like gelatin or a tightly strung cord. But if they were opened a little with the fingers there was a furrow that descended and went on afterwards to the mouth of a strange flower of blood hidden between pubescent locks of hair whose dampness faced the sun to receive all the colors in the world. The man who'd undressed Josefa tried to close his hand tightly over that coral crack and trembled all over again. His fingers squeezed the whole imaginary loaf of those corals and his teeth tightened so he wouldn't explode in his delirium. Then, quickly getting undressed, he raised up a kind of mediocre limb that grew out from between his legs, an animal tree irrigated by twisting nerves, and that branch penetrated so deeply into her that it may have run up against the walls of her stomach. Josefa didn't even quiver. She generously received the muscular guest of her insides and was already absorbing its strength in small cylindrical movements. Then a strange machine with an accelerating piston dug furiously into her womb, more and more urgently, and an erotic explosion circulated from body to body, warmed the hands and groins of all those lost females and ended up setting them on fire. They say that love and death are supreme states of symbiosis, but making love like that was nothing but a way of undoing everything down to its origins, as the whole being admits another different being into itself, deeply, and loses it, starting with the first center of solar gravity. They experimented in taking them from the front, then from behind, and from the front again, and when they did all that, they went back to eating with the expectation of soon being able to repeat their copious fornication. But death was arriving. First it slithered in like a worm or a fetus, curling up in the entrails, immediately changing into a deathbed convulsion, and right after Josefa was already announcing, between vomiting,

"I'm on my way out, have pity on me."

Her throat was on fire and she was rolling back and forth on the ground, back and forth, in a perfect pendulur movement, begging the others to bring her water and counsel her to wisdom. The others were lying about all the while with identical afflictions and howling in the distance with their hands clutched over their innards. The pickles poisoned with a strong dose of rat killer were spreading death all around her, and vomiting, shrieks, howls and curses could be heard, and the men were scratching on the walls with their fingers and downing jugs of water, while the women were crawling out into the street, naked and desperate suffering from the gastric fire, but intent on coming out to die under the rain of fragmenting stars.

When the eclipse had passed and the population had returned to the parish, people came upon the dying, all entangled with each other as if they were worms defecated from a monstrous womb, and they saw that they were still twitching in one last spasm. They ran to get Father Governo, asking him to come and absolve those souls for their sinful poison, but with great firmness he refused them extreme unction.

"Since they're going to hell," he said, "they have no need of the Church's blessing. Let them instead ask the Devil for his benevolence."

So they were buried in wild land, with no funeral rites, and without the weeping of professional mourners, in a place outside the settlement normally used for animals. The very next day and into the night their ghosts began to wander through the four corners of the parish in search of relatives and friends. A short time later they began to attribute all new misfortunes in Rozário to the accursed dead. If a calf disappeared in a ditch, if a mare split a hoof for no reason, or if the mahogany axle of a cart broke—and other like troubles—it was to the accursed dead that such misfortunes were attributed. They went back to ask the priest to re-

consider his decision and once again he refused to transfer
the bodies to hallowed ground. Those dead needed to be
pacified in the fury of their destruction and that's why they
decided to give them redress. They took up a collection among
themselves and somebody got the opportune idea of placing a
burning bush at the place where they'd been put into the
ground. It was a barren, unsheltered place where no unac-
companied soul would dare pass after nightfall. The dead
certainly had their memory, or a right to it, so over the ground
of their entombment a kind of bony luminosity was erected
that spun like acrobats in a circus, and from the woods it followed people from a distance. Josefa's ghost was even seen
in the most diverse places in Rozário, first in Burguete, at the
crossing of its three deserted roads, and she had her arms open
and her eyes were phosphorescent, as if she'd been crucified
in life; later on she appeared to two old men up on the New
Road and they were able to verify that it was she, followed by
a strange retinue, all of them also with arms open and fiery
looks. Her vinegary voice invariably asked for a resting place
for herself and her guests. After much insistence, the priest
became convinced of the need to transfer the bodies to the
cemetery by the square. He played hard to get one more time,
but without his previous conviction and stiff, temperamental
stubbornness, until he finally gave orders to proceed with the
rites. He strongly attacked prostitution and once more vowed
Hell to all who dared repeat the example of those outcasts
of the earth. Full of wrath, he inveighed over and over
against the wiles of the Devil, his voice hysterical and his
eyes flashing with hate, and he turned all the women to weeping with emotion, while the men gravely received his tribunal
voice and admitted that Father Governo, in order to speak
with such eloquence about the greatest pleasure in the world,
fornication, had most certainly been castrated at birth or
during his preparation for the priesthood. Finally, when he
had finished his sermon, he went over to the pit and recommended that the common grave be dug a little deeper so the
accursed dead not commit the foolishness of returning to the
world again. He supervised the operation until it was finished
and was only satisfied when the men had rolled a boulder as

tall as an ox on top of the grave and trod the earth down all around.

"And let nobody, absolutely nobody, under pain of excommunication by me, go back to spreading any new falsehoods about the end of the world," he warned, finger in the air, before leaving the cemetery. "Our earthly destiny belongs to God and not to the whims of the stars. There are a lot of dunderheads hereabouts who have to get that foolishness out of their heads."

The next Sunday, during mass, he himself was able to confirm that life had returned to normal. The eyes of his parishioners had found the purity of symbols once more and were ready once again for reconciliation with God and his angels. In his sermon he lingered over the need to create a historical event capable of celebrating the return of the prodigal children to the house of the Eternal Father, and he put forth the suggestion of a three-day festival in honor of Our Lady of the Rosary, the patroness of Achadinha. So that festival had its start on the last Sunday in August and its tradition is still kept today. Out of it, however, they drew no joy or glory, but only the time, the heartache, and the memory of our despair to prolong the duration of the world.

4

THEY HAD ALREADY
FORGOTTEN THE EPISODE OF THE WANDERING
DEAD AND THEIR CURSES, WHEN THEY BEGAN TO
NOTICE THAT ROZÁRIO HAD GROWN AS SWIFTLY
AS A GIRL AT THE CRITICAL MOMENT OF HER MEN-
STRUAL PUBERTY. HAD GROWN HOW?

It had ceased to be a tiny, dismembered body of the Island of São Miguel, Arcanjo, and had become a civilization. Roads had been opened in several directions and people had begun to leave. Others arrived, led by those who'd decided to return. They were, in general, white girls with a strange pronunciation and calling *Mother* the mother of a man from Rozário whom they'd promised to love and respect for the rest of their lives. Businessmen also arrived, men without a trade or wives, hard workers. No one knew for certain what civilization was after the arrival of so many people from other parishes, but there were those who understood it be a kind of perversion injected by the strangers into the people of Rozário.

In the course of the third week of robberies and assaults a committee of men lamented the fate of the parish and presented themselves at the residence of Father Governo to demand severe measures against the lawlessness of those outsiders, who, in addition to their habit of theft, had a barbarous and insolent air. They cursed the robbers of corncribs and bean bins, insisting that the priest take up the defense of proper behavior. For them, all foreigners were nothing but an organized gang, coarse and impious, who worked at night and spread panic. There were also those who were tame and inoffensive, it was true, but they bore a strange greedy look or were always lazing about in corners and biding their time until they would be accepted by the people.

"How can it be," they said, "that our women take them as husbands or lovers while our men have to go elsewhere in search of wives?"

The case of Jesus Mendoça, much talked about of late, ended up becoming a weighty argument against the mixture of populations. Jesus Mendoça, they all remembered, was nothing but a poor old man whom a strange illness had deprived completely of a desire to sleep. Not a madman, but an insomniac. He was in the habit of spending his nights puttering in his yard, involved in the quirks of his sleepless temper, until he caught a blow from a scythe on the neck and went off to die in the hospital at Ribeira Grande, almost decapitated. Not even he had been able to reveal who it had been and who it had not been since his damaged gullet prevented him from naming his attacker. In view of the men's determination, Father Governo pondered deeply behind his grouse eyes and began to conceive the vague idea of setting up a way of reinforcing and making unquestioned his authority in the parish. It was necessary, according to him, to look at the example of other places, Achada, Salga, not to mention Fenais da Ajuda or even Algarvia, models of law and order that overcame the machinations of any civilization. He was prepared to assume the future of Rozário as his task. Hadn't he already given dozens of years of his life to those people, to their land? Hadn't he set up the cemetery, hadn't he restored the church and the parsonage? Well, there he was. Besides, the gentlemen knew that it was urgent to gather men of good will together again and start some more repairs on the church. He had already drawn up a progressive plan for improvements. They had to remodel the sacristy, gild the baroque altars, remove and replace the glass panes in the windows where the wind whistled over their heads, because time was devouring everything. Had they taken a good look at his vestments by any chance? There was no more room left for any mending of albs, chasubles, or stoles. Religion was in a state of poverty!

"So, you gentlemen might conclude from this that since I'm the first person responsible for the order and progress of these people, I've also been the person most forgotten."

From there he went into a serene lecture on the evils that threatened the kingdom. He spoke to them of those who obey and the one to be obeyed, and if they would permit him a touch of vanity, all over the world priests stand a bit higher over the earthly dimensions and materialism of men. They had a world very much their own, touched by the inspiration of the good. And since he was the representative of Christ Himself, he was someone poor in spirit who pointed life not in the direction of His death, but toward His resurrection. Thereupon he spoke to them of the mysteries of God, of His designs and the many ways of understanding His truth about the world, and he was soon getting lost in the metaphors and parables of the Gospels when the men looked at each other with annoyance, not understanding the thrust of such preaching. Father Governo then gave signs of having understood he'd gone too far and turned to practical things. He offered them all a mug of the wine stored in his cellar and laid out his project:

"In the first place," he confided, "we have to name a mayor." He sought in vain to observe the effect of that idea on those present, for they remained impassive, thinking this wasn't the product of some flash of illumination. They'd thought about it for a long time.

"So, finally," he added immediately, "you gentlemen now have the floor."

The men then shuffled about a little because they were beginning to agree with him. The subtlety of priests, furthermore, lay in that way they could read the eyes of darkness deeply and quickly.

"We've got to look for honest people for the official posts that will be created," he went on with some euphoria. "People with spirit and a clean slate, in whom no one can find the slightest blemish."

After a few moments he encouraged them to make their decision right there, something, according to him, that would go down in the history of Rozário and stand in the memory of future generations. He brought out a tray with little pieces of paper he'd cut out with a knife, and he rolled them up in full view of them all, with one having a cross marked on it. The mayor would be chosen by lot and the nominee would be announced later on in his sermon on three consecutive Sundays until the royal services of the Northeast ordered the edict of the appointment posted all throughout the Council territory.

By a whim of fate the little piece of paper marked with a cross was unrolled by the fingers of a monstrous figure. His name was Guilherme José Bento, but he was better known by the name of "Goraz," elephant fish, because of his bulging red eyes. He weighed two hundred and fifty pounds, as bovine as a stud bull and his elephant-fish eyes put fear into children as well as dogs. He was famous for other things, too, most of which had to do with his brute strength. According to some he was a good man for grabbing a steer by the horns and bringing it to the ground all by himself, without breaking much of a sweat; according to others, he would lift up five men lying in a tangled heap, drink down five quarts of wine in one swallow, and was the only living creature on that side of the Island capable of straightening up a house that had threatened to collapse in the last earthquake. Tipsy with drink he wasn't just a muscle machine, he could be an almost tyrannical hero. Once at the cattle market in Achada das Furnas, up in the hills, he'd laid eight knife-wielders low with his fists and tossed the ninth up over a fighting bull. His horse had been the first victim of that muscular, brawling temperament. On one occasion it had escaped from its stall, driven crazy, they say, by the solitude and the flies, and plunged full speed into the streets full of people. The animal was frothing with fury and its eyes were burning and feverish like those of a raving lunatic, because they say it was pulling the stucco off buildings and the stones off walls with its teeth and sniffing the moral food of its perdition in the air. No one dared approach the animal, but Goraz was waiting for it at the intersection of Ramal and Eira-Velha after it had passed through plowed fields and fallow ground. And approaching it with his arms outspread, he fetched it such a clout in the middle of its forehead with his fist that the creature shuddered all over and fell unconscious to the ground. It's claimed he even picked it up in his arms and carried it back to the stall, although that has never been proven.

Whether from his strange look of an elephant-man or because of the exaggeration of his feats, the men gave a sigh of relief and Father Governo cast a papal blessing over him, wishing him discernment and rectitude in the fulfillment of his new duties. Guilherme José didn't waste any time in putting all his zeal into the job of mayor. He immediately hurried about as if he'd been invested with the duties of a cabinet minister. He began by transforming the oldest and most unused room in his house into an office into which he dragged a heavy acacia-wood table, three chairs, a cat-of-nine-tails, along with a pair of rough and rusty handcuffs, a ledger, two rolls of cord for tying calves, the horse's packsaddle, a spittoon, and even the doghouse for his guard dog. He also prepared a small box of sharp pens, an inkwell, and a pad of thick yellow pages where he would scribble down fines, complaints, decrees, and autos-da-fé. Since he needed a place to pin up his writings, he solved the problem by nailing up two wide boards along the wall facing the window so that everybody could see clearly how much the new obligations were spread through his government. He set out at once for the parsonage, first to settle the progressive steps of the new order with the priest, then simply to expedite some small matters. He listened to the priest's advice in silence and even tried to find inspiration in some of his suggestions. As the first families had emigrated from the Island for distant countries, he made him feel the necessity of appointing someone to the post of mailman, since correspondence was brought to the capital of the Northeast and took several weeks to reach the hands of its addressees.

"The pain of watching a family leave is bad enough, so it's all that much worse not to get any news from them. We've got to get connected with the world right away."

"Our mayor," the priest replied smiling, "is quick to see some light in the darkness. The idea of a mailman had never occurred to me, but that must be due to the fact that I'm not a man for great ideas. Let's think about the appointment."

If the reverend father didn't object, he'd already thought of a solution.

"For that job," he explained, "a person with my strictest confidence is needed. My brother-in-law Juliano."

He was a man who could defend himself along those highways from people hunting dollars and old Brazilian cruzeiros. As a matter of fact, he had a red, almost opaline, color, and his breath was so alcoholic that it caught fire on contact with the air during the hottest times of the day. It was said his mouth was a maelstrom, because he would devour a pot of baked beans at every meal. The central mail service of the Northeast, on the intervention of the Achada sector, supplied him with an oversized denim uniform and set his salary at three hundred patacas a month. Living in Achada, he'd been widowed by a sister of Guilherme José, whose family was scattered all over, and since he hadn't remarried he was still considered his brother-in-law. He usually carried a canvas sack under his arm, just to put thieves off the track, because they say he stuck the letters under his clothes, next to his belly. His daily trip between Achada and Rozário was so regular that farmhands, used to judging the time by the height of the sun, came to calculating it from his passage at five in the afternoon, knowing that his route, the same as his steps, was something just as spiritual as the movement of the sundials.

After Juliano's appointment the mayor's most notable undertaking consisted in setting up the election of a Parish Council, whose provisional seat he assigned in advance as the foreclosed house of the Raposos near the Largo de Cruz. The elections took place two weeks after the publication of the edict, and the single list of candidates had the express approval of the priest after a sermon in which he exhorted the parishioners to buckle down in their plan of action. In addition he blessed its president right at the beginning of mass, commending him to Our Lady of the Rosary, just as bishops had done for kings and navigators in other times—so that no one was surprised, not even his enemies, who were prevented from voting, by the fact the list was elected unanimously. For that reason Father Governo publicly congratulated himself on the weakness of the opposition. According to him his enemy was utopian; maybe they should invent one just in case one was ever needed. Jeremias Furtado, the elected president of the aforesaid Council, was solemnly invested in his post and he was the third in line in the Rozário hierarchy, below the spiritual supervision of the priest and the governing action of the mayor. At the inauguration ceremony he spoke voraciously about his utopian plan of action, which was as prophetic as it was poetic and religious, but which, even before being started, had undergone postponement for many, many years and even for generations. It was his plan, he said, to build a permanent seat for the Council, pipe water from springs to fountains and from fountains to houses, replace oil lamps with gaslight, since electricity was still unknown, and open highways and roads to the interior of the island in the direction of tillable land and parishes on the other coast.

"As for the parish," he added, "the least this Council must do is pave its main street from Canto da Fonte to the church, establish a mother-and-child center, and relying on the worthy service of our priest, open a parish hall for the children's catechism and the enjoyment of adults."

The people listened in great numbers on the street to that sort of proclamation of progress and immediately began to react as a crowd. Crowds, however, have a thought and a philosophy, and this one heard those promises with the prudent reserve of slaves in captivity, thinking that it always behooves politicians to promise and the people to learn the lesson of disappointment.

"Therefore," the president went on orating, "in order for such noble goals to be attained, it is necessary to build up income and funds under the governing power of the Council over which I preside, because miracles are not produced by words nor are public works brought about with scant municipal resources. We need to feel the inspiring breath of economic power, receive it in our blood, and know how to generate budgetary contributions. What's work for one will be work for all, by all and for all."

The crowd began to move, soon flowing off in all directions and breaking up into groups. Words were already being bandied about regarding Jeremias Furtado, he being known up till then for having the makings of a scholar and even a poet, but nothing of a man of action. When he finally let the people know that the authorities of Rozário had established a consensus as to how the budgetary deficits would be overcome, the people sharpened their ears and immediately rose up against the first betrayal by their representatives. The president had just put forth the idea of decreeing a harvest tax of one percent, adding that it was the only possible way of building up a fund for public works. He even made it know that said tax had been put into a decree and signed by him as well as by the mayor and even by Father Governo. The edict of the harvest tax stipulated yet other things: the obligation that no more houses were to be built without the prior consent of the Council or independently of municipal permission, and in like manner there were norms governing the admission of outsiders into Rozário. It was a little text in a wavering and vaguely legible hand, with orthographic figures like those on papyrus documents, at the bottom of which was the signature, for the good of the parish and the world, of Jeremias Moniz Furtado in his status as president elected by the people. Such an odious document brought on any number of harangues and talk and at night it was ripped down after being posted on the front of the church.

Faced with that deed, the mayor, roaring with rage, organized a night watch in the hopes of nabbing the first careless person caught in the act—and so he acquired the habit of spying on the population's every movement. He did it progressively, first in the darkness in search of suspects, then in the light of day when he threatened jail for a man who had the courage to denounce publicly the new impunity of the government and the ecclesiastical betrayal. But the resistance was so tenacious that the mayor exploded with rage and began carrying his whip and lashing out everywhere. Like all powers that stiffen when in danger, Guilherme José, fearing a riot or even a popular uprising, armed himself with all his gear and was determined to confront his enemies. He now no longer went anywhere except on horseback and with his guard dog on a leash, and he would fiercely brandish his whips and handcuffs.

When he was summoned by Father Governo so they could reformulate the text of the decree that had disappeared, he made him aware of his plan not to acquiesce to the revolt and heard him react angrily:

"I don't understand the way these people think. If we leave them loose in this vale of tears without protection, it's our fault, we stir up disorder, theft, and corruption. If we bring order, it's even worse: they start accusing us of all the monstrous things the fantasies of their minds can stir up."

Guilherme José didn't seem too impressed with the priest's fit of anger and wanted to get down to practical things:

"That's it, there'll always be people talking against the favors done them, Father Governo. It's just that our consciences should be clean as far as we're concerned. Let's rewrite our decree and you can leave the rest up to me. You, Father, take care of the religious problems; what's left in the world is my part."

The priest's hand trembled noisily as the decree was rewritten, while the mayor smoked, pacing back and forth. His boots squeaked so much on the floorboards that the priest became consumed with all the anguish of that afternoon's end and solitude, at the same time an almost lazy irritation was overtaking his stomach and filling his mouth with gastric juices. When he finished writing, his face was a blood-red sheet. Without reading it, Guilherme José ran his eyes over the text and blew on it to dry the ink.

"Now I'll take it to our president for him to sign, I'll have a few copies made, and it's just a matter of putting them up in the usual places. I'll be dammed if someone is going to destroy our decrees again, Father Governo, I'll be damned."

Jeremias Furtado read it twice before he was ready to sign it and he was so terrified by its content that he threatened to resign. At the same time he realized that his resignation was impossible because the mayor just pointed to the paper, not even waiting for him to agree. Almost in panic, as if they were asking him to sign his death warrant, the president broke out in a sweat with his shirt soaked about his shoulders, chest and armpits.

"Did our priest think all this up?"

"All of it, it's just the way he said it. The rest will come later," Guilherme José replied enigmatically.

"Since when do priests take the place of governments in legislative matters?"

"As far as I know, since always. In one way or another they've always governed the country. They govern everything, even the ones who govern, and it's not for nothing that our priest is named Governo," the mayor philosophized.

"But this isn't a decree; it's a writ of slavery."

"So what? I don't care whether it's a writ or a decree. I assumed the responsibility of putting it up today and seeing it's carried out. That's all."

"I never could have imagined such an abuse of our people. I never promised to enslave them. You know my character."

The mayor put both hands on his hips, brimming with anger, and put on an evil face:

"Listen, Jeremias. Listen well to something I'm going to tell you. The greatest difference that separates men of action like me and politicians of your stripe is this: I never promise anything because I don't know if I can carry it out. I follow my head. While you, on the other hand, know that you can never carry out any promise and that's why you win elections. That's why I'm a man of action and you're a bucketful of intentions."

"That's easy to say, especially since you don't have to sign any decrees."

"In that case I'll sign it myself and you can consider yourself relieved of your duties. Quite simply I'm placing you under arrest for negligence and betrayal of the people and I'm going to dishonor you in front of the whole parish."

The president of the Council couldn't believe what he was hearing. In one quick instant he understood that power doesn't exist except as it devours itself internally. One part of power devours the other, the other devours the next one, and so on until the last one is left feeding infinitely on itself and is no longer aware of its existence. He immediately picked up his hat to leave, because he needed room to breathe; he would have to gather the people together quickly and make them aware of the monstrous enormity awaiting them. He would, in addition, have to present his immediate resignation to the priest and the people. No sooner had he got up out of the chair than the mayor grabbed him by the shoulders and made him sit down, at the same time disdainfully handing him a sharpened turkey quill that had been dipped in the inkwell. He had the wild face of a horse with the beard of an old man and two eyes so wide and thick that the president thought he could see himself in them and was seeing his image in the whirlwind. Whale teeth floated in his smile and they, too, seemed to give back his double in that mirror of the Devil.

"You're getting more and more difficult, boy," he told him in an almost confidential tone. "After all, it's just some unimportant shitty edict, one among thousands of edicts handed down around the world."

"But it's over my name," Jeremias replied, offended.

"And I'm the one who'll carry it out, not the one who signs it."

"So there's a difference: you order what's to be done and I execute it. I exist and you invent. Or I don't exist because you so order."

"Exactly," Guilherme José approved merrily. "Precisely, Mr. President. You don't exist because I so order."

"I'm just not going to sign that, I'm going to resign."

"And I'm going to break every bone in your body and kick you out of this parish," the mayor replied, still softly and with the same confidential and sarcastic voice.

"Then I'll sign it and resign afterwards and the decree will be invalid. You'll be stranded."

"In that case," the other man concluded with the greatest calm, "I'll follow you to the ends of the earth and snuff out your life."

The strange thing was no rancor was heard in their voices, because they were just bouncing little paper balls back and forth along with little drops of saliva, saliva that flies and doesn't hurt its target. Jeremias then got up out of the chair a little, without saying anything, leaned over the table, and, showing signs of the most absolute calm, signed the text, received the horse laugh in his face, full in the face, and refused to look as the mayor went off toward the door.

"Mr. President!" Guilherme José muttered disdainfully, "What do you know? Mr. President!"

When he opened the door to leave he had to duck not to catch the inkwell flung by Jeremias at his head, and for a few moments he stood in the street listening to the other's roar. He was breaking every small object and doing it in such a natural way that no one could have suspected it was the noise of things being broken up. When Jeremias left he carried inside a determination to disappear from the face of the earth. He locked himself in his house and began a cycle of drinking binges. Two weeks later, unshaven and drunk, his eyes vacant, he was a man heavily castrated by drink, because he'd come to fear his own lucidity as much as the very light of day. From then on his life was completely reversed in the cycle of time: he would spend the night getting drunk and sleep all through the day. He'd become as well a pensive being in the way, calling to his wife or one of his children, he would say:

"Bring me a bottle of brandy so I can get drunk!"

In his look of an absent and wretched man the well-known theory of the mayor began to show itself, according to which it wasn't even necessary to wipe out enemies; he preferred to render them inoffensive. Guilherme José had managed to get him out of the way and he'd started maneuvering as well toward rendering the priest silent and neutral. He'd conceived the plan to take over Rozário all by himself, and he was still thinking about that when he began putting up the edict in several places in the parish. As he redoubled his operations of vigilance he sensed people were starting to avoid him, a sign that his strength had already taken on the necessary density and he could shortly begin to venture into new ways of seduction. In the beginning he would seize delinquents by the arm, or even by the neck, and lead them by force to his office and make them read the precious edict aloud in his presence; later on he would only take the offender to task and sentence him accordingly. Sometime later he even dispensed with those bothers and began beating people up. Since the infractions persisted and became even more numerous, he ordered Calheta the sexton to read the text on the church steps after Sunday mass. Since the sexton was illiterate, however, the mayor took care of the matter personally and bellowed it aloud to make clear that nobody could invoke as his defense ignorance of the law. And he read:

Jeremias Moniz Furtado, prezident of this Parish of Our Ladie of the Rozário of Achadinha, in full uce of the powers given him by the ilectors and outher temporale & religious authoritys, makes known to the people of the same what can be read here:

Article 1—Be it known that the citizens of this our land have as their duty and obligation better public sanitation and other necessities, and since this Council cannot perform miracles, it is decreed that a tax bee imposed called the Harvest Tax witch shall be one bushel of crop for every hunerd bushels harvested and wich are to be deposited at Council headquarters or shalle remaine under the care of Mayor Guilherme José Bento so none of the same shoulde go astray.

Article 2—This oure mayor by name Guilherme José Bento known also as Goraz states that anyone who does not fulfill or misstates his quota will be imprizoned for a month and pay a fine of two hunerd patacas for each delinquency or delinquent in addition to what is decreed in this edict.

Article 3—He also makes the following fines for acts of misbehavior or rashness:

a) Anyone letting his cattel stray in someone elses field, a fine of fiftie patacas in accordance with the laws set forth above;

b) Anyone who damages his naybor drastically or in other weighs, twenty patacas cash and he might get a publick flogging as well;

c) Anyone building a house or hut or hovel or workshop without permission and on his own five hunerd patacas and a demolition;

d) Anyone damaging the goods of an other his naybor by destruction, profanation, or removal or any form or reason another fifty patacas;

e) Anyone caught in the act of robberie let him be truly warned because it will be jail for him, a cut on the wrists, a beating about the ribs, and on top of that a fine of two hunerd fifty patacas and an appearance before the Judge for the Northeast;

f) Anyone who insults, offends, demeans or causes different annoyances will be dealt with according to circumstances;

g) Anyone who says God doesn't exist or insults our religione, the church, our priest, or is reason for scandal among children, will make publick confesison, suffer degradation, and the appropriate physical correction according to the seriousness.

Everything that is to be legislated from here forward will be only through these means of decree, which will be presented to the people in the usual places destined for all notices. Therefore pay close attention to the following words: NO CITIZEN CAN INVOKE IN HIS DEFENSE IGNORANCE OF THE LAW REGARDING THE MAINTENANCE OF GOOD BEHAVIOR!

Done this tweny-seventhe of the monthe of May of this Yeare of Our Lourd Jesus Christ by the

Presidente,who signs for the good of
the parish, the kingdom, and the world
Jeremias Moniz Furtado

And after that, one afternoon, with several harvests already quite advanced, the first accusation appeared at the mayor's office, for the Council's edict had immediately aroused hate and disagreement among several families in Rozário. Agostinho da Canada, according to the denouncer, had harvested his potato patch in Macieiras Velhas at night and, contrary to the rules laid down by the new administration, had stored his crop away by stealth in his bin. Scowling as always, Guilherme José listened to the man's testimony with euphoria and set out for Agostinho's house. He covered the distance with great dusty strides and lashing the ground with his whip, already half-intoxicated by that opportunity to teach his enemies another lesson. Those who saw him pass that afternoon thought they saw on his face a mysterious pallor that contained not only the wrath of the Devil, but most of all the passion of death. The space between the infinite wrinkles on his face had filled with a look of lusterless copper, his visible and somewhat blue fire, and his body was already tilting forward, ready to head into action. When Agostinho's wife opened the door, nothing stopped him. He charged right into the house and began rummaging in all the corners, from the kitchen and bedroom to the attic with its trunks; then he went out into the yard and, passing by the cowshed, scared off the hens that were brooding eggs in nests of cornstalks, stepped on a mouse which scurried through the crack between two boards, and, going up into the corncrib, found what he was looking for. There were sacks, baskets, and bowls of potatoes. He weighed them and turned a deaf ear to the insistent pleas of the poor woman, in whose terrified eyes the specter of dark fear was beginning to arise when the mayor faced her sternly and asked about her husband.

"He ain't home, suh. He went to see after the stock, up to the hill, and he won't be back from there till after night."

Guilherme José quickly concluded the woman was lying to him because she said all that in an afflicted way and as if she were looking around and listening for the smallest sound. Therefore he began to search inside and outside the house again and finally came upon Agostinho hiding in a vat. He didn't grab him by an arm or by the neck as he normally did on other occasions, but by the tip of his nose, and he dragged him along the street that way to his office.

"You great swine!" Guilherme José cursed. "You flinty dog, I'll burn your guts for you!"

As he was shoved through the door, the man lurched and went straight up against the wall where yellow sheets of paper ran along in a row, among them a copy of the decree.

"There it is," the mayor said. "Read! Drawn up by the hand of our priest, to be respected and obeyed."

"Oh, mistuh! Oh, mistuh! Pleases, have mercy! Cain't you see I'm a poor man and I've got a wife and kids to take care of? Oh, mistuh, oh, please!"

Goraz immediately lost his patience and gave him such a whack that the man stumbled toward the wall again and slumped onto his back. He fell half-knocked out and when he came to he was weeping. Nevertheless, the tears and the whining, the same as the twisted talk, produced just the opposite

58

effect desired in the mayor. He decided to let Agostinho choose between jail and the payment of a double harvest tax—and the man, bathed in tears and secretly swearing a string of vengeances against Guilherme José, ended up picking the second alternative. In exchange he obtained from the official the following promise: the case would be buried deep, quite deep, in the tomb of oblivion, and there would be no more talk about it: but the man should note well in his excommunicated head of a stubborn ram: the authorities had their laws, the edicts were there to be obeyed, if not, there would be trouble, great trouble, everybody pulling his wagon in his own direction, which would make it hard for him, the mayor, in his mission of policing such an ungrateful gang of unscrupulous lawbreakers. Agostinho guaranteed then, and repeatedly, that he was well aware of his duties and obligations, and he swore by the holy faith of the Church and its martyrs, by the doctrine of the bishops and the Pope, the one they also called the holy father, by everything, everything, in short, that was most sacred in this world, and since there was nothing more to swear by, he took advantage of the moment to philosophize a little, since all there was left in this world of forgotten people was to die, let the sacred scriptures and the serene will of the saints and the archangels protecting us abundantly in the midst of the shadows and snares of life be fulfilled. A moment later, convinced of Agostinho's repentance, Guilherme José went to get two glasses of liquor and a dish of roasted squash seeds, and there began the peace treaty between two men who had mutually cleared up an unimportant mistake.

They say, too, that it was a pact of life and death, made to take effect under the best and worst of circumstances in the future. Others add they got drunk that afternoon and even became accomplices in some unspeakable chicanery. That, however, was not immediately proven.

5

THE SIGN OF THE GREAT
WEEPING OF ANIMALS TOOK PLACE ONE SUNDAY
AT THE END OF THE DAY WHEN A FEW LAGGARD
HERDERS WATCHED WITH SURPRISE AS THICK
TEARS POURED OUT FROM THE EYES OF THEIR
COWS. NO ONE COULD EVER REMEMBER HAVING
observed a similar occurence before because it was generally
known that suffering and the ways it showed itself were strictly
human privileges. As a matter of fact, they were accustomed
to weep only for the dead and the absent, because they alone
were capable of having feelings for all of life's situations. In
that way it became evident that despair was a form of suffering common to all animate beings, and so terrible that it could
even modify the hidden face of things. Following that the
cows, dogs, sheep and goats wept—and thus a reason to
believe in the universal phenomenon of prophecy arose, for
the lament of the animals was naught but a sign of the time,
as visible as its future grandeur. So if that was how things
were regarding beasts, and especially the females among them,
why not admit then that trees, stones and the earth wept as
well when at night they received the loneliness of water and
moaned, submerged in dampness?

Alarmed all the more by that manifestation of despair, the
men crowded together at the top of escarpments and from
on high were amazed by the way in which the weeping
spread out silently toward the sunset and became gilded
by it, washed by the salt of low tide. An immensely afflicted look, it became immobilized all over the empty spaces

on the Island, broken in its outline by the spine of the mountain, as if the courage of past days had slipped forever inside. It took a long time for the origin of such an unusual phenomenon to be revealed, but it was finally attributed to a nostalgia for the very process of the earth's formation.

"The fact is that animals," Professor Calafate explained after some stubborn mediation, "also feel the melancholy of the place we inhabit." If he spoke that way it was to allude to a kind of communion of despair between man and beast: "Just like us, they sense that they're the property of this land and the prisoners, perhaps, of the sea, the water, and the salt."

The fact is, the professor's explanation was only plausible because the turns in the knowledge of the world were going through an equivocal stage, and it was formulated on the basis of continuous and new hypotheses. Empirical science, in spite of having been born of mankind, was still random and unsystematic. There was, however, a foreboding that something definitive was to happen one day, for the age-old destiny of man and beast was written and lacked no other sign beyond death. No one inhabited an Island; it was an insular prison, with its eternally low ceiling all seasons of the year, a sea, a round space, like respiration or the movement around an axis—and nothing else. It might be that the sea there would rise up to the highest parts of the mountain one day and everything would sink into its great bosom of a mother whale, or that the very Island would devour itself from within, attacked by the colic of the earth's mushrooms, the volcanoes, and thus fulfill the ancestral prophecy of the biblical waters that would leave no stone standing nor any living creature on the face of the earth. Professor Calafate could find no explanation for the fact that all the children on the Island had been born with blue eyes, notwithstanding the fact that their parents had the inexpressive and colorless gaze of people born everywhere in the world. Perhaps they were the children of the resting sea and carried with them the memory of the waters ever since creation. Even the copious rains that went on for ninety-nine days without surcease had to be interpreted as a kind of endless cycle between birth and death. And if that was what the professor thought, he said it even better:

"The difference between our children and the grownups is that they've taken the destiny of the sea for themselves, while the adults put forth roots into the land like plants, out of fear of going away again."

Following the weeping of the animals came the sign that the yam was an edible tuber when its properties began to be appreciated by the more famished mouths. At first they cooked them with the skin on in large clay pots, where the roots floated for a veritable infinity of boiling; later they experimented by putting them into the oven on tin trays piled high with earthy crusts, concluding thereby that the husk was an accessory as useless as its digestion was arduous. Faced with the unexpected discovery of the yam, the monstrous hunger that had been silently growing in many houses in Rozário until then was soon reduced to skin and bones, like donkeys when they become filled with the patience of their old age and start losing their lives. All over the Island, along the banks of streams and beside the sluices of water mills, yams grew mingling with chicken feed and rows of watercress, to the point that it seemed inevitable for that unexpected novelty to be introduced into their diet. All that was needed then was to pull them out of the ground with a great tug and wet them with *tabuga* leaves. Even the pigs, tearing the stalks and roots with their teeth, got fat in the space of three weeks and were ready for slaughter. Even though their flesh had taken on a carbolic taste similar to mold, a lot of people opted to raise swine. With the arrival of the sugar beet there was a sight of pigs, cattle, and other animals all aglow, fat and hairless, as if that unusual and final blessing of the land had made it creamy and thick with sugar and been transformed into sap in the animals' bodies. The herd grew overnight and presented the same trim look as when they came back from the Mato do Povo, the people's woods, at the beginning of Autumn. Finally peach trees appeared, coming directly from the lands of the Persians, and the force of their growth showed itself at once to be so uncontrollable that any idea of planting them was unnecessary. Drifting about, the pits sprouted in damp places and then opened up into a leafy plant that soon after put down roots and flowered the following Spring. There were, lastly, skinny banana trees scattered through the cane brakes or along the edges of gullies, in places that had been out of the way until then, but where groves soon came to be. At first, mixed in among brambles, boxwoods and rushes, the banana trees grew, sickly looking and bearing no fruit; afterwards, when they'd cleared away the brush, the farmers supported them with stakes and made them face the Sun—and then they became fruitful with cow manure out of the bosom of the earth itself.

One day the Rua Direita was trampled all along its length by the largest herd of cattle ever seen on that side of the Island. A confused bumping of heads and horns for a distance of over a thousand feet appeared at the end of the parish, coming from the Moio flats. Hostlers and drovers whistled continuously at the guard dogs, which would nip and then try to get out of the way of kicks and butts. They used goads, switches, and whips made of whale skin to control the bulls and stop the calves from running away. It was already the month of October, the rains had begun, and the world had turned itself around to show the face of the coming Winter. The herd was strung out along the street in front of the horses, quickly taking the route to the pastures. The trampling hooves dug deep into the mud and scattered pebbles. The street was transformed into a lardy bog where stuck out stones, pieces of submerged logs, and wood chips rotted by dampness. The animals displayed an aluminum ring in their ears that identified them as the property of Leandro. But due to some confusion, someone had marked the cattle with a branding iron in a twisted, curled figure that stamped on their haunches an L with two small stars at either end. People came to the doors and windows and couldn't keep from crossing themselves in shock.

"What a mystery of animals!" an old blind man said, his ear cocked to the sounds of the world. "There must be more than a thousand, aren't there?"

Father Governo, up on his balcony, hard by the flank of the church, blessed the herd and began to open up with the smile of an elderly archangel as he tried in vain to count the heads bustling about beneath his feet. He laid claim to all the signs of Rozário's abundance for himself and he enjoyed with carnal pleasure the wealth of the men God had entrusted to him. With the same gesture he blessed the cowherds, who took off their hats as they passed, and he waved from a distance, just as he'd seen bishops do, to all those who'd taken up positions on steps and in doorways to admire the cattle. They noticed, with surprise, that his hair had begun to turn white around the temples and that the beginning of a bald spot was already at work atop his leathery head, where the remnant of a tiny and now distant sun reflected. They were especially startled at the way in which that smile was slowly cutting across a face that never smiled, because the wrath of his Sunday sermons would be prolonged throughout the week until the following Sunday; such was the picture people had of that furtive being who policed their sinful souls, censured their bearing, their thoughts, and every small action in their lives from the day of their baptism to their extreme unction.

Children were habitually terrified just seeing him from a distance when someone called him or whenever he took the initiative to visit some sick or sad person. They would go kiss his hand with the air of someone condemned to slaps and tugs on the ear, even when it wasn't catechism day:

"Who is God?"

As a rule they would answer him in a chorus and quite vigorously, because his ear required it that way—and they would do it with a rush of words, with dread, repeating the stated wisdom countless times. Thereupon Father Governo would point his finger in the direction of a face and order it to repeat the holy doctrine all by himself.

"He's our Father in Heaven, the creator of all things on earth, who sent His Son into the World to die on the cross for our salvation."

If a child tangled up his speech, he would receive immediately a furious look, with a bitten lip and spit shining in the corners of the mouth, and then the pinch or swat on the head. The children's infinite weeping became then inevitable. Their little hands desperately rubbed their temples, the tops of their heads or their painful earlobes, thinking there must be some father or older brother, a father with the strength and anger to

64

punch the priest in the mouth, in his fat smile, in that face of his as beastly and maybe just as sad and cruel as the wrath of his religion. His roars echoed through the nave of the church and were encased for life, they say, in the blameless look of the children of Rozário. He couldn't admit that those children didn't even come to resemble the ones he'd found in the parish at the time of his assignment, for whom the teaching of the catechism had been unnecessary. He just couldn't understand that time had degenerated the human mind so much that intelligence and the evolution of mankind and things had acquired a different logic—that of growth, of progress through the inner growth of the civilization of the world itself.

"Oh, what dunces! What asses, may the Lord forgive me! Uncouth swine like these can only be found in the depths of Hell, to the shame of my countenance!"

Many years later his voice, which in the beginning had been too large for this world and seemed to explode even inside rocks, had changed into a painful gasp like the squawk of a hen with respiratory problems. His legs then required a high-backed chair to be set up before the faithful. He ordered teachers to introduce doctrine in arithmetic problems, in dictations, in the names of rivers, mountains, and countries, because, he said, his temporal strength was as frail as the legs of insects and it no longer permitted him to teach catechism. As for the rest, when they watched him celebrating mass sitting down with his back to the altar, they thought with relief that death was the wisest event in life and that it most certainly would not be long in meting out its justice.

When the herd disappeared over the Canto da Fonte, a tide of manure was spread over the street and urine ran down the gutters and from there into the drains. Silence brushed past open doors, for no one had as yet become accustomed to such noisy passing. It wasn't even probable that another herd of those proportions would come to stand before their eyes again someday. The calm of beams and the crackling of firewood, the awakening of steps on the floor of tamped earth in almost all the houses, their voices, the reborn voices of the women, and all that had existed before were being reborn, making one think at times of the ghost of an abandoned or long-deserted settlement. That was when the horses, running up the street at full speed, repopulated the nakedness of the walls and carried off with them, in the beating of their hooves and the tossing of their manes, that infused and unreal silence. The bones of the afternoon were clad once more in the layered thickness of paint, of salt and oxide, of all the invisible axles, of the restless rolling of balls and bobbins on sewing machines, and then the afternoon took on its animal look again, and the breathing of craters and conch shells went back to being monotonous and absent. It wasn't a sensation of bone splinters, but the perception that the whole Island was nothing but the product of a combustion of acids and inorganic matter and was now and forever waiting there to be able one day to slide off to another land. Like us, the insular umbilical cord suffered from the fever to return to the maternal womb, because it, too, sighed with the breath of uterine heat. And for the selfsame reasons that children become distracted, lose the hand of their mother, and spend the rest of their lives looking for her in the midst of the crowd, so too in bygone days its body had floated out to sea, as the moss, the algae and the smell of the volcanic *bagacina* rock still attest.

They were living at that time through the tribulations of the decrees that Guilherme José went about putting up in various parts of Rozário. Sometimes they would see him with soap paste or chewed lumps of bread putting up the small, handwritten sheets. He would hang them on the three doors of the church, on the wall of the milk stand, on the windowpanes of the Parish Council, on the barbershop of the poet and dentist Francisco Heitor, and, finally in his office and on the front of his house. They were texts scribbled out invariably on yellow sheets of paper all through his sleepless nights when the winter weather already came along outside and cats fled their rooftops to seek shelter in sheds. Guilherme José had even entered a creative delirium, for he would compose and tear up and compose again until he got the final form of the decrees concerning contributions and fines, notices with no rhyme or reason, and a repetitious roll of names and relatives of the dead and the newborn; and sometimes it happened that his shoulders would hunch over and take on, with a touch of modesty, the solitude of inglorious creatures at the moment of inventing in writing what has no need to be created, and along with the solitude of the night they doubly spawned his nocturnal insomnia, until day would begin to break in the distance and the mayor would feel an interminable urge to die. *What are we to preach to the fish today, Father António?* With this voice that cries out in the wilderness we shall preach an animal smile, one without malice, a dog-smile that doesn't bark but bites, and no ordinary dog, let it be understood, but a different one, with his mouth watering—because only water doesn't terrify fish. Guilherme José ended up shredding all the sheets of paper and standing up with his enormous bulk. His brain was floating inside a desperate weariness and his body was pleading, at last, for death. Then he went to awaken his wife and pulled her drawers down to her feet. He liked her smell of sleep, of dead saliva, the smell of her vulva at rest and the heat of almost rotting hay that the breath of her body had. He would pick all that up in his arms and hold it in the air above his head and stand for a moment scrutinizing the woman's sadness, not feeling like, she would say, opening up her legs for him. But when the woman began to weep, he would only say to her, "Stick it deep inside of you, you'll see that it doesn't hurt," and she would stay there chewing a corner of the sheet and moaning, moaning, moaning until she passed out. That was when Guilherme José would fill with steely excitation: the woman's sobs burned his body within her skin and communicated deeply with that perforating organ that still grew inside her dead groin. A half hour later he would come back again and fuck her slowly, almost passively, because the woman had stopped moaning and was beginning to smell of menstruation and sweat was running from all the pores that had yet to faint in her pain. Immediately thereafter he would fall asleep and the woman would get up from the bed and go wash herself to put out the fire in her ravaged insides and start thinking that if God existed there must be some kind of leprosy, anything, that could start eating away at that monstrous body weighing two hundred forty pounds on top of hers every morning; two hundred forty pounds and a bull, she thought, waiting for flies, bees, and spiders to get together someday and divide up the sponge of his testicles among themselves, or maybe cholera, poisonous mushrooms, the curling worms that children get, and every plague possible and imaginable to make a nest of shit out of his guts and eat him up alive. Still and all, Guilherme José slept imperturbably, all curled up in his peace, and no illness was ever to afflict him. In the turns that life takes, he had married that submissive creature who suffered amidst tears and silence the charges of his horse-like virility whenever a thing resembling the handle of a plow came out from between his thighs and tore into the woman's infertile womb. In that house love was a creaking of joints and clasps rusted by dampness and the very voice of the woman imploring him for an impossible respite had become rusty and old, because the mayor never loved her: he was only thinking of new decrees while he fornicated, or he would write them out on top of her, feeling her going to sleep from fatigue. If his imagination didn't serve him, he would go into action again on top of that body, so irrepressible was his hunger for the woman's thighs. It was said he even liked to look for her on days when her menstrual flow was most abundant and that the sight and smell of the blood gave him an inconceivable erection. Others thought he was also desperate to enter her body because he'd sworn to kill her if she didn't give him a son and that he would continue fornicating in her even after she was dead.

There were those who'd promised to lie in wait for him behind a hedge and cut his throat, but that and other threats kept bouncing off his indifference or soon became part of his glory of ordering his enemies around and affronting them. He put them on the list of unimportant things because no one had yet been able to stand up to him and never would be. One morning, before the tolling of the Angelus, as he went down the street with his pockets full of new decrees to put up, he noticed that the herdsmen no longer answered his greeting. They looked away and prodded their mares, but their eyes were quite full of rage and they didn't even notice that Guilherme José was laughing in their faces and that he'd finally put an end to the good manners of offering a greeting. That time he squeezed the paste between his fingers with saliva and pounded the pieces of yellow paper onto the main door of the church. He stood there waiting for someone to come along because he was spoiling for a fight, to lay his hands on somebody and knock him down. Still, not a living soul came near. Everybody had decided to ignore his decrees. By acting so, the people imagined this to be the only way of turning everything to disdain, because boils are either squeezed or allowed to come to a head until they burst, and, in any case, they always do burst. Guilherme José immediately tried to counteract those tactics and he did so in such an expressive way that he soon recovered the advantage the powerful always hold over people. So, since a decree from the king had arrived in Rozário in the hands of an emissary ordering a review of all titles of ownership of lands and houses, the mayor felt the warlike spirit of an entire army reborn in himself. He spent the whole night interpreting the royal decree to the last detail and then he drew up an edict to be read on the steps of the church after mass. And, imagining the effect it would have, he took such care in its writing that he ended up putting together a text much more tangled in its twists and terms than was the king's own Latin. It stated that *it being meet to give every owner his due, as the holy scriptures have determined, let all people avail themselves of proofs and writings and come to attest at this mayoralty to the legal possession of lands and houses and all belongings conventionally held by an owner, so that said registrations may be reviewed and an end put to old and contentious disputes.* The philosophy behind the edict lay in the fact that Achadinha had been built up in a haphazard fashion on that flatland of hydrangeas, brambles and hazelnut trees, so that its plots were, for the most part, areas acquired by simple occupation. Lands and houses passed in that way from fathers to sons and from them to new sons, and no one ever questioned those conventions. After reading the royal decree and his own edict, Guilherme José admired the fearsome effect of his laws and withdrew to wait for all those who were to come and see him. As the days passed, human animals, dying from fatigue and anxiety, began arriving at his office. They carried rolled up in their hands papers containing the artless proof of their ownership of things, while others nervously fingered their hats and could only offer their word of honor. They looked up and down at those walls covered by the most obscure resolutions as they waited in line. They adjusted their frayed shirt cuffs, and the effort of arguments concerning remote inheritances and family traditions brought out streams of sweat on their temples and trembling fingers as they sensed they might be close to the moment of poverty and shame. Then they would resume larval faces and their bodies would hunch over in humiliation, since the secret of success with Goraz could only be guaranteed by that humbling attitude. They regaled him with bows and slimy smiles, calling him *Mr. Mayor,* but they were also thinking that in the presence of reptiles the first feeling one gets is the dampness of their coils and the greasy water of their track; nevertheless, facing Goraz, that sensation immediately went away because his face had the look of a toad and his bulging eyes inspired vomiting. The long human lines generally became as brittle as fish bones as they waited for the mayor to fill his books with his sluggish writing, interrupted many times by doubts and all manner of objections, to a degree that it was necessary to repeat all the arguments in different words and pull the signed document with the seal of the mayor's office out of his hands. With that guarantee they could travel to Nordeste and register the deed to their lands.

That was when the tale of compulsory restitutions according to the criterion of Guilherme José got started, or, in other words, the simple abandonment of lands belonging to no one to be added to the already incalculable holdings of the Council. On the other hand, no one could swear that the mayor wasn't taking advantage of the occasion to enrich himself at the expense of those dispossessments. There were at least several indications this might already be taking place. He'd ordered his wife to clear out the small spare bedroom in order to store all the products of the harvest tax there, and lying inside were piles of potatoes, bins of corn and beans, squashes, pumpkins, baskets of fruit, bushels of wheat. When the time drew near for those products to be sold at auction to carters, hucksters, and all manner of middlemen, it wasn't just the spare bedroom that overflowed, it was the granary, the attic of the house, the cowshed, and even the pigsty. It had become impossible to distinguish between what was his and what was supposed to revert to the Council and its works program. There were, however, accounts to be figured and the bickering of those middlemen by his door over prices and forms of payment and his wife's and his prosperity had become quite visible. So perhaps it might not have been improper to suppose that the fate of some of those lands had already been programmed in advance.

The land registration operation was still going on when someone got into his yard and set fire to the granary. The way in which the mayor fought the fire would be remembered for more than a century. He roared with rage as he ran, barrel in hand, going to the front and to the rear and throwing monstrous waves of water onto the flames, although the efficiency of the attempt was in doubt from the very first instant. Then he bellowed for people to help him and he called with frantic gestures to those standing in the nearest yards, watching from there the inexorable progress of the flames. When he saw how they all turned their backs, a kind of torpor made him drop his arms alongside his body, and once and for all he was certain there would never be a hint of reconciliation between him and the men of that land. And when Agostinho Moniz arrived running to help with the fire, Guilherme José merely cast a discouraged look in his direction and decided that the two of them would sit down and watch the flames. In little more than an hour the fire had consumed everything, ashes were piling up over the embers, and the granary had been reduced to a shapeless carcass. If Agostinho's gesture inspired a remnant of friendship in him, it didn't prevent other Rozarians from deducing something else. Matters were beginning to make sense, since they all remembered that Agostinho had recovered certain pieces of land that in times past had belonged to some farmers from Salga. Quite simply, those lands had remained abandoned and never been cultivated. It wasn't just by chance that people swore Agostinho enjoyed immunity from the harvest tax. Guilherme José went on to be the only visitor to his house, recovered now from the poverty of rusty hinges and crumbling walls. For the repairs he had to hire stonemasons from Algarvia, since no master mason in Achadinha was ready to take on the work. Neighbors even swore the two men abandoned themselves to drinking all night long while planning together new obligations for the inhabitants of Rozário.

João-Maria was one of the last people to enter the office with the provisional titles to his lands in Fontainhas. It was a morning of new buds, one of those that offer the promise of peace with the world for our souls. With the approach of Spring the fig trees were beginning to be covered with leaves again and carts with manure went up the Rua Direita to the seeded fields. João-Maria trusted that such bureaucracy was nothing but a way of formalizing uses and customs, and beyond that he couldn't understand how it could be any other way. When he faced the mayor he saw that he had before him a set of eyes watery from hate and drink. They even had the insomniac and almost afflicted look of a madman, because Guilherme José was in one of those ups and downs of life where despair had taken over his complete physiognomy. He'd given his wife and horse a drubbing, he'd written the latest decree seven times and torn it up seven times, he'd run to the pigsty another seven times and there had defecated with yellow dysentery the same number of times. The cramps in his guts had printed the expression of an acid stomach on his look and when things were like that the world hung by a thread. On such occasions his wife vaguely felt growing the hope that a fatal illness was devouring him and when she said so she was beaten senseless. So when he faced João-Maria and saw him hold out some papers already half-eaten by dampness and the spiders in cupboards, the mayor leaped up and came over to him as if trying to stop him from entering the office.

"Here," he cried peremptorily, "everything is done properly, as has been set forth. With order and justice."

The other man didn't understand the full import of those words right away, but he had the feeling of someone who'd lost out due to hatred. He stood there facing him, not moving the most insignificant organ of his body, knowing, however, that he was making a great effort not to fling his hands around his neck and tighten them until he strangled him.

"To each his own, João-Maria! That land in Fontainhas is mine and very much so, as you well know. Bought by me in your father's time. You get yourself off there in the time laid down by the law or else I'll arrest you."

"Nothing of the sort," João-Maria retorted coldly, still not moving. "You know just as much as I do that you never paid my father a penny. That's why I've got here the deed in his name and here I am as his only heir."

At that point Goraz began to grow, inside and out, and became the size of an old dragon driven from his lair. He picked up his whip and called to his guard dog. Still, João-Maria's almost deathly pallor was so fearsome and his face so covered by lines and shadows that the mayor withheld his impulse and spat far off toward the spittoon. The people witnessing that from outside came a little closer. It so happened that courage still existed, they thought, courage as old as the sweat of their armpits and the memory of their work.

"The land is mine," João-Maria repeated, with the greatest calm, holding out the deed again. "You're the one who, if you set foot there, will have your head cut off. I'm not leaving."

They all crowded together in expectation of the mayor's attack. In fact he did aim his whip at João-Maria, who received the blow and staggered, confused, up against the wall. He fell under the formidable blow of a punch and then a mountain of flesh closed over his body. He tried using his knees to get out from under that sort of whale, but it was all useless, even impossible. Guilherme José grabbed him by the hair and began beating his head against the wall, and he was certainly going to kill him with no effort at all. Suddenly João-Maria could see that people were leaping into the office from the street. They were flying in through the window, as light and euphoric as bees in heat, and in a short while it was a matter of boots and cudgels and terrible mouths biting, biting still with the mayor's first cries, and they began to drag the whale into the street, and they finally understood he was nothing but a great unconscious mass, out of whose mouth a green froth like octopus spit was blooming. They left him in the care of his wife, who, when she saw that her husband was swallowing his tongue, thought: "Now I can kill him," and paid no attention to his epilepsy. They came to get him, however, and dragged him to Cadete the healer's sick bay. The next day, still not fully recovered from the terror of dying, he ran to the borough office and ordered a police platoon. He went from door to door, set up ambushes, shackled all his attackers, and had the men under his command avenge him with their rifle butts. He himself drew up the sentences for imprisonment and the fines for attacks against authority in small hearings with the *corpus delicti* proven by the bruises on the plaintiff himself.

There was rebellion all over Rozário. The weeping of the women and children was completely useless, however. As for the men, they were kept at a distance by the whirlwind of animals and the threats of rifles. João-Maria was one of the first to be marched off to jail over the protests of Sara and his sons, and he only had time before they shackled him and broke his nose to shout that chains weren't forever, one time would follow another, and he would settle his accounts with the mayor when he returned. When they saw that crowd of men being dragged off to prison, the women gathered together and ran to get Father Governo, whom they begged to intercede in such an outrage. They ascertained, however, that the priest had gone almost completely deaf, because it took them half an hour to make him hear and understand. During that waiting time the prisoners had disappeared under the watchful eyes of their escort.

"Have you ladies gone mad? What? Your husbands arrested? Well, go complain to our mayor."

When they explained that the arrest order had come from him, the priest quickly disabused them. They shouldn't get involved in the affairs of a bunch of rowdies. That's what civil authorities were for. He must leave them in God's little peace because he, His minister, had no power against the sign of the times. Nevertheless, his vinegary voice the very next Sunday was able to roar out against the perversion of the evangelical spirit of the parish where the iniquitous not only didn't respect God, but were now attacking the defenders of order and morality. His sermon even conferred an exceptional dignity on the tincture of iodine and the mercurochrome on the face of the mayor. At that moment, anyone who turned his head would have seen him in the central nave of the church, sitting in a large chair and completely apart from the men. His injured trunk had straightened up a little and his eyes moved around him. There was in that look, more than on his lips, a dull smile challenging one and all again. One and all were once more being challenged by that smile.

Soon, in that way, the Rozarians felt the rigor and the violence of the law's iron hand on their flesh. Its tentacles came there gloved in the invisible person of the citations and summonses carried in the canvas bag of Juliano the postman or in the slim fingers of municipal policemen, from whose belts there now hung revolvers and a kind of horse's phallus wrapped in leather that the caustic sun of the highways had long ago wrinkled down to the bone. The surreptitious movement of all that disorder drove the mayor into a verminous state for a long time. Fines levied on drying lofts and laid on doormats, new contributions to lands deeded to him, and ecclesiastical tithes were now things far removed from his position of a mastiff temporarily retired from the crime patrol. Even the collection of the harvest tax had become almost automatic because fear had taken on a shadowy look and nobody dared violate the edicts. It was inevitable to conclude that the authorities, after the episode of the arrests, had put into action a general plan of pacification, putting behind a first cycle of violence. Nobody could guarantee, however, that it wouldn't be repeated. When the prisoners returned to the parish they spread the word that the mayor had tampered with the writing on the deeds because he'd put some of the lands of the absent owners in his name. João-Maria, learning about this before the others, consulted with Sara as to the way to recover his Fontainhas land, and he set out again on the road to Nordeste. He contacted solicitors and bribed people at every level. Since nothing came of this, he offered temptations to men with alpaca sleeves and eyeglasses who dragged their idleness and poverty along behind old deserted counters. He talked to clerks, requested an audience with a judge, wrote to the bishop and to the king—but all roads were barred to him. He quickly came to understand that all through the kingdom there was a kind of consular empathy among functionaries and that the whole chain of connections worked against anyone who only knew how to beg for a little attention. At the end of a month of insistent requests, he'd spent a thousand three hundred patacas to no avail, had lost his lands, and was in penury. As he got off the jitney that brought him from Nordeste, he bore a look of destruction and he came smothered with hate. His old companions from prison, his sons José-Maria and Jorge-Maria, and his wife Sara heard him say:

"The only thing left for me now is to kill the mayor."

He took his sons by the shoulders and held them tightly against him, sensing that they were crying. They were still young lads, but they'd been reared with a great love for their father and they were capable of weeping during times of affliction. When they got home, Sara faced her husband with tenderness and seeing his eyes quivering, ran to embrace him, and they both wept.

"You're not going to kill anybody, man of mine," she said, "What we're going to do, all of us, is defend our home and our family. That's all that's left for us to do."

"You're right. We've got a home and a family left. For how long I don't know."

Guilherme José went on to become a great landowner. Wanting to cultivate his new land, he offered extraordinary wages to the men who waited at Canto da Fonte for someone to hire them and he watched with surprise as they all turned their backs on him. So the plots remained abandoned since it was impossible to find anyone willing to sell him the strength of his labor. The solution was to look for unemployed workers in the nearest settlements. Later on, beset by threats and ultimatums, the outside workers also ended up beating a retreat and the lands went back to sink into their now chronic idleness. The mayor then conceived of a devastating plan. He went on to find reasons not just to preserve order, but also to avenge himself on everybody. He would put an end to all resistance once and for all and assume the role of a great lord, the absolute master of Rozário. If necessary, he would hire men from the other side of the Island, would arm them well, would wage war. When one looks at a reptile the normal feeling, as so happens, is one of dampness as its skin touches our tactile sense from a distance. When one looked at Goraz, however, it wasn't that way: he had something of a frog about him, his jowls puffy as they were and his hair twisted about the top of his head, as well as the fact that his eyes bulged out over the outline of his cheekbones. In addition, his body was completely like a toad's and his way of walking, always in heavy oscillating strides, made his trunk float frontward, while his misshaped hands were like those of a famished crane, making one think as well of the leaps of a frog. It was necessary to look at him crosswise or simply look away and keep on going forward.

After the tumult and the arrests, the authorities of the council had furnished him with a huge horse pistol that he kept holstered next to his belly on a canvas belt. With that instrument hanging along his thigh, Guilherme José acquired the habit of caressing his weapon with a smile or even his horselike grin that completely broke any tension around him. He also began to change in appearance. One morning he showed up in public with his beard and mustache so stiff that people almost didn't recognize him. It was necessary to pay close attention to the way his broom-like hairs rose up toward his nasal passages so that his small mustache looked more like a prolongation of the tufts of hair coming out of his nostrils than the other way around. Those tufts, along with the others poking out of his ears, ended up transforming him into a hybrid figure, half-bull and half-frog, as if he'd been the result of some miraculous crossing of animal species quite distant from each other. His plan consisted of a tireless hunt for lawbreakers, at the same time that he decided to double the amount of fines. In order to tighten the circle of his vigilance, he secretly hired some informers and began to make his rounds on horseback at all hours of the day and night. He'd recently taken over dozens of goats and heifers, confiscated sucklings, and even arrested a group of children who were experimenting at breaking all the windowpanes in the priest's house by throwing stones. He made their fathers whip them in his presence, lending them his own switch, and the fathers had to choose between giving them five lashes on each leg or paying a twenty-five-pataca fine. As for the animals, if they were caught grazing casually in a vineyard or a cornfield, he would proceed to catch them and apply a hundred-pataca fine. Later on their owners could redeem them at the mayor's office and hand over their old stained banknotes, always at a distance and without any argument, because the hearing concerning the *corpus delicti* had for witnesses only his two eyes and if anyone argued about a lack of proof, he could be taken care of with a whack...

Until the day Fernando Cabral stood up to him over a heifer that had run off. The animal had slipped into a cultivated field, then trampled down some wheat; following that it leaped into an orchard, and then a dog ran after it and bit it on the belly, so the heifer retraced its steps and, entering a house, ran into a table and panicked a young new bride, making her urinate all over her legs; it immediately went back out of the house and ran up the street followed by a dog, then another and another, and there were already so many dogs that the poor calf ran into everything in its way until it finally stopped, facing the open arms of Guilherme José: he was in the Canto da Fonte and seized it by the ear after scattering the dogs, and he waited there until Fernando Cabral, drenched in sweat, said very angrily:

"Even animals have got a reason to go around nervous with all the sentences handed out in this place. Aren't you ever going to die, Goraz, you son of a bitch? Your mother made a mistake when she gave birth to you: she should have shit you onto a dung heap!"

Guilherme José picked up the heifer bodily and put it to one side, and then his back curved over, just like a little spider defending itself against a bee, he began pushing him toward the ditch with an almost diabolical urge to

78

provoke him, and with a strong desire to lay hands on his body and send him out of this world.

"You hit me, mayor, and I'll pay you back double," the man said to his face, still retreating toward the ditch. Guilherme José then grabbed him by the bottom of his pants and lifted him up into the air, saying:

"This is what I do to men like you," and he threw him against a wall. "This," he repeated. Cabral slid down to the ground and looked him up and down with such hatred that for the first time in many years the mayor became a little thoughtful and lost his nerve. He even forgot to levy a fine on that crazy animal going along now under the rope lashes of its owner.

"I'll still see you darker than horseshit someday, you big swindler. You'll be kicking like a hanged man." And, turning to his heifer, he kept on whacking her on the flank and shouting along the street: "Death to Goraz, death to Goraz, death to Goraz, death to Goraz!"

Then, as if a popular uprising were about to take place, doors and windows opened and from house to house, from yard to yard, that cry multiplied like the echo in a dynamited quarry: "Death to Goraz, death to Goraz!"

Guilherme José went into his house and immediately went to fornicate with his wife. Until she died by his hand, that creature with no spiritual existence had only been seen by neighbors a handful of times, generally in the backyard hanging out wash or dressing pigs and chickens. It's said that the night he killed her the mastodon fornicated six times without stopping, roaring for her to give him a son. On the seventh attempt, filled with an inexplicable rage, he closed his hands around her throat. When he saw that he had a still warm corpse under him, he got up and began to dress her. Then he fixed a rope and, hanging her, faked her suicide.

6

"THE SEA? THE SEA IS WHITE," CADETE THE
HEALER SADLY THOUGHT, TURNING TO STROKE
HIS FANTASTIC PERPETUAL BALL IN WHOSE
TRANSPARENCY HE WOULD HABITUALLY WATCH
theSea of the Azores. Loose and skittish in its foam of razors,
raging snakes, monsters, invisible perhaps and snorting salt
and sand, the sea was white because it went about sprinkled
with the desperate saliva from the continuous biting of whales
and serpents. And death was loose there, as when the monster
Centaur passed the chariots of the sea gods. The pale horses
of the gods were certainly not visible in the agitation of the
water, but they would stir it up when they galloped in the
direction of the wind and as the sea went belly-up they turned
it white to Cadete the healer's eyes.

It wasn't even necessary to look too far away, because a
goodly portion of that sea had been closed up centuries ago in
his fabulous perpetual ball. A man's real power consisted in
dominating the sea, keeping it inside a ball, or, as it were, in
possessing the wisdom of Moses, the prophet who separated
the waters of the Red Sea—Cadete, however, supplanted it
all with that object of great utility by whose means he'd learned
to examine the cosmic signs of illness and human destiny. In
truth, those facts were projected on the great colorless iris of
the sphere and were revealed with the extraordinary clarity of
Baudelaire's twin mirrors.

At the end of the day, after the last patient had left, the
healer felt all the solitude of the world and wished for death.

When it rained, his sadness would look around and grow soft as it lighted on objects, just as once oxen's eyes would reach out to the sunset and fill with tears. Then, thinking, "I'm going to die soon, I want to die," he would start arranging the impressive series of materials and instruments of his science and the astrology books, his notebooks with maritime and meteorological calculations, the greasy, worn notebooks with lists of illnesses whose secrets he'd studied, and starting to stroke the magic sphere, he would apathetically review the last few years of his life and admit to himself the nearness of his hour of departure.

The sphere had the fat-bellied shape of an ordinary globe of the world, a bit flat at the poles, but it was graced with inlaid tentacles and the spectrum corresponding to the signs of the zodiac. He'd bought it years before from Bárbaro the pilgrim, during the time when he was still convalescing from the bite of the poorly castrated horse. Bárbaro had sought to guarantee him that the aforementioned sphere was the invention of a primitive monk from Tibet, the hermit Apanaguião. Its properties were infinite. And not the least of them was the rather uncommon way in which the four elements of nature floated inside it without ever mixing. How was that? Something quite simple: the water of the sea, with suspended algae and moss and the remains of the corpse of a prehistoric fish (perhaps a teleost that had disappeared a long time ago, according to Bárbaro), coexisted with fire in the balance of the vacuum in the same way that the air enwrapped the earth and was its respiration—all that by the work and grace of the magical breath of the monk Apanaguião, Asian hermit and philosopher. In addition to that, Bárbaro asserted with eloquence that whoever handled such a precious object would most definitely assume the very spirit of Apanaguião and become his disciple and the heir to his limitless wisdom, just as the apostles had been of Christ the Master in other times. Well, wasn't it true that he, Bárbaro, had the strength of an ocean liner in spite of his age? Did friend Cadete know what an ocean liner was? Something quite simple to explain: just imagine that suddenly, just before we fall asleep, we look out at the sea and a palace appears before our eyes floating on the waves, not one of those palaces with the cavernous front of a church, but a palace built on a keel and equipped with a powerful propeller and engines with the power of many thousands of horses whipped along with a stiff crop. That was an ocean liner, just as Bárbaro had seen them in the sea off Ethiopia, between the Zaaed Strait and the Mediterranean coast. Well, there it was, Mr. Cadete.

The healer ended up convinced of its usefulness, because Bárbaro had held that pale and gloomy eyeball up to the rays of the noonday sun and thought then that inside he could see some kind of convulsive walls surrounding a castle or fortress with the vague look of an ocean liner. It was, without a doubt, final proof of the magic and ageless antiquity of such an amazing object. Because wasn't white the most ancient color in the world?

"Absolutely, absolutely," Bárbaro guaranteed gravely. And attesting to it were his own paleness and his strong albino hair. Bárbaro's face was an enormous ball of tallow, with cheekbones as prominent as two pumpkins, and ashen skin touched by the serene crystals of sainthood, giving him a vague resemblance to a prelate. He had, furthermore, the fat smile priests have and, like them, he would belch thunderously and bless God as much for the calamities as for the magnificence of the world. He was going on a hundred and two years old, according to what he said, since he had already lived everything possible for a human being to live. But he still had enough energy left to wander continuously around the Earth in search of Eternity. He was familiar, furthermore, with every stopping-off place in the universe because he'd already followed not only the routes of the non-solitary navigators but also the endless pilgrimage of Fernão Mendes Pinto himself, a spice merchant and his forebear. In his youth he'd sailed unknown seas, unheard of and never before explored, had been in combat with Greeks and their sea gods, armed with terrible tritons and whose look was obeyed by all monsters. He'd even bested Adamastor on one occasion when that phantasm had had the effrontery to block the Strait of Magellan. He'd loved the Nereids and nymphs of the Euphrates on the Invented Isle off Bombay and had prayed in the sacred sites of Galilee where he heard the voice of Christ in the depths of a conch shell, and he'd been sold to the Chinese and the Japanese and taken captive by corsairs on the sea route of the Rotted Sun. Once publicly whipped by the Huns, another time crucified by the eunuchs of Mongolia, he'd made his way to Tibet on a commercial trip trading marten pelts for mysterious objects. At the conclusion of which, friend Cadete, over the twists and turns in this world, I reached Tibet, a land of lunar gravity, and I plundered a native tribe that held the wise monk Apanaguião kidnapped in a cavern whose ceiling was supported by columns, and in exchange for his freedom I obtained not only the perpetual ball but above all the secret of the elixir of maximum longevity.

How did you diagnose an illness with such a fabulous instrument? Well, very simply: you spin the sphere in front of the patient. Like this? No, no, gently, gently, so as not to awaken our hermit's spiritual breath: you spin it in a spiral, like a top, on the surface of a table, and then the elements, the sacred elements of Nature, touched by the breath of the monk Apanaguião, Asian hermit and philosopher, would go into temporary imbalance. When the ball stopped, the healer would immediately hold it up against a luminous focal point and then decipher the data. If the sea appeared (white, without a doubt, friend Cadete), the patient's ailment was liquid, and you would have to encounter it with the opposite element, fire. But if land appeared, then the cure would have to be effected through the gaseous element—air—and so on successively *ad infinitum*. A simple matter of logic, that's for sure, whereby it was just the same in practice: fire is opposed to water, as earth is to air, and water to earth, and air to fire, and the latter to earth. In Apanaguião's perpetual ball, however, these elements coexist and are never mingled.

Cadete gave repeated signs of understanding. Bárbaro swallowed his spit and his enthusiasm grew. In a short time he was explaining that hot intestinal fevers, gastric guts, febrile hallucinations, burning shingles, and even hepatitis or cerebral migraines required water, lots of water, while rheumatism, sciatica, and lumbago could be overcome by the action of fire. As for earth illnesses, such as kidney and bladder stones, calcareous cysts, fecal verminosis, prolapses, swelling, and intestinal cholera, they could be eliminated by the power of plenty of cupping glasses or by the action of infusions and applications of steam. Cadete had difficulty repressing a lively nervousness as he saw that he had the greatest bargain of his life before his eyes. Ultimately, with such a magnificent object, he could quickly forget his sad past as a gelder of horses and obstetrician for difficult mares; he would pass from animal medicine to the science of humanity, and from that to the supreme glory of traveling on those ocean liners that Bárbaro spoke of, and he would try to discover the trail of Christ, the places, states, and names that time invented—because the world existed beyond the world and he'd always had an ambition to go off and discover prophecies. Then he made his quick decision. He accepted Bárbaro's proposal—he received the perpetual ball from his hands and turned over to him two ill-tempered mules that were frothy with rut but barren as stone.

When he saw him leave, he shut himself up in the rear of his house in an old garret eaten away by spiders and mice and spent five days and five nights in experiments, intense reading and meditation. He'd completely forgotten to eat, urinate and sleep. After that he busied himself for a few hours with the task of cleaning out his bedroom, taking the bed, dresser, crucifix, and his personal effects to the garret, and he began to organize the future consultation office in his former solitary bedroom. Then, one by one, he tested all the qualities of the perpetual ball.

At the time Cadete was only curing cattle, goats, horses and other animals that came from far and near, from distant parishes on the other side of the Island, attacked by a medley of illnesses and epidemics, and he'd become an expert in healing animal blisters and fistulas. He'd even invented an unguent based on white ginger and cloves, to which he added seeds-of-paradise, nutmeg, and orange rinds, a mixture that spent many hours under infusion in an alembic and which also had the curious virtue of getting rid of lice, nits, green ringworm, blisters, scabies, and scabs. Difficult births in cows and mares were taken care of with eaglestone and jasper, and in the case of poison, domestic parasites, fungi and hay fever, he created the most unusual antidotes. Enthusiastic over such results and with the insistent quest of those people distressed with their animals, he ventured into new research. From the City he ordered different sets of vats and retorts, aromatic plants, little bags of exotic seeds and leaves, and, in a short while he discovered the fascinating properties of rosemary. First he eliminated plant lice and blowflies, responsible in his opinion for the principal infirmities of animals, then he learned how to offset vomiting in goats and jaundice in dogs by mixing liverwort with the white of turkey eggs. Right after that he applied pig dung and pellitory to hemorrhoids in some oxen. He also experimented with parsley, hyssop, wormwood, spearmint, mugwort and shamrock, and in that way he conquered quartan and tertian agues, which in the short space of a week would bring death to whole herds of pigs and flocks of Plymouth rock hens. One day he cured a ewe blind with cataracts, on another he completely deflated the spleen of a horse and the dysentery and nasal fluxion of a breed goat, and was in sight of a remedy for swine sciatica, healed a stray dog's gout, overcame sterility and black rabies in a thoroughbred bitch, cured the bovine deafness and clotted placenta in a sow that had just given birth, and when at the end of seven more days and nights of stubborn investigations he looked ecstatically at his own hands, he accepted two hypotheses about himself: either he was a genius, a sage or a madman, or else he was delirious with fever, that terrible fever of insomnia, when he completely forgot to sleep again. At that time, since his fame had spread quite thoroughly to the four corners of the Island, he began to receive the nocturnal visits of a few men with syphilis and other inflammations of the male member, and passing on from there to the secret for childless couples was a task of simple, natural inspiration for his creative genius. One time a lady from the Adro, the neighborhood by the churchyard, entered through the backyard, carried in a hand-chair, emitting a tremendous menstrual flow. She was as white as linen and rolled her eyes at him with the complete look of person who'd lost the very notion of despair. Cadete asked to examine her in private. He applied a thick poultice of cuttle-fish shell to her stomach, then a powder of burned bones soaked in roadweed juice. He immediately removed that poultice and applied another of seashells and chimney soot with egg white and the sap of dead nettles, and he sent her away in peace because the hemorrhage had been stanched in a few minutes. And as he recommended three doses of barley flour with night-shade a day, as he always did with animals, he concluded that his destiny had changed course again, because human nature was either only a prolongation of animal nature or it was surrounded by the same needs. He could stop concerning himself with animals and dedicate himself exclusively to people! He spent another eight days and eight nights without going to bed, forgetting about sleep and seeking inspiration in the vigil of the holy man Apanaguião, and in the end he decided to change his life.

He had Calheta the sexton make a proclamation after mass on two successive Sundays, by which means he made known to one and all of his distinguished citizens that he was prepared to examine men, women, and children and that he guaranteed relief from each and every suffering through the scientific method of the perpetual ball, proven more than a century ago, as guaranteed by Bárbaro the pilgrim, by the spirit of Tibetan monks. Then, like a person on the eve of going off on a journey with no return, he went down to the sacristy and asked for the blessing of Father Governo, from whom he received the guarantee of evangelical missions, prayed beside the tabernacle of eternal light, went up through the parish, and sat down at the three-leggedl table amidst his fearsome instruments, and waited for the first patients to appear. He knew they would come. Indeed, seeing how Cadete was eagerly toiling with his objects and getting ready to accomplish scientific work, people weren't long in seeking him out. It was already known that he'd performed his first miracles because he'd almost completely suppressed the need for sleep, set up a laboratory endowed with an alembic, vats, test tubes, strange cupping glasses, hermetic pots, the seeds and roots of varied and unnamable tropical plants, essences of rose, rosemary, musk turpentine and sandalwood, and all of it was arranged in pouches and on shelves with their respective labels, formulas and dosages. As for his own appearance, it, too, had made unexpected advances, convinced as he was that everything in this life demands a dignity adequate to the person displaying it, and he began to shave closely every day and use a little brilliantine on his hair, first patting it down with sugar water. From the City he ordered overalls, like they wore in America, a pair of glasses with grave, oblong frames, a cane sofa, and a screen with opaque curtains. Topping off all that new equipment, he had some pieces of cardboard framed where he'd written in bold letters the ever so wise declaration of Bárbaro the pilgrim:

> **IS WHITE**
> **NOT THUS THE MOST**
> **ANCIENT COLOR IN THE WORLD?**
> **Bárbaro said so, and it's been proven!**

In time new writings and sayings were framed, some of his authorship, others anonymous or attributed to unknown philosophers from the age of fire or even the age of swamps. In the end he'd taken on a cranky and reserved temperament, with great frugal gestures and a neutral expression befitting a sage, and the rigorous air of someone who meditated incessantly and had withdrawn into the elevated contemplation of complex phenomena. It was then that he got the idea of expressing himself in short phrases with lapidary meanings so he would never be mixed up in the vulgarities of the world. In that way the three inscriptions of his most noteworthy and also most disquieting affirmation appeared:

the	**The**	**THE**
sea	**Sea**	**SEA**
is	**Is**	**IS**
white	**White**	**WHITE**

The day of his first smashing victory over lukewarm people finally arrived. It was even more smashing from the fact that it had been practiced on his worst enemy: Francisco Heitor, poet, barber and dentist. He'd come there to his office in the flesh asking for help. Cadete was appalled by his fecal pallor full of hate, and he certainly would have struck him if he hadn't been so impressed by the swelling of his jaw and his pitiful look. The man was struggling with a terrible toothache caused by an impacted wisdom tooth and his eyes conveyed so much suffering that he seemed to be begging more for a *coup de grâce* than any other form of relief. He wept like a little boy, stating that he hadn't slept for more than a week, and that neither his poetic art nor his experience in dealing with gums had been any use for that demonic illness. So he was a man rotting away from a week-old relentless insomnia, with the look of a madman and a growth of beard, and there he was before Cadete because he'd lost all the rancor that had always kept them on opposite sides. Even if all that was left to him was to starve and thrash about on the ground until he died, he begged him to free him from that excommunicated tooth, which had neither any birth or any use. Well, the reason for such hatred was no longer a secret from anyone, because Francisco Heitor, in addition to being mediocre, was spiteful over his enemy's success. He was practically in poverty ever since the day patients stopped coming to see him in the torture chamber that was his place of business. As a poet and as a dentist he still used the obsolete methods of pliers and twine, poultices of earth and urine, and gargling with salt water. And his house was as foreboding as a coffin to the eyes of someone near death. It was said that his poetry disheartened peasants and frightened cow herders' horses for being absurd, uncomfortable, and overly persistent. He would tie his patients to a kind of gelding rack and, working his pliers with eager brutality, recite hateful tercets and lavish quatrains, dramatic odes, and even a few epigrams against the government of Portugal. Torture and poetry became associated to drive terrorized people away, and it reached the point where a herder, as desperate over the rhymes as the pain, took him by the throat and suggested he shut up and free him from the tooth tormenting him.

So Francisco Heitor put in an appearance before Cadete, his face flooded with shadows, and he was so beside himself that he dropped onto the doormat sobbing. There he began to spew a thread of purple saliva, as if he were vomiting mulberry juice. He begged to be killed, to be killed! Cadete was surprised by the fact that he felt no rancor whatever toward the man who'd shown him the most ill will in the parish, and he hastened to wet a cloth in water tinted pink with roadweed liquor, purslane and vinegar. He also brought out some pink olive oil, chamomile tea, marigolds and henbane roots, convinced that no human pain could resist such mixtures. Then he became filled with lively diligence, thinking, like Guilherme José the mayor, that all enemies could be gotten rid of without violence. It was merely sufficient to render them inoffensive. In a few minutes, relieved of his suffering, Francisco Heitor was sleeping like a just man without memory. When he awoke, many hours had passed. Cadete was still watching over him and immediately declared he would have to pull the tooth. Francisco Heitor shuddered and immediately became wide awake. Leaping up with the most ferocious appearance in this world, he looked for the door to flee. He was so dizzy, however, that he stumbled against the wall and could only murmur:

"What you want to do is ruin me, you big asshole!"

Cadete took a deep breath and called on his superior patience, the calm and leisurely patience of a fat man who sweated a lot on his hands, in his breath, in the flabby lines on his face, and even in his eyes:

"Get a hold of yourself, man! You can just leave if you haven't got the courage. What kind of a sudden fit is this? So, c'mon…"

He went inside and brought out a flask containing toasted lizard powder. He softened it with a spoonful of spiritual water, working zealously like any pharmacist, and for a few minutes he rubbed the martyred gum of the poet until it became completely numb. Then the pliers worked so swiftly that the operation seemed more like a trick of black magic than the vulgar and sordid art of pulling teeth. Radiant with himself, Cadete displayed a molar with two roots twisted like hooks. He showed it to Francisco Heitor, and his wolfish smile filled with saliva.

"Hah! Hah!" Cadete went on, almost euphoric. "I've just won a race, even though I don't know who I was running against. Let it be clear that our war continues, because I'll never make peace with any of my enemies."

That wasn't the opinion of the poet, however. He'd opened his arms as a sign of truce: not only was he not a man to harbor grudges, but one who even proclaimed the genius, the efficiency, the abnegation of our healer. Perhaps someday he would be able to compose an ode to him, because poetry, he said, has the supreme grace of conferring immortality.

"When I write an ode to someone it's as if a statue of him had been erected, " he confessed humbly, prissily spitting out the blood from his crater. "I remember one day I myself came to imagine that someone would erect a bust of me. Today I admit I've lost my last opportunity."

Saying that, Francisco Heitor bowed to him and went on his way. He had a despondent air and Cadete, still with his wolfish smile, couldn't tell whether that body, from the way it leaned forward, was carrying a load of vexation or just the weight of its last defeat.

The second notable of Rozário to pass through his consultation room was Father Governo, which was a great surprise for Cadete. It was a stormy night and dusk was closing in with the sound of wind and rain when he heard somebody knock twice at his door. At first when he laid eyes on the priest, he was afraid he'd been caught by the censure of the Church. But he concluded at once that the priest had the withdrawn air of someone trying not to be seen. He was only an animal wrapped in a cape up to his ears, and he had the pleading look of each and every traveler seeking food or shelter. Cadete went to get the lamp and raised the wick. He didn't have a priest before him but some huge half-open nostrils peeping out from the cloak, and he stood there stupefied, unable to admit that a man like that could ever complain of anything that wasn't heresy and bad behavior in his parishioners.

"Might I be of some use to you peradventure, Holy Father? Or have I sinned against God and for no reason?" the healer inquired.

"No, nothing like that. And leave off kissing my hand. I've come here with my complaints."

Cadete told him to sit down and gave him a blanket to wrap his wet legs in. Because it was true: the priest was complaining of a galloping deafness and a strange buzzing in his head. No, not all the time: there was a kind of cycle to his illness, worse with a change in weather, so-so in Summer and real misery in Autumn. Like dogs and flies, he said, he'd got so he could predict rain because the buzzing would become an almost supernatural whistling. Cadete was writing these facts down and he soon felt his calm recovered, his sour manner and his sweat returning. During times like that he thought, "I'm going to die soon, I have to die soon." He spun the perpetual ball in front of the priest, once, twice, and both times he verified that the luminous center was making the fire sparkle in the direction of the patient's eyes. Intrigued by the enigmatic way in which the healer was stroking his chin, the priest admitted that perhaps he was already profaning, more than the secrets of his body, the shrine of his soul.

"Is your shuffling walk congenital or was it acquired in some fall, Your Holiness?" Cadete inquired finally, raising his eyes from the entry book. The prelate opened his eyes wide and didn't understand what relation could exist between his deafness and his ever so discreet way of limping. He swallowed and looked him up and down before answering:

"Congenital, man. It should be obvious that it's congenital. Valgus knees, understand?"

Cadete didn't reply and fell back into heavy meditation. Sometime despair would start there, with the questions he was obliged to ask his patients, with the not very clear and even evasive way in which they would respond. Despair was setting in and Cadete, in order not to wish for death again, quickly picked up the luminous focus and the perpetual ball once more, and everything was dark and redundant around him until he remembered to go on to the next question:

"Who were your parents and what illnesses did they have?"

Thereupon Father Governo began to squirm in his chair. His face suddenly became flushed as it circled about over his knee bones. Seeing him lower his eyes, he repeated the question as a sign that perhaps he hadn't heard him.

"Unknown," he replied annoyed, certain he was revealing the greatest secret of his life to a stranger. "Are you putting together my dossier?"

"A bastard, then?" the healer replied, without any sarcasm and as if he hadn't understood. "Then you sir, Father, are you a bastard child?"

Quite nervous and irate, the priest got up and was going to leave, but quickly resumed his seat when Cadete began interrupting him again:

"Have you ever had any dubious relations with loose women or animals with sexual diseases?"

"Relations with women or animals?" He reacted by standing up again, trembling all over and convinced that the healer was most certainly mocking his dignity. "What kind of talk is this, now? Me a minister of God, messing with animals, with prostituted women? You deserve to be burned at the stake! Oh, Holy Inquisition!"

The other man, however, went back to not hearing him. He was scratching his scalp with his nails, debating nervously with himself and removing pieces of gelatin from that strange mortal parchment.

"Your Holiness will have to forgive me, but I can't help you. You, Father, sir, have the sickness called syphilis. It's a typical case of cavernous syphilis. You will shortly be attacked by total deafness, then by blindness, and you will die of kidney failure. Your feet and your arteries will swell up and the blood will explode in the vessels in your head. There you have my prognostication as to Your Reverence's case."

It is said that then and there Father Governo's infinite sadness began and also his growing revolt against death. Years later, when an old servant woman came upon him with his eyes bugged out toward the ceiling, his ears were as large as a donkey's and his stomach as hard and swollen as a sack of sand. On that day, if he could have visited him then and hadn't hanged himself before, Cadete the healer would certainly have seen the proof of all the phenomena in his record of that illness and, weeping inside, would have thought once more, and with identical sadness:

"I'm going to die soon, I want to die."

Finally passing through the consultation room on the Caminho Novo were those ill with the plague, the unfortunate and lost people with the incurable plague, and they were newly old men and grimy women, the women just like all women in the world who are about to die and pray: Sara the saint came through with her ashen cough, still not resigned, and said: "You must save me, sir, so I'll be able to live just a wee bit more for the poor innocence of my children, for the forgiveness of the world, and for Christ's last look, you must save me from dying, sir"; the man without a face passed through, the one who'd once said, "Let the dead bury the dead," as Inês the fox-woman also passed through and begged him: "A miracle, healer, sir, just a little miracle so I can get rid of this cross." His glory was spreading beyond the parish and it reached the settlements along the coast like an echo. From there it progressed into the interior, crossed the mountains, and women and children came from all parts of the Island, and all of a sudden someone proclaimed in Fenais da Ajuda that he'd invoked Cadete's name and had been saved from a ruinous rash. In Algarvia, in Feteiras, in São Pedro Nordestinho and other parishes within the council territory, people formerly possessed swore that they'd been snatched from the clutches of the Demon by the simple invocation of his name, and the name quickly began to be murmured among the names of all the saints and apostles, and a child who'd been born with a huge hydrocephalic head showed signs of a solid cure when his desperate mother fell to her knees on the ground and wept and prayed for Cadete to remember her misfortune. Then the healer abandoned sleep completely. He was sought out at every hour of the day and night by people who came from afar to entrust their afflictions to him, and he always stayed home, always on watch, so depressed by solitude that he thought again: "I'm tied to death by a thread, I have to die." Everyone had something to love or suffer under, had a feeling, a truth, or a time to recognize that life was a lie; the dying themselves, when they dozed off forever on the maternal bosom of their death agony, had a name on their lips, the name of Cadete, in the hope that his Tibetan spirit would arrive in time to revive them. Only he had nothing, except the greatest, most complete solitude in the world. "That's why I'm in a state of wishing for my death," he thought.

On the day he'd decided to kill himself and was preparing a noose and a stool, he saw an enormous inanimate mass coming into his consultation room in the arms of ten men

who were kicking its head and spitting on its mouth. He
thought: "I'll hang myself sometime this afternoon," and he
heard the thud of a pumpkin, because the men had dropped
the mayor's body with the great hope that it would shatter on
the floor. The men's saliva met the saliva of that mass, it was
one loathsome thing atop another, and one of those who'd
brought him, his eyes filled with misery, implored:

"Fix up a good dose of poison, Cadete, free us from this
pile of manure cooked in hen shit."

The hatred was a confusion of twenty arms dragging an
unconscious body rigid like some dead whale: there was the
urge to beat on the whale, inject its arteries with the liquid
breath of arsenic, and thereby put an end once and for all to
that infinite, unslept night, and finally there would be an end
to the nightmare of women and the breastfeeders, their children, and death would take charge of the sea monster that
dwelt in the body of Goraz, the wife-killer, son of a priest,
son of a million priests.

The mayor was slowly devouring his tongue and the men,
laughing behind their hands, grabbed hold of him: "A good
dose of poison," one of them kept begging. Cadete the healer
had decided to kill himself, that was true, but he could still
believe perhaps in a country with no night, because, he thought,
"More important than having the Sun is being able to leave
the night and go meet it, and more and better than that meet-
ing is the power to invent it, to say it never existed." A thread
of blood flowed from the tongue of the inanimate whale,
because the mayor continued devouring it and spitting it out,
and the healer, thought: "It was, in fact, a good time to relieve
him of life." He spat on the mouth as the others were doing
and left the room. He went through the door to the backyard,
closed the latch, pushing it to the heart of the stone, headed
his body with a twisting motion toward the *canas-da-India*,
went through a hole in the garden hedge, and climbed the
fence that separated it from the sown plots that reached up to
the woods, and from the woods to the crags and from the
crags to the sea, he continued through the trees in search of
the place where in other times he'd built a lair in the darkness
of the dead, went in through the straw, lay down on his back,

and with his hands crossed over his stomach and calling softly upon sleep, he felt it approach and take him over, first in the hands, then in the lower members, and finally in the head, dozing off at least and remaining asleep for fifteen days and fifteen nights, at the end of which, returning to his consultation room, he found they were weeping for him, thinking he'd disappeared from the earth.

7

AND MANY OLD MEN IN THIS OUR LAND OF
ACHADINHA SAY THAT JOÃO-MARIA, ON FINDING
HIMSELF IN PENURY, FOR THE FIRST TIME IN HIS LIFE
FACED THE HOUSE THAT HE LIVED IN AND STATED
IT WAS IN THE MOST DEPLORABLE STATE OF RUIN.
Up till then he had been unaware of the existence of the things
that grew and changed around him, as if there had always
been an invisible partition between them and his body. But as
he grew old the world had become degraded and almost all
his points of reference to it were already disappearing. Looking about only meant to him seeing how things were growing
inside that destruction, falling apart little by little in the
profile of time. Hedges and trees were straggly. The cycle of
life and death had attacked the walls for the forty-fifth time.
Dampness had corroded the deep skeletons of wood and
stone as suddenly as the phases of any growth. And Winter
had always been precisely Winter, while Summer had never
existed to be repeated from one year to the next. His arteries
had burned out completely. The Sun and the fire of blood that
illuminated them had been completely consumed and had
passed into his body in such a way that it would never be
repeated outside. So the sudden sight of his house called the
careful attention of his eyes upon it and the meaning of life;
his body awoke to the feeling of material degraded by time—
and it brought him to the conclusion that the material was
rotten and as ephemeral as the solution to his poverty. And it
wasn't just old age that was slipping along over the surface of

things; it was the body glued to the bare walls, without white-wash or paint, with the cement framework showing; it was also the profile of the body sneaking away in the nails of the rafters and broken down doors, on whose hinges rust was crumbling the iron and steel of screws and plates. It wasn't the house but humanity that was gushing outward.

The House.

The House breathed through the cracks in the roof where the nests of brown rats had multiplied by the dozens and the rodents dawdled at night in the spaces between the slats. That breathing could be heard through the mutilated windows that the wind battered sadly from frame to frame, even through the iron of the beds and mildew of the rotten wooden floor around the beds. The House was a kind of lung of mildew and salt and water, a lung with a sickly look, as if all humanity had been transferred inside its walls. And there was a breath that smelled of latent porosity. When it rained, that breath would increase in all the rotting matter, in its apparent thickness. And all of that had the name of ruin.

The general feeling of such unexpected decrepitude made João-Maria move his eyes along the tiles of the roof. That look moved slowly from board to board, was wounded by all the nails, became granulated with every piece of grit; then it flew over furniture and walls and ground, and once more walls and ground, and their hollows; it hung down from the twisted beams, measured the space between the knots in the wood like the space between the wrinkles on his face; it dug in when it came upon the foundation and found the stone. When the stone was found the look wept from inside the salt of the earth. And when it finally discovered the worms and black ants it communicated deeply with the earth—and wanted to die.

Going along the walls in ruin, it turned its body over his body; it gave the body the final immobility of stone and once more he wanted death. But what might death be? It demanded, no doubt, that every little quiver of life disappear from the body: the cell strangled at birth so as to be unable to reproduce, strangled by a strong pressure on the eyelashes, and the breathing suppressed, and the space of the body deserted in its surrender to the last and definitive rigidity...

He'd heard of the possibility of making death depend exclusively on the will to renounce life. For example, a man would look around him, say goodbye to everything that had once been his, and announce to his family: "I'm going to die." It would enough to control the flow of waters, invert all pulmonary movement until bones and organs fell apart, and that was dying. The alternative of hanging from a beam or simply slitting his wrists, along with dying in the rolling waves of the sea, were alternatives that didn't exist because João-Maria had always decided to reject them. What is certain is that he wasn't and never had been crazy. In addition, the true courage of death consisted in being a little like heroes when they discovered they were also children and could weep in their mothers' laps. João-Maria waited for the look of his sons and his wife. When that look caught his, he was already on the other side of existence. Death was the continuation of another life different from life. A new birth of another way of being born.

He'd withdrawn into a corner. He'd crossed his legs and, leaning his back against the wall, was letting his body slide down until he was sitting on the floor. He thought

WHAT CAN DEATH BE LIKE?

I don't know if it hurts or if it's simply darkness. I don't know if it will just be the untying of cords and the undoing of knots, or if there's the solitude of a great bird with its wings open and floating in the air. What aches in the teeth from worms and perhaps its obvious sobless weeping, that taking over of the wailing when death begins to be a silence that hurts and is afterwards prolonged in the gelatin voices and cursing of priests. I don't know, besides, how to cross through a night with only trees: I always needed Sara's hand, the hands of the little ones, the way I used to need and still need today my mother's hand in the dark.

João-Maria hesitated a bit before his wife's look and was able to understand immediately that the time to say goodbye to her and his sons still hadn't come. He felt a tingling in his legs—and it still wasn't the moment to announce that farewell to her, because Sara's eyes went against the very idea of separation. They'd filled with the same despair, it was true, but they rejected panic. They were calm there in front of the

mirror in which she was surprised at her husband's terror. So he immediately broke into a weeping right there that was quite without rhyme or reason, and he took the opportunity to see how the tears began to come out of the eyes of his loved ones to meet his. For quite a while, suffering like that, they flowed, without anyone's speaking. And as if no other way of appreciating that life belonged to him occurred to him, João-Maria went off with all his despair in search of some cane liquor and he guzzled the bottle down to the dregs. And he got drunk. From then on he preoccupied himself with having that pint bottle with him, its neck sticking out of his jacket pocket all the time. He developed a great loss of appetite, lost interest in his wife's body, stopped listening to his sons. "He died then," José-Maria, the elder, thought when he came to tell him of Sara's death, doing so without any emotion. "He died on the day he lost his lands and never again found the peace that their possession inspired in him."

One day Sara came across him filling the cows' manger with sheaves of corn as if he were preparing a bed. The woman fluttered around him for a while, intrigued with the metallic whistling coming from the corners of his mouth, but she didn't dare ask him anything. Lately her husband had been grumpy to all sorts of interrogation. He pretended to be unaware of all matters and she no longer knew of any way to untie the knot of his tongue so he could put his heart in his hands. She was certain, furthermore, that her husband was not only going about in a state of permanent drunkenness, but that he'd lost his speech completely, trying to go mad. Maybe he'd even ceased to recognize people and to love her and their sons. Resigned, she took charge of the house. From that moment on she began bringing him a plate of pork rinds and a thick crust of yellow cornbread at his express request. At first he rejected the chowders, the baked beans, and the steaming broth—and he demanded fried yams and blood sausage. After a few days, declaring himself to be sick of everything, he recommended to his wife that she only bring him pork rinds and some sprigs of fennel to chew on along with some sips of cane liquor. Sometimes he would look at his meal in such a strange way that Sara had to accept the fact that he'd lost his memory of

things. She experimented then at spoon-feeding him. Beard and grease would become mixed together on his face in the same way that the straws of a broom pick up oil or rust. His look ended up striking fear in the children to the point they stopped visiting him. They would spy on him from a distance, however, and their eyes would open wide with surprise, for their father wasn't just changing in his habits, he was even changing in his looks. The little ones couldn't figure out the secrets that motivated the man's withdrawal into the darkness there, lying at the bottom of the manger, sleeping insatiably in the place for cattle and, always with monotonous avidity, draining the same bottle of liquor, filled repeatedly at Capão's store at some imprecise dusk hour. One or the other, each would be sent there every day to buy soap, paprika, or sugar. Their mother would then come and hold out the small liquor bottle, always in silence, and they understood immediately what they were to do.

Sara decided, finally, to remove herself somewhat from her husband's behavior. She got all fussy inside in a sage domestic burst of energy. She began to get up earlier and earlier, long before the sun came up, possessed in the groin by a kind of early-morning wrath, and right then and there she went into a complete revolt: she emptied the wash basins in the trough for the pigs and chickens, she poked around in the nests for eggs laid the night before, she busied herself cleaning and clearing paths and fills and dumped the stagnant water onto the dung heap. Then she would bounce to the fountain with a jug on her head and supply all the vessels in the kitchen. If some herdsman surprised her in the middle of the street and stood there following the trot of her mahogany clogs with his eyes, she would quicken her step, her head down, as if she feared being raped by that look. She would quickly slip into the first doorway, hiding so that no one would ask her any questions about her husband's disappearance. His despair had also become closed up inside her body. It was a worm that was secretly sucking down to her bones and an overdue curvature began to make her lean over and bend her back. The inevitable little blue veins finally broke into sprays of vessels and ended up giving her skin the look of an old woman,

trembling slightly. Every morning that creature would run about in a lively, infernal sweat, thinner and thinner, but ever more energetic. Her face was filling with hollows, shadows, and wrinkles, and her beautiful blue eyes disappeared behind a bony nose that was like a stick sharpened with a razor. Until a gray cough feverishly took over her mouth and never left it again.

Caught up in the whirlwind of that surge of activity, the sons also began to slosh forward, always in a hurry, sent out for thistle and yams for the animals and brushwood for the fire. Forbidden from going to Professor Calafate's school, wearing clothes torn but immediately patched, they experienced forthwith the weight of the hoe, scythe and adze. Sara had a real obsession with cleanliness and order, and she'd decided to turn that house of rats and vermin, smelling of mud and volcanic rock, upside down. She decided to begin by closing up the attics and redoing the ceiling, threadbare where some slats were rotted by rainfall. She even departed from her normal ways and backed up her new matriarchal authority with the use of her broom handle on the back of the older boy, whose face already had a bristling fuzz the color of rocks covered with moss. José-Maria had turned reddish almost as suddenly as a phenomenon of transfiguration, while his blue eyes maintained their strong liquid incandescence. They were already staring beyond people in a kind of sensual restlessness, capable of undressing the first passing female. As for Jorge-Maria, the younger one, he was still only quite a snot-nosed child. But the same blue eyes as his mother's and brother's also seemed to pass through walls and communicate strongly with the mysteries of stones.

Sara had begun to worry because the young ones had entered the age of growth and were devouring inconceivable amounts of food at every chance. There was no more stew or salted fish left. Immediately thereafter, as if thrown into a funnel or a drain, all the products in the house were disappearing in the face of such voracity. She'd reduced her own food to the minimum so that nothing would be lacking for her husband and sons—and hunger filled her eyes with a feverish and pensive glow. When everything was used up she

cooked kale and greens and began killing the hens. She was going to do the same with the pig when she remembered that the dog had died a month earlier. And she decided to dig him up. On a moonlit night, when everybody was asleep, she dug in the garden and scraped the animal up. He smelled of rotten intestines and hairs poisoned and cooked by the earth, but, even so, he would be boiled for several hours and compensated with extraordinary does of peppermint, garlic, paprika and fennel—and the youngsters not only didn't find the taste strange but didn't even dare inquire what kind of animal it was or where she'd found it. In that way, for a week, she hung onto the illusion of the survival of the last animal, the pig, even though she knew that she would have to kill him too the following week. When the time came she faced the hog's reddish eyes with anguish and broke into sobs of pity for the animal, for herself, and for everything that was left in that house without a man. Then she sent her sons off to beg alms at the doors of Rozário. She, too, left then in the direction of Salga and Lomba de Maia. She finally became so confused in her shame and timidity that she put aside all forms of humiliation and went to present herself to Leandro the farmer seeking jobs for her sons.

She begged him on his health and that of his family, by everything that was holy in Heaven, and for the peace of the Earth, for the souls of the angels, of old men and men without memory, and not having anything else to plead by, she rolled upon the ground and asked him to take on her two poor sons, still so tiny and so much in need of earning a living, as herdsmen for his flock. She wept and wept and Leandro the farmer smiled with his gold teeth, and Sara faced that refusal to take her children into service so tenaciously that Leandro the farmer began to fill up first with coldness and then with tedium. He even seemed like a person offended in his principles and he tried to persuade her it was all nothing but the foolishness of a heartless woman.

"They need more sleep and play than your drive to make men out of them. How can you think of waking them at five o'clock in the morning and sending them out into those cold woods in the mountains where they can freeze to death or come down with rheumatism?"

Sara had just as many arguments, however, and in a short time got work for her sons under conditions that Leandro the

farmer considered fair: a quart of milk, Sunday afternoons off, and five patacas a day.

"But look," she countered, upset, "won't you even let the boys attend mass and appear before people with their feet washed and in proper clothes to see Our Lord God?"

"Beggars can't be choosers. Take it or leave it, there are lots of people who'll take it and for even less. Lots of them," Leandro made clear, bored to death but still smiling with his teeth. When she arrived home Sara got dressed all in mourning and sobbed for the rest of the afternoon, waiting for her sons to arrive so she could inform them of her decision. They took the news without blinking, as if they'd already expected it and at once began their preparations for the first trip to the mountain meadows.

João-Maria could hear all the sounds from the house in the distance, but he let those drunken days run by, stretched out in the manger. Lying like that, sprawled on the sheaves, it was as if he were laid out in profile in that diagonal space among plowshares, mahogany ox-bows, rakes, harnesses and ropes. Everything smelled of things at rest, close to rotting away, and the space between things was filled with cobwebs where fat, tin-colored spiders strolled about. When the gusty rainstorms came, the thick, dirty morning rain of the Island, the dampness descended along invisible cords. Then the rats would dig holes searching for kernels of the now crumbled corn, would look for bread crumbs lost in the grass and squeak as they attacked each other with their teeth. João-Maria would amuse himself by watching the way the rats gnawed at some tasteless shinbone. They would attack it with their velvety paws, then grapple with their teeth, and it was sad to see them chew at the hair because the rats' eyes were generally a liquid blue, feverish for death. João-Maria felt a vague joy when the animals discovered a crumb of his yellow cornbread or the pulverized remains of a piece of pork rind. He was almost dazzled at being able to witness the diligence of the hairless rats, from the grandfather rats down to the small white ones with ash-gray eyes; he would hold his breath and, as motionless as a dead person, his eyes wide open, he discovered that the rodents' haste was that of an afflicted and frail last moment of life. At first they would face him from quite far off, their snouts sticking out of the walls, and they would be frightened at his slightest movement. Little by little, however, an intimacy inspired in mutual acquaintance grew between him and the animals until out of that approach all that remained was the fear of fears. When they went away he would take advantage and drain the bottle of cane liquor and summon up his courage: he'd become accustomed to the visit of the rats. He knew now that they had fixed hours for appearing and that hunger was repeated like the clocks in belfries or the cries of the shearwaters at night. The fiery liquor burned his throat, scraped all the walls of his mouth, and exploded like poison in his stomach, coated in saliva. Once more, with the rats' appearance, he would hear their steps in the silence and repeat to himself inside the muffled shout of death.

"I've got to die very soon," he thought, "so these rats and worms can devour me." The mother rat might begin by gnawing at his clothes, opening a passage to his body, and she would most certainly dive into his thighs in search of the spongy food of his testicles; she would walk over his eyelids and suck out his eyes, the way needlefish do to corpses lost in ocean plants. He was a bit horrified by the idea of his own body being sucked up: the horror of a scalpel opening his flesh or even the heat of the earth in the bite of worms. But it was as sure as the Bible that creatures, all creatures, depended on each other and nothing could apparently change that balance.

His hair stood on end from the shock of such imaginings. It was sticking out from the four corners of his head, with grease, pieces of leaves and awns all mixed together. His beard, too, because it was so thick, had the gleam of fat and sandpaper. When the rats withdrew to their lairs, he would remain with his ear cocked for the steps of Sara and his sons, and then an old, misty tenderness seemed to emerge and announce his love for them. A sluggish love, he had to admit, a slow love, never urgent, for he'd decided on his eternal separation. From time to time, in order to keep it alive, Sara would visit him in the manger and, in silence, offer him her punished body. Finally, when he found out from her that his sons were working from sunup to sundown and had been left without a childhood, João-Maria made the decision to deny himself the desire to touch and possess his wife's skinny body, and he stopped speaking to her. Still, the unsophisticated heat of her vagina lingered with him, her huge, superior grandeur of a woman with a narrow nose and a mouth as round as an apple, always avid for one more death in love after love, her white legs that grew quite thick toward her buttocks. He hungered to squeeze her tightly and fill his hand with the dampness and smell of that half-open flower and just one more time, very deeply, sink his penis into her soft urgent belly. His courage would begin to hesitate and his blood would throb under his fingernails, and once more his penis would come out of its animal repose and stand up very tall toward his navel. Something was breaking up behind that force and João-Maria would let himself go in sobs of rage. He was annoyed with the rats and the spiders and he took the phallus in both hands to masturbate. It was raining and he hungered all the more to roll about on Sara's thin body. It was a rain of soot, however, which was breaking apart and thickening into scabs of water, a wild rain that wet the pores of an impossible death agony and attacked with a sacred and black sleep like a signal of death. He thought

WHAT CAN DEATH BE LIKE?

He was thinking what death could be like in the darkness of his eyelids, in the pain and darkness of his dead eyelids, when, rising up a little in the manger, he saw, without any surprise, that his body was changing into a gigantic, yellowish rat. His hands and feet were cased in velvet, his face was snout-shaped and a little worried, and his stomach was as smooth and trim as the keel of a ship out of water. Even his nails, longer and hard down to the limits of their thickness, made his hands longer, almost giving them the terrible look of claws. All he needed was to grow a tail, no matter how small, to be able then to consider himself a perfect rat...

8

THOSE DAYS CAME ON TO DIE, THEN, BY THE EDGE OF NIGHT. AS NO RAIN OR DEW HAD COME, AN AD-MIRABLE SUN WAS FADING INTO ITS DEATH AGONY, slow and far away. It was a sun that was squeezed between the branches of the fig trees and the rough gables, toward where it now directed the shadows in their lunar movement. Field workers passed with bundles of firewood for the Saturday bread-baking on their backs, along with the oxen and the mares and also the dogs who hunted rats and weasels—but it was the sweaty men with their aching bodies who filled the silence with their sharp steps. They swept away all the halted shapes of dusk from in front of them, hastening night on its journey towards the origin.

At that time the women still maintained the whole ancestral ritual of waiting, seated on doorsills delousing their children: their fingers went after nits and their hasty fingernails left welts where tufts of hair had been pulled out. The children would groan at such torture then and cry to be let go.

"Quiet down there, girl!" the mothers roared. "Naughty girl, you won't let me do anything to that head of yours."

As for the lice, they presented a round and mustard-colored appearance as they popped between the fingernails in an almost metallic explosion, squashed into a substance similar to the foul snot that caused ulcers in some children's noses.

Night's advance was already visible in the gusts of wind turned loose by rainstorms out at sea, a sad wind, wet like a dog's nose, at that vague hour when things submerged into a stew of disappearances. The tolling of the bells was the night's elegy as it said farewell to day, as if a hint of death were touching things. The running of bolts on doors had a sound like that of garrotes and guillotines and silence settled down inside houses like the blink of candles in a church or the buzz of flies around some ears of corn hanging down in the middle of the house. But when a stranger dragged his boots down the Rua Direita all that movement halted the talking from door to door for a bit and the women's eyes followed with amazement the anticipation of those steps. At the same time the silence seemed to breathe and throbbed like a drum. Anyone who has experienced tolling bells knows that one can awaken from a sleep of sadness and see strange and voiceless people arriving from the ends of the earth, coming from who knows where, carrying mysteries in the steps of their boots, people brought here by some twist of fate. Well, at that time a person could swear that no creature like that had ever arrived in Rozário until then, because his appearance was rough and immediately brought on a fear of misfortune. He was a terribly ugly man, with a horse-face and the great eyes of a hallucinated ox, bearing little or no resemblance to the human species. In days gone by José, the man with the levers and the wheels, had arrived with his polished, eager fingernails, an austere face split by a cleft under his chin, and his hair greased down with brilliantine. He'd impressed the women with his sweet, solitary, almost feminine sadness, with his most affable and somewhat erotic way of referring to the sewing machines as if they were an invention of his own genius. He seemed to chant his explanations, sketching out lingering, magnificent gestures over the machines with his air of some kind of accomplice. José, the man with the wheels and the levers, had settled down in the community and was quickly gathered into its affection; oaths of love and passion as fervent as wine would pour down onto virginal laps, to loving, mystical women to whom a sublimely effeminate smile lent the promise of limitless abundance. There was a tacit impossibility in his only promised gift, however, and some of the boys, spiteful over his acceptance by the women, began to spread dubious and malicious rumors about his sexual capacity. No stranger with such beauty had ever arrived there after him. Therefore it was with huge interest that the women stopped delousing their children and let their eyes follow that man grimy with soot, with two rough hands like the claws of a bird of prey capable of tearing off their clothes and raping them in public. He was as big as a bull-god carved in stone, although his majesty had nothing sacred about it, but rather, precisely and nothing more, a slow and heavy bovine bearing.

His only luggage was a saddlebag slung over his shoulder with mundane insouciance and a kind of cage or rat-trap full of secrets and treachery that he held, also carelessly, with his hand and whose mesh seemed indisputably complex. Seen from a distance as he was already turning the corner of Boqueirão, he seemed taller than the houses and one might have imagined that at any moment he might rest his load on the roof of the nearest one or lay his head down on top of some eaves. The children immediately went off helter-skelter following in his footsteps as soon as they saw him pass the end of Ramal and turn down the Rua do Cruz, and from a distance they followed the way those huge shoulder-blades went back and forth oblivious to everything. He must have had the strength of a horse, because his look was not only confident but even insolent. He looked about at people's eyes, making them get out of his way while his shoulders rolled high up, clumsily, like two haunches of beef. After a few minutes, when night had already closed in over the church steeple, they watched him pound his fist twice on the mayor's door and fling that indecorous and strange burden to the ground. He was, no doubt, a member of Goraz's family. Seen clearly, he displayed the same tufts of hair coming out of his ears, his face somewhere between that of bull, a horse and a frog, and there were those tremendous hands that never alit on objects, but rather flew over their surface.

The mayor took a long time to open the old door that hung loose on its hinges and broad on its screws and bolts, and he stood there, paralyzed with rage as he laid eyes on his brother. They stood facing each other like two circus wrestlers about to grab one another by the shoulders and butt heads as the vapors of rage from the one mingled with the other's breath, with Goraz barring entry with the impassable barrier of his bones. He was scratching hard his head, either from apathy or nervousness. Then he rubbed his brow noisily, raked his fingers over his neck, and, snorting through his bellows of a nose, realized that he'd finally been found out in that part of the world and couldn't run away any more. Without saying anything audible, he slipped in through the panels of the door and dragged his brother and his luggage behind him, fearful that someone might go off and immediately announce to the parish the arrival of his double. José Guilherme avoided greeting his sister-in-law, who huddled in a corner of the kitchen, having lost forever any form of courage. He only observed that she was twisting her apron and had begun to weep without any explanation. She had the look of a rat sucked dry by the jaws of other rats, and her neck was flabby, her breasts flat, and she was much older and less a woman, in his opinion, than when he'd known her when she'd been hunting men in other places on the Island. With a simple grimace, his eyes flew over her and were lost in the observation of the kitchen's beams and cupboards. Up until then he hadn't proffered a single word. In spite of the fact he had never been there, he seemed to know every nook and cranny in the house. As for the sister-in-law, he'd always imagined that his brother would pick out a silent, expressionless woman like that so he could almost ignore her existence. He'd always preferred them so, anodyne and easy to command, in bed and out, and the sister-in-law doubtlessly combined all those attributes because it was obvious that his brother ridiculed her body the same way he did her conjugal misfortune.

José Guilherme lit the oil lamp, hung his saddlebag and trap on one of the hooks in the kitchen, and went over to the cupboards to get something to eat—with ever the relaxed air of someone in his own home. No manner of bashfulness even

stopped him from opening his four-bladed knife and carefully slicing a loaf of cornbread in two. Putting one half aside,
he opened the other and filled its center with a slice of raw
bacon. Guilherme José, his brother, still stood in his corner as
if the sight of José Guilherme were some kind of demonic
apparition that paralyzed his mouth whenever he moved to
speak. Curled in her way, watching him devour slices of
bacon, the sister-in-law seemed to be writhing in pain,
imagining that those horse teeth might also devour her, and
that her blood could well be the fat now dripping down his
chin. All of her intimacy was being violated, touched by the
bites and caught up in that vigorous chewing. She already
had one monster inside there. Now she was going to have to
struggle with him twice over. Guilherme José leaned against
the kitchen door, quite pale, completely blinded by rage. By
what devilish fate, he thought, had he never been able to
disappear from the view of his family and deny their existence? He folded his arms, ready to explode with hate, and he
began to froth like an octopus. He was only waiting for both
their looks to cross so they could start talking. At the same
time he felt like beating him up and kicking him out of Rozário.
José Guilherme, on the other hand, showed no sign of nervousness. He was cleaning his teeth with his tongue now,
and the only sound he had emitted so far was a belch and sign
of gastric distress. Then, as if an unexpected thirst had awakened in him, he tipped up the jug. In spite of its containing
vinegar, he wasn't bothered by the sourness. A thirst that great
had grown in the dust of the road and in the soot of fireplaces
and sheds all over the Island, in his strange profession of a
hunter of rats and weasels. An endless chain of secrets about
what he ate rested in that thirst and also about the places where
he dragged out his days. It was the story of a man without any
destiny whatsoever, for whom straw served both as bed and
food on rainy winter days, going from parish to parish offering at doors his experienced art of saving corncribs and fruit
lofts from rats. They would hire him at half a pataca per rat—
but the reputation of being a swindler began to follow him,
because he would carry the dead animals in his bag and
collect for their number over and over. That being the case,

the plague kept on devouring corn and seeds after he'd passed through. In addition, his finicky nature contrasted with such a strange profession and his customers grew all the scarcer as inventions and products for extermination began to appear. He himself had recourse to scientific inventions, preparing and serving up indisputably deadly recipes, always trying out new ways of death by poison—but he still preferred the noose, because, he would say, there was no method of killing as perfect as the gallows. Nevertheless, people caught on quickly and were wary of these and other methods, so José Guilherme soon had to seek out other parishes and new places, there to proclaim his gifts and guarantees, even if in vain.

Two hungers coursed through his body in the middle of winter, one in his stomach and one in his spermatic animal, and his great despair for food and women came to turn his loneliness to rage. He became branded with the condition of those who are always passing through places and past people, and women fled from him out of fear of his monstrous size, while men refused him the shelter of their lofts. In the end he would supply the necessities of his stomach with the rats themselves, roasted on a spit over the fire; it was a meat of tender cartilages with the taste of velvet and the smell of a tannery, so he ran out of his provisions of resold rats paid for at half a pataca each until they smelled rotten. Then the despair for women awoke inside his body the drive of a volcano controlled by valves and emptied out in a jet against walls until one day he attacked a cow in rut and made her low all through the night as if she were being butchered alive. The unexpected discovery of cows compensated for that loneliness in part, but it ended in blood when he was caught mounting a jenny ass which had curled up into a ball of affliction under his attacks. Sickles and cart poles appeared, hoes and axes, and a whole aroused parish tried to corner him in the woods with such fury that only the priest was able to save him from death. He was on the other side of the Island at that time and he went deep into the mountain forests, using the shelter of trees and caves to rest in and heal his wounds. He cooked herbs, tried poultices, boiled urine, and removed large crusts from ulcerating wounds. At the end of a week, completely healed, without a single scar, he decided to set out on the road to Achadinha because he'd been told that his brother had settled there years back and had even been one of the architects of its progress. He would have to traverse the whole island, cutting across the mountains diagonally until he reached the People's Woods, where he hoped to find some living soul who could provide him with a bit of food and point out to him the shortest way to the coast. He didn't find anyone, however, except cattle and goats lost in the forest, animals turned loose into the underbrush a while back which ran off or stood bleating at a distance. He didn't have the strength to attack any donkeys in heat again, and it was also true that his body no longer called upon him for those forbidden acts that could end in punishment. He left there walking wearily uphill, half-faint with hunger. In a short time he discovered in the distance, hard by the sea, the jumbled houses of Rozário.

He'd spent three days crossing the Island, but he'd recovered his former energy. He was even hopeful that word of his perversions still hadn't reached the coast on that side. He was counting, furthermore, on the help of his brother, whose fame had spread everywhere, and he would find some way to use his snares in the hunt for rats. So when he reached those parts he was surprised neither by the silence nor the air of mystery that surrounded his path to Guilherme José's house. Sadness opened up like an ear of corn on the faces of those people. It was a sadness that looked without seeing or hearing anything, a sign that his brother's shadow once more hovered everywhere with the same invisible claws that had been poised over his own absence. Now, sitting across from him, his gaze roving about the house was as red as the glow of a bonfire left to go out by itself. He searched in his vest pockets for a twist of tobacco, chopped it into small, regular strips, and rolled them up in a corn husk, which he lit from the chimney lamp. He was taking a second puff when he uncrossed his legs, got up, and took a few steps back and forth, always facing his brother, trying mentally to pick up again a discussion broken off long ago.

"So," he said, "you're the one who owns these people."

Goraz's body trembled and the woman almost cried out

with fright, but neither of them said a single word. José Guilherme hadn't expected him to answer him in any case because he hadn't really asked a question. He began to scratch the side of his head and he belched again from too much fat and vinegar. He walked back and forth a little more, this time in a circle, closer to his sister-in-law, whose body was like a broken egg alongside the clay water pots and the china closet. She seemed to be moaning from cold or fright, but she'd stopped weeping. José Guilherme still sensed that his brother felt threatened by his presence, especially visible in the way they avoided looking at each other, because if they did a barrel of wrath would have immediately poured out between the two of them, one still filled with past times and an ancient, chronic and repeated discord coming from before their last separation.

"That's the reputation you've got all over the Island," he added, leaving the kitchen and walking toward the office. He was moving about the house as if everything were familiar to him. He knew, for example, that there was no bed on which he could lie down for the simple reason that in Guilherme José's house there would never be room or even an invitation for lodging anyone. In view of that he immediately decided to fix himself up in the cowshed or the storage loft, or even in the corncrib, among the sacks of potatoes and sheaths of corn. When he went into the office he wasn't surprised by the chaotic look in spite of its airs of a royal chamber. The rows of yellow papers covered by twisted writing where norms were profusely decreed and the eventualities wisely punished were there atop each other, tacked or glued to a surface of planks propped against the wall. He wasn't dazzled by the display of all those written decrees and edicts, but his eyes sailed up and down in the midst of that sloppy orthography that composed tangled terms and uncouth orders. When he read the decree on the harvest tax, he reacted with a whistle, feeling that there lay the secret of secrets concerning his brother's prosperity.

"There it is," he thought. "The same as always, everywhere, wherever you find him." His ideas were falling into place. His brother was in his blood, or course, but it was misunderstood blood, the kind that was always in a permanent and spontaneous ferment between hate and tenderness. He knew he was standing behind him with his hands on his hips as he felt his breath on his neck. He'd never felt that close to the back of his neck a breath so anxious and at the same time so upset. He could also imagine the way the arteries in his neck must have been throbbing. If any feeling was imminent in his spirit, it could only have been this: grab José Guilherme by the arm and drag him out of there, because his presence in that office was a profanation. Goraz had to gather together all his strength of spiritual containment in order not to explode. He'd been taken by surprise with his brother's arrival and his only desire was to discover quickly a way to send him far away, not because of the space he was going to take up there, but because that presence represented an obstacle. He had decided long ago to be all alone in the world, without family or any other bonds whatsoever, and his coming to Achadinha precisely signified that exceptional option. He'd even forgotten where he came from, what had happened to him in childhood, who his parents had been. He was only interested in having his memory concentrate on a new exist-ence and a new place. When he got there Achadinha was only a collection of animal pens watched over by a half-dozen large families, bound by multiple ties that verged on incest with relationships so dubious among them that they were more like a tribe of the same blood than a community of several generations. There was a single street, with the school and the church, and even the existence of those things was more the work of his imagination than that of their hands. Guilherme José had immediately begun by developing a movement to put houses in order. He went to neighboring villages in search of stonemasons and master carpenters; he gave residence to vagabonds and wanderers with no destination; he brought in a cartload of women whose origins no one ever could explain, nor did he reveal; he distributed land, plows, oxen, and rams, had all the people baptized again, hired a priest, a schoolteacher and a healer, and busied himself at such el-ementary tasks as registering people as to their pairing or bachelorhood, and he found out that there were at least twice as many men as women. By the end of all those operations he felt he was an important man for whom the people perhaps couldn't help reserving a place of honor, and he decided to go and admire the work he had brought about. He climbed to the top of the Caminho Novo, the new road, up to some still wild land, and fell into a sort of fascination, because there before his eyes he had not the old tribe, but two rows of houses that lay sleeping in the sun like snakes. He finally could admit that the freshly plowed lands were irreversibly tying those nomadic people down to Achadinha. There were several native-born children already and life was taking on all the rituals of rest and fatigue in its daily work.

Any other person would have wept with emotion, but Guilherme José didn't; he'd lost the basic memory of how to cry. He would die in perfect tune with the things created by him or others. There was still the cemetery left to establish, and the hiring of a new priest, other teachers and more women was urgent. In addition to which the church was calling for a complete restoration. That only came about with the arrival of Father Governo a few years later, when nobody any longer remembered who his predecessor had been or what he'd done there. Coming down from that sort of plant nursery after admiring the village, he made the great decision to end the isolation of his life among others and conceived the idea of sharing his solitude with someone. So, among the women brought in by his wagon years before there was one who still had no husband, even though for some time she had been offering herself for seven patacas to the men who sought her out. Her name was Glória and she lived in an unprotected hut beside the sacristy, on the other side of the church. She ate cooked grasses and peeled roots, wept often, and had a syphilitic thinness. When Guilherme José went to find her in her hovel and entered, bending over down to the ground, she wasn't surprised or startled because she'd stopped being wary of the men who showed up there. She immediately began to undress.

"Get your things together, you're going to marry me," he announced. Glória quickly obeyed and, gathering up a bundle of clothes, she followed him to the church. The priest at that time, whose name no one could recall, received him without any fluster despite being surprised in his intimacy, for he had been lying on the bed in his drawers sleeping his siesta.

"For me to marry you I must first hear you and her in confession and be convinced of your repentance. Then I will need four sacramental witnesses in order to celebrate this wedding."

"Then get yourself a servant, because Glória is going to be my wife right now today."

He crossed in front of the church, heading for the shop of Francisco Heitor, barber, poet and dentist, and he interrupted the intense flow of his odes against the governments of Portugal: he needed four witnesses. He pointed to two old men, a boy, and a huge woman with large breasts and a smile as fat as the vassals who penetrated her insides. That marriage was memorable because Guilherme José provided drinks for everybody and led the celebrations in the yard until dawn. The nameless priest drank and danced, his sleeves rolled up and his cassock open at the chest until they carried him off unconscious, so drunk that he'd turned as yellow as cider and suddenly aged so much that it could have been said he was transfigured. Few people remembered his appearance, which was as bilious as diarrhea. But someone swore that his liver had burst at all its seams. Guilherme José's first night with Glória was also a frightful thing, as full of her cries as it was of the amorous fury of his seven uninterrupted orgasms. From that point on her body was tortured and deformed, and that was why Glória said to herself that all she'd done was exchange one unhappiness for an even greater one. At the same time she felt a great hatred growing for that man who was causing her slow death, because of his uncommonly huge penis and his eyes of an ox halted in the small death of an unrequited orgasm. Insensitive to that hatred, Guilherme José became a different man, destined, as he judged things, to rule over others and acquire new status. For that very reason his brother's presence was an obstacle, even though he believed his appearance in the parish was simply part of a trip between two places. He would put him up for that night. Then he would find a way to get him out of the parish the way he was accustomed to do with undesirables, with the recommendation never to come back there ever again.

If that was what Guilherme José imagined, he didn't admit it, even to José Guilherme, because in the meantime he'd opened his arms to him with a trustful air, not taking his eyes off the harvest tax edict.

"You," he said, "are going to draw up a decree on rats this very night."

Guilherme José reacted immediately, pounding his fist on the table top. And the inkwell flew off, breaking up into dozens of blue particles. Tongues of indigo ran down the wet plaster and an indescribable rage took hold of him. Then, for the first time after so many years of separation, Guilherme José and José Guilherme stood face to face, looking at each other from the depths of their eyes, and concluded that as brothers all they had was the bond of blood and perhaps not even that. In everything else they diverged completely. Guilherme José was a spirit always on the brink of conflict, ready even to kill if necessary, while José Guilherme held within himself the tiny patience of rats and all small creatures, even having their damp and afflicted iciness. As well, his spirit grew fat as indifference governed his relationship to the world. There was no memory of their ever having separated without a fight, not just between the two of them, but between hostile groups. Those, however, were bygone times. Both their lives had taken a complete turn and, like a ball, had rolled and rolled and rolled until stopping, stuck in the mud. The mayor's face was ruddy and puffy and the tiny veins and branches across it stood out, while José Guilherme's was impassive, like a pale statue, loaded with a chill peace. His brother's eyes couldn't bear the strength of his: they fled from that perverse force and went wandering over objects, a sign that another form of tameness was encircling him front and rear and stopping him from thinking clearly. He wasn't surprised, consequently, by his weakening as he heard him lamely protest against the demand of finding a place to live and work there:

"Fuck the rats! You're not going to find any kind of life for you in this parish. I guarantee you that."

All of Guilherme José's mockery fell on him in a guffaw made up of disconnected sounds that shattered the night like breaking glass or tumbling stones in the silence of a glade. It was a clear, absolute laugh. It shook that ox stomach in its aging age and made his triple chin quiver. Guilherme José reacted nervously, feeling the other was laughing in his face, and he began to admit there was a definitive and vital difference between his brother and the common run of people: José Guilherme felt no fear in his presence, while the others, all the others, shrank before him and scurried far off afterwards like rats, afraid of being squashed by the heel of his boot. Do they know what Fear is like?

Fear is an elephant with blue eyes and a belly that sags down to the groin—and Guilherme José was that proboscidian in whose body fear grew in size and took on volume, like a balloon blown up to the limits of its insides, or like an avalanche pouring down a hill. The people didn't exactly fear his strength, but rather more his cruelty, even when that strength dropped and needed repose. They also feared the sound of his voice, because in it they imagined all his muscularity and conspiracy. José Guilherme, on the other hand, felt at that time the space his hands took up and he thought about their size: men make the world or destroy it with their hands; with them they love or beat women, wipe their behinds or their mouths, hear themselves in them while they talk, because hands can open space for light in the darkness. Nothing exists or lives in man that doesn't have to do with his hands.

"I know rats are your civilization," José Guilherme said, and he left his brother paralyzed with surprise, because that same phrase had been spoken in times past by Father Governo. "Small, noisy, bony. They're all fucked up, rats are, did you know that? But you're afraid of them, while I can strangle them. That's the advantage I've got over you. Want to see?" And without waiting for an answer, from one of his pockets he took out an all white rat and put it in the palm of his hand, right next to the mayor's nose. It was an animal with a pink snout and little feet, purple as if from cold, whose movements consisted in sniffing the furrows in the large hand that wasn't shaped like a hand and then curling up beside the thumb. The only thing remaining outside the curled up bundle were its eyes, and Guilherme José found them ashen and murderous, which made him push that hand away from his eyes.

"See? You're shaking with fear, just the way I sometimes do along these Island roads, trembling from hunger, the hunger of rats that I skin myself and chew from one winter to the next while you grow fat here at the expense of these people."

With that, he put the rat's nose up to his mouth and Guilherme José began to vomit out many of those creatures, rats of almost every color: green, blue, mustard, crab-colored. There were rats and more rats softened into a spongy mass, full of saliva, and the enormous elephant belly emptied itself of them in short, vigorous spews, to the point that José Guilherme was pale with wonderment as he watched such a prodigious quantity of rodents coming out of his mouth like that. Then he felt pity and disdain as he saw him sit down quickly at the desk, his hand trembling and listless, and begin drawing up one more decree prohibiting the existence of rats:

Whoever reads this must keep in mind what I have set down as follows: the evil and curse of such pernicious creatures of rats being known, all are guilty who oppose their destruction by poison or traps, whether they be garrotes or snares, in accordance with the methods best advised for their total extermination. And as our land has them by the millions, all the illnesses of the world reside in them along with death, which they bring on in a direct or devious way. I, Guilherme José Tavares Bento, mayor by grace and confidence of the citizens of this parish, order that all be advised that a brother of mine, José Guilherme by name and my twin at birth, will proceed with his profession of killer of said animals and receive from it the payment of half a pataca per head, which can also be made collectively if he so understands, with the whole population of Rozário being obliged in this until the end of this holy year of our salvation in the world. This brother of mine will begin to undertake the task of disinfection street by street and house by house, and whosoever opposes will immediately be called upon to defend himself against the charge of being an enemy of the people.

José Guilherme noticed the way his mouth twisted in a convulsive weeping that had no tears over the very motion of that goose quill crudely sharpened with a pocket knife as it slipped along. His mouth chewed on the pain and chewed on the writing, and he thought that maybe there were people whose weeping was absorbed in their saliva, in the teeth that chewed on sorrow and the thick hands working so forcibly. And he smiled with an almost demoniacal wickedness: the smile was red and from it droplets of vapor round as bubbles, pouches of poison, slipped out.

Then he made the decision that never again would he kill a single rat in that land, knowing all the while that they were reproducing by the millions and that one day, perhaps, they would be able to drive men off it or even devour them alive.

9

JOÃO-MARIA HAD JUST HEARD
THE TOLLING OF THE TRINITY OF THE MAIN BELL
OF ROZÁRIO WHEN HIS ELDER SON CAME TO TELL
HIM OF SARA'S DEATH AND DID SO WITHOUT ANY
show of emotion, in the same tone of voice with which one
announces that it's stopped raining or that a rather unwel-
come person has arrived. The lad simply said, "She died,"
and more than the expression on his face or in his eyes, his
voice was pensive, even desperate perhaps, although it didn't
carry the thickness of a sob nor the usual agony of death.

The rats were roaming freely and in small bands over his
body, and they were so tame by that time that they would lick
his hands and face and breathed unworriedly between his
fingers. But when João-Maria sat up in the manger, taken by
surprise at such news, the boards creaked and his whole body
exploded like the spring of a joint eaten by rust. Then the rats
became frightened again and flew out of the manger onto the
floor, using a winged mechanism similar in all ways to the
wings of a bird, and they quickly sought out their distant holes.
There were so many that the boy opened his eyes wide, almost on the verge of terror, suddenly surprised that his father
hadn't been devoured by so many such bloodthirsty creatures.

João-Maria had meanwhile begun to destroy the netting
of cobwebs that had been woven over his head and soon his
fingers were green from squashing spiders as fat as boils. But

his face remained serene and unaltered as his fingers squeezed small spiders and huge ones, because nothing had apparently happened in the course of his hibernation except that the space between his wrinkles had narrowed a little more and his whole face seemed to have been patched by an intense covering of shadows and creases. As to the rest, his body had suddenly ceased to resemble that of a giant rat, unlike the time when he'd made ready to await death, because the simple movement of getting up had brought back to him his former human appearance, adding it to the mortal spectacle once again.

All the while the son was finding his father's delay endless as the latter turned to the detailed destruction of his nest of leaves and spiders, slowly rising up out of the bosom of death, shaking the awns from his hair and beard, and he judged it more prudent to stand aside from that ritual of return to the other meaning of life. In spite of the fact that his face was unchanged, José-Maria didn't doubt that his father was weeping convulsively. But not in any visible way. He was weeping with the invisible organs of his eyes now that tears would never bloom on the surface of their lashes, but only circulated inside the optic nerve. It was a weeping as carnal as the revelation of an illness or a sudden terrible pain, and he had such an urge to hug him and everything so much like him that his body experienced a convulsive feeling, while his ruddy face and lecherous eyes stayed impassive and absent. "My old father," he thought, "my old, finished, bitter and tender father," and his lips trembled and his breathing became difficult, on the point of turning into sand and slipping through his bronchial tree.

His father rose very slowly, his bones cracking, and he, José-Maria, said to himself, "He's already dead. He died by his own decision on the day his land was stolen and he's going to die again now because mother was the last being he possessed and she no longer exists; some hidden force is devouring father to the rhythm of lizards and silverfish, that's why he'd dead already—I'm only talking to myself, all alone with what there is of him floating in my arteries, his breath, his voice inside my voice." José-Maria was even convinced that only a reason as serious as death could have succeeded in dragging his father out of that manger, because neither the plague nor the scientific hunting of rats undertaken by José Guilherme, the man with the absurd snares, seemed to have impressed him or even distracted him from the obstinacy of dying. João-Maria had come there with the firm proposal of doing without life and dying, and he'd striven totally to learn the only possible way of wanting it, believing in the possibility of weaving it with his saliva or through some alchemical process like that of spiders. The most he'd managed to do didn't go beyond the semi-paralysis of his facial muscles. It's true he'd reached the initial stage of metamorphosis into the body of a huge rat. But not even for that reason did he cease believing that death merely depended on an exclusive act of will. Besides, the rats and the spiders, the spider webs, the nest of vermin, the rotting bundles of sheaves, and his own excrement lying in a pile in a corner of the cattle shed already presaged death, and João-Maria felt himself rotting away day by day in contact with the feces and the dampness. Like him, things were giving off a residual stench of age-old matter, rain on the mildew and the aged whitewash.

Finally, when José-Maria saw his father rise up out of that hole, he found him to be a miserable creature. His beard had grown until it had the greasy gleam of sandpaper and it was quite long now, naturally, and pierced by awns. As for his clothing, it was fluttering in denim stripes the same color as his flesh and was full of holes made by the rodents' teeth. The rats had disappeared completely into all the burrows beneath the flagstones, in the spaces between slabs, in the small dens dug deep into the very marrow of the plaster and sand. Their sound of frying eggs had disappeared, the smell of pissed-on corpses had also gone away, along with their little steps of spongy fleece, because a convulsion similar to a war of extermination of all living species had come to that last redoubt of existence. So solitude for João-Maria was just that, the absence of rats and the memory of the last buzzing insects and, for José-Maria, it was being all alone facing his father and the silence, sensing, nonetheless, his convulsive weeping that showed no signs, looking in such a way that he drew back from the inevitability of having to embrace him and express to him all the world's despair. He was a bit bothered they hadn't embraced each other yet, crying out, for that would have been the most natural thing between two people attacked by the grief of having lost half their life with Sara's death. For wasn't it true that every act of man was marked off ahead of time like a liturgy or an unconscious habit?

It was beginning to grow dark when the father went through the backyard, crossed the kitchen and embraced Jorge-Maria, the younger son. At the door to Sara's room, before going in, he felt faint and the boys noticed that he grabbed onto the door jamb in order not to fall. Then he vomited. The vomit was a kind of jet of blood, but it was green and brought up threads of saliva with it the shapes of dead animals, Apocalyptic rats and spider webs in a procession of lumps that descended down along the blue threads of saliva and phlegm. The father's eyes finally opened, like a muscle, at the sight of Sara's corpse; then they hesitated between maintaining their dignity and the less austere way of dragging their grief over to the body to embrace it. Somehow or other, his approach was so slow that it made one think of some dying animal dragging itself along. He began reeling upward, as wild as a pendulum in a roofless house, brutish, drunk with nausea, still unable to face his sons as new vomit came out from inside him like a spring released in his guts up toward his mouth. Seeing him like that, with his beard so filthy and his eyes red with madness, Jorge-Maria, the younger son, said, "My father's a werewolf, a werewolf with the signs of infinite fatigue perhaps," and he fled out the street door to weep. His blue eyes were like those of a puppy brutally separated from the maternal breast, his nose full of snot, and he had the absorbed air of someone abandoned in the solitude of a desert with no trees or mirrors, and no repose either. When he approached again he came with his head lowered and he looked at his father from the side and no longer recognized him. He could have been just a man, any man in this world, standing there beside his mother's corpse. Sara was lying sidewise, and her beautiful thin nostrils, turned blue by death, were even fleshier on the tips. It was impressive to see such a deep peace in a body that had been so habitually vibrant, moved by the force of the countless stiff levers that had ultimately transformed her into a machine that moved about and worked over the whole space of her days. João-Maria stood looking at her for a moment, refusing to believe that death and still hoping to see her awaken at any moment, ready to take up immediately her bustling activity of a woman who once again had no nights. He had to tell her about his new and miraculous energy then, "Woman, here I am," and give her his hands so she could rise up more quickly from her sleep: they would have a horse again, a pair of oxen, two plots of land registered in his name, João-Maria de Medeiros, his father's only heir. He believed in things so absurd that he even came to call her twice by name, softly, Sara, Sara, sure that she would turn her face in his direction and, opening her beaten blue eyes, recognize him immediately. When he realized that he was acting like an idiot before his sons, he dropped onto her body and emitted a howl of an animal stabbed in the belly and then broke into sobs. The sons, too, immediately let themselves go in wails and moans and the whole house filled with the mingled and tragic weeping of those three mouths. José-Maria scratched his nails on the cement, hopped about as if an unbearable knife-thrust had caught him in the middle of his testicles, and then his mouth filled with foam, while Jorge-Maria, lying on the floor, rolled back and forth and shouted, coiling and uncoiling like a snake, "I want my mother, I want my mother, I want my mother," and the shouts from his orphaned mouth were such that people came right away, a lot of wondering people, coming from all the neighboring doors, wanting to know what was going on in that house usually so peaceful, where the people only flitted about, flying over the shapes in the dark.

João-Maria then went to the door and chased away all those people with a wave of his arm. He made a sweeping gesture over the multitude of heads, and most of the people didn't recognize him either. Since they didn't move an inch, he picked up the bar to the door to chase them off and began insulting them with the names of rare animals: parrots, spitting snakes, ostriches, hyenas, wilidogs, veincutters, and deliropedes. He immediately threw the bolt, put the bar up behind the door, and went over to embrace his sons once more. They all wept until ready to drop from fatigue, in a chorus, lying on the floor, and that embrace would certainly have been fatal if João-Maria hadn't suddenly been struck by the most exceptional of all suppositions: he was going to revive Sara. But how?

Without her, life would have no use or meaning, besides which the sons, too, wouldn't stand living a single day longer without the presence of their mother to guide them in life. Therefore, he was going to revive her and ask her to return to the living incarnation of her energy, because only she put the same irrepressible euphoria into all her actions, from the moment she got up until she went to bed, and the memory of her lost steps, movements and sounds, that memory had already been transmitted to the very configuration of objects, to the way they'd been forgotten in the corners of the house and only had any use at the most propitious moment. Then João-Maria lay down on the bed again beside his wife and he strongly embraced her terribly thin body where there was only fatigue, the fatigue of death. He began by caressing her with tiny, urgent touches, like the moments when he would prepare to make love to her, and he tried to touch all the nerves in her body. But that breathless sleep went on and João-Maria, seeing that he wasn't succeeding in bringing her back to life, began to say louder and louder, until he was shouting, "It's not true! It's not true! You're not dead!" She wasn't dead, she was only sleeping because she was tired. And he was watching over that sleep so no one would disturb her.

He invited his sons to come lie down on the other side of the corpse. They came and wept in long, drawn-out sobs. Finally they fell asleep, worn out from weeping, and night fastened all the latches and there was only the howling of dogs in the yards outside; and the wind howled over hedges and roofs and night birds and trees and sick music shells, and the sea was the womb of all the howling that spread through the night. When the first cock crowed, and then other cocks crowed, dawn arrived to find João-Maria awake and still muttering, "It's not true, you're not dead," she was only sleeping, slowly and without memory. Then day came and the sons awoke and started weeping again. They bit their hands until they injured them and bleated, "Mother! Mother!" for the mother who would never again be, nor her courage, nor her smile, nor the sacred kiss for someone going to sleep who wouldn't be all alone with monsters. The mother commands and mountains move, she has the sweet, primitive breath of land and water, mother, mama, my mother of waters, and never again would it do any good to open their eyes and call things by name, because you, mother, were in the shape of everything that received a name one day. They bit their hands and said, "Mother! Mother!" and the mother was the very taste of the smooth syllables, as if they were eating her; as if, greedy for her face, they were eating it. With the break of day João-Maria realized that she would never wake up, that she was definitely dead because outside the rain of ninety-nine consecutive days continued and there was still plague. It was completely impossible to revive her. Only a miracle, he said. But time had already fallen apart like the ruins of his house and there was nothing miraculous about that. Each and every thing inside was so destroyed that only a new creation of the world could have restored God's thoughts to Earth. Let the Land, the Seas, Fire and Air be created then. Let Man be created in our image and likeness, and João-Maria gave a start because suddenly he saw Fear before him. He gave a leap and fell to the ground, and Fear was there, crucified in his body. He stood up again and fell and stood up again and thought: God. It was necessary to challenge Him, blackmail God and revive Sara. He was going to set fire to the house because fire, he thought, would devour his misfortune, Sara's body, his, the bodies of his sons—unless God intervened to avoid that holocaust. Wasn't He the supreme defender of children? That was what priests said, even if they lacked proof. The problem was that maybe God didn't even exist. That was why He couldn't even be challenged. Besides that there was the rain: it was continuously filling the land with sadness and it might render the effect of the fire useless. It had also been proven that children could dominate fire with their looks and order its flames into the most unforeseen and spectacular directions. And even if it weren't so, the fact is those two young ones were his sons, the adored and loving boys of his sin, as handsome and docile as swans. They were sleeping with their heads resting on their mother's stomach, as if lying with her on the same side of death.

If it was no use putting God to the test of fire, it was also a fact that He would never be able to see those little hands burning like torches. Thinking through all those hypotheses, João-Maria was moved to tears and quickly reached a decision. He ran into the yard in search of some planks, lathing, and beams. He went to the forgotten tool chest, brushed aside the cobwebs, and broke apart some rat nests. He gathered scattered nails together, sharpened his chisel on the grindstone, tightened the handle of the hammer, fastened on the head of the adze and drove a wedge under its blade; he picked out just the right drill bits, set aside the square and the level, found a pouch and some screws, patiently assembled the plane, took a file and cleaned the rust off the blade of the adze and the teeth of the saw, sharpened the charcoal pencil with a razor, and weeping without tears, began to sort out and measure his best lumber. He was at it hour after hour until by the end of the afternoon he felt he'd finished his wife's coffin. He was drenched with sweat and his body gave off a strong smell of ammonia, and a whiff of ether had dried his throat completely, giving his breathing a sound as agonized as that of someone dying. He gathered all the strength he had left, however, and called his sons to help him carry the coffin into the house. He dressed Sara in black and placed the body in a comfortable position in the casket so she wouldn't be fatigued by that last long trip into the interior of the Earth.

"We must bury her," he said, more in the tone of conferring with his sons than giving an order. "We must bury her in the yard under the fig tree so she'll be ours forever."

The sons fell completely mute and said nothing. But the tears were still rolling uncontrollably from the depths of their eyes, in pairs, ever thicker and slower. They agreed, finally, that their mother should be buried that very day, before dark, so the spirits of night wouldn't come and carry her off. They also accepted the backyard as the ideal place for her grave. In that way their mother would always be near them; they could spend the rest of their lives consulting her about each and every practical matter. They would obviously taker her advice: they would ask her for courage and for her blessing, and she would always be there to receive and nourish them. When finally they died, then they would be led by her to the hidden places, to the lost places of the Earth, such places to which priests commonly gave the name of paradise and where eternity had been invented.

They were in the midst of this when the three bells of Rozário began tolling the death knell and a damp wind, salivated by the distant sea, scraped across the whole surface of the almost empty streets and raised red clouds against the walls. João-Maria asked his sons not to be moved by the tolling and recommended they stop crying.

"We must be worthy of her memory," he said. "Sara mustn't at all imagine us like this, without the courage she herself taught us."

He dried their tears and wiped away their snot with his hands, because he felt strong and had renounced forever his own destruction. He now had great reasons to survive that destruction. First, he would avenge Sara's death and the boys' orphaned state, he would recover his land, the honorable land of his father, João-David Maria de Medeiros, stolen by the mayor, Guilherme José, whom they called Goraz because of his large bulging eyes and his heavy elephant-fish body. And all that would be accomplished in a very well-planned way, one carefully put together.

He didn't get to finish his thought, however. At that moment a small crowd was approaching the house and João-Maria, through the cracks in the boards, saw first a cross, then some yellow and black surplices, six professional women mourners all dressed in severe black, and finally, bringing up the rear of the group, dragging his clumsy boots along, Father Governo in surplice and stole, a ridiculous dark cap covering the host mark on the back of his head and a forbidding crucifix hanging around his neck. João-Maria immediately threw the bolt on the window and went out in the direction of the cowshed in search of a sickle for clearing brush, swearing between his teeth that Sara's hour of justice was at hand and no human force would steal his dead beloved away from him.

When he returned with the sickle over his shoulder, the cortège had taken up position in front of his door and all that could be heard were coughing and throats clearing in expectation of some first words. A short time after someone tried to communicate through the door with a few timid knocks, hurriedly rapping with his knuckles, and the person who knocked got the sure and startling impression that on the other side of the door was a house that had been deserted for many years, such was the echo produced in the silence.

"Let me bless your wife, João-Maria," the priest then moaned, with a shudder, as if he were speaking at the surface of the waters in which he was drowning. He waited in vain for an answer, for no sound rose up on the other side of the door inside the house. He always felt ill in such a situation. That distant shudder now ran down his spine, the saliva in his mouth was drying up, and his hands began to tremble uncontrollably.

"So, did you hear what I just asked you? I've only come to bless your wife's body. I'm only fulfilling my duty."

They were silent again, awaiting a reply. This time, too, silence reigned. All that could be heard in the house was the creaking wood: a frontier silence between the trenches of war. There wasn't the slightest breeze of a movement in it capable of betraying the position of those dug in or even their hiding in the shadows. Their ears cocked, people looked at each other and shrugged their shoulders, then turned to the priest and saw his mouth half-open and his face dripping sweat from every pore.

"You can go to hell, Father," João-Maria suddenly roared when everyone was expecting some sign of irritation on the part of the priest. "Use your religion for justice for the poor or leave them in peace once and for all."

An indignant buzz was heard, then a tearing of surplices, and there was already a sound of boots on the street when someone repeated João-Maria's words to the deaf clergyman: *"He says for you to go to hell, Father; to use your religion for justice for the poor or leave them in peace once and for all."* And the repetition was so exact that the priest immediately began to froth with rage, as red as a glowing ember, his mouth all twisted. Never had there been a more stupid expression on a human face, João-Maria thought as he peeked through the window slats again.

Didn't they know João-Lázaro?

His voice was blank and his look satanic and tragic when the boys would sick dogs on him or throw stones and clumps of sod from ditches at him. His hands burned permanently with that arid, blond fever that anticipates certain forms of madness and anyone who studied him up close would see that he looked like a god of misfortune, with his ragged clothes on the winter roads and a solitude as incurable as his skin unleavened by dryness and old age.

They weren't sure where he'd come from. He'd arrived in the parish on a rainy pilgrimage day in Lent with a canvas sack tied to a staff, an acacia branch curved at the end which supported the weight of his legs—and they'd soon come to see him at doors begging for crusts and cracklings. It was said he expressed himself in a completely incomprehensible language at that time, as remote as a ritual from the most distant of memories, some asserting it was Latin because of the bird whistles, others that it was Hebrew or some language from the Pentateuch, with long, open monotone syllables. What was certain, it was discovered later, was that he'd been conceived in the womb of a sister and that he always carried with him, in places where he wandered or was spoken of, all the signs of that incestuous descent. From his father he'd inherited the blank voice and satanic look, they said, and from his sister, his mother, the interrogative reasoning of a child. For that very reason his mouth painfully tortured the sounds of speech and out of his parchment lips emerged only the warm prayer of beggars never given anyone's understanding or pity. He had, in addition, the primitive face of pre-historic beings and like them, had already been around the world several times.

So it happened that one day as João-Lázaro was wandering around that place he spent the night in a cowshed with a group of pilgrims who were paying for their sins on the deserted highways of the Island. It being his habit to lose himself, out of continuous fear, in obscure solitary byways and reappear later in the middle of the group, after a few leagues he already had the colorless pace of the Earth's eternal pilgrims, as much as his sick wits would permit. So it came to pass on the following dawn, when they took up their walk around the Island again, the pilgrims didn't notice his absence or ask about him. In that way the leader gave the order to leave and the pilgrims, half-dead with fatigue, gave a goodbye look to Rozário and set out toward Moio in the direction of Achada, where the people and Father Amores were expecting them for the ritual of penitence. They not only lost him from sight, but also from their memory, and thus, when they returned just as soon as Lent came around again, they didn't ask about João-Lázaro. Nor had they heard any news regarding his name.

The town had received him while it was dozing one day and his raps were as mad as the doors that opened to him and where he invariably asked for crusts and cracklings. At that time he had a sumptuous red beard, woven with threads and strands, in the midst of which glowed two sky blue eyes, the color of Earth angels. His bare feet had become disfigured from stones on his eternal wandering: curved and callused, with huge old and sacred toenails resembling the talons of some lost bird, for he was a bird-man, with an almost rounded nose as thin as its bone. Wrath and goodness boiled and hissed in that bony, blood-red nose as the liquid blue of his gaze fastened on the things and beings before him that he seemed to want to transform forever.

It didn't take long for news of mysteries and miracles about him to spread, similar in every way to the nervous powers of Cadete, the parish healer. Some said that João-Lázaro had become a suppliant in the time of Christ and had been brought back to life by him; others that he was nothing but a common vagrant with no origin or destination, wandering about the world in search of truth; finally, they reached the absurd point of swearing that Lázaro was all that, no doubt, but only to disguise himself, because it might well be a matter of an exiled prince or even a bishop subjected to excommunication by Pope Iliderius IV, author of the schism of the four

132

theories on dogma. In that way, all that was necessary one day when the dogs were set on him was for his satanic look to explode at the beasts, paralyzing them and leading one to suspect that João-Lázaro was a beggar only in appearance. The dogs stopped barking and stood off at a distance, struck by the discharge of his demoniacal look. Then they tried to stone him, but the results were the same: the projectiles veered on an arc between the arm that threw them and his head and were lost on distant targets, windowpanes, as if some mysterious force had turned them away far from that body. They sent other dogs against him, horses and uncastrated bulls, but João-Lázaro shouted curses and maledictions, and appearing overcome by a great supineness, all those animals came up to him with such tameness that they looked more like manipulated tools than wild beasts running rampant. Furthermore, they would recognize him from a distance and bellow a greeting when they saw him pass. The oxen would stick out their necks toward the west, as if they were glimpsing death, and weep, walking beside or leaping around him. As for the dogs, they would come over with familiarity to lick his sores, and the unguent of their saliva cured them so effectively that João-Lázaro joyfully absorbed that relief from his suffering.

They couldn't hit upon any way to expel him from the parish, therefore, as the prayers, conjurations, and blessings connected with Father Governo's exorcism could do nothing against his strange weariness. It was even supposed that such powers challenged God Himself, as the priest guaranteed, inveighing once more against the heresies of the people who followed him everywhere. For that reason he stubbornly tried to expel him as quickly as he could. But how? First he took the advice of Cadete the healer, who cooked up some balsamic herbs wetted with snake anise and invoked the spirit of the apostle Saint Matthew against the Devil; then, since that had no effect, he summoned God, in hope of an oracle—but God didn't illuminate him either. Then a group of men armed themselves with their work tools and went to encircle him on the banks of the Salga, where they were certain he dwelt in the Cave of No Man's Exile. They finally came upon him on the outskirts of Achadinha, and he was surrounded by such thick underbrush against anyone who dared approach that the mob stopped and turned pale with rage. What most startled them was the fact that their own dogs, their respectful, trained and submissive watchdogs, were with him. They drooled furiously against their masters, turning continuously around João-Lázaro, in whose eyes the virgin water of sainthood flowed. They lost their boldness then and, turning about, quickly went back down the road to the parish. Cadete had striven hard at the invention of a complex and fatal recipe, capable according to him of wiping out a dinosaur with its odor alone, but he soon admitted defeat: no power could surpass that satanic look and no command was sufficient to go against João-Lázaro's singular blank voice. He then tried to calm down the emotional climate of the population of Rozário because he feared seeing the art of his miracles and cures weakened.

"It seems to me that this man is no mendicant. He could be a biblical prophet," he guaranteed. "You should give him room and board, reward him with clothing, and let him relax in the peace of destiny."

They did in fact make available to him a hut that had been in ruins ever since the last earthquake and they dressed him in a coarse woolen cloak. From that moment on they began to welcome him at their doors with a mixture of holy terror and hateful pity. João-Lázaro was not impressed by such a radical departure in people's behavior, however. He was going about at that time working other miracles with his look, teaching the mysteries of silence from village to village when the year of hunger and epidemics reached Achadinha. Fearing all manner of contagion from strangers, people quickly barred their doors, fled from his look, and began to get used to the way in which death was knocking on doors from house to house in a strange visitation. First, almost all the old people died, then some men and women of indeterminate age, and Achadinha was already filling up with that nameless despair, waiting for the time of the children also to arrive to complete their misfortune once and for all. While the plague spread, only two shadows dragged themselves from door to door, illuminated in yellow by the sun of the world's last breath:

the priest, blessing the dying, weeping with the sad and deprived people, commending souls to the saints of his devotion, burying the dead, and João-Lázaro, only a poor unsheltered man invariably asking for crusts and cracklings. The women no longer had anything to give him. But at times they threatened their children with his figure for their mischief and misbehavior, other times against the aversion to death that was sucking at them inside, seeming to disfigure them. During those days that blank voice would be calling in the wilderness, in the rain, when it was windy, calling out in the midst of sick cattle and maritime waves, calling out and calling out as if the whole world were weeping in that voice, the very voice of death, and his unintelligible and warm singsong ran that way down all the streets and entered all the closed-up houses. It was the only audible voice of God, they said, because people were dying, begging His mercy for the children—but God didn't come, didn't exist, or hadn't announced Himself yet to men.

10

IT WAS NECESSARY TO TURN THE SUN AROUND AND
QUICKLY LEARN THE SECRET OF ITS HIDDEN FACE.
ONE SUNDAY FATHER GOVERNO, SEEING THE
CHURCH ALMOST EMPTY OF THE FAITHFUL, COM-
MENDED THE SOULS OF MORE THAN A HUNDRED
dead people, asked for the healing of two hundred forty-nine
people ill with the plague, and felt himself taken by an unexpected emotion when he conceived the idea of the miracle of
the Sun. Until then he'd limited himself to the role of a neutral pastor who heard people's confessions, officiated at mass,
and gave the sacraments to the newborn and the dead. The
faithful recovered their beliefs as they invented a different
way of praying: they wept to themselves by just imagining
death, while the cycle of the plague was taking place in the
bosom of their families, for now there wasn't a single day or
night when the eyes of the dying wouldn't all of a sudden
stand stock still. So only the miracle of the Sun showing its
other face would bring back hope to that faith ruled over by
misfortune and illness.

On that Sunday the vicar decided to proceed to the invocation of the Great Spirit that navigates by walking over
the waves, passing over all abysses, calming wind and
storms, stanching hemorrhages, and he was thinking about
that possibility, clasping his hands tightly together and closing his eyes and weeping, when he came to develop a kind of
alchemy, which consisted of catching the tears in his hands

and then emptying them into the chalice so they could be consecrated. And, calling upon himself the grief of three hundred entire families, he took over their weeping, and the tears his eyes shed were those of a maelstrom, so thick and in such quantity that in the space of a few minutes the chalice began to overflow with that liquid, as sharp as a diamond, which slowly began to acquire color until it was as ruddy as the sun that bloodied summer mornings. Thereupon, consoled by his own weeping, he covered the chalice with the stole hemmed with marine animals, opened a path through the faithful clustering in the center of the church, and ordered them to form into a procession behind him to the entrance, for God would certainly make the Sun move and show its hidden face to those who'd never admired it on their feet. Some sort of miraculous thing must finally have been about to occur: the manifestation of God through the sun of creation, the miracle of the cure of the epidemic of the plague, the rescue of those despairing castaways, so that people would finally move away from death and also bring back to life their dying spirit and their flesh, burned by that sinful sun over so many centuries and centuries without change.

It was a bright day, a day with birds fluttering on the top of hedges, walls and trees, and the voices of the birds had a strawberry sound and their light flight reminded one of the swift breath of white acacias on their perpetual voyages around the world. They were unknown birds whose glass voices lit up the day with secret breathing, birds with no form of existence and without the look of affliction of insect-birds, and everyone waited to see them in the air, not in flight, but swimming in the day, when they realized they were only inventing them. In fact, when they reached the steps only the rain persisted, the witches were mating without trilling, and an everlasting rain of ninety-nine consecutive days had turned the Sun damp and whitened its very light. A white rain powdered the face of illness. The priest lifted his stole to conjure away the malignant flash piercing the eyes of the sinners, and, behold, the flash took on the look of a metallic mouth that passed through the weave and the embroidered fishes on the stole and, diving into the chalice made holy by the tears of so many eyes, drank up the bloody contents and disappeared again into the firma-ment. What tongue of fire was it, they thought, that had come, sent buy the Occult One with no other word for the suffering of that people? It was the supreme sign of the wrath of God because they were challenging the power of the Sun and the power of God over the Sun, and that challenge was as hell-bent as heresy. Father Governo stood there, pierced by panic, and ordered everyone to take shelter in the church, which they did quite quickly, not upright, but dragging themselves down the main aisle, along the sides, and also throughout the sanctified laby-rinths. They dragged themselves to the main chapel where the confession of their sins was supposed to take place, and there was weeping and gnashing of teeth, while outside the Sun was spinning in a spiral to go off laughing toward the distance above the clouds. And the clouds were changing into a cone of brambles on the back of a man with a pair of big ugly boots shaped like the map of Italy, when lightning flashed and a bolt opened a rift in space. With the opening of the rift a handful of thunder-stones fell announcing the storm. Frightened animals became agitated in their pens, attacked by the announcement of death. Hens flew and bumped into things that had never existed and had certainly not been in those places and, not reaching shelter, they spread out on the ground and moaned with an asthmatic wheeze of sand and feathers, while cattle pawed the ground of their sheds and struggled against the halters of their perdition, as pigs climbed up the walls of their pens and bit stones in two with their teeth.

Then it was the rats' turn: they emerged by the hundreds, in uncontrolled bands, fleeing the holes where they'd hidden from the Sun, to slip into the nearest sewer. Such a fatal thirst burned inside them that they swallowed all the rotten excremental water of cesspools as if some superhuman had also poisoned them, they sprawled in ditches, belly up, with the stiff legs and imploring snouts of tiny soulless animals. They remained that way for a few minutes until they cooled off, because immediately following bats came and devoured them in that noble and civilized way bats use everywhere in the world.

It was, however, the time of the magnificent imposing rain of ninety-nine consecutive days and the plague was still as widespread as the rats, the rats that were growing, multiplying, and not going away because they'd fallen asleep in their nests.

"You can go to hell, Father," João-Maria roared again as he tried to make himself heard without the intervention of strangers. And once more the buzzing grew and the same voice came to the rescue of ecclesiastical deafness: "*He's saying again that you can go to hell, Father.*" Father Governo, however, turned an even deafer ear and tried to maintain his gravity:

"My Church orders, João-Maria, that those who die in Christ have holy burial. We must bury her in holy ground, in the cemetery, like any Christian, don't you think?"

"In that case you're on the wrong side of the world, you go around betraying your Church."

"What do you mean?"

"Simply this, you, Father, go around blessing the rich and cursing the poor, because you bury them in mausoleums and us in the cold ground. You yourself are the richest man in this part of the world. Your holiness can bless my backyard, but go away afterwards. It's there I intend burying Sara's body."

The intermediary once more transmitted what João-Maria had just said: "*You can bless his backyard because he's going to bury his wife there.*" The priest began to grow moist with an old greasy and resinous sweat, salivating inside and outside his body, and he was walking back and forth in a furious, stumbling excitement, beating the stones with his cane. When he stopped, he pointed the tip of his cane in the direction of the door and made his first threat:

"Free yourself, my man, from the punishment of God. If you don't do what I'm telling you, you'll regret it for the rest of your days. I might even request the bishop excommunicate you for heresy."

"Nobody in this parish is a bigger heretic than you, who've lived alongside the powerful and never wanted to hear about my poverty. You, Father, collaborated in the theft of my land and the destruction of my house. I have no reason to obey you."

Surprised and indignant exclamations resounded again. In the midst of the babbling the priest's voice asked, "What's he's saying? What's he saying?" and since nobody answered,

Calheta the sexton got up his courage and warned João-Maria in his illiterate's language:

"You're offending God's ministry. It ain't just the father priest you're offending. This here's dumb stuff. Hey, buddy, people's talking about going after you."

"Stick your dumb stuff up the crack of your ass and go off to mass with him. You're nothing but a stinking little priest without a frock," roared João-Maria, so worked up that he was pounding on the inside of the door with the sickle. "The life of a stinking priest is fine for sad characters like you, but it doesn't do poor people's troubles any good."

This time, too, a great annoyance ran through the flock of black afflicted birds. They were waving their stoles in a discreet flapping of quick movements, the mourners moaned in the stone bosom of their lamentations, and the priest, they say, was weeping then, humiliated and ready to settle things with blows as in the cold and memorable days of his youth, and was about to do so when the mayor began to clear his throat and spread his nostrils as puffy as a pig's bladder.

"Stop!" he said, "The ruling authority will take over here. I charge you, in the name of the law, to open the door and allow the Gospels to be put into practice. If you don't open up, it will be knocked down."

João-Maria hazarded a quick smile, as if he'd been waiting all the time to hear Goraz, the smile of a serpent-angel who promised to raise up the mayor's head on a tray and drink greedily of his blood:

"As for you, I'm going to cut your throat. If not today, someday. But I'm going to cut your throat."

Father Governo, desperate from his deafness, cupped his hand behind his ear, and his broad nostrils opened and closed while the horrible cavern of his mouth, lacking a good number of teeth, looked like a sponge wet with strings of saliva.

"What a willful man," he opined, beside himself. "He should be brought before an *auto-da-fé* of the Holy Office, accused of insulting the Holy Mother Church."

"It's no good repeating that. You're getting things mixed up. I've lost my faith in you and those around you, but I haven't lost my religion."

"Insolence, insolence," the mourners murmured sorrowfully as they immediately began to keen like wounded cows, squatting with their heads resting against the end of the house. João-Maria consulted the look on his sons' faces again, because he was going to need the courage of his forty-five years and days in order not to surrender an inch in his conviction. The eyes of José-Maria, the elder one, suddenly struck his, communicating a strong impulse, and even Jorge-Maria, the younger, in spite of the terror in his look, was experiencing the most perfect moment of his childhood. He would never forget that perfect instant of his first greatness, because he'd just heard the other side of truth from the mouth of his father. They knew then they would forever share something: the balance of forms with things and that kind of blood-pact whose validity, more than supernatural, was without beginning.

"Ask whatever you want, Father Governo, sir, so I can answer you. In that way you'll be able to learn something about my religion."

"Who am I except a minister of God on Earth and His representative on this Island? You must submit to divine rules, not to my wishes."

"Then ask me quickly. But these people have got to go away. I'm not going to confess in the presence of my enemies."

"What enemies? We've come here on a mission of peace, as people of good will, and only to carry your wife to the gates of paradise—that's all."

"Get that idea out of your head. Priests and land grabbers don't enter my house."

"You can bury a cow, a goat, a sheep and even an unbaptized child in your backyard, but not a creature baptized according to the rites of our Church."

"Well, there you have it. It's all a question of the love a person has for animals and people. An unbaptized child is still somebody's child. And as for Sara, she's only going to be buried in the place she loved most, her backyard."

"In that case I'll have to challenge you to prove that was her last wish, because we too respect the memory of the dead."

"I'll prove it before God, I don't need any go-betweens."

"And who is God?"

"The Almighty, the Creator of Heaven and Earth, who came to earth to save us; he became a man and died crucified on the cross."

"And revived on the third day, don't forget that."

"That's what I've heard tell, have no doubt about it."

"Do you believe in the prophets of the Bible?"

"I'll believe in everything you want me to as long as you bless this house and go away for good."

"Do you believe in the Holy Scriptures, in the story of the people of David?"

"In the wisdom of King Solomon, who divided a child in half and distributed the pieces to two women, in the lamentations of Jeremiah over the destruction of the city of Jerusalem, and in the strength of the giant Goliath. What more do you want to know?"

"Do you have some pact with the evil spirit, the Devil?"

"I'm not about to have a pact with anybody. I'd rather break them."

"Do you believe in the sacraments of the Holy Roman Church? Do you believe in the pope, bishops, priests?"

"In all of them when necessary. Except in you, as you well know."

"Then," Father Governo shouted, enraged, "I have no reason to bless this house. I'm being insulted. You're not ready to be heard in confession, this is a matter for the office of our mayor."

"No, sir. The only matter having to do with the mayor of this place is you yourself in person. It's your morality. You defend peace with war. The people no longer believe in your peace."

"The people live in silence, they're not like you. You talk out of the mouth of Satan and you may be possessed by him."

"It's easy to prove the opposite. Try by putting the mayor in jail and you'll soon see the people break their silence."

"It's no use talking to you. You refuse confession because you don't believe in your sins. You only accuse others of sin."

"I confess to the saints of this world and the other, I don't confess to criminals like you, much less before a man who elected himself to ruin us."

"Then, I repeat, I have no reason to bless this house. I'm going away and I leave you with my curse."

The priest gave the order for the cortège to disband and, before going down the street, the mayor put his enormous hands to his mouth and roared, "You'll pay for all this another time." The sexton crossed himself and the mourners threw some stones at the door, while the men took off their surplices and picked up their crosses.

João-Maria was suddenly filled with a strange fervent calm and again took counsel with his sons. Embracing them, he asked them to keep their courage up. He told the older one to take his place at the door and not to open it for any stranger, and he left. He was carrying the sickle tightly under his arm. He passed by many eyes frightened behind the opening of their windows. Cautious men, hidden in the doorways of their barns, done in from fatigue and as sad as death, scratched their necks and said nothing. Their souls were already so chagrined that their faces were permanently wrinkled. They were sweaty, emaciated, silent men whose spines bulged in the middle of their backs; men wise from suffering who forgot their voices so as to see more clearly in the dark. They carried night in their very breathing, a thick, purple night where eyes forgot to sleep. And the women, too, were courageous animals as they saw him pass in such a hurry: they sang under their breath of the strength of the first man in the world, discerning perfectly, even from a distance, the way in which his veins were throbbing, full and twisted. And even the sad children watched him pass and stood there until they saw him disappear far off, larger than any man they'd ever seen, because he was carrying in his hand a sickle for clearing brush and fens and was walking above the street as if he were flying along at roof level. João-Maria knew then that there were people inside the houses and that inside the people there might be things other than solitude. A short while later he entered the priest's house and surprised him sitting on a wicker couch devouring his breviary.

"You, sir, are a jackass and you don't deserve my respect, but you're coming with me now, without any altar boys, to bless my house and Sara's corpse."

Father Governo was startled because he was immediately taken by the certainty that a sickle in the hands of a criminal was a terrible instrument of earthly justice. He pretended to be even deafer, hoping to gain time until someone could come to his rescue, and his face was inflamed by successive sheets of blood that formed scarlet disks on his jawbones. Only his eyes were pale and almost lifeless within two large circles of lusterless copper.

"Are you kidnapping me, João-Maria? Have you gone mad?"

João-Maria put the sickle to the priest's nose and pushed the nostrils up a little, making him look ridiculous: his nostrils were as wide as the sleeves of his cassock and inside them the hairy tendrils were damp with sweat and snot. He seized the couch with both hands and began to hoist himself up by the strength of his wrists, so terrified he was chewing on his tongue and swallowing saliva and breath at the same time. When he saw him standing before him, João-Maria drew the sickle back from his nose and placed it in the middle of his back. It was a sight to behold as the priest walked in front, stumbling, talking to himself, head down, jaws tight. He was a humiliated man who didn't greet those who came to peek out of doors and windows, nor did he hold out his hand for children to kiss as was his custom. Father Governo realized now that he'd never had a vocation for dying in the service of God because he had a great love for the things of this world. The enjoyment of infinite things for the things of this world. The enjoyment of infinite things in life had nothing to be compared, however, to the glory or the ephemeral joy of death by martyrdom. And if he were a martyr he might see himself put forward for sainthood, all that was necessary were four canonical miracles. But he wasn't sure he would bring them about after he was dead. That's why he didn't make the slightest gesture to contradict the furious grandeur of that madman completely out of his mind. He only sensed that a great many hidden eyes were keeping watch on him all the way to João-Maria's house and he wasn't sure they were friendly. When he entered his kidnapper's house he was all sweaty from that stickiness of affliction that turns the skin greasy like remorse, like a great unlimited fear, and he decided to pacify the looks of the two boys by smiling at them with apparent calm. He even tried to win over the feeling of great grief hidden in their eyes, making ready immediately to bless the body of their mother. He was so careful with his funereal Latin that emotion enwrapped his voice and it became as weepy as the lamentation of a family member. Immediately thereafter he blessed the young ones and the house and withdrew to a corner the better to admire the dignity of the dead woman and those mourning her. Before slipping away, since night had come and he was afraid of the barking of dogs in the dark, he brought up the matter of someone lighting his way. The dogs were howling, their noses pointed at that house, they were howling in the direction of the waning moon and they were just as fearsome. So that Father Governo begged João-Maria to pity a little his old age and illness. The latter was, however, firm in his decision:

"I'll take you home, of course, as long as you consent to be a witness to Sara's burial and won't go about saying afterwards a sacrilege was practiced here."

Father Governo himself helped carry the coffin into the yard and he waited patiently while João-Maria dug the grave a little deeper, fearing the dogs would come and dig it up to eat the body. Then, when the earth was pushed back, the sound of the hoe and the weeping boys moved him to tears. He wept with such despair beside the sons that João-Maria immediately forgot his rancor of many years and, trembling, not feeling at all like consoling a priest, laid his hand on one of his shoulders, seeming to give the impression that the prelate was the one left a widower and not he. And they embraced each other, all of them weeping, kneeling on the ground, when without any such expectation they saw all the leaves fall off the branches of the fig tree, leaving it completely naked with a sound like the winter wind. Alarmed, the priest's eyes filled with copious white tears, for he'd come to the conclusion that the great miracle of his life was taking place: that is, he said, the leaves of the fig tree were only the wings of invisible angels sent down to Earth to fetch the soul of that saint. Such a manifestation could only be divine work.

All it needed was to be interpreted carefully. God took some of His elect to His bosom, that was true, but His choice was shown in the most diverse ways. In the case of Sara, who was a saint, the angels had come to get her disguised as the leaves of that tree.

"Let us pray," he implored with emotion. "This fortunate lady that you had for a wife and mother is saved and has just traveled to the gates of paradise."

There was an opportunity a short time later to attest to the veracity of that miracle. As the fig tree had withered away in just the space of a week because of the very fact that its leaves had been transformed into redeeming angels, João-Maria decided he would cut it down at the base and convert it into firewood for the hearth. He and the young ones undertook the delicate task of removing all the dead roots in order to allow only lilies and begonias and white roses, the most beloved flowers in Sara's life, to grow in that spot. They dug around the coffin in search of small rootstocks, digging in the soil with their hands and speaking to her with tenderness and suffering. Soon their longing made them dig deeper and still deeper in their excavations until a hoe brought out a deep thump like the sound of a drum on the surface of the coffin. They decided then to look at her and admire her one last time. When they opened it they were filled with terror and began to call for help. People came. And people came one after the other and proclaimed everywhere that Heaven existed, not up there in the firmament, as they had been taught, but most certainly in the interior of the earth, because Sara's body, buried in it, wasn't there. She had been resurrected.

It was the ninety-ninth day of water and the rain suddenly stopped. They'd become so accustomed to it they no longer remembered noticing its existence.

11

WHEN JOÃO-LÁZARO REAPPEARED IN THE PARISH
DESPAIR WAS ALREADY A GREAT BLACK BIRD
HANGING WITH OPEN WINGS IN THE MIDDLE OF THE
RAIN AND HIS LUCIFERIAN GAZE STOPPED TO CON-
TEMPLATE DEATH FROM AS CLOSE AS A HUMAN
CREATURE COULD WITHOUT THE RISK OF BEING
struck down by it. The same arid, blond fever was burning in
him with uncommon intensity on that day and his white voice
had grown somewhat hoarse from weeping. That was also
unusual in his life without memory where he had always felt
an almost fantastic clarity as visible as illuminated crystal.
His sumptuous red beard, woven out of many threads and
skeins, in the midst of which two earth blue eyes glowed, his
feet callused and curved, just like his ancient sacred nails, his
whole bird-man being with a hooked, bone-round nose, suddenly filled with that despair because the plague had already
brought death to a few children and was secretly continuing
its visitation from house to house. It had already been seen,
according to what they said, sitting on the bed of a three-year-
old boy reciting psalms from the Bible, and it was a faceless
woman who expressed herself only with gestures and spread
a sulfurous breath over every object she touched. Others swore
that his own smell, sulfurous and toxic, perhaps scorched the
air forever.

Jõao-Lázaro went back to begging cracklings and crusts
with his innocent white voice out of paradise, crying in the
wilderness and touched with pity to the point of weeping over

the misery of the women and the suffering of the children. As they had neither cracklings nor crusts to give him, they began to offer him white and black coins, but João-Lázaro would only accept the dark money, since it was of secondary value. His poor man's pouch was growing empty and hunger soon obliged him to eat roots and wild mulberries. He wandered about indifferent to the rain and the lightning and began to render small domestic services and take the place of men who were sick or even dead. In payment they would give him a bowl of barley or pumpkin soup and he would sip it without relish, as if concentrating on the act of feeding. His inexhaustive energy of a rawboned, obstinate old man led him to grab his ax and chop piles of tree stumps without the slightest drop of sweat. He persisted until he took on all the other chores, and he did so with such a feeling of service and delivery that soon after cutting firewood he would clean cattle sheds and pigsties and even after that repair broken fences, huts knocked down by the wind, and plugged drains, and he would whitewash buildings and walls, reroof houses, seal up cracked fireplaces, and proceed on to a whole endless series of other services. Sometimes people had to invent senseless tasks, such as arranging rows of sacks that were in perfect order, sweeping the street, or watering plants already drenched, because João-Lázaro would only desist when the Sun went down, considering just then his work at an end. No one ever managed to understand a single word out of his mouth, but when they gave him instructions in Portuguese they would explain what had to be done first, detailing everything needed, and he showed signs of perfectly understanding the language. Nevertheless, it was impossible to converse with him since his speech consisted only of bird whistles and great open, monotone syllables. They tried to pay him with bright silver money, pork and chicken meat, or simply a few ears of corn, a quart of beans, eggs and other items of food, but João-Lázaro persisted in his immediate refusal and would only accept dark coins, cracklings and crusts. If there weren't any, he would show no sign of annoyance whatever and go on his way.

The days went on like that and the rain kept up, furrowing the ground, knocking down walls and opening ditches in plowed fields. The roads were practically impassable because of washouts and the yellow water swirled along the streets in a flood until it split into successive branches. In a short time Achadinha had withdrawn into its original egg, shutting itself up inside its houses to let the downpour fulfill the prophecy of biblical waters. At the same time the hateful fevers of the plague, with its vomiting and agony, its delirium, headaches and nausea, was leaving people bilious and with tongues the color of brimstone, possessed with a sinful thirst, unable to urinate and their bodies covered with sores. They would die sometimes in the middle of a gesture or a step as they were getting out of bed, they would die with their arms flexed and their legs stiff and would blink convulsively as if they had received an arrow in their heart. Death took on all those sudden forms, brought on by thirst and unusual suffocation, and people's afflicted mouths would open to give passage to a tongue burning like a lit match. João-Lázaro went about indifferent to such family tragedies, not hearing the wailing, the cutting shrieks of mothers over the beds of their children, the short, spaced sobs of men without wives, the moaning of children and animals as rats devoured each other and would sometimes burst from drinking rainwater. João-Lázaro didn't even see the almost continuous funeral processions going by in the rain with the priest sheltering himself under a kind of bishop's canopy, and he was even far-removed from the meaning of those pine boxes on top of oxen carts. By then they had completely forgotten his miraculous blue eyes and the old effect his look had on dogs, bulls, and stones, his unexpected meekness, and because of that he'd gradually been assuming his status of a beggar once again. Quite simply, he'd stopped wandering around the Island in order to be useful during the misfortune of death, and once more boys turned to throwing stones at him and sicking dogs on him, thinking that João-Lázaro's arrival had coincided with the outbreak of the plague and the rain that had gone on for ninety-nine days without end. They even ended up considering him an idiot, because it had never been possible to glimpse any indication of wisdom in him. On the contrary, everything led to their treating him with scorn, allowing that only a person of weak intelligence would reject silver coins and jealousy guard dark money.

João-Lázaro averred furthermore that he was a child of a tender age, saying so with a gesture of his fingers: when a boy asked him how old he was, he showed him two fingers and was rather annoyed at the laughter his gesture prompted in the onlookers. And when asked where he'd been born and where he came from, he turned his back and went off up the street murmuring rude things in his strange language. Then the boys got up their courage and went after him. They began by pulling his hair, then they tore his jacket, and one of them showed him his erect penis, saying he was going to stick it up his ass. It was then his fearsome wrath made use of his acacia staff and he swung it about with satanic energy, capable of smashing the first head it hit. The boys swore afterwards that his eyes had grown in an inconceivable way and that serpents with forked tongues were coiled in his eyeballs, because the gleam of those eyes was liquid metal again, exactly like that of snakes and the poisonous bite of their saliva.

One day somebody noted a startling circumstance: the plague was disappearing and, even more noteworthy, it was doing so in houses where João-Lázaro had gone to lend his services, where it ceased to torment people and animals. The sick people would suddenly awaken from their larval sleep, as white and transparent as wax from being unwittingly in the shadow of death, and they would immediately arise from their beds and look around, all flustered, scarcely believing what was happening to them. Children of a tender age, in turn, with their heavy purple lashes, began to stretch and immediately sought their mothers' breasts, ending in that way their mortal duel with darkness.

The one who'd begun to put the acts together and jot them down in his notebooks was Cadete the healer, whom the plague had already deprived of a long list of patients. The man had embarked on a stubborn marathon against death. He'd tried to invent a chemical product based on multiple mineral-vegetable essences, first by cooking and then distilling off a syrup, and finally using an alembic to clarify the product of the mixed herbs, the result of numerous and patient experiments in alchemy. Everything had been in vain, however. If he did manage to stanch the diarrhea, he couldn't suppress the fever or hydrate the body; if he eliminated the high fever, then the diarrhea would gush and the thirst become even more devouring—and death was only inconvenienced in its passage, but not abolished from the bosom of families. Having lost heart, confessing his impotence, he went back to consulting the stars, hoping to attain through astrological means what he hadn't produced in other ways with the slightest practical effect. One night he stopped. There were phenomena on this earth that were strictly within God's competence and not that of men or even the stars. He tried to pray, but he didn't know how. If God did exist, it would have to be the same for good as for evil. Therefore prayers could go fuck themselves. Wasn't it in God's purview, then, for Him to act directly? What was the use of praying? Here in the world, among the tiny little gods of the Earth, help had been invented out of selfishness, which was forbidden to God—because God was a winged being who flew above all objects and obstacles. He could very well dispense with listening to any pleas for help. Cadete judged the rigorous inscription of his motto to be useless and turned it toward the wall. Then, with the same impulse, he turned all the other inscriptions around, from the one that said THE SEA IS WHITE to the other one, the formidable phrase of Bárbaro the pilgrim: THEN ISN'T WHITE THE MOST ANCIENT COLOR IN THE WORLD?, and successively in that way until his consultation room had a Lenten look about it, as when the saints are forbidden to observe the world. Then in a spell of discouragement he sat down in his chair and tried to doze. But seeing João-Lázaro pass on his way back to his animal lair at the far northern end of the parish, he leapt up and remembered it was Saturday, the day when that soul there was accustomed to flit casually from house to house asking for cracklings and crusts. He then decided to follow his tracks and, taking his hat, went walking behind him, always at a distance. João-Lázaro didn't walk, but rather kind of floated, like a dozed bird looking for its nest to sleep in. Cadete felt a vague fascination with the tiny little steps he took and the way he would rise up at times above the walls along the street.

Cadete the healer mentally reviewed the details of João-Lázaro's passage through the parish, from the first day of his appearance with the crowd of pilgrims to the news of his prodigious and mysterious acts in surrounding settlements. Cadete had led the initiative for his expulsion at the head of a group of rowdies and he'd been able to witness the strange magnetism his eyes had for dogs: it was an ophidian and batrachian gaze, as the boys and a few superstitious women could testify. At that time what had really worried Cadete the healer was the eventuality that hiding in João-Lázaro's wisdom was some occult power capable of competing with his art of expurgating illness and curses for sick people and believers. So famous was the word of his deeds in the parish and on the Island that it became known that all one needed was to invoke his name, the name Cadete, or to look toward his house and certain lesser illnesses would immediately disappear in a breath and cease to be a secret or reason for concern. So that since a new enthusiasm had spread with the arrival of that biblical prophet, Cadete had undertaken to exorcise him: he convinced the priest to give public testimony of his pact with the Devil, and in order to excommunicate him, he lined up some of the most fervent defenders of good morals, thought up new smokescreens to embalm his spirit, spread the most biased versions of his white voice, and proclaimed his madness.

João-Lázaro's expulsion was imminent when a new outbreak of plague invaded Rozário and then new and profound efforts were asked of Cadete to discover a cure for the epidemic. He shut himself up in his laboratory again, ready this time to challenge God himself, and on the outside of the door he hung a sign bearing the stern inscription:

| DO NOT DISTURB: WISE MAN AT WORK! |

It was a slate inscribed with chalk and hanging from a piece of greasy twine and as sacred as a hieroglyph, which the usual frequenters of his consulting room, chronically ill people with numerous repeated and unusual ailments, respected to the point of panic. For six days and six nights he confronted the smell of sulfur from the flasks and test tubes with a stubbornness that carved thick blotches around his eyes. It was the despair of the agony and death of others against the despair of the plague, as was known. But the tense inventory of its origins and causes, his tests, his therapeutic experiments, were all for naught, and Cadete the healer recognized his impotence once more, this time in a definitive way. Only God, in the case he existed and wanted to, could suppress the epidemic, not ordinary men, not even wise men.

The whole cycle of death by plague went along until the day João-Lázaro was at last accepted as a harmless being, closer to animals and children than to adults, and he began his chores and small services from house to house in exchange for some cracklings for his dinner. Wherever there was suffering he would arrive while the day was still young and knock on the door and his euphoric energy, his bony nerve, and his great sacred feet would be turned over to the small tasks of people's homes, cutting firewood with vigorous blows of the ax, grasping a dung fork to clean out pigsties, unplugging muddy drains, pruning reeds and boxwood hedges. Without anyone suspecting so, there his miracles began.

Cadete the healer, following him from a distance at dusk on that Saturday, made one last effort to understand the most extraordinary coincidences in his sentient life. He worked all kinds of miracles through science, but he was a long way from that supernatural power of curing the plague with a look. There were still at that time many sick people lying abed in all four corners of the parish, but it was quite obvious the illness had not only slowed its advance, but had ended up leaving children on the Rua Direita alone, as well as the animals in their houses.

"Well," Cadete concluded, "it was precisely along that street that João-Lázaro spent his days toiling from sunup to sundown in exchange for dark money, cracklings and crusts."

Everything had been revealed, no mistake about it. Cadete suddenly felt the poor flesh of his mortal parchment seized buy a shudder, as if he'd seen the Devil on a street corner, and he took off down the street at a run, fearful of being chased by the faceless, eyeless creatures that habitually inhabit the night. The enormous mouth of the darkness was wide open behind him except for the specks that indicated lights on houses or the doors of taverns, and a mixture of euphoria and fear drove his heavy protuberant body forward, stumbling along the way as he fell into ditches and his steps echoed at intersections. Panting, sweating, his eyes wide from the terror of his deduction, he slipped into Father Governo's house and dropped his shapeless elephant body onto the first seat, fanning himself and mopping his neck with his handkerchief.

"I've discovered everything, your holiness. I've just discovered everything, everything…"

The priest's hearing had grown stiff, like rope that becomes firm in water or grains of corn in a frying pan, and he had acquired the habit of speaking in a very loud voice, like a person with an absolute need to hear himself through others. The people, as well, had been contaminated by that unusual way of roaring and they themselves would speak louder than advisable.

"Come, come, my friend, get a hold of yourself. What is it you've discovered?"

He was wracked by a coughing attack, like an insect buzzing inside the neck veins and stiffening the tongue, and the priest was suddenly filled with irritation, impatience, because he wasn't used to receiving anybody at that hour of the night and, being a practical sort, he wasn't used to delays and superfluous talk.

"The man," Cadete finally said. "That man has got the art of a wizard, or an apostle, or maybe a doctor of the Church. He can cure the plague."

"The man? What man? What's going on in your mind?" the priest roared from the depths of his confused deafness. And he got all worked up, sticking his spine out of his collar like a tortoise waking up out of its shell. "This is getting to be land of poison!"

Cadete spread his hands wide before himself to calm him down, and went on to lay out the scientific basis and the details of his theory concerning João-Lázaro. It might be a case of reincarnation, he whispered. Or a lost soul locked up in the appearance of a human rag picker. But he could guarantee one thing: a house that João-Lázaro had entered was a house free of the plague. But let your holiness see for himself…And he enumerated with excessive and lively detail dates and facts related to João-Lázaro's comings and goings and so thorough and complete was he in his convictions that the priest's body straightened up suddenly and he went into a kind of volcanic convulsion. He stood up, sat down, and stood up again, and there was a driving force in his legs similar to a sewing-machine pedal and his face grew as ashen as lichen on busts in public squares and a chill of pins hitting their mark ran through the lobes of his ears, huge and arched forward and always so devoid of sound and understanding. His practical spirit then made a desperate appeal to his carnal forces and demanded action of them, and suddenly his legs and his arms seemed to take on all small actions, like the pieces of the great heroic machine of his life, and entered into a cold accord with logic. His former energy, which had restored the church, had opened the cemetery on a level tract of land, and had conceived the cement and the crosses, that energy propelled him into the great bosom of the night in whose sightless eyes the priest stumbled, limping, swift, driven by the invisible hand of God, who was leading him to the encounter with Lázaro and his drab unsheltered den. He went along so wrapped up in his thoughts that he didn't even notice the crowd already following him and spreading the word from door to door, like a rebellion against the corsairs and invaders and plunderers who had threatened the parish in other times after its founding.

"There goes our priest. Let's go along, let's go."

Boys had already taken the lead of the splashing of aimless voices and galoshes shuffling along the pavement, and women came to the windows and said,

"Lord in heaven, what sort of a mystery is this?"

And, going up the Rua do Caminho Fundo in the direction of Eira Velha, the crowd grew and a few torches appeared. The gray-haired old women, wrinkled by weariness, posted themselves behind their windowpanes and murmured prayers and exclamations that couldn't be heard outside. But children were crying, dogs were barking with their snipper shouts in the direction of the Moon, and the uproar was a maritime thing that carried horses and waves in its bosom and ships and a feeling of danger and shipwreck until the moment when

155

someone climbed up the church tower and began to ring the nocturnal bells, and the night was broken again into many pieces of sound and breaking glass. When they finally reached João-Lázaro's shelter they saw him emerge from a hole, coming from the center of the earth, and his body was pale in the light of the torches and he was as rigid as a core of rock; he seemed encased in copper or bronze. They stopped at a distance, admiring his majestic red beard woven of threads and skeins, his bare feet curved and calloused, with old, sacred toenails; his clothing consisted of shreds and rags, his pants ending halfway down his legs, but his hair was so thick and long that no one noticed the half-nakedness of his body. Then Father Governo made a sign to the crowd, with a grave gesture similar to the multiplication of the loaves and fishes, he approached João-Lázaro and had the sudden feeling he was face to face with the Messiah himself on his return to Earth to save mankind. Their looks crossed and they could have fallen into each other's arms, but the priest forbade himself such a vulgar gesture and held out his arms, shouting from the depths of the silence watched over by the flames of the torches:

"João-Lázaro, spirit of good and of peace, be ye saint or sinner, I command you to follow us and practice charity for the sick and dying of this land!"

João-Lázaro trembled all over with the animal fear of a beast alone and at bay, he slowly cast his eyes over the houses of the parish and then onto the priest and those following him, and his shoulders shook like the two wings of an eagle taking off on its last flight and, without anyone's knowing how or for what reason, he burst into sobs. Still weeping, he put on a woolen jacket and walked at the head of the crowd to the first street in the parish, entering every door then and it was prodigious to watch the way in which his eyes awoke children prostrate in the sleep of death, and on contact with his hands the women and the men received, in spirit, a command, the command that Christ had given the paralytics in days gone by, "Arise and walk," and they would immediately rise up from their beds and felt cured and praised God for having sent His Son into the world again to save them. Witnessing all that, the people were so taken that they began to say to each other:

156

"It's all a dream, nothing is true, we ourselves haven't yet been born and that's why we don't exist either," and they asked each other to slap and pinch them so they would awaken and that was what they did, but in the end the miracle of the cures continued and João-Lázaro went on touching bodies and the bodies were saved and there was so much Joye then that Men & Women & theyr Children and even theyr Friends and theyr Animals had naught wish then but that they should kisse and embrace and go aweeping and yea all did blesse the Lord God the Father, for a Mercy n'eer seen nor wondered at anywhere in this darke World.

It was dawn when the visitation to the dying ended and by then there were only a few people around the priest, Cadete, and João-Lázaro, because the others had scattered to celebrate their second birth with noisy and prolonged euphoria. They slaughtered lambs and goats and offered them up in sacrifice, and they drank wine and cheap liquor while night was still on. So it was they didn't see or sense a white coldness of death suddenly coming over João-Lázaro's body, feverish and tarnished with sweat as he became strangely disfigured, as if all his flesh were being devoured by fire or attacked by quick-lime or some corrosive acid. His face suddenly filled with a great mortal weariness, his mouth disgorged a vomit of crack-lings and saliva and his tongue became as yellow as brim-stone, while his body puffed up and became covered with sores. All of that as sudden as the coming of rain or the birth of the Sun or lightning or the crumbling of a wall, so that in a few seconds João-Lázaro fell to the ground and began to die, and Cadete was grave and bellowed into the ever so deaf ear of his holiness:

"He's absorbed all the plague on the Island, Father Governo. He's going to die. He's going to die, holy father."

And his shout of "plague! plague!" echoed again and flew over the houses of Rozário, reached every empty place, turned and came back all alone because no one could hear it any-more. Everyone was drunk on the wine and on the blood of the lambs and goats they had sacrificed to God. Father Governo, having quickly crossed himself, found the moment opportune to flee from the plague and recommended a like procedure to Cadete. Before fleeing he covered his nose with his handkerchief and blessed João-Lázaro's corpse, saying:

"So may you be fortunate, oh, poor man, because the Kingdom shall be yours and not this world!" and he ran stumbling to the church to anoint himself with holy oils and holy water and the salt of baptism. He went to the bottle of sacred wine and got drunk on the blood of Christ. Then, calm and fatigued, he thought about going to bed, because no epidemic could enter his body sprinkled with the wine of the sacraments.

The next day they placed João-Lázaro's body in a triangular wooden box, brought a cart drawn by two mules, and put the coffin on it. They buried him in a restful spot in a corner of the cemetery between two rows of boxwoods beside the wailing wall. A week later hair had grown on top of his grave, and it was imagined that a white voice was crying out inaudibly from the bottom of the earth, because his body was still breathing and the ground itself was slowly going up and down in time with that respiration. But if a person asked whose body was buried there no one would remember his name, because there were really only two hypotheses to consider: either they had completely lost any memory of his acts, or it was certain, then, that João-Lázaro had never existed.

12

JOÃO LÁZARO'S RESURRECTION TOOK PLACE ON
THE DAY OF THE VISITATION OF THE DEAD AND THE
DEPARTED FAITHFUL, AND MANY PEOPLE WIT-
NESSED THE EVENT WITH THE VERY EYES OF THEIR
OWN FACES. THERE WERE MOTHERS STRETCHED
OUT OVER GRAVES WEEPING FOR THEIR ANGELS,
their milk-doves, and bold women, trembling and in a panic,
were talking convulsively to the earth where their old wax-
colored husbands were sleeping forever; there were hands
arranging the branches of boxwood shrubs and the roots of
rosebushes and lilacs; and the mausoleums, open like
sacrariums on Sunday, gave off the smell of candles and
incense; there was still the undecipherable whisper of funeral
prayers, as monotone and ancient as the breathing of the stones
themselves. So that the silence was only a vegetable thing
with hands pruning its roots, and the scattered sobs were black,
like the great black bird of death—of a weary and afflicted
death.

When the first signs of João-Lázaro's resurrection
appeared, Father Governo was methodically using his hyssop from grave to grave and his Latin that omitted syllables
here and there floated about like a sonorous mist above the
figures: *requiem aeternam dona eis, Domine: et lux perpetua
luceat eis.* He was calling on God and men in such a terrible
way that the November wind, blowing in sparse gusts, made
whistle the bodies of the cypresses and the bamboo. It was a
bitter, sibylline wind, like the sound of the women's wails.

159

He'd made a complete turn around all the flowerbeds in the cemetery. He'd blessed the earth with holy water, and, in Latin, he'd once more warned the memory of the living and the dead of the temptations of this world, for it was written in God's wisdom that all beings created by Him had been born of dust and would return to dust one day, just as all food returns to the maternal breast of the earth of our creation: *memento homo quia pelvis es et in pulverem reverteris.* Then he walked to the small funeral chapel, stumbling, his face tightened with deafness, and he was surrounded by crosses, surplices, purple banners. There he prayed with a honeyed tone made up of liquid sounds and brown syllables accompanied closely by the response of the faithful. He rested in peace the dead and those afflicted by death, reciting for them the psalms of the Hebrew poets:

> *Dies irae, dies illa*
> *Solvet saeclum in favilla:*
> *Teste David cum sibylla.*
> ....

It was vinegar weather, the damp, oppressive weather of a barren island, with wind and fog, and the cold curled the grass and twisted the cypresses until they took on the geometric shape of cones. When that happened the people cried out in terror in a chorus alongside the wall of their lamentations and from there they broke into a run searching for the priest: at that exact moment, as if by some miracle of God, the earth began to breathe with life, heaving up like a set of bellows and slowly going back down, and it opened up with a boom. It was an enormous forgotten and magical chest that opened up with a sound of rotted fittings, and from its bottom they saw a short man with a long and sumptuous red beard woven into threads and yarn emerge. He had, that man, eyes as bright as phosphorescence and his hair falling down over his shoulders made him look so much like pictures of Christ that the people immediately stopped running and began to kneel on the ground, believing at last in his appearance. Jesus of Galilee was in the habit, it's true, of visiting sad people on his earthly pilgrimages. And he's worked miracles with paralyzed and starving people and distributed bread and fishes, walked over the waves and restored sight to the blind, health to lepers, and life to the dead. Jesus had been water for the thirsty, food for the poor, and clothing of the naked who bore the sack of their misfortune along byways and through deserts. But now he was there in front of that still incredulous people, at whom he gazed with the sapphire of his calm and saline merciful eyes. It was like the look of a satanic lamb, as in bygone days when he'd driven the money-changers from the temple. And his great large hands, almost transparent, had slender, knobby, pink fingers, like the images on altars, while his soft flesh, like that of a child on the body of a man, assured everyone there was still the possibility of a new birth for the dead.

Father Governo was quickly summoned to come witness that apparition just when he was reciting the psalm of the Hebrew poets. Coming out of the funeral chapel, he limped over to meet that stranger and stood before him in ecstasy. His mouth fell open, revealing the toothless crater, and he stood mute and anxious for a long moment as his body became covered with a froth of sweat—a strange blue sweat that speckled his forehead with drops and dripped across the small spaces between his wrinkles. Then standing face to face, as in the year of the plague, they didn't recognize each other. But João-Lázaro smiled at him with kindness and, opening his arms wide, invited him for a holy embrace. The priest's body reacted quickly with a shudder of terror, for he thought that if he embraced that man returning from death he would inevitably be embracing his own death and would immediately see the end of his days. Facing such a possibility, he realized full well he wasn't yet prepared to die. So then a sudden temptation to cry out and flee far away from there came over him. He was so old and lacking in strength that his legs started to shake and the veins in his neck throbbed strongly, to the point he felt he was about to have a stroke. Inside his spirit floated a cloud of affliction and amazement, a kind of fainting calm mingled with the disorder of all his senses. He was certainly going to flee from the face of death, flee from its embrace, because fear was showing through once more and flooding his face with sweat when he noticed that his human sheep, as afflicted as he, had knelt down and were praying, and João-Lázaro continued smiling, still motionless, seraphic, inviting him into that holy embrace. Should he really challenge him?

In a flash he realized that everything had already happened to him in his life: the miracle of the wise children illuminated by God at the time of his appointment to the parish, the mystery of the weeping animals, the cure of the plague, the disappearance of the body of Sara the saint, stolen away by the angels who came down in the leaves of the fig tree, the ninety-nine consecutive days of rain, and, lastly, the resurrection of that strange luminous and satanic being. He could even die, because nothing more miraculous was certainly going to happen during the rest of his days. He only needed one last breath of spirit to understand the secret of such and so many divine signs. Unable to gather them from those surrounding him, he took inspiration in the earth.

He looked at the Island rising like an amphitheater into the mountains right before his eyes, and he admired the majestic grandeur of the Pico da Vara, where later on he would see the airplane fall, and beyond that the eternal clouds that ran like sprites made of delicate glass, hovering over the mountains whose march toward the south had the sway of every dozing shape. On the other side, to his left, Cadete the healer's white sea, the sea of the Azores, was roaring with the despair of its Apocalyptic horses, and there were gods on its surface armed with tridents whose white horses, winged and heavy, moved the very bosom of the waters. The gods were along standing in their swift war chariots and the sea was as white as the wrath of the passing crosswinds. Crushed by the steamrollers of such affliction, he decided to question the man. A kind of physical resignation was already calming the tremor in his legs and softening the rush and heat of his sweat glands.

"Tell me, my good, man, who are you and where do you come from?"

Then a distant white voice, snaking out like a serpent uncoiling from its nest, came from inside the man and could be heard with perfect clarity, to such a degree that the priest thought his deafness had come to an end and the nostalgic sounds of the world were clear:

"I am João-Lázaro, the one who died one day to return from the future," the other man replied. And he explained, rather softly, that he was sent there by the wisdom of people and nations to announce the fleeting joys of life and soften the suffering of the men of the Island.

"I bring you the proven science of peoples that they call progress and growth," he added with humility.

Fright. Fright is a spring that leaps out just as flowers, sponges and mushrooms explode at birth; a spring that opens mouths and broadens nostrils, enlarges eyes, brings unexpected wrinkles to the brow. It's an animal ill with jaundice, fright, a green and bilious November animal, while João-Lázaro's white voice was even more illuminated now inside and suddenly began to pour out for those men and women who were so amazed to hear it and over the fabulous distant worlds of the great imagination of poets and, perhaps, of madmen; the worlds where men are not the sad and worn-out creatures of an Island, but the creators of joy; where machines are moved by the electricity of lighting, and war and peace make use of such machinery with the precision of the Sun and Hell, and where the days in May always announce repose from great weariness. And as he said that, men and women began to rise up slowly and move closer to João-Lázaro. His face was profiled against the landscape, as soft as the breeze that flickered in the bosom of the trees.

It wasn't long before they were following him in a procession through the streets of the parish, without even knowing they were walking: something like that had only happened once in the history of Achadinha, when the bishop of Angra had come to confirm the whole population. They went to greet him at the top of the Caminho Novo, carrying standards, guidons, and flowers of every size. That visit had been surrounded with such majesty that the slightest gesture by the prelate was immediately interpreted as a blessing. The bishop made use of a solemnity only comparable to that of a pope or of the very Christ of the Resurrection, with his little purple biretta, his great sapphire ring, and his ample vestments that

163

transformed him into a kind of voluminous and real lady as the people followed him to the church in silence and sobbed with emotion. As for João-Lázaro, as he went down the old road, he gently waved at the people watching him from their windows. A smile of milky quartz, thick and motionless, made him look, amidst his dignity, like an exalted and grand biblical patriarch, dressed in his perfect denim, smelling of musk, and softly placing his wooden-soled sandals on the ground, as during the time they had dressed him and put shoes on him to conjure away the plague. As so many years had passed since those events, it was frightening to see how his bearing had become filled with solemnity and his former status of beggar had been abolished from the memory of all the people, and his body didn't have the dull tone of days gone by but the secret and nervous incandescence of fire. In spite of that, the dogs recognized him, because they came to lick his hands and howled deliriously. Babes in arms also greeted him, extending their hands in his direction with a smile still without memory. He wasn't recognized by the old and middle-aged people, however, because they'd completely lost any knowledge of his name. And, furthermore, João-Lázaro had never existed in any part of the world before his resurrection. He probably was, according to what they thought, some crazy foreigner who had come from God knows where, speaking in a strange way about the transformation of things, of other unknown places, names and powers like electricity, radio, motors and telegraphs. They listened to him, amazed and incredulous, without understanding any of the things he named, but as if seized by an invisible lodestone by the warmth and absurd velvet quality of his white voice.

"Where are the white trains?" he inquired at one point, turning to the crowd.

White trains? they thought. What trains? They didn't know, they weren't things that could be seen on an Island as distant from the world as that one, they'd never heard of trains, what were they—white, on top of it all, because whales were white sometimes when they passed in the distance and in view of the children themselves or came to die and rot on the shore on the eve of the eternal rains, and the sea was white, the sea of the Azores, according to Cadete the healer, as white as João-Lázaro's voice, not the trains, had always been.

"What about steamships? What about airplanes? Haven't any steamships or airplanes ever reached here?"

Steamships, airplanes, white trains, none of that had ever happened on an Island so far-removed from the world. The houses had thatched roofs and adobe bricks; the roads were made of tamped gravel and rubble and lumps of mud, and the horses and oxen were docile, but there were no steamships, or airplanes, or trains. You left the Island on the sailing vessels of corsairs and wandering navigators guided by the astrolabe and well-placed winds. João-Lázaro then asked if they knew of the existence of other peoples and their languages, and he experimented by speaking the dialect of sirens, the languages of the Saxons and the Gauls, and he sang the music and poetry of the Greeks and Trojans. He invoked the civilizations of Phoenician merchants, Armenian warriors, Eudonian peasants and Beterastian shepherds. He spoke to them of cities and terrifying countries—but they'd only heard of Egypt and the cities of Jerusalem and Babylon, places in the Bible. They'd also heard tell of popes and bishops, of conquering kings, of crude navigational things and secrets of good seamanship for any course. Their frightened looks still went back to the times of shipwrecks and the last earthquake, without forgetting the solar eclipse and the prophecy of the biblical waters that were to submerge everything one day and not leave one stone standing nor any living creature on the face of the Earth. They were forgotten men and women, accustomed to looking around and measuring everything by the spinning direction of the Sun that gave them their view of the sea and time. As for science, they possessed the science of the tides, the winds, and the great eternal rains, and they had scientific knowledge of the cycle of orchards and harvests, the age of rut in animals, the fiery sermons of their great faith in the saints. As to instruments and machines, they had ox carts, plows, packsaddles for donkeys, harrows and rakes, hoes, scythes, saws with which they patiently guillotined living trees, a gibbet for every animal condemned to the servitude of men, infinite skills to accompany an infinite number of work tools, beginning with the task of carpentry all the way to staves and work in vineyards. They also had their hands, and hands again, and more hands. João-Lázaro countered all this immediately with great agility of thought: mechanical devices for farming, clocks, the surprising advantages offered by electricity in all its applicable forms, and he envisioned someone someday comfortably seated in Achadinha talking through a wire to somebody else on another continent, or listening to a radio by means of a wireless. And he also explained the delicate system of machines that did everything all by themselves, precisely because that occult force, electricity, had been endowed with intelligence and discernment in order to supplant men in the most complex and costly operations.

"The intelligence of electricity has been proven absolutely by the superior state of electronic intelligence. Machines talk, machines handle numbers, discover and treat illnesses. The white trains themselves fly along commanded by that ultimate intelligence, the way airplanes and birds fly."

The people were startled by the revelation of so many hidden things missing from their knowledge and pestered him with questions: was it true, then, that airplanes held themselves up in the air belly-down like hawks? Was it certain, then, that the white trains flew?

"Without a doubt, yes. They fly through deserted landscapes with no beginning or end carrying people from one kingdom to another," João-Lázaro assured them. He wasn't from their time but had returned from the future to teach the people on the Island the proven science of peoples and nations which is called growth and progress.

In a short while he was surrounded by people ever more amazed at his revelations. Whole families even began to fight over him, offering him bed and board and all the comforts normally dispensed only to notables and on special occasions. He invariably spoke to them of the flying apparatuses that crossed cosmic space in a number of hours no greater than the fingers of the hand, overnight, going from torrid climates where it was hard to breathe to frozen places; about the white trains, about underground trains that flew along beneath the marvelous cities of the world through tunnels and huge silos like rats and other vermin; of automobiles, of threshers and other agricultural machines—stating finally that the time of the great island revolution against the tyrants was at hand, against intriguers and priests, the great revolution of men over the obligation to work and suffer until a miserable unjust death.

"People must make ready for the change, then. They will have to take it on as a good thing and as force for change." And he explained: "Revolutions are made in the craziest ways, sometimes against God, other times against men in their status as animals."

And the people were struck to the nerves of their faith:

"Are revolutions made against God? What revolutions?"

"Well, now my friends: Not against the visible God, but against the absent gods you worship," he answered abstractly, so people couldn't find much to understand right away. But then the voice of a young man hidden in the crowd broke the silence, a euphoric voice, vaguely feminine in its suggestiveness, saying from the rear:

"Why, of course, we have to revolt against the priest and against the mayor!"

Challenged rebelliously in his wisdom, João-Lázaro then visited Cadete the healer in his consulting room one day and began to listen to him go on about his proven art of curing illnesses. Cadete showed him the fabulous perpetual ball invented by a Tibetan monk, where he scientifically read cosmic signs, announcements of the future and of death. He performed a few small, quick demonstrations with his alembic for distilling aromatic herbs, gave him some of the miraculous essences of his invention to smell and made him test cures and harmless substances, from the pill made of garlic and Satan's nails for uric acid and roasted snake basil for internal hemorrhoids to lixivium unguents and the foul-tasting elixir of the twelve vegetable potions whose minor effect replaced the process of decline in any spermatically aged or fatigued animal with new sinful joy. It had the vague smell of roasted almonds, and João-Lázaro remained pensive and silent with the sorrow that such primitive things like that brought on in him. A short while after he spoke to Cadete about the scientific methods of cures through medicine, through endless complexes and sensitive ausculation devices, X-rays, surgical operations on the lowermost nerve of the spinal system, and he dismissed, with no cruelty, a few strange and fatal illnesses like tuberculosis, malignant volvulus, and primary leukemia, ailments overcome by science long ago, he said. He gave the healer such copious information concerning the new products of chemotherapy that Cadete slowly lost his color and enthusiasm and was soon run through with terror. His spirit was overtaken completely by a feeling of being crushed physically. And when João-Lázaro assured him that all his methods and ways of thinking were obsolete since the illnesses to which they were applied no longer existed anywhere in the world, the healer, who up till then had possessed the power to cure everything and expel the Devil from the angels' place in the body of any ordinary possessed person, realized he was an ignoramus. He grew so visibly sad that João-Lázaro began to feel upset and thought:

"He has tears in his mouth and his voice is already weeping."

Then he took a complete run about the office and began to read the framed writings placed along the walls. Even over his head there was a slate hanging from a string, and João-Lázaro pondered for a moment the stern inscription it bore:

> ## DO NOT DISTURB: WISE MAN AT WORK!

He thereupon began to be filled with vague pity for that man who was fatally mistaken about the meaning of life, and he continued to read around him: WELL, ISN'T WHITE THE MOST ANCIENT COLOR IN THE WORLD?—*Bárbaro said so and it's been proven!* There were other sayings still, among which was Cadete's fabulous maritime discovery, framed in three versions of increasing size, as if each were in turn successively more profound than the previous:

the sea is white
The Sea Is White
THE SEA IS WHITE

"Illnesses like that," João-Lázaro stated suddenly, pointing at the hanging inscriptions, "are the product of polluted imaginations."

Since the man was sobbing and blubbering now with renewed intensity, he was filled with new affliction because he had before him not a man caught in a flagrant crime against civilizations, but that soft and equivocal species of a delicate animal with no barbs. He began his therapeutic explanations again:

"There's no such thing as a person possessed by the Devil for the simple reason there's no such thing as the Devil. They're people who've lost control of their nerves through the work of the religion of priests and overcome with hysterical crises, the ones you mentioned. Hysteria is an indescribable state: it can be suppressed by psychic treatment. Psychic treatment studies the mind in its hidden part through the ogival process and through the logical reactions to shock treatment."

The healer then stopped listening to him and made a broad, desolate gesture all around, a gesture that meant the destruction of everything, sweeping the objects to the floor in an imaginary way. He threw a glance of merciful pity at the perpetual ball, the test tubes and retorts, the small boxes of herbs and the alembic, after which he dropped onto the nearest stool and thought:

"Now I'm going to die."

In fact, he'd already decided to renounce existence once and for all. If he disappeared forever he would at least remain in the memory of his objects over the length of so many years of curing. They, yes, would make him eternally loved. They might even go so far as to erect a statue of him, as he'd been reminded by the poet and dentist Francisco Heitor on the day he publicly recognized his creative genius. If not death, what other things made sense in life anymore?

It wasn't true he had absorbed the science and magical breath of the wise Apanaguião, the Tibetan monk who had invented the perpetual ball, according to what Bárbaro the pilgrim guaranteed. Nor was it clearly true that people could be cured from a distance by the simple act of invoking his name when some ailment struck them down. But how was it possible, then for all those things to have happened? Had someone invented that fable? Maybe it had only been the exclusive product of his mad imagination of a former bull-gelder, because just as he'd been guaranteed by João-Lázaro, a man of the future coming directly from death, there'd been born into the world a new genius of wisdom to defeat him in the most perfect way. Against such a power, then, what could his herbs and essences, his incenses and beverages, and the proven faculty of the perpetual ball do? What could his old despair of so many years do against João-Lázaro's new euphoria of the world? Nothing, nothing. Ten times nothing.

He would die, however, with the world whose end was also quite near. In fact, humanity had already gone through all the cycles of its existence on Earth. It was going to devour itself. It was going to initiate the process of its long, slow inevitable extinction. He knew that this, and nothing else, was the destiny of the world, of man—of them both.

13

JOÃO-MARIA

WAS SQUATTING TAKING A CRAP IN HIS BACKYARD WHEN IT ALL HAPPENED. HE FIRST NOTICED A NOISE LIKE THE CRUMBLING OF THE WALL IN A QUARRY growing in the distance and coming to meet him, overwhelming the sonatina of the waves and the prophetic bustle of the shearwaters. On nights like that the moon covered the whole crest of the Island with flour and all that could be seen were rising shapes, the unusual and austere shapes of the earth that slept and kept watch, and the audible lure of the dampness drawn out of the hedgerows persisted, making the old bones of doors and gates creak. Those shapes were startled by a kind of face above the sea forgotten over the ages, a face with residual saltpeter, inside of which night hid the fossil of the isle.

He was immediately upset by the origins of such a sound, because looking at the low-hanging fog, all he could see were the rolling clouds and the shapes agitated by the wind. It was a night of fleeing thieves, because the dogs were chasing the silence helter-skelter and he was afraid the children's bogeyman had been turned loose or that some suffering souls from the other world were wandering about there. As a rule, when something like that happened, people foresaw earthquakes and waited for them in panic, while cattle lowed and rats went into such a state of madness that they deserted their nests, bumping blindly into the first object.

João-Maria, however, was convinced at once that it wasn't time for an earthquake, because a noise like that, in the case of earthquakes, never came from the Pico da Vara, but from the center of the Earth. It was an unusual mountain, with a tilted head and a belly as thick as the hugest lunar pregnancy, like shit when it hits the ground, he thought, and the mountain was there with its shape of a god sitting on his misfortune. Something was moving in the midst of the clouds and around an axis, however, and that thing had a misshapen belly, out of which lighting flashes were shooting. And the thing was completely out of control, losing altitude and about to crash, because the attraction of the Earth on that falling ball of fire could be felt.

So, as João-Maria was squatting and taking a crap in his back-yard, he gave a jump and immediately got the feeling a terrible collision was going to take place between an object shot out of the sky and the peaceful mass of the highest mountain on the Island. It occurred to him that it was one of those mysterious and unbelievable sky chariots that in times gone by João-Lázaro had given the name of airplane, a heavenly chariot in which the unknown angels of the earth traveled, just as the white trains crossed deserted landscapes with no beginning or end carrying people from kingdom to kingdom.

Suddenly there was a great explosion. At first it was like a slow, stabbing knife penetrating the sleeping back of the Pico da Vara, so slow and soft that João-Maria would later swear before others that he'd heard the ground moan with pain, as if wounded deeply in the stomach. Then the stones exploded. Strips of fire formed a gigantic corolla of flames and the mountain was imme-diately transformed into a mushroom of smoke. João-Maria got a perfect view of how the curious object struck and split in two, its tail twisted so freakishly that from a distance one could make out a hooked nose sticking up like the beak of a great bird that had been stabbed to death, and that bird was flouncing about in the night transformed into an insect. Later on, along with the others, João-Maria would say he'd had a feeling of floating on a wave of voiceless cries, because a broken voice had asked for help from the unnamed beings or gods who'd never been there on the Island. And he thought:

"These things can't be happening to me, things like this don't happen in the life of a person without any history," in the same way João-Lázaro was an invented object that invented imaginary trains and chariots and exotic languages and denied the existence of God, because maybe João-Lázaro wasn't the body of a man, but someone sent from the future and the occult world.

He wiped himself hurriedly on some dry shavings and buttoned up his pants on the run. From that time forward everybody would say, "In the year the airplane crashed…" It was there, perhaps, that the aging of the distant nights without memory in which the old and trembling tellers of tales still located the start of their time. There had been the year of the plague and the ninety-nine-day rains, the year of deadly hunger, the year of earth tremors, the year of the American locusts, and during those years the escalator of death had passed across the Island, because a kind of circular trip was turning life like a carrousel that spun forever on its axis. At that moment, leaping over the pigsty, João-Maria caught the sound of the parish in an uproar.

There was someone in his long underwear halfway up the church steps bellowing to all the souls in the world to wake up and see with their own eyes the little incandescent pieces rolling down along the mountainside and breaking apart. Everywhere and in every direction sparks were leaping and flint stones were whistling, and the man in his underwear saw veiled blue tears exploding on the Pico da Vara, and one might say that a volcano was being born in the mountains because the phosphorescence of the lava was already sliding down in a smear of smoking syrup, making the hair stand up on the backs of people's necks and loosening their bowels. And fire would soon break out in the nearby woods, with tongues of twisting flames, and then the trees would be strangled.

A strange desolation came over the men in the midst of such disaster. The smell of brimstone caught people at their street doors. Those people had the drowsy face of someone sniffing the night and not understanding it, and then the women and children went into a mad whirlwind and the cattle lowed with lethal anguish and the dogs ran in packs and barked angrily at the edge of then night. When Calheta the sexton ran to the tower and rang the big bell, an old blind woman wept and said, "Our Lord is dead," and another woman next to her said, "Nobody's dead, the world has died," and a faceless man remembered a fatal phrase and said as Jesus Christ had said, "Let the dead bury the dead, for the love of mercy will you women shut up and let me sleep," and a young woman shouted, "You be quiet there, sir, my father shouldn't be speaking heresies," and the young woman's husband said, "Light me a lantern. Light me a lantern," and he ran down the street in his long johns in search of the disaster, joining the others. The Rua Direita was filling with the sound of wooden clogs and the tripping of bare feet, and people came to their doorways and asked those who were running:

"What was that? What was that?"

And one of them said hurriedly and with an almost haughty knowledge:

"It wasn't anything. A volcano exploded up on the Pico da Vara, that's all."

But then Calheta the sexton stopped ringing the bell and hollered from up on the tower:

"A plane crashed!" and his shout made a fantastic echo over the rooftops and remained there infinitely repeating itself:

A PLANE CRASHED, A PLANE CRASHED, A PLANE
CRASHED, A PLANE
CRASHED, A PLANE CRASHED, A PLANE
CRASHED...

and he remembered to go wake Father Governo to bring him up to date on the situation. He went inside the house without being startled by the fact that the doors weren't locked. He found him sleeping, all wrapped up in death, an exceptionally ugly old man with those donkey ears sticking out of his head, snoring so loud the walls shook. On the night they found him dead there the priest was sleeping that way and had the same eager ears, but he was as swollen and tight as a bass drum. He called to him, shouted, clapped his hands, and he ran off terrified bellowing: Our priest's dead, Our priest's dead, Our priest's dead, Our priest's dead…

There were now flocks of people running about, people running into those in front of them, stumbling in the darkness, and the people were being joined by the first harnessed animals coming at a mincing trot. So a confusion like that, something difficult to narrate, would be remembered in years to come: there were nameless people perched up high in the dark and naked blue women were flying around the chimneys of the houses, and children and the ever-present dogs and their monotonous howling at the hedges in the lost lands that bordered on the crags, and the night was being pushed completely toward the sea, because all the other animals were turning toward the shore and roaring with the voices of marine amphibians. People say that a weaned young steer profaned the house of God that night when it was released from its stanchion and ran off, leaping right up to the main altar. The animal seemed fascinated by the lamp hanging from the ceiling and stuck out its snout toward the tabernacle; it bellowed for God, just as people are accustomed to do in times of affliction, but God gave it no answer and, then disillusioned in its faith, it paraded down the main aisle, leaped over the space between the prie-dieu and the pulpit, and took refuge in the baptistery. There it drank up all the water in the baptismal font without noticing that it was holy and therefore not fit for drinking. It opened its bowel in two diarrheic streams and when people come to corner it, it attacked its pursuers with lowered horns. They broke two benches over its back, squeezed its testicles, and led it off by force. After the episode of that disorderly animal had been settled, all the people went back to concentrating on the flames curling up in the distance: it was a sea of fire, seen from atop the demolished walls, and with the enormous combustion the earth continued to moan, stabbed in the stomach.

The first animals were being harnessed in front of the church when João-Lázaro appeared. In the darkness he had those same globular eyes of a mare, and Cadete the healer, beside him, was burning with fever, shivering from cold and thinking again that he would soon die, and José, the man with the levers and wheels, followed João-Lázaro's slight gesture with the soft look of his temperament and Francisco Heitor, poet and dentist, was in the seventieth night of drunkenness and poverty from the day he lost all customers for his torture, and then the priest arrived and roared for Guilherme José and with him there also came his anomalous twin brother José Guilherme, the rat-catching man with his absurd snares, and his face was so full of rust that it was as if a nocturnal ball were perched on his shoulders and, finally, João-Maria, who, facing the mayor, filled his voice with hate and swore in public that he was going to kill the Great Enemy of Rozário, while Calheta the sexton kept on bellowing from up on the tower, "A plane crashed, A plane crashed, A plane crashed…" João-Lázaro mounted the third step of the church entrance and asked for silence, and once more his eyes, half-lit in that night of torches, were satanic; he asked them to spread the word from door to door, through the nearest pathways, so that all available men would come there, because it was urgent for those poor people, the travelers of death.

"We've got to help out in that disaster," he said.

Well, the most amazing thing of all was the way in which the mayor was submitting to the orders of João-Lázaro, whose eyes were quivering like those of a small boy surrounded by dogs. And it was said that Father Governo, too, had lost his authority when Lázaro faced him without saying anything ever since the Sunday when he rudely interrupted one of his sermons and said:

"You're talking like that about the poor because you've filled your belly on their misery. You know quite well your God doesn't exist because that God isn't the one of the poor and the downtrodden," and João-Lázaro's look had the same fury as Christ's when he drove the profaners from the temple.

For a moment, detaching themselves from that terrible, death-dealing look were the old bifid snakes of earlier days whose saliva stung from a distance like that of Baudelaire's snakewoman. Such confusion reigned in the church that Father Governo came down from the pulpit weeping, blushing with humiliation, and he immediately declared mass over for that Sunday. To his wine cellar he summoned the mayor, the president of the Council, José Guilherme, Agostinho, fat Cadete the healer, and a few others, and he sought from them an agreement concerning his immediate resignation from the parish and, by means of a petition, the dispatch of a new priest, a priest capable of understanding the times and facing up to the rebellion of his enemies. As for him, he would simply retire to an old folks home, to a hearth and winter cloak and he would begin his days of meditation on God as he awaited death.

"What's happened is that communism's come to Rozário. That João-Lázaro, from whom we hear so many heresies, is nothing but a communist who came here with the mission to destroy us all."

With everyone present startled, Father Governo caught his breath and made himself comfortable on the bench he'd sat down on. Didn't they know what that communism business was? Well, then, let me explain. First of all, it's a counter-religion invented by the Anti-Christ. Its minions are a bunch of cannibals, because it's been proven beyond a doubt they feed on children and old people. They kill priests and bishops, they pillage churches and cemeteries, they take houses, land and livestock away from their owners and come into possession of everything. Do you know how it's done? Property is no longer in the name of its owner and everything goes into the same heap. There it becomes what they call the common good. From that they get the name communism.

Guilherme José and Agostinho reacted immediately and brutishly to the priest's revelation: so, have those people come now to steal what's ours, only ours, and very much ours? As for José Guilherme and Cadete, intrigued by that unbelievable madman's fable, they immediately left the priest's house and went in search of João-Lázaro. The latter had rebuilt his life completely in a shack by the new highway near Cadete's office, and he'd gained fame as the best master carpenter in the parish. He specialized in building furniture, for he'd invented the art of smoothing wood with sandpaper, vioxene alkaline solution, white wax, and varnish. He had become almost an expert at a skill that was recent but already sublimated in his voice as he spoke with a vocabulary chosen from the daily reading of the Azores newspaper and his row of books on *The Practical and Methodological Sciences of Life in Primitive Communities, The First Stage of the World's Modern Civilizations* acquired on his last trip to Ponta Delgada. When he saw them enter his workshop out of breath, João-Lázaro stopped sanding a dresser, shook the red wood dust from his thick hair, washed his eyes in a basin, and sat down calmly, immediately guessing the visitor's intent:

"I'm quite sure the priest has grown old in his brain, he's getting more and more soft in the head. He can't put two correct words together anymore. But the mayor, that brother of yours, there's no excuse for him nor any pardon either. As for the president of the Council and that sad character Agostinho, they're a minor worry. The secret lies in our getting a quick replacement for Goraz. Once he's been replaced, all the others will become harmless."

With no further words, he went back to his work, and both Cadete and the rat-catcher sensed they'd been dismissed and went about their business. Seeing them disappear around the corner, João-Lázaro closed his shop and flew over to the priest's house. He caught them by surprise in the wine cellar and could see they had the drunken, tense and hypocritical eyes of the eternal money-changers in the temple. Agostinho and the president of the Council ran to take refuge between two duns, while the priest's breathing rose to a whistle. Guilherme José, Goraz, stood before him then, barring his way, but he received such a bump on the shoulders that he lost his balance and fell back down onto the spot where he'd been sitting. He was immediately sure that the man there had supernatural strength and a faith capable of moving a mountain, because his red eyes showed a sun of malediction in the center of each pupil and were as wild as those of an animal threatened with death.

"You," he said, addressing the priest, "can request your replacement from the bishop and it would be good if you did so as soon as possible. But first you'll have to see to the arrest of this man, give back the lands stolen from the people, and set up the election of another mayor. As for the rest, don't worry. The poor can take good care of themselves. From here on in it will only be a matter of replacing the power of the rich with the rights of the poor. Everything else is the fantasy of a priest, the lies and malicious talk of a priest, and that's why, because of that and everything else, you're condemned to hell.

"We have to help out in that disaster," repeated João-Lázaro, still standing on the steps of the church. Someone had brought him his horse. It was a noble animal, as aggressive as a bayonet, and everybody feared it because its deadly teeth caused wounds and welts that never healed and its kicks knocked down sheds and shelters, mangers and fences. They even said it flew over obstacles like a boat over the white sea of the Azores; but the magnificent animal filled with unexpected docility as soon as João-Lázaro approached to pat its haunch and nose, speaking tenderly. It communicated with its owner by signs, by strange, deep bows and curtsies, rising up on its hind legs to celebrate his appearance, and it would smile and franticly flash its eyes. Its joy was that great, a horse as white as the sea for whom João-Lázaro was the sun of its day, the divine, burning, daily sun of intelligence and joy.

There weren't enough animals for so many volunteers, so it was decided right away that two men would ride each mount and so they rode single file along the Rua Direita toward the new highway and from there, with a bit more urgency now, took a narrow cattle path between a tangle of brambles and hydrangeas in bloom, stone eggs the size of poplars, round and fearsome barriers. They rode for the rest of the night through the Escampado pastures, forded the creek at Achada, endured the mountain dawn, and when the animals were lurching up the side of the Pico da Vara, the Sun came out and they ran into people from Algarvia, Feteiras, and Santo António.

Those people were also coming in a hurry, on foot or on horseback, but they were merry, merry people, chattering and talking about marvelous things falling from the sky that night. There was, of course, lamentably the dead, but, patience: maybe they could pick up a few valuables, get some precious support for life, earn the blessing of some gold item, a small harmless gift from that chariot from heaven, because that illuminated bird had fallen there and it wasn't known where it was coming from or what route it was following...

When they finally caught sight of the wreckage at the top of the mountainside they stood stock still with amazement and remained marveling for a moment at the unbelievable destruction of the landscape there abouts, where there were scorched trees and rocks now and a magnificent heap of broken parts. Was that an airplane, then? João-Lázaro assured them that it was and explained briefly its composition: there were two propellers that were the sign of the last gasp of the motors, the cockpit, two wings, the cabin, and landing gear— but all that was as much in pieces as a whale butchered on the morning of its misfortune, because the belly of the machine had been consumed by fire and was all curled up from its impact with the ground at a speed a thousand times greater than any cyclone wind.

Suddenly João-Lázaro's hair began to stand on end, full of electricity, and his face went completely pale as he realized how they were all behaving like savages before a spectacle as primitive as was the death of others. Then he spurred his horse and galloped the whole distance still separating him from the aircraft's wreckage. Right beside it the horse reared, taken by panic because its hooves were treading on skulls and other remains of blackened corpses. Bodies shriveled like decomposing fetuses were strewn about and there were crushed heads on the gravel, and arms hanging from the aggressive branches of the scorched acacias, and brains pecked apart by birds and intestines scattered by the claws of kites. The earth had sucked up the images of that destruction so ravenously that death itself no longer existed in spirit, nor could any of them even imagine it.

João-Maria accompanied João-Lázaro in exploring the site, but he quickly lost his courage at the sight of those bodies. The sweet smell of blood mingled in his brain with the smell of flesh turned to ash, and a feeling of nausea and illness came over him that made him lose the will to be alive once more, the same as on that remote day when he'd desired and decided to die. He sat down on a log still warm from the fire that had devoured it during the night and he felt a sudden longing for Sara at the same time that despair returned to his pale spirit and he was attacked by a kind of fatal illness.

"I'm going to run away," he thought. "I'm going to run down away from here and find a place where nobody in the world can see me."

But his limbs were already so worn out that they soon did away with that idea, and João-Maria limited himself to closing his eyes with the old tightness of his rejection of life, as if he still believed in the possibility of taking leave of the world that way. He'd never imagined that his life could have gone on so long after Sara's absence. He wept for her every day, however, hugging his children, the children of his sin and his love for her.

"It's horrible, horrible!" João-Lázaro suddenly murmured beside him, his face disfigured in such a visible way that his whole appearance lost that almost incandescent glow from his way of looking beyond things, that gift of looking inside stones and the trees themselves and also into the hidden part of people in the dark.

Once more he was the bird-man from the time of the plague beyond memory, with his bony nose tightening into a whistle and his dull, earthen skin, while his eagle face took on the vertigo of all solitary beings. And his voice went back to being as white as the voice of the eternally damned of the Earth.

And it was horrible indeed, horrible: the slaughtered corpses, almost torn to bits, bodies with no faces and faces with no eyes, and hovering over them that horror of someone who dies without the conscious breath of his final moment. João-Lázaro went from one body to the next, repeating aloud the last word on their mouths, halted in the middle of a syllable. On the mouth of a child was still half the word *Mommy,* and on that of a young woman without arms whose legs opened her broad abandoned flower to the Sun the syllable of the word *love,* and there was a man, a man with the ruddy face of a priest, whose mouth was smiling as it exclaimed without tragedy, *Oh my God, my sweet God*; and an old couple had held hands and squeezed their fingers together to the point they were melded. Their names most certainly must have been Jim and Debbie, judging from the oval shape still showing on their lips. Then, farther to the front, a middle-aged man, fat and perpetually hungry for love, had a pair of solitary eyes where the birds had pecked away the irises opened toward the trees. His lips had stopped in the middle of a verse, still mouthing *Her smile gladdened me, the blue-eyed love.*

The horror that João-Lázaro had proclaimed was still on the face of a blue woman whose lips the kites had eaten and whose gold teeth smiled at death with half her fractured mouth. And another body, that of a blond lad, had burst apart against a pile of stones from where a mass of blood and feces now trickled, and the huge crater of his crushed cranium gave off a white vomit of saliva and brains. Then the girl appeared.

The girl was sitting on a log and leaning her head against a rock. João-Lázaro and João-Maria looked at each other and thought she must be sleeping. She isn't dead yet, they would call to her and the girl would awaken from that dream of oblivion and turn her face toward them, and she might even recognize in João-Lázaro the man who'd one day returned from the future and from death. What could her name be? João-Lázaro made an effort to remember: a girl like that must have had a blue name like that of the angels who come down from the leaves of fig trees and fly inside the Earth. João-Maria had seen them carry Sara's body away and then he remembered they had had the same metallic transparency in their flesh as that girl asleep against the rock. It was like a fledgling dove on a quivering flight, and João-Lázaro said Get up Cindy! and João-Maria said Get up girl! Get up, Sara! and they both saw the angel remained in the same place and her sleep was as irreversible as the secret of a name never spoken.

At that point the others had taken the strange still fortress by storm and were beginning to show off boxes, mysterious suitcases, gleaming articles, shining metals—and the mayor, Guilherme José, was making use of his muscles to split open effortlessly a small chest filled with camphor. He opened his eyes wide and his smile filled with saliva when he discovered it contained gold. He laughed out loud, for he'd drunk four bottles of rum with Agostinho Moniz and both proclaimed to the wind they were rich. Calheta the sexton got control of his trembling hands and ferociously took possession of the coral necklace of a fat lady whose belly lay squeezed between two panels with lines crossing and joining the continents; José Lisboa was bloodier than ever because he'd forced open an armored case—and there were pale phosphorescent coins, and gold plates, and some piece of sepia paper on which *Bank of America* could be made out. When he realized he was in possession of a great fortune, he ran to his horse and fled. On the other side of the airplane people from Feteiras were fighting with people from Achadinha, and a man from Algarvia broke four teeth on someone from Santo António and also fled down the slope with a small box under his arm, while the fighting increased with men fighting a ways away when José Guilherme, the rat-catcher, stuck out his fist and then sniffed through a broken nose. Cadete the healer worked slowly and his fat man's look made his movements particularly heavy as he struggled with the ruby and sapphire rings that the fingers of a stubbornly rigid corpse withheld from his greed. There was only one solution: he opened his gelder's knife and sliced off the knuckles, one after the other—and he lost, who knows whether or not for good, the wish to die. People were still fleeing with bags of clothing, tightly sealed trunks, the ever mysterious suitcases, while José, the man with the wheels and levers, was dismantling the plane's equipment and seemed startled at the complexity of its mechanism. He ended up taking away a noise-making apparatus where aquatic voices blossomed in some unknown language.

João-Maria was then overcome with fear as he examined the daguerreotype of a family with six members. There was a thin woman, a man as round as a top, and four children smiling as they looked off into the distance. They must have been happy people, there on the other side of the world, but João-Maria, when he identified the girl sitting on the log with her head leaning on a rock in the photograph, became upset by her and began to weep. She'd been the last person to die and as he tried to imagine her loneliness among the corpses he thought he was also inside her and the desire to die returned.

He was wishing for death when he heard a whistle coming from somewhere and then a kind of roar of stones rolling toward him. It was the sound of stones mixed with footsteps. A bird called out in the distance and all the people looked to the place from where those mixed noises arose, in the midst of which was the fury of a roaring sea with whales attacked by harpoons and the steady arm of harpooners. Then a brutal howl covered the mountainside and the horses reared again, as if the spirits of the delirium possessed the bodies of those animals. A few horses ran down the slopes, kicking up their heels, and a mare, falling into a gully, moaned, her bones broken against a cliff.

Suddenly the whole mountainside filled with weeping, angry shouts and phrases uttered in an unknown language, and the men tried to carry sacks on their shoulders and control the terrified animals. Then the dead began to rise up from the ground and went back and forth with the bustle of people preparing to defend their homes. Heads flew from one side to the other as they found decapitated bodies, and legs ran all by themselves in search of their trunks, and behold the dead opening wide their arms then and running in a pack after the thieves, and Cadete, in a panic once more with those cries of harpooned whales down by the shore, stood with his hair on end and shouted:

"Death is coming! Death is coming!"

They fled in every direction, spurring their beasts and clutching at the boxes and sacks like drowning men. They ran and ran and death came after them and fell sometimes, losing its strength. Exhausted, death was flying over the surface of the ground and bumping into every obstacle; it moaned in pain from each fall and then was left behind. When they had succeeded in escaping the pursuit of the dead, they stopped at a distance and stood for some time watching those levitating. They were threatening them from afar with obscene gestures around the airplane in a dance without weight or thickness. The smiling faces now showed their enormous and definitive pain of pardon and forgetfulness. They waved goodbye, then, and saw with surprise that the corpses were answering their salute, even though they were already very far away, unable to make out at that distance.

In the midst of them, alien to everything, João-Lázaro sat down on the grass and, stroking the sleeping girl's hair, wept incessantly and inconsolably, because he'd ceased believing in the possibility of restoring her to life. They called to him several times, first one by one, then in a chorus. But João-Lázaro wasn't listening, nor did he really see how the dead were spinning about the wreckage all around him. Later it was discovered later he'd stayed there for more than a day negotiating with God, proposing that he take the place of that girl in death.

God, however, always refused such proposals: He had never conceded humankind the privilege of knowing one's fate beforehand or the judgment or choice of the final gasp— the one that closes the door of time, turns the key, turns out the light, and orders man to conform to the arrival of his hour.

14

ON THE DAY OF HIS MOTHER'S DEATH JORGE-
MARIA DISCOVERED THAT HE LOVED HER TO THE
POINT OF SIN BECAUSE EVER SINCE THE DAY HE
SAW HER NAKED BEHIND HE'D STARTED MASTUR-
BATING. HE ALWAYS KEPT THE SECRET TO HIMSELF,
however. His brother José-Maria was showing all the signs of
puberty then, with the first growth of a beard sprouting and a
voice hardened with the announcement of the second stage of
childhood, and he would masturbate in bed before dozing off.
He would hear his breathing grow and thicken until it flew
off to the sound of the corn leaves in the mattress and his
fingers were so vigorous in their manipulation of his penis
that he was immediately taken with an intense urge to weep.
His brother's chest was also producing the sound of a bellows from the wind of that energy, and he opened his eyes
wide in the darkness, feeling invaded by all the terror of that
wakeful state.

One day, watching her pee in the pigsty, he admired the
superb whiteness of those squash-shaped buttocks cut by a
fissure and as fat as two cheeks covered with pubescent fuzz,
and a mysterious warmth immediately came over his body.
He crouched behind a woodpile and observed the extraordinary erection of his penis, the blue veins that crossed it and
the thread of gelatin moistening its opening. And then he imagined his mother embracing him: a broad smile crossed his

face, puffy with pleasure, and inspired the confidence in him that images of sin had kept dark in his soul until then. He pictured himself loving her with great fervor, sure that he could feel the heretical and incestuous warmth of that body and the hot passionate kisses coming from the other side of tenderness. There were wise words in her look, never spoken by any mother in the world, and he listened to them with his hands on the buttocks that swayed and twisted a little up on that body.

His mother was big, of an almost inconceivable whiteness. She trembled all over, like the nervous legs of centipedes as they feel out lit surfaces. She had, that woman did, a broad, soft belly and her voice was whitened by passion, a voice that loved him and therefore was saying, "My son, my son…" Then Jorge-Maria would offer himself the endless possession of that body, masturbating over her image several times a day. It was a volcanic love, oblique like the sea, in which he found shelter from the cold and fear of night. Mysterious waters circulated through the tangled network of his nerves until he would feel himself explode inside and spurt out a jet against the firewood. Witnessing that first ejaculation, Jorge-Maria, although overwhelmed with happiness, was frightened by the sperm. Hiding in the rushes he tried it another time, and another, until he was exhausted and his legs were shaking. At the end of the third attempt he was covered with sweat, his ears were ringing, and he began to vomit. When he realized he was crying, he said to himself, "Damned fool!" and then broke out laughing, laughing to the point of tears, laughing at himself and his vomiting and in that almost convulsive laughter he finally fell asleep, filled with happiness. From then on he began to follow her from a distance, waiting for her to go pee in the pigsty again. When he was finally able to observe her huge vagina from the front as it filled the whole space between her thighs pale as minerals, he murmured to himself:

"My mother is mine."

He put himself in her, from the outside in, and in that way he'd entered her purple hole, never to reappear in the world. He took the feeling of that possession of his mother so seriously and saw himself so involved in it that he went two nights without sleeping. He could no longer bear for his father to have recourse to that body, nor was he certainly going to allow her to give in to his nocturnal impulses. When, in addition, he heard her moan under her father's body, he would get all upset and awaken his brother. Then both of them, not moving the smallest part of their bodies on the mattress, would be witnesses to an almost violent encounter. The father was stabbing blindly down below at the hidden site of her dampness and murmuring in one continuous breath, "I love you, I love, I love you." Then he would breathe very deeply and fall on his side as if dead while she also fainted away beside him murmuring "Oh-oh-ohh…"—and then fall asleep from fatigue. Jorge-Maria grabbed José-Maria's hand with unusual strength and squeezed it. He was choked up with tears and they both felt betrayed by their mother. They were both certain that if they loved the maternal body in equal measure, an undefined hatred for their father was growing in them. Maybe they would never stop hating him.

Because of the theft of the land, by order of the king, and João-Maria's withdrawal to the barn where he vainly waited for death, Sara took charge of the house. She took the sons out of school, got them work with Leandro the farmer, and turned to supervising every step they took. She would wake them up before dawn so they could accompany the cattle herders to the Escampado or Outeiro-de-Cima pastures, and receive them at dusk to wash their feet and give them dinner. She never heard them protest against their life, but from the very first moment she was certain that those sons had forever lost their joy. No matter how many years they lived, that feeling would never return to their eyes because life, work, and their father's withdrawal had completely castrated the joy of their youth. They would get to be old men but they would never know what it was like to have had a different way of being alive in this world of darkness. When she would watch them fall asleep at the table, done in by fatigue and with no urge to eat, Sara felt her heart breaking. They were the poor, the ever so poor children of her unpardonable sin; the children of the sin of love with the man who'd gone to sleep in the manger and left in her a final weariness of living.

In spite of her mother's death, Jorge-Maria continued to love her with the same vigor. First he possessed her in the way he saw her in death: she was lying on her side with the serene look of someone sleeping and her thin nose, turned blue by death, had become more fleshy at the nostrils. As for her body, the same countless levers of that powerful machine for moving about and working were there but weren't vibrating. Then he watched her leave in a linen-lined box and waited for her to visit him. Because wasn't it true that she would come at the start of night to lie down beside him and remain looking at him while he slept and stroke his hair with the same trembling fingers as before?

Sometime back Jorge-Maria had acquired the custom of receiving the dead at nightfall. Grandfather João-David would fly, habitually, in his manner of a ghost, from the hedge of *pica-ratos* to the grillwork of the garden gate. Catching the wheeze of his asthma, Jorge-Maria would wait for a pair of strange feet, more imagined than flesh and bone, to emerge sometimes from the kitchen's tamped earthen floor and stop before him, right there on the first boards of the floor. Then he would turn toward the old man and gather that his body was levitating at the level of the walls' chestnut wainscoting. He was never sure that his mouth was moving, but his voice would move to tell him in a sibylline gasp about the suffering of his soul with no final rest. He wandered back and forth through the world in search of the peace of the dead, the blessed and lyrical peace of the dead, and Jorge-Maria could never be sure that any eyes existed in the stiff glass of the corpse's sockets. His grandfather's body was, as well, riddled with multiple craters. It looked like an almost shapeless piece of matter that was falling apart, but it had the dim glow of the cutting and terrible objects of night. As for his smell, it was that of death: a sulfurous breath that reminded him of the rotting dampness of the holes in the wall. Twice his grandfather had told him of his affliction: that someone must pay his debts and promises to Saint Cyprian the Just, father of all mercy. They consisted, those debts and promises, of going at midnight to Rozário's church, lighting two red candles as tall as a man beside the niches of Saint Cyprian the Just, and reciting, with eyes wet from many tears, the severe prayer of someone who forgives all the evil in the world and forever renounces his hatred of the living:

Oh, my beloved and fortunate Saint Cyprian:
talents and treasures I leave you here;
oh, my saint and my angel, I come to leave
my final pardon here;
oh, my book, my knowledge, of you done
and dedicated to you, I come to return;
oh, my most holy name, I leave my hate,
I leave my name, and may your glory
be forever praised. Oh, my holy
and good Saint Cyprian, shepherd of Mother Church,
let peace for the world and the dead come from you,
let your eternal peace come to me.
      Amen.

Jorge-Maria immediately calmed his grandfather: he would fulfill that function of allaying the tyrannical spirits persecuting him from the other side of death itself. He had become a perfect Christian, however, something he still wasn't so long as he hadn't received the sacrament of confirmation. Did his grandfather know what a bishop was? A bishop, my Grandfather, is a fat thing with spangles and rings and gold teeth in his smile; that thing glittered under canopies and blessed people's heads with the solemnity of a pope; do you know what a pope is, Grandfather? It's another thing like that, all in white, with a very thick neck and a skullcap; that thing, white as a dove, was guarded by some very pale cherubs armed with tridents traveling in chariots of fire from heaven; the chariots of fire were pulled by thoroughbred horses and the white thing said a lot of things, a lot things, and he blessed the world right and left with his rings from God; when the white thing orders the fat thing with spangles to come here to Achadinha from Angra to confirm all the children I'll be a perfect Christian and fulfill my grandfather's pledge: while I'm still at the age of venial sin. And the grandfather said:

"Keep on your toes, my grandson. The spirits are malignant and vengeful. And this fire that's burning in my rib cage might pass into your head one day. You'd never be a completely sane man again. Have you seen your mother?"

"Mama comes every day, after your time, Grandfather. Haven't you ever met her on the road, Grandfather?"

190

"No, my grandson. Your mother dwells in a different part of death, where I can't go until I'm rescued from this fire."

The glow in his craters suddenly grew dim, the levitation of his body finally gave way to the sound of asthma and the sulfurous smell became thick again. Finally a pair of fantastic feet bore him away and Jorge-Maria was left thinking about the way his body slipped along through closed and bolted doors, walls and everything, and he had to conclude that the dead had a really strange means of moving through objects.

He remained waiting for his mother. I open the windows. The people sail by out there in the small darkness of the day and I wait for my mother so I can fall asleep, thinking that the old shiny rats were only sniffing out their nighttime holes before slipping into the first crack. I remain waiting for my mother because her death is like the dampness of drains sucking up the water in gulps: the dampness makes everything in its passage grow, in places with mold, in all the openings in the walkway and the walls. It's that dampness that makes the brown rats, frightened by death, squeak noisily from drain to drain. They're searching for the crumbs of lost bread, they put them in their mouths and flee—and then perfect silence comes over the night and I myself am my mother in that dark fear of being her orphan, her angel, her bird, her castaway.

My mother had almost arrived when at the top of the Rua Direita a coffin appeared, bouncing along on somebody's back. By the prissy pace, multiplied into thousands of rigorously measured little steps, he concluded that it was Manuel Setenta—one more step and he'll collapse! The bells had been tolling all afternoon from one hour to the next and the sound was gangrenous, in which one could picture the whole cycle of keening and lit candles. Bodies would ripen in long waits of pain and insomnia, feeding on pennyroyal tea and chicken broth until the black hand of death was lowered over the nostrils of old people and asphyxiated them as something that belonged to it. Along the way there was the ritual visit to the dying. It all began with the visits of Cadete the healer, a fearsome man as awful as wild yams, in the opinion of Jorge-Maria, because he would say something like "the sea is white" and bellow into the clogged ears of the sick:

"Have you shat yet? What was your shit like? White? What about your spit, was there any blood?"

Normally the sick people would limit themselves to nodding and holding down their gasps a little. They had fearful watery eyes, however, where delirium was burying absent visions. After the consultation the healer would search in his pockets for a notebook and, whistling under his breath, note down the names of syrups and unguents. He rarely came a second time because the next visit was that of the old priest. Crippled, paler than his sacristy, he dragged himself up the street and blessed death in the ferocious language of the Latin poets. Then someone would remember Manuel Setenta: a man with the reputation of a vagabond, quite averse to work. With time he had even turned into a vegetable being, his skin broken into small veins and tiny capillaries. His thatch house was located next to the Fonte do Boqueirão: nothing but a square hut with two large beds and a mat. When the weather or the moonlight wasn't cooperative for his nocturnal raids on the granaries and corncribs, he would offer his services for funereal tasks like that of going to Fenais da Ajuda to order coffins and carry them to Rozário on his back. That was where the best funeral carpentry on the Island was located, they said, because they worked with good woods like cryptomeria, acacia, incense wood, and mahogany, and for thirty patacas and a half day's work a casket good for the earth could be had. Such a low price, along with the skill of master carpenters, gave death a kind of last comfort, and, often, it was matter of thriftiness. Grandfather João-David had put aside a small veneer coffer where he kept all his cruzados, the guarantee of that comfort beyond the grave. He'd done it with such enthusiasm that Jorge-Maria, in spite of still being a very young child, thought that people decided to die at the most appropriate moment. He wasn't surprised, therefore, when his grandfather told him one day:

"It's sad to die in the third week of January, my grandson, because of the rain and the storms. I'd much rather wait until the coming month of May."

They carried him to his grave in an acacia coffin, and Jorge-Maria only remembered that the wood creaked from his grandfather's weight. It had been necessary to reinforce the planks with three cured beams; they said his grandfather "weighed more than a creature from the sea."

Passing before him, Manuel Setenta mentioned something about settling that gloomy load better on his shoulders. Standing, he gave a little leap. He adjusted the cushion made of dried grasses pillowed in a canvas bag that hung down like a hood from his neck to the bottom of his back. His thickset body under the casket was being consumed by a sweat that would have put the most docile of natures into a frenzy. When he tried to adjust his load better with another jump, he groaned, and Jorge-Maria saw the coffin slide off in front of him like a sinking ship and thump like a bass drum as it hit the ground.

He was waiting for his mother, then, when Manuel Setenta, with another step and an explosion, broke out into harsh curses, May lightning strike that devilish old woman again, that vinegary whore of an old woman who got it into her head to die on that bitching day, by the soul of my mother and that old whore's too, never again will I get involved in a trip like this with the devil on my back—and Jorge-Maria turned his face away from sin and smothered a laugh—because that leprous old woman, Setenta was saying, can go straight to Hell, a little more of this, a little more of that, as he consigned that soul to God and the Devil, and Jorge-Maria was there waiting for his mother so he could go to sleep when the man stopped mouthing all his curses and roared at him, only at him:

"Hey! Hey, soul of the Christ-Child, lend a hand here for the repose of your mother and help me get this load on my back!"

The small body of the Christ-Child put his belly onto the window sill and slid down to the ground with his knees against the wall. When he got quite close to Setenta he thought, "He's neither an animal nor person," and he felt the breath of his cough and the smell of rusty saltpeter coming from the mouth on his face; something, some sense of salt came from the stubby body of that animal-man whose face, cut with a knife, emerged from the fatal filth of his skin and sweat, very much in need, no doubt about it, of a bath in a tub or a basin. On the man's upper part was a head of grease-colored hair that grew wildly about the nape of his neck. When they looked each other in the eyes, Jorge-Maria saw fear and thought, "He's surely going to kill me," and his insides trembled, what are the insides of a person full of fear like? Maybe like mushrooms, because death was like that, too, intimate, timid, like a mushroom in the middle of the guts. With the dead, yes, he was able to chat, because he was in the habit of receiving them at dusk. But at the feet of that animal-man his guts felt as if they'd been stabbed, since his eyes were large and glowed in the night like two coals being blown on. There were old accounts to be settled between Papa and Manuel Setenta. One day Papa had caught him stealing firewood in the Chão da Cancela and there was a row: You devil out of Hell's fire, I'll take this ax and cut off your head like a turkey's, Papa had said, but he only had him jailed in Nordeste, the police and the judge got involved, and Manuel Setenta locked up his hate inside himself, all his hate for all people, and was still waiting for the moment when he could take revenge on the parish. Like a knife-edge in the dark, his wolf's gaze showed his desperate body: blows with rods, curses, the bites of guard dogs, he'd gone through everything. So as Jorge-Maria was pondering all that, he saw Setenta lean his back forward and turn it before the flat part of his load as the lid of the coffin got loose from its catches and the whole thing hit the ground again with a loud noise, and the hollow sound went boom! boom! like a bomb. The nocturnal drum obliged the man to clutch the casket impatiently, lift it up to his shoulder with his hands, what a shitty life I lead, he said, and he started up with his little leaps again, that bouncing little walk with the tiny steps of a thief in the night. Jorge-Maria was going to slip away from there, full of fear, when he heard behind him again the invisible voice of the rats of the earth:

"I'm never going to get a coffin for your father, he can go to his grave wrapped up in the beating he gave me once. But you're an innocent. I've got children your size. If I wanted to get vengeance I'd put my hands around your throat and the Devil take me if my age-old account with your father wouldn't be settled. It might happen someday, my little one, I know all kinds of poisons…"

194

Then Jorge-Maria took off from there at a fast run, feeling the eyes of the animal-man climbing up his rear end and his words sounding the prophecy of a coming martyrdom. He was going to leap through the window when he saw a great bird take off through it in flight and land on its feet in the middle of the street. That bird in all aspects looked like a young boy grown into a fury, a boy hidden in the night in the place where Mama would appear to watch over the sleep of a boy brooding over the dead. It was his brother José-Maria who must have been waiting for her arrival and in the silence heard Setenta's threats. The brother flew through the dark and laid his terrible hands on the back of the animal-man. His hands dragged the coffin free and flung it to the ground, and the great black box again gave off the sound of a drum, and his brother flew over it again and grabbed the animal-man by the shoulders and, still flying, gave him a butt with his head on the mouth followed by two punches, and Manuel Setenta shouted, "Help, I'm dying," but José-Maria fetched him a low thrust with his knee, right in the center of his stomach, and all that could be heard was a groan that lasted until he fainted. Jorge-Maria thought he was going to kill him and shouted for his mother to come quickly and calm his brother's hate.

What happened after that? Nothing happened. José-Maria put his arm around his shoulders and was talking to him in the secure and ample calm with which one protects a child from the imagined things of night. For wasn't it true that Manuel Setenta, the mayor Guilherme José, Agostinho, and Father Governo would one day pay for the evil they'd done Papa? The years and Mama's death had turned Papa into something soft before his enemies, with no bones or nerves. He was slowly growing old, that was certain, and his old age had been transformed into time without hope, believing that justice and punishment could only be the work of a new generation.

"We've got to grow up fast," José-Maria said as he laid him down, adjusting the bedclothes over the small body. "Papa's only waiting for us to grow up so he can die. He'll die on the day he looks us up and down and says, 'My sons are two men now; I can take leave of the world at last.'"

Jorge-Maria silently received his brother's revelations, but he was still so confused in his head that a glass fever, not the hot fever of sick people in winter, but the colorless cold of the night when he waited for Mama and she didn't come, made him wrap himself up in the bedclothes for he was beginning to shake with cold.

"If I wanted to I could cry now," he said, "but I'll go on waiting for Mama until sleep takes me in."

José-Maria went over to lie down beside him and waited for a long time until he fell asleep. When only the sounds of night remained swaying between them, they heard the rats walking inside the roof tiles and the lathing. They were running through the house in small bands and in every direction, the rats, always the rats, and they seemed to be arguing noisily among themselves over the very air they were breathing among the rotting laths. The voice of the rats would always be the most terrible thing to hear in the midst of all the present and absents sounds of the night.

"I'm going to cry," Jorge-Maria thought, still shivering from the cold and moving a little closer to his brother's warmth. But before beginning to weep he still had to tell him, "I want Mama to come back to me." And José-Maria would inevitably answer, half-asleep already, defeated by the fatigue of the mountains and the work there:

"The dead don't exist, little brother. Mama is never coming back to our house."

15

IN SPITE OF DEATH,
JORGE-MARIA CONTINUED LOVING HIS MOTHER
FOR A LONG TIME AND FAR FROM THE WORLD,
WHICH IN PEOPLE'S OPINION, WAS IMPAIRING HIS
GROWTH. AS A MATTER OF FACT MUCH TIME HAD
passed. People were growing old and the exceptional transformation of things went along without the slightest surprise—
but only Jorge-Maria showed no sign of development, either
in body or in spirit. Cadete the healer had been called to observe such a strange phenomenon because it wasn't natural
for ordinary people of this world to reject life's transforma-
tions. The order of things had only one kind of balance: the
Sun. The Sun dwelt inside trees, in the circular and eternal
soul of their fruit, and it would combine with the earth to
raise creatures a little bit above the ground. What was going
on with that child, then?

His childhood companions began to leave the parish and
go off in search of work and wives; new generations were
already arguing among themselves over the space in their
world, while others kept on taking leave of it forever. Only
Jorge-Maria remained indifferent to all and everything.

The healer asked to examine him in his consultation room
on the Caminho Novo and João-Maria quickly agreed. Until
the death of his wife, his son had always shown a peaceful
manner, intelligence, and the will of any smart child, with no

mysteries: at school he'd learned writing, arithmetic, the basic geography of the World from Professor Calafate, and had even developed a fascination for the secrets of animal life. Besides that he'd always distinguished between love and hate, had made his father's friends and enemies his own, and nothing and no one seemed to disturb the natural course of his growth at that time. He'd shown himself to be, also, a careful guardian of cows in the service of Leandro the farmer. He'd taught a dog of some brownish breed how to bite without breaking the skin, how to round up herds and lead them to watering places along stream banks; he'd matched strength with the boys his age and beaten them all. Besides that, he'd thrown bullocks and rams wild with rut, and, to all appearances, there was nothing about Jorge-Maria that could offend the traditions, customs, and teachings of the oldest people. So on that day João-Maria was filled with worry and began to scratch his mop of hair, not knowing what to do with his life, when Cadete, lighting up his pipe, cast his eyes on the little one and immediately suspended the operation, alarmed at what he saw:

"Say, doesn't that boy grow? He's always the same size! What kind of a pitiful man is he going to make?"

João-Maria looked at him with the same surprise. He'd never noticed. It was obvious, however, that his son had become stuck in childhood forever. His little body had become solid, his look had the firmness and penetration of intelligent boys, everything about his manner of being was quite natural, with the exception of one essential thing: the wise joy of children was missing in those eyes, the carnal joy of a person living out the pleasures and fascinations of this world. João-Maria didn't know how to explain to Cadete the reasons for the apparent darkness that had cloaked his son's spirit. He could, however, guarantee that Jorge-Maria had never shown any signs of reacting against the drives of nature.

"He doesn't even dislike anything, that boy of mine," he said.

Cadete, perhaps not quite convinced by that story, rather seriouslyconcentrated on the matter. His face filled with shadow and even became pale with worry:

"Are you in the habit of giving him eggs, milk, cracklings and beans?"

"I give him all that and he eats it," João-Maria guaranteed again.

And he would hug him every day, and sometimes they would weep in a group during the sad and lonely hours of a house without a woman, and he would divide the bread into three equal parts among his two sons and himself; they had all the harmony possible in a family without that sun, white in its brightness, that came, as is well known, from inside women and only from them, the unique and white sun that only a woman can give to life in a family house, and, just imagine, Mr. Cadete, Sara died so many years ago and nothing new has since happened in that house: the same objects in the same usual places, the eternal sound of her footsteps, her voice, her way of looking and laughing, the bony energy of a woman who's dead but hasn't died, understand? It's all inside there, intact, like her memory, the care with which she'd wash the boy's feet at the end of another day of working for Leandro the farmer—the poor boys with the love and sin of them both. A man, Mr. Cadete, closes up those notions inside without her presence as a woman, thinking someone is still putting their hands on their shoulders, and if they cry with longing it makes it all the more certain. When, all of a sudden, an outsider like you points his finger at the boy and asks if he doesn't grow, I feel that I've been wrong about everything in life, because I wanted to die once and I left off because of them. I was never able to straighten up in life ever again. I'm still alive, that's for sure, but crouching, crouching down before the world and if I stand up straight my eyes can no longer see into the distance, not even across the street. Something like that may have happened to the boy, because boys like him grow and stand on their own two feet in life, while he's got sadness clinging to his flesh, and sadness already in his bones. Can it be because it mines people inside like that, sucking at them until it eats up the marrow of their bones and nerves? Can it be because sadness ages a body even before it grows up and becomes a youth so it can reproduce itself?

"It's quite possible there's a little of all that," Cadete said without much conviction as he went back to lighting his pipe. "It could be that the same thing happened to the little one as happened to you when you decided to die. But there must be a scientific explanation, maybe. Bring him to me this afternoon, at the end of the day."

He recommended that he keep well in mind his need to know everything about the boy, the date of his birth and the exact time of his coming into the world, the way and the time in which Sara was carrying him in her womb. It would have to be the both of them, he said, interpreting the phenomenon in its deepest origins if they wanted to eradicate the causes and the gloomy tendencies of that inhibition of growth.

"But how?" João-Maria asked, perplexed.

"We'll see," the other replied. "I'll consult the stars and the elements of my perpetual ball. I'll take him into my dark chamber where I'm accustomed to find the inspiration of the peaceful spirits—but it's absolutely necessary for you to supply me with every detail relating to the boy's life."

Cadete gave some examples: sometimes, in cases complex in appearance, there are solutions as simple as those of a riddle. Did he remember Mandonça do Burguete's son? The boy had grown like a weed, too big for his age, but his right hand was withered like a wolf's paw. After making a few investigations without giving up, putting aside all hypotheses of a scientific nature, he'd decided that the atrophy could only be due to one fact: at the age of seven the boy had slapped his mother, a poor woman, nameless and homeless, which had been interpreted as blasphemy or an unnatural act. The obvious solution: Cadete prescribed for the boy the obligation of going out into the world in search of his mother, of embracing her, bringing her back home, and gaining her forgiveness. Once that was done, the hand immediately recovered the previous energy of growth that had been punished. He was going about in this endless world again, serving the king in the trenches of Africa, and what a handsome and perfect young lad he was! On another occasion he'd received a girl from Algarvia who had all the signs of lacking sanity, because she was going on twelve and she drooled, wore diapers because she wet herself, and could only indicate things with monosyllables. When he focused light on the iris that was halted between her eyelashes he discovered that her brain was blocked and empty, as if two invisible panels were pressing down on the mass of intelligence. A solution for that was both simple and obvious, friend João-Maria: the girl was still carrying her umbilical cord. No one had ever remembered to remove it and her spirit continued to be fed through the fetal channel. She was still breathing the blood and energy of pure animal substance through her mother's body.

"The opposite of the illness of cerebral gigantism may have happened to your boy, understand? Bring him to me this afternoon, after sunset but before it gets dark. Right when the sun goes down, so the solar influence over him will be completely neutralized."

João-Maria led the boy in by the hand and felt him trembling with panic as he faced the disorder, the darkness, and the mysterious instruments of that consulting room. There were different inscriptions on the walls along with cobwebs and damp stains that looked like navigational maps and sea routes. The soft, sweetish smell of smoking herbs and essences, the warm acid of substances in a state of fusion, all intoxicated him a little. He made a last appeal to his former courage and led his son into the presence of the healer. Surrounded by all those symbols, amidst stacks of books, twisted retorts, and unknown apparatuses, Cadete was transformed into a strangely luminous insect and inspired spiritual notions. His green forehead, burrowing under his mat of hair, reflected a bright gleam of silk and taffeta, and his body passed slowly among the shapes in the dark or the beams of light coming through cracks in the wall and the window. He passed by, dense and slow, like his look, and his breathing could be heard above all the tiny sounds that came from outside, from the bosom of the dampness and the axis of the stones. There was the drift of sand among the roots of grasses and solitary plants in that breathing. João-Maria studied the heaviness of his wolf eyes for a moment—could they be moist with tender feeling?—and he waited endlessly for the moment when they, the eyes, would assume all their mystery. Cadete was taking his time, however, admiring the order of his objects and the way in which he himself worked in their midst. He was deciphering data and writing things down in those clumsy grease-stained notebooks like some popular scientist eagerly awaiting the impossible hour of his glory in this world; he was softly whistling through the same gap in his teeth where his breathing also passed, and his frog fingers were making almost distracted little taps on the surface of the table as he concentrated. João-Maria thought he'd been forever forgotten, because all the gods in this world fed on the same vices: their glory began in the hopes and patience of men and ended with their disappointment. And he was still imagining himself forgotten forever when the healer sighed deeply and the cobwebs in front of him quivered to the breath of wisdom, and he thought:

"My time has come."

And, looking at his son, he felt a distant thud and had an urge to grab him, pick him up, and kiss him the way a person devours a piece of fruit so as not to die of thirst. Jorge-Maria had sat down in a corner and was playing in astonishment with a skull from Cadete's mortuary collection, fascinated, no doubt, by the fact that his fingers could go in and out of the eye sockets and fly about like butterflies inside that cathedral with walls as harsh as sandpaper.

"Bring me the small one, then," Cadete ordered, tamping the bowl of his pipe with his fingernail.

First he rolled the perpetual ball once, twice, in front of the boy—and he saw right away that he wasn't suffering from any physical illness. Of course that revelation didn't surprise him because he'd already suspected something much more hidden there, in the realm of the mind and not the body. Then he felt the top of his head and saw that the knitting of the fontanel was as solid as that of an adult. He immediately experimented by pointing the focus of light in his eyes and when all of Jorge-Maria's face was lit up by it, his look filled with panic and the little one began to cry out.

Cadete asked João-Maria to have him blow his nose, because he had to investigate all the openings of his body. After examining his ears, his nasal passages, his mouth, his anus, and his eyeballs, he was filled with a sudden impatience and began to mutter foolish little things. An obscure force coming from the boy's soul was resisting the magical impulses of his hands and his eyes, and something inexplicably strong floated on the surface of that absent gaze, full of worms and tiny ophidians.

"The symbol of the serpent," the healer thought, "is related to the Devil. Can this boy be possessed by some evil angel? Is that why he doesn't grow?" And turning to João-Maria, he shook his head without saying anything, but already concerned by the imminence of a foreseeable defeat.

He made two attempts to put the boy under hypnosis, but that look full of worms and serpents kept resisting concentration and the healer began to sense defeat, translated into affliction now, dampening his fingers and throat. João-Maria was puzzled by the beads of sweat running down the age-old wrinkles on his face. A lively impatience filled his fingers, which stopped being gentle like the movements of an octopus and were now moving about restlessly.

"Like flies," João-Maria thought. "Like flies caught in a spider web, caught on the sticky surface of that spit glue—treacherous, hopeless."

Why was that boy's innocence resisting him so much? He got up and took him by the hand, leading him into the small room for spiritual cures. This is where he lives at night, Jorge-Maria thought; a tiny little chunk of night among dark hangings, cosmic symbols, and maritime deserts, and death had been shut up in bowls of mercury, in tubs full of stagnant water with white stones at the bottom. In one of them there was a sample of the sea, really white, he thought, and a small clay-colored octopus had all its cups up against the glass and was lying there asleep, for many years, perhaps. Cadete sat the boy down in the dark and consulted the perpetual ball again. He rolled it between his fingers in front of the oil lamp, lit up its transparency, and opened his mouth a little with surprise when he saw the four elements of nature remain motionless in their places. Fire had gone out, water had acquired the thickness of ink, a patina of grease like the white of a turkey egg, while earth showed a reef-like surface and an uncharacteristic metallic color. Only air, perhaps, was maintaining its spiritual existence. Well then, from those frightening signs only one conclusion could be drawn: death. Cadete grew even more confused in his affliction in face of such evidence. He thought:

"How could the boy have died? Because he breathes walks, talks, and has all his senses intact."

He couldn't recall any devilish thing like that no matter how much experience he'd had struggling with all sorts of inexplicable enigmas. It was, furthermore, obvious that Cadete wasn't going to say to João-Maria: "I can only conclude that your son is dead. He lives, breathes, sees, observes, and reasons, but his spirit, that's what, has died." "But how could he have died?" João-Maria would retort. "Are you making fun of my troubles?" "He's died for the world spiritually, maybe. How and when I don't know. What his death is feeding on I don't know either. But just that he died, only that he died." And João-Maria would say: "I'm going out of my head with this. Do you mean to tell me that my son is only inventing or faking that he's alive among us?" He made an effort to concentrate and then he felt all the pores of his body open up with affliction. Mushrooms of sweat burst out in the root of his leathery head and were running down in back toward his neck along the furrows of his mortal parchment. He needed to go and breathe the night air, convince himself that some living thing was still inside him and keeping watch, keeping watch, keeping watch.

He took the boy by the hand again and brought him over to his father. It was true that he, Cadete, was experiencing a crisis in concentration. His spirit was galloping along to meet old age and he'd already lost a good part of his original reflexes. Maybe he'd lost his genius. But how could he not guarantee, even if it sounded absurd, that the boy was lying in a state of death without having died?

"So far," he said, going over to sit down by his work table again, "nothing abnormal to my observation, friend João-Maria."

Nevertheless, he'd begun to twiddle his thumbs like someone rolling up a thread of nervousness, as when João-Maria went before Guilherme José with the deeds to his land, and he felt pale, hollow, without the courage to look at the man who remained motionless before him and in whose look a perplexed caged bird was roosting:

"Well, if my friend Cadete says so, why should I think otherwise? This son of mine and I are in your hands."

They were in the midst of that discussion when they heard a voice coming out of the darkness that said:

"Can't you mend your ways, Cadete? Are you still going to keep on hoodwinking half the world?"

They looked up to see João-Lázaro. The healers hands immediately curled. They even grew icy. Then his voice and his blood turned to ice. How had João-Lázaro got in there, because the door had been bolted on the inside and the latch was still in the same position? He must have come through the wood, because he worked wood down to its soul as no one else had ever done in those parts. Their gazes touched for just an instant, because out of João-Lázaro's poured a feeling of fury ready to suffocate the world. They were two snakes, the abundant and thin saliva of snakes without a nest as they prepared to strike. Cadete turned his tearful eyes away. He'd been caught *in flagrante delicto.*

"Now I really can die," he thought.

"You, Cadete, are a common intriguer with no scruples, we already know that," João-Lázaro added without giving him time to reply. He began walking back and forth the whole length of the consulting room with his hands behind his back and went on: "The only tragedy in these parts is their three fatal diseases: the priest, the mayor, and you. But while the other two have already got the people against them and don't need to be denounced, you, Cadete, being an ordinary case of hocus-pocus, sing to them like a siren on the surface of the water. It's a simple case for the police, when we get a proper version of them in this world."

The enormous body, almost crushed down, swayed in the large backless chair: nothing but a mass reacting with small nervous convulsions as when air bubbles burst on the surface of a vat. In a quick glance, his eyes moved around toward the perpetual ball, the twin mirrors, concave and convex, the pouches and the books that contained the hope of all the villages on the Island, and they'd been feeding on the same depression ever since João-Lázaro had come there and proclaimed the art of curing the ill with medicine. From that day on, Cadete felt all the signs of the condemned of the Earth weighing on his shoulders and decided to end his life. He wouldn't do it in some peaceful way, however: in any case, he had a cat's nine lives and would make use of them all.

"A case for the police, you say? Then just try denouncing me to the people so they can put me in jail. Then we'll see whose side the people are on."

João-Lázaro nodded his head like someone accepting a challenge without any hesitation. He stopped pacing a little and went on:

"I'll hand down the jail sentence myself someday when I put myself at the head of the diggers. Do you know who the diggers are? They're the people who think right and work on the right side. They themselves will ask me to proclaim a revolution against that priest, against the mayor, the president of the Council, and the thieves from the airplane crash. It will be a revolution of the poor against you and all the others."

"Fine," Cadete said calmly. "Your revolution can start right now if you want. Explain it to the people and ask them to be the ones who decide my fate."

"I'll do that, you can count on it. It will be easy to make them see that you've been tricking them all these years with home remedies made out of horse manure."

"It won't be all that easy, João-Lázaro. You said you came back to life, isn't that so? You said publicly that you came back to the world to explain your experience to the people. But so far you haven't done it and nobody's going to believe anything except that you're crazy. Will you be able to explain, for example, what mysterious thing is going on with this child, João-Maria's son?"

"Nothing mysterious beyond his sick imagination, Mr. Healer."

Saying that, João-Lázaro picked up the child as he'd seen the Messiah of Galilee do in days gone by and spoke as He

206

had spoken, suffering the little children to come unto Him. Handing him to his father, he declared:

"This little fellow's illness is not and never has been in him; it's in the world he was given to live in. He refuses to grow in a world like this without the presence of the mother he keeps demanding. And that's how he'll go on, João-Maria, until the day you bring about either Sara's return or, at least, the substitution of the mother he lost."

João-Maria couldn't believe what he was hearing, but he seemed horrified at the absurdity of those theories. His voice and his movements began to tremble as if he were not talking to a furniture-maker but to a soul wandering in a world of shadows:

"But what can I do about the substitution since I gave up everything when Sara left us? You, João-Lázaro, must know that I'm dead, too, and I can't wait for your revolutions. I'm here in the world like all the others, alongside my sons, just waiting for them to grow up and choose what they want to be in life."

"Precisely for those reasons this child isn't obliged by any commitment that he myself won't take on. You've transferred your hurry to die to your sons and that doesn't help their relationship to growth. Die if you want, but let them make their own decisions. Let them leave and fly away."

After that João-Lázaro kept on trying to explain to João-Maria all the mechanism of the process blocking Jorge-Maria's mind in an emotionless state. But nothing came of it because he'd stopped listening to him. The son was going back to being the old-man child of his unforgivable sin. The father, sinking once more into the wretchedness of that ever opaque gaze, ceased believing in the simple hypothesis of any redemption. When he departed from the consulting room and left the others still arguing about revolutions, he was crouching down facing the world again, and his look no longer reached the other side of the street, it had become so dim so suddenly. It wasn't only the darkness of the night out there, or only the dogs barking or only the silence that flew over the Island night and put to sleep in itself the bodies and the consciences of all the enemies of a man like him; it was his very soul that was growing dim in its vision of things, with no light. He felt himself staggering a little then because he'd become filled with old age and had lost all notion of the space around him. Watching him feeling his way across the small paving stones of the street with his feet and fearing the shadows, the boy took his hand and began to guide him along the way, saying:

"Papa, I'm not afraid of the dark. I'm big now, Papa!"

João-Maria said yes, his dear son was obviously a man, all the people in the parish said so. And he thought, "Like a little dog," starting to sob inconsolably, without the boy hearing him. "Like a little dog leading his blind friend, so mild and humble that he no longer knows how to bark or claim his place as a dog, as the son of all the other dogs."

16

…IN THE MEANTIME
JOSÉ-MARIA, THE OLDER SON,
HAVING DECIDED TO LEAVE ROZÁRIO FOREVER,
WASN'T LONG IN DISCOVERING THE GROWING
DRIVES OF HIS BODY. AS WELL, HE DISCOVERED IN
MARIA ÁGUA'S TENDERNESS ALL THE GOOD
THINGS A WOMAN CAN OFFER A MAN.

An unfortunate girl from outside the parish, very much liked by its people, however, who in their homes offered her a nest, bread and blood sausage, and in addition kindness and a pale charitable smile, one day she faced up to João-Maria's drive and ended up his wife. Many years earlier, when she'd arrived there with her hair drenched from the downpour and thick crusts of mud clinging to her cheekbones, she was still a child all yellowed from abandonment; but the people were immediately filled with pity for that small solitary being, thinking they could already see pulmonary fever turning her eyelids purple from a lack of sleep out in the great world. It was said in those days that not even the eyes of a baby calf could be more docile than those thin eyes sunken in shadow, nor could the cold of winter be more naked than the mute aspect of her disillusionment. An indifferent, sleepy creature, but with the great smell of a sick mother who had suckled her until her breast gave blood, and the only memory she had told her that it must have been a woman with breast tumors, always bathed in tears and consumed by weeping. As for her papa, he would hide in every corner of the house, coughing in the dark and vomiting everything he'd swallowed, and his urine was so blocked that he swelled and swelled until his bladder burst with the sound of a balloon. They were found in a state of putrefaction a long time after they'd died for lack of help and all of Salga smelled of dead dogs in the road and people guessed that the air was full of some kind of animal plague mingled with a smell of public toilets: anyone who went there to urinate or crap came away with a fetid smell that stayed with him everywhere he went and for the rest of his days and he would immediately be marked as an inhabitant of those parts, even before he said where he was going or where he was coming from.

Maria Água was just a little girl, full of freckles and with yellow pus running down her badly infected nose when from the yard she witnessed the removal of the half-rotted bodies infested with flies and the burning of the straw mattresses, furniture and clothes. Watching the fire devour as well her beloved rag dolls stuffed with grasses and awns, an intense delirium whirled in her fever and burned out for good all signs of her joy in life. And having finally reached the conclusion those people were abandoning her or weren't even aware of her existence, she decided to follow the procedure for going mad, but never succeeded. She'd begun, in fact, by undressing at the church door with the only result that the priest ordered them to stone her and drive her out of Salga, alleging that Maria Água was not only a bearer of all contagious diseases, but that she was especially possessed for the perdition of men. The following day she was sought out by two boys whose hands sweated as they gripped her body, then by a married man, after that by another man, also married, and at the end of nine weeks she'd been had by half the male population. Judging then that it was impossible to go crazy that way, she became filled with hate and attacked the last man with her fingernails until she felt avenged for her parents and her dolls.

Her trip to Rozário in search of sustenance began at that time. As her fame as a woman of immeasurable love

210

had traveled rather quickly, from the beginning there were men with excited eyes and boys consumed with passion waiting who gave her money and food in exchange for her warmth.

On one of those trips José-Maria went to wait for her in Pasos de Ribeiras, way ahead of all the others, certain that she would pass that way and not refuse him a little tenderness—and that's what happened. When she set eyes on him, Maria Água was afraid of being murdered and tried to run away, but she stopped when she finally saw the boy's eyes were as beseeching in their amorous intent as hers: the brightness and transparency of the angels of birth were in them and they were illuminated by the lonely determination of motherless orphans and wifeless mourners—and she received him right there in the middle of the woods, lying on her back in a clump of ferns.

José-Maria was dazzled by the beauty of that body where no mark of sin or the violence of men and no other smell and no other memory of anyone existed or had come before everything she herself had brought to give him. It smelled, that body, of an earthy substance with the sap of a growing tree, and its color was certainly as acrylic as it was diaphanous and lukewarm like glass transmuted into crystal by the hands of master potters, or even like the mirrors in the water of her name.

He loved her first from the front and then from behind and from the front again, and on the last try he caught the formidable reply of her body. Her nails dug desperately into the ground and her stomach twisted around an impossible axis as he pierced her until touching her intestines. After that Maria Água began to smile and José-Maria forever carried in his memory that smile of a woman who'd been loved to a point of pleasure, destroyed and renewed like a cell. She was still lying on her back when he saw her eyes open with amazement and remain motionless, like the sky that shared their color, perhaps unable to believe in the discovery of such happiness.

"I've never received that pleasure from a man," she said bashfully, almost sobbing with embarrassment. "Never, never, never."

Hearing her talk like that, José-Maria began to weep with emotion and decided right there to take her as a lover. She would be his and his alone and would finally replace the maternal image of his nightly orgasms. So much so that he started to wait for her every Sunday at that shortcut, always ahead of the others who also came to wait for her in vain and then he forbade her to come to Rozário. He was always possessed by a corporal fever and only the peace, pleasure and smile of that woman could sate him. He even conceived a plan to take her over completely and for that reason began to bring her wheat bread and honey, honey with crackers, mulberry jam, fried bacon, and now and then milk, carob beans and almonds. Giving her all those things to eat, he would wonder silently at her almost unconscious hunger and thought that a woman like that held the secret of the night beyond night, held all the burning signs of the Sun in her look and even had the eyes of God alighting on her. Love had entered his body like a violent fever on a rainy day and a new excitement arose in his groin, putting his stomach muscles into an uproar and entering his head with the thrust of a stab, spreading out in a gush right to the marrow of his bones. Then he got the energetic itch of growth.

Seeing such strange things being produced in him, Maria Água opened her mouth wide, wanting to cry out, but finally controlled her fright. She'd dreamed many times about a similar operation that transformed the world around her. In those dreams there had always been something that communicated with her blood. Once a horse had stopped before her and spoken to her with the voice of her dead father; another time a dog frothing with rabies gave her news of her mother, she hadn't died, no, her mama was only sleeping in the peace of the Occult one; and still another time a huge maritime creature with blue scales rose to the surface of the water and told her:

"I am God and your life is about to undergo a great change, Maria. Pay attention to the breath of the stars and the rain of the moonlight, because your life is going to change."

But they were dreams, only dreams, she thought, while her astonished eyes couldn't believe the radical change in José-

Maria's body. First his wrists and muscles grew thicker, then a beard the color of moss on rocks sprouted out from all the pores of his face, and finally the bulge of his Adam's apple, the apple of Eve and the serpent-woman, stuck in his throat. Hair was also growing on his chest, arms and pubis, and his spermatic animal shook with a seismic convulsion, becoming immediately thick and erect like a pole. Crowning that growth process, José-Maria's body underwent a final muscular stretching, making his clothes burst and tear apart at the seams—and she had before her now a man as solid as concrete, in whose eyes a great will to dominate the world was already sailing about. When in addition he asked her to get undressed to make love, she noticed his voice had hardened, too, full of the brutal sounds of the sea when it smashes against crags in midwinter, and she was loved with a perfection never before experienced in her relations with other men. In his breath there was a heat like potholes of volcanic mud and that heat manifested itself in an absolute form in the possession of that woman, moist as when the first animal on Earth discovered a female and invented love with her.

On that dim Sunday afternoon, possessed five times, Maria Água thought like this her happiness: a force that carefully squeezed her womb at the moment of penetration and afterwards a thorough dampness of heat, sweat, and the infinite pleasure of flying within oblivion. Even without saying so, they'd already thought about joining their lives together forever and living in common.

"Now," he said in a voice muffled by emotion, "there can be a place for us in Rozário. We're husband and wife and we're going to take a trip around the world."

All they needed was for someone to bless their union, as was traditional. There was only one person in the world capable of carrying that out quickly and without scandal: José-Maria's father. Ever since the death of Sara the saint, all religious rites had been abolished in the family. Papa had not only fallen out with the authorities of the kingdom and with the mayor because of the theft of his land and Goraz's outrages, but also with Father Governo and the Church because, in his opinion, they'd transformed the elementary principles of religion into corruption. João-Lázaro had been the first person to give substance to the idea of the non-existence of God, but he must have been referring only to the God of the poor and not the one of the powerful people in this world. That God existed in themselves, in the very person of rich people: in the gold-toothed smile and in the bounty of the things that teeth like that sometimes ruined even without chewing. Nevertheless, neither João-Lázaro nor the others had yet challenged the power of the priests. But his father had, he thought, first at the time of the death of Sara the saint, when he went to fetch the priest at his house under the threat of a brush scythe, after which he always refused him entry into his house on visits to those disconsolate because of death and illness. Papa made no distinction between his hatred for the mayor and the abominable decrees he invented and the ecclesiastic inspiration of those laws. He was a whole man in his dignity and revolt and he couldn't help but approve the union of his son with a woman like Maria Água, even if that was an affront to the order and morality laid out until then for the people of Rozário.

If that was what he thought, José-Maria acted even more quickly. Taking the hand of his young wife, he went down to Achadinha and immediately noticed that many things had changed in the parish. How many years had passed? He would never be able to tell because he'd traveled around infinity and had lost all notion of time. He even thought it natural that people and things had accompanied the transformation of his spirit and his body during the time he was absent. The same heavy women sweeping the street now showed the graying hairs of age. In their pale and quite wrinkled faces they had mouths softened by a twilight of affliction and duress. Some of them had even lost all their teeth, while others smiled at him through the great caverns of their gums or with a single rotting tooth swaying in front of their tongue. The rest were so sucked dry down to their bones that either their stomachs didn't even exist or had become lost amidst their guts or had become dried-up and sterile from old age. As for the men, with the exception of João-Lázaro, who, they said, was as eternal as a rock that couldn't be moved, they'd become covered with wrinkles and walked all bent over with their hands on their kidneys or leaning on a stick. Their hair had the look of dirty wool, dead and dull, but they were, now and forever, the good, cautious, wise men of hopeless suffering whose voices showed the way in the dark and who carried the night in their breathing. They smiled at him and waved in a friendly way as they watched him pass, while the lads of José-Maria's age, after doing the same, stood admiring the rather exotic beauty of Maria Água, with her wheat-colored hair and delicate skin, softly bluish like a pearl.

"Hey, José-Maria, old pal! You've shot up, boy. Jesus! What's happened to you?"

José-Maria told them about himself and his union with Maria and in turn received a running account of the past few years in Rozário. He went along stopping from door to door and shaking hands with those old men who had the same Asiatic eyes as other old men, as all the old men on the islands. He told them the story of his travels with Maria from their discovery of the City and its cemetery over a league long and the Holy Shroud and the docks with their ships to the sight of all the Islands of the Azores, and from the smallest detail of his activities as a whaler to the sure navigation of a ship that sailed continuously and everlastingly along the route of the nine Islands.

"Tell me one thing, José-Maria: ain't it true them whales is by no means wicked critters and they even runs away from a man in the water without doing him no hurt?"

José-Maria explained that whales were like the mothers of men: they offered themselves up to death in the place of their young and moaned with oceanic grief as they covered their bodies to receive the deadly harpoon.

"They're maternal animals, like eggs," he explained, fumbling for a metaphor. "They give their children the air they breathe even when they're dying from suffocation."

Then the old men, who'd never been more than a league away from Rozário, listening to him now talking about the existence of other Islands, about whales and ships, became astounded by such tales and exclaimed:

"Lord-a-mercy! This world is a big place for sure. I wish I could take a trip like that at my age!"

215

José-Maria vainly tried to clarify things about the world for them, however: in addition to the nine Islands of the Azores there were a lot of countries with their own names, cities, and people; there were continents and seas, people of all different colors, white, red, yellow, black, and according to what José-Lázaro had said one day they spoke strange languages that couldn't be understood, and they'd invented the progress of our dreams, our imagination, supernatural mysteries and fables for themselves. So that after Rozário there was the Island of San Miguel Arcanjo and after our Island there were eight more of different shapes and sizes, some a little sharp, others rounder; and after all of them there was Portugal in Europe, Cresmalia in Asia, Tabanão in Africa, Semfim in the Americas. So much of it, he said, that when they taught me all that I figured right away it was impossible to go around the world, it was so endless, and I headed back to Achadinha, which is always the little place we carry in our hearts. The old men didn't understand all that immediately and they closed their eyes so they could imagine it better. For the first time in their almost century-old lives they admitted that death wasn't darkness; it was never having been able to see a little farther in the distance.

After listening to the chronicles of the past few years in Rozário, José-Maria was able to conclude that the parish had started to progress again. It was no longer that clump of half-ruined housed in darkness and poverty with muddy streets, crumbling walls, and the atrophy of its sad everyday life; the streets were full of small businesses, there were new stores and workshops and houses had multiplied and grown in size and splendor. Two-story buildings with broad balconies on which maidenhair and dwarf ferns, begonias, and fuchsias were growing lined the Rua Direita, finally covered with paving stones all the way to Lugar. Fresh façades, whitewashed every year, gracefully received the sun and reflected its rays like mirrors under a chlorine sky heavy with dampness. Rats and spiders were practically extinct species, but, on the other hand, birds were numerous and doves flew low to their nests under eaves and in granaries. One could breathe the warm, light, clean air of the girls who sang as they shook rugs out windows or sewed on upper floors, and music machines and loudspeakers bellowed from vendors of dry goods, knick-knacks, and children's toys. Nor were they anymore the mule drivers of olden times with their little donkeys and mules loaded down with gaudy household goods; they could have been their sons or grandsons: they wore leather vests and jackets and flashed carefully polished nails, gold wristwatches and Gypsy rings of the tribes scattered throughout the world. In addition, they wore smiles as familiar and friendly as the polished talk of politeness and priests skeptical of the usefulness of celibacy.

After Cadete's death, Rozário had received the visit of its first doctor, or not quite that: a dour crow with cold hands who listened and hurriedly gave treatments and was rapidly prospering in Algarvia. He had, in addition, the skeptical eyes of the rich with the inappropriate color of his syrups, a crow with the disposition of a shearwater, and he smelled so much of X-rays that people went back to venerating the memory of Cadete, having erected a tiny marble sanctuary to perpetuate his name and the services he'd rendered humanity. Taking advantage of that wave, Father Governo conceived the idea of a monument and ordered it built in Canto, above the public spring. It was a wedge-shaped affair, twenty-five feet tall and decorated with tiles depicting the fires of Purgatory. The souls were suffering in silence amidst the flames with their arms reaching out to a divine hand that prayed for them in their uncomfortable punishment, intending to lead them back someday to a well-earned eternity. In the center of the monument and in a place quite visible to passersby, Father Governo had them cement on an apple-colored plaque where a dramatic poem was inscribed:

> Prayers for holy souls
> Are duty, not devotion;
> Who forgets the dead
> Loses his Christian soul.

Going down the street a ways and stopping continuously from door to door, José-Maria admired the whole transformation the parish had undergone since the plane crash. Old Libânia tugged his arm and spoke to him secretly, as she had always done in any case: did he remember José Lisboa? He was the one who'd pilfered an armored suitcase containing coins, gold bars and Bank of America checks from the wreckage. With the product of his plunder, according to the old woman with secrets, tired of conspiring but never disenchanted into silence, that man had built a long, low palace from the windows of which hung pots with azaleas, and dry goods stores, groceries, cobbler shops, with sewing machines and everything you could imagine.

Years before, while still a child, José-Maria had witnessed the operation to recover the goods purloined from the ill-fated airplane. Some policemen had come from the town of Nordeste and asked door to door about a list of unheard-of riches, and both the mayor Guilherme José and Agostinho Moniz, along with Jeremias Furtado and Father Governo as well, harangued the people together, some condemning the despoilers of the dead, others demanding the restitution of the pilfered goods. Guilherme José went so far as to go into houses with the brutality that bloomed and bubbled in his blood and turn over mattresses and empty out cupboards and drawers, leaving behind a jumble of damaged and destroyed objects. Cadete the healer, that saint, quickly returned the rubies and sapphires, his soul grimy with remorse, and went back once more and forever to the solitude of his laboratory.

"He was never the same man again," Dona Libânia swore, bathed in tears. "Our divine healer faced the basins, siphons, labels of essences invented by him, remembered what João-Lázaro had told him about illnesses on the day of his resurrection and immediately made his decision. The people found him hanging from a beam and they ran to save him from that peg. They saw that they'd arrived too late and then decided to make use of an old idea of Francisco Heitor, poet and dentist, by erecting a monument to him."

As for his father, João-Maria, on the day they asked him about the riches from the plane, he forbade the mayor to enter his house, went inside and brought out the daguerreotype to give to the police, and with such dignity that no one even dared suspect that he'd kept other things. That was the last time, perhaps, Father Governo had looked deep into the eyes of a poor man and into the clear and untrammeled look of his nobility.

A few houses down, quite close to home already, Dona Estefânia came out to stop him and tell him about some new events:

"Did you know that we've got a new priest now, son?"

He was a very skinny man, according to her, with aluminum hands and the smile of an angel; he still spoke timidly of justice and equality among men and of the necessity of distributing the wealth. While Father Governo was alive, "an old man as deaf and stubborn as a ram," in the words of Dona Estefânia, he was an underling in parish functions. But the serenity of his civilized ways began to bear fruit, because the church started to fill up with faithful again on Sundays and the younger women developed a passion for him, both for the glad tidings of his words and his unaffected and harmless beauty of a young priest whose smile, they said, had been polished and inspired by God's own wisdom and which inspired in them a certain skepticism regarding celibacy.

Along with all that growth people had come. People called more people, of course, and with them they brought projects, skills, and ideas. They bought houses, cows, and land and the cows gave birth to calves and great herds were led to the People's Woods once more. With such a mixture of people Achadinha was divided in two, those inside and those outside. That division gave rise to another: on one side were those who loved the new priest and went on to believe in the existence of God and the commandments of His Law; on the other were those who still placed conditions on their beliefs in the future of religion. In between the two factions, João-Lázaro asked they sit down around him and he stood amidst them, just as he'd seen Christ do with the Apostles one day and later on with the multitudes who went with Him everywhere and bore faith and witness to his miracles.

"A revolution frees the people, it's made with them and for them. It's the work of the poor for the poor, against the rich and powerful of this world. It must be made by the famished, the naked, men who have no work or land, or, if they do have these, by those whose spirits are moved and revolted by the misery of the peasants. It's enough for all men to become aware of their work, their suffering, and bring about the great spiritual union that will transform the world among them. That's all."

Nevertheless, his ideals were getting farther and farther away from reality because the rich had taken possession of everything again: the name of things, the name and essence of things and of men; Leandro the farmer continued smiling with his gold teeth and showed off rings set with rubies and sapphires, and he rode fabulous horses with camel hide saddles; Guilherme José, the mayor, had deported all his enemies, had replaced Jeremias Furtado in the presidency of the Council, declaring him crazy, and he sneered at Father Governo's deafness. José Lisboa himself had taken Francisco Heitor, poet and dentist, into his employ, lording it over José, the man with the levers and gears; he had four sons studying Navigational Sciences in the City, he presided at festivals and made installment loans to afflicted men without funds; he was already talking about buying five tractors, a truck, a taxi, a threshing machine for wheat—and maybe someday he'd be a priest, a mayor, a doctor, and everything else in this world that could be bought.

He would have to confront all the rich men in the world, however. When he embraced his father, José-Maria got the latest information about everything that had happened in Rozário during his several years absence and was moved to tears by the decrepitude of that skinny old man, almost sightless. When he saw his face light up like that of the father of the prodigal son, he embraced him for a long while, asked his forgiveness, and vainly tried to stop crying. He had his old, bitter, and tender father between his arms, and João-Maria was only standing because the bony, swift energy of his thinness and hunger had converted his body into a lightness of movement similar to the breath of survival.

Papa immediately bubbled over as he properly received Maria Água into the bosom of the family. The very thought that into that equally decrepit house so beautiful and young a woman was entering after so many years of solitude made his eyes fill with tears that rolled with euphoric gratitude. It had been worth the trouble after all. She would take Sara's place in managing all household affairs, she would be the white sun of its illumination that came from inside women and only from them, the unique and white swan that a woman gives to a family house, and she would also offer the new hope for children. With a woman inside like that life would take a great turn. It was necessary to fix up a house, turn it completely in the direction of that sun, people it with the sound of new footsteps, things that the solitude of a man without a woman could never bring about.

José-Maria stood for a moment looking at the pitiful state of this childhood home. The beams had been eaten away by smoke and the walls were completely stripped bare, and the floor of tamped earth had so many hollows that the table and chairs and the log benches, with four legs and a plank like sawhorses, had to stand on ever larger wooden shims in order to be steady. The roof showed old cracks through which needles of light and drops of rain poured, and the lathing had been completely devoured by rats.

In spite of everything, after so much solitude João-Maria was grateful to the world and thought perhaps he ought to forgive all his enemies. He hurried to transfer his old things to the loft in the barn, the torn and dirty blankets of raw linen, the winter clothes chewed by rats, the boots of a digger in someone else's land and the instruments for working another's holdings, which had lain there since Sara's death with no hope of any rich man hiring him. He had the income from two hillside plots in Moio and a vegetable garden and he'd managed to buy a goat, a pig, two hens, and a pregnant rabbit. He was in the middle of his moving when José-Maria, finishing his inspection of the house, came back to see his father again and stood before him, just looking at him, as if he hadn't had time to do so before. Only then was João-Maria impressed by the way the boy had grown during his absence. Just the opposite of Jorge-Maria, he'd flown from the height of his nest all alone and in that way had disappeared along the flyway of migratory birds from the South. There was certainly no other man as strong in all the territory of the council of Nordeste, for his shoulders gave the impression that the boy had spent one part of his life destroying the world and another developing his muscles rebuilding it. Not even Guilherme José or Vitorino de Sousa could be as strong, in spite of their legendary colossal statures.

"I've come from far away, father, to protect you and also to get back everything that's ours. But first I have to know if my father will bless my marriage to Maria Água."

"I bless it, of course, my dear son, but let's call Jorge-Maria first. He's probably playing by himself out there in back."

He immediately went out into the yard, sorry to have forgotten about his brother's existence, going on tiptoe, without making any noise. He hoped to be able to admire the work of time on Jorge's body and imagined a sandy head of hair like his own, a pair of broad shoulders, and the same lusty look in his eyes from the time when they'd both worked for Leandro the farmer. That look must have been at the age of undressing the first female now and the great event of amorous possession. He was drawing near and was surprised by his brother's silence when, peeking through a hole in the backyard hedge, he was horrified by what he saw. Jorge-Maria was sitting on the ground and sticking his penis into a hen's rear end as his haunches worked eagerly in search of pleasure and orgasm. He was immediately filled with sadness to find in him once more the same growthless child, still caught up with the dream of Mama's white flesh. He waited until he let the creature go. Then he himself gave a tremendous kick to the hen, which flew off like an elliptical wild ball against the hedge. Jorge-Maria leapt to his feet and was astounded to recognize his brother in that stranger. How was it possible for him to have grown so much in such a short time away? Was it really José-Maria? His brother leaned over to embrace him and picked him up. He felt himself smothered under the weight of the love of those inconceivably strong arms where every muscle quivered like strings tightened to their limit.

"I wasn't the only thing to grow and get this strong, brother. Time grew, it changed everything in our age."

He carried him to the house with his arms around this neck and went along talking about the crucial seasons in the life of men. There were things in time very much like the ripening of fruit or the cycle of trees, things comparable to the tides, perhaps, in their rising and falling. That's why time grows inside men and things and not the other way around, because every man was only the measure of that transformation.

"This is your sister-in-law. Her name is Maria Água and she's going to stay and live in this house with us," he announced without any ceremony but with the hope that his brother would understand in that way what he'd been saying about growth and transformation.

"Is she going to stay here forever, as if she were our mother?"

"Mother died and she'll never come back here, brother. Maria Água is going to be blessed by our father and she'll be my wife. You can kiss her now."

Maria Água was immediately moved by the liquid and so deeply unprotected look of that ageless child and she felt that she had loved the boy ever since the beginning of the world, even when she was unaware of his existence. She took him in her arms and carried him off to give him a bath while José-Maria, sitting down beside his father, began laying out to him the plans for rebuilding the house.

"Before the house, my son, we've got to talk about you and the world you went in lost to us. They say you were hunting whales on the high seas, is that true?"

"All right, father. You can hear it now."

Against the old man's slight protests he tried to set him up in a more comfortable place. He wrapped a blanket around his knees and brought him his pipe, already lit by a coal from the fireplace. He sat down by his feet and began the tale of his voyages. He still had the same innocence of the boy of yesteryear, however, so clumsy in his humbled ways and in his muscles and so sure that nothing would have the least bit of importance in the end that he omitted a great many episodes in his maritime odyssey. He invented others, many others, and he ended up convincing himself of the fable of his life, just as acrobats do in the circus or priests on Sunday at the hour of mass.

On the first day they walked along the shore, loaded down with their personal effects, and they were able to conclude immediately that the world was just the same everywhere. The same grimy houses, some of stone, others of thatch and blood-colored adobe, up on stilts, laid out in rows, invariably facing the sea. Sad people with the look of someone who hadn't slept for centuries went about from morning to night among the plots and houses and presented the same look cooked by dampness and salt, also with a burnt and solitary voice—like us. Later on, as they tried to get to know the City, they headed in the direction of the mountains and covered the whole interior of the Island. When they got to the top of the mountains they caught sight of the sea again from the other side of the land and immediately felt encircled.

"There was sea on both sides and the land cut through the middle of it, just as it must have done in the times when lava slid down from the volcanoes and formed the Island."

They spent some time resting there. Then they slept in a cave, covered with some dry ginger lily stalks, and they remained listening to the night with its wandering birds and rotting, audible dampness among the trees. The next day at dawn they watched the sunrise from up there. From the bottom of the sea, from far off, from among cobwebs and balloon clouds, the Sun was a bright spiral coming toward the Island and its movement was like a celestial swirl opening up toward the space of shadows and everything there inside them. There were gullies deeply cut into the middle of the earth lighting up in their breaks, there were nests of ancient earthquakes and forgotten craters and also wrinkles of lava scraped by the immeasurable hands of God. And great lagoons of a colorless color, father, with stones sticking out of the middle of the water and black silence, and the trees, always trees of sleeplessness and oblivion, receiving birds, birds, and still more birds, and José-Maria had never been able to imagine himself as the inhabitant of such a place, so primitive in its wisdom and in its ignorance, too. He'd never even been able to imagine that going over those mountains to the other side opposite Rozário he would be able to see the sea again, sitting on a large stone as smooth as glass but streaked by the rain. He'd never been able to imagine a world like that with two equal faces, even in their appearance, with the same infinite sea in front and an Island with the memory of an animal whose members had been transformed into roots, which, too, were sinking infinitely into the depths of the water.

"How couldn't I have imagined an Island so beautiful, so proud and a thousand times more wonderful even in its solitude, father, and at the same time with so many people suffering on it for all their lives when this could have been the paradise of our first parents in the Bible, before Eve sinned?"

Taking Maria Água by the hand, he stood up next to her and said, "Every people, every village, and every country has its desert of sand, sometimes right before their eyes and even under their feet in the place they've chosen to live in; at other times in themselves, when they look inside and find out that in their souls they're carrying the black chant of a solitude many centuries old, with parents passing it on later to children and those children to their children. Because people, even the most victorious and barbarous among them, never argue among themselves, they simply invade their solitude."

"As for us here on the Azores," I said, "I still don't know what could have happened to us. Papa was used to saying—remember?—that our world is this infinite sea with its desert of water in front and no way out, where you can die of thirst or from too much of the water that surrounds us."

Flocks of birds were crossing the morning in their freedom, coming out of the middle of the woods and invading the silence when José-Maria and Maria Água decided to begin their descent from the mountain range to the shore on the other side. By midday they'd caught sight of new settlements and had passed through them, always in the same direction, toward the South, oriented by a strange vibration. It must have been the City, because they say that all cities have that distant and prophetic buzzing even when they're not within sight of the people looking for them.

"Old men sitting on stoops, father, were receiving the sun in their veins made rough by age, leaning on the staffs of their weakness, and they always pointed out the road to the South to us. According to them we should head in that direction and where the road ended we'd see a row of ships tied to the docks and, by the cranes, by the birds roosting on the masts and on those cranes looking about, we'd finally discover the City."

"And what's the City like?" I asked one of them.

"It's full of white bustle and people running around for no reason at all, big houses with machinery in them called factories, and cemeteries more than a league long."

"Are there any animals?" Maria Água wanted to know.

"No animals, child. Only machines, ships, a lot of cars as noisy as hell itself, and those long cemeteries. Animals always die when they're taken to the City. Not even the birds get very used to flying in a sky like that."

So, shown by those old men, father, we kept on walking South without tiring and alert only to the buzzing that awaited us in the distance. In our feet we could feel the hidden vibration of that animal whose heart was beating on that side of the mountain and we were irresistibly taken by its almost hellish seduction, because other old men sitting in the sun now had a look that was even more defeated by age and for that reason were absorbed in smoking their sailor pipes. Old men like that would blink their Asiatic eyes in a solitary way toward the South and listen to the memory of the City that was growing harsh in their veins. José-Maria and Maria Água were already drawn by the smell, by the sound, and by the emotion of a City promised them many years ago in their childhood, because no childhood ever existed without the dream or the promise of the sea and the city. So when the road ended, father, we walked along a white wall more than a league in length. Looking over it on the other side we caught sight of more than a million gravestones, mausoleums, tombs, and simple memorials written on slates all along there through rows of box shrubs and beds of dahlias, lilies, and amaryllises. Alongside those paths were trees with birds dozing in their branches. Trees like poplars, cypresses and cedars have a look as if they were hung with birds and they make you think of death. Who could have thought to make up death like that with such show in a cemetery-city inside the City?

The sharp smell of wax, incense, and musk reached them and, enwrapped in that smell, the voices of a thousand priests and millions of dead people roared in a dull way over the sounds of the City like a maritime, vaguely spiritual wind. All the men's widows were there because it was the day of widows. Their clothes were torn from indignation, as in Rozário, and they were defeated women whose weeping wailed over the graves of their turtle doves, their child gods, or simply the children of their hearts; others knelt and laid their hands on the ground as if still touching hands with the only men of their bodies and their joy.

"Then," José-Maria went on, lowering his eyes now so as not to look his father in the face, "I remembered Mama that way, on the day they went to bury her in the backyard, and I stood there a long time deciding whether or not I should turn back to Rozário, to my father's house, or keep going on as I'd promised Maria Água."

They stopped watching the white orioles in the cemetery and ended up going through its austere gates, fastened solidly to the walls. At the end of a drive with poplars whose leaves were yellowed by the oxide of birds stood the famous hermitage where the Holy Shroud had been placed centuries before.

"Holy Shroud?" João-Maria asked.

"A tunic with holes made by the thorns and flagellation whip, the Holy Shroud of Our Lord Jesus Christ of the Miracles had reached the Island, brought from Jerusalem by Hebrew navigators fleeing pirates. Every year at Lent pilgrims arrive there from their walk all around the Island. They receive forgiveness for their sins, leave, and then go back to sinning year after year until they die without forgiveness."

"That's what those jackass priests say, at least out of their assholes and into the ears of dimwits. But the only people who believe it are the ones who want to."

A world so shaken by forgetfulness, father, that the orioles roost and grow old there until they turn white and big like pigeons or even like seagulls tired of flying along the coast.

From there they finally left for the City and, dazzled, went through its flat streets paved with tar and Maria Água had never seen so many automobiles or so many clothing stores, and she even tried to imagine herself dressed like that to love her man in luxury, and then she imagined José-Maria dressed in one of those suits on the dummies sleeping in the shop windows. He would look like the Prince Lupert of her dreams as Princess Argentina. She noticed that all the people in the City had bird faces; some were finches with elegant crops and full of light, others were fierce, with their terrible alcoholic eyes, red from so much sucking of the blood of land birds. She was frightened by all those birds and asked him if they could hurry towards the docks because she wanted to see the ships from close up and breathe the wonderful air of their holds.

"Well, father, the ships were funny things, shaped like galoshes, and the arms of the cranes hung over them, the rigging stood out up to the crow's nest, and in the middle they had the mouth of a whale, just like the ones I'd seen in the sea off Pico, that was swallowing up lead-sealed boxes, steel crates, bundles of all the practical things we see being born out of the earth here, and even terrified animals. Hanging from the cranes, the calves spread their hooves wide and bellowed in panic; the blond goats rolled their goat eyes around a lot and the sheep floated in the air and went mad in full view of people, returning then to their original pale color. Finally bales of straw followed, flying up to meet that mouth of hell, that whale's mouth served by pulleys and noisy cables. Everything was so rusted, too, father, that it frightened Maria Água's eyes the way it frightened mine seeing a ship there day and night swallowing living things and which would never be filled up by the time it was to sail."

We should have left on one of those ships, of course, because we'd gone without eating for two days and we didn't have any money to buy anything at all or even to rent a room with a bed for the night. Maria Água was beginning to wake up out of her dream of Princess Argentina loved by Prince Lupert and would soon be crying from unhappiness, leaning against me. I went up the ship's gangplank and offered my services and hers to a man with a heron nose walking back and forth on deck with his pot belly sagging. He had a bird face like the rest, too, but with a touch of poetry in his eyes.

228

One of those men, father, that you look at and say, Now this here fellow is a man. He listened to my explanations silently and seemed to grow pale as I told him about our troubles. He was, without a doubt, the famous Captain Desmandos, a hero of the sea and the wolf of his people.

"Why do you want to go looking for your future if you've got it all so set on our Island?" he asked.

I replied with the story of my childhood in Rozário: Mama dead, Jorge-Maria not growing, not waking up to life and always receiving the imagined visits of the dead, and so I had to leave, emigrate far away, and then, one day, every inch the man, return to Rozário and put an end to the hell of this house.

"What about her?" Captain Desmandos asked, turning his bird's eye in the direction of Maria Água.

"She'll receive the blessing of two peoples and new priests," I assured him quickly, with absolute conviction.

The man with the bird face and a touch of poetry in his eyes lit his pipe and started walking back and forth across the deck again with his pot belly sagging. He didn't say anything, but he was pondering his decision. He could turn us over to the Harbor Police, to the City authorities, to the old priests, who would send us back here to jail, or he could take us away in search of work and a place to live without Guilherme José, without a deaf priest, and without the smile of rich men like Leandro the farmer. In that sharp bird face with poetry there was the howling, and I heard it, of a weary dog that wanted to die or maybe command a gang of diggers and proclaim a revolt. That puppy of a dog was barking in the night over the sea and must have been frightening off the night birds that existed in his face.

"But this ship of mine," he put in, "only travels between Islands. How do you plan to reach the world on it?"

Then Maria took the initiative and spoke up:

"Maybe, sir, there'll be an even bigger ship later on. Or maybe even this one will end up sailing out toward the world someday."

The man didn't seem immediately convinced by any of those arguments, but he admitted that deep down, he, too, was waiting for the day when his ship would change course.

Really, he said once we were at sea, I've been wrong in all my notions of life, I'm a solitary figure in the world, too, as solitary as you people, your father, Jorge-Maria, and all the people of Rozário. He was in the habit of carrying clandestine people on all his trips and he could see that there were no other solutions for the people of the Azores. Everybody wanted to go off blindly to distant countries, some to Brazil, others to America, others still to Europe, like rats in flight so as not to be eaten alive, he said out at sea. Wasn't there enough wealth for them all? There was. The problem was space and its distribution. The rich, always the same ones, all ate like one happy family, while the poor, them, had children, children, and more children. Only free to distribute their poverty.

I worked on board washing the deck and greasing the hawsers. Maria slept or cooked for us, and that was when my annoyance with the world began. For months we made the circuit of the nine Islands, always with the hope that the ship of our destiny would cross paths at sea with another even larger one, maybe a ghost ship that couldn't be seen sailing along by the Azores. Finally we decided to go ashore because that ship didn't exist or would never pass by. We were on land again when people invited me to go hunting whales sixty feet long. Those maternal animals breathed through waterspouts and mouthed endless oceanic cries. The Pico is their sacred mountain, without innards; it looks like a pile of manure shaped by a hoe. São Jorge, which is an almost submerged crocodile, has flat lands on the edge of the sea covered by flocks of mist, and I ran fleeing along the coast always hoping that in the Channel on one of those nights with no shelter for men the big ship would pass along the route of the whales. I asked about that ship on Faial and Graciosa, they said it passed by sometimes in the direction of Flores and Corvo and that it continued afterwards toward America. An Island as sad as Corvo, where people even forget their forgetfulness, gets into us and turns us pale, father. You get the impression you're seeing the land floating on the water, floating on the water like orphans in the dark, and there I began to think and I thought: I'm only a man of the Azores in any part of the Azores, I'm encircled like a wolf, and here I am going around trying to match my strength against the strength of innocent whales. If I could conquer their sixty feet of length, their cries, and even their muscular tyranny, I might also be able to return home to the Island and get my revenge on the rich, the old priests, the mayors of the world, in general on all those we consider our enemies. That's why I'm here, Papa, to protect you, Jorge-Maria, and my wife and to get the land back, my grandfather David's land, the land where Mama would have been buried if only she'd died sometime starting tomorrow morning.

José-Maria began to weep convulsively and through his tears floated before him the figure of his father who was weeping, too. He listened to his weeping for a long time. It was like the rain, his wail: it poured out ceaselessly and, suddenly, it thickened with the same emotion as a cloudburst, the wind, a storm at sea. He thought right then he would soon die because he'd been waiting to weep like that all those years before taking leave of the world. Frightened by the eventuality of that death, José-Maria was afraid there wouldn't be time to rebuild the house and make their enemies come there seeking punishment or pardon. He'd decided not only to get the land back but to bring down the mayor and the old priest and join the revolution that João-Lázaro had for many years been quietly proclaiming in Rozário, for when the diggers deemed the time was right.

He immediately began to nail up and replace beams and boards. In the space of only five hours he repaired the three beds, replaced the leaves in the mattresses, tightened the screws on tables and chairs, cemented the fireplace and the oven and, afterwards, began work on the floors in all the rooms in the house with the exception of his parents' old bedroom. Using a bucket of water he wet the floor and chopped it with a hoe, leveling it then with a plank. After that he went out into the yard and brought in twenty-seven bushel baskets of earth and with all that his father was frightened by his strength. In order to support such a big basket all by himself on his back José-Maria must certainly have had the strength of a Hercules and could stand up to any animal without any risk and, even better, to any man in the world. He spread the earth, sometimes with his hands, sometimes with the hoe, distributing it in thin layers and mixing in black sand to cement the old earth to the new. He went back to using the plank to level the surface and he wet it with more splashes of water before starting finally to tamp it down. He spent the rest of the afternoon pounding it with the blade of the hoe, back and forth. He would stop sometimes to ask his father for advice and immediately pick up the work. He delivered such terrible blows that Maria Água came running out of the kitchen to say the whole house was shaking from being hit by an earthquake. At the end of the day, covered with sweat, José-Maria considered the job done. The house smelled of plowed earth, of the ripe plowed earth of his memory, of new wood, and even bubbly cement. In the days that followed he eagerly continued the reconstruction. He called on the young men his age to give him some help after work. Seventeen came and the house first had all the tiles removed from the roof and then was covered with new ones. He took it upon himself alone to fill in the cracks in the walls with cement and mortar before whitewashing them. Then he called in the seventeen lads again and had them paint the front of the house, the molding, and the interior. When that was done, he pulled up the flooring of what had been his parents' bedroom and, still with the aid of the seventeen boys, planed the boards smooth and adjusted the crossbeams. At the same time, with kerchiefs on their heads and wearing colored calico aprons, Maria Água and the young men's wives scrubbed all the cupboards and windowpanes and lined the shelves and drawers of the china closet.

When he saw the old house transformed into a noisy place smelling of paint and cleanliness without the dead air of rotting beams chewed by rats, João-Maria recalled the day when he confronted his misery and found himself in a complete state of ruin. Now, instead of the desire to die he'd felt then, he was overcome with emotion and stopped believing in the facts that had made his life a disarray of death and solitude. It was no longer true that someone had stolen his land or that his wife had departed so early from this life. Sara's great spirit continued to glow over the house like a forgotten candle that still eternally burned. That spirit had turned into the arrival of José-Maria and his wife. He was ready to return to human company, to rest alongside Sara.

"Give me your blessing, father," José-Maria asked before going to bed.

As he embraced him, João-Maria examined his face again, the face of his son, and he found it closed over by a most absolute determination. He was frightened by the strength, by the capacity for violence, because he was catching sight of vengeance against all enemies in it and life would soon be filled with the same despair as years before.

"Listen, my son," he said, without the spirit for any more of it. "I only wanted to die. I was only waiting for you."

José-Maria pretended not to understand and sat him down in a chair again. Then he made a gesture roundabout, very slowly, a gesture of love and tenderness for those boards, those walls, and the floor of the house, and he sat down beside him like someone who had something very important to confide.

"This is your house again, father. It wouldn't have made any sense at all for me to come and rebuild it if my father was going to leave it now."

The old man cast his eyes around, but he would no longer see anything except the walls in front of him and a few objects from his memory in their usual places, in the places destined for them by Sara's hands. Blindness was growing in those half-dead eyes, almost translucent from weariness, and he'd grown to find his way more by touch and smell. He could understand, however that the house had been going downhill in time, but shaken like a cracked egg now it was as comfortable as the early nest where he'd loved Sara and seen the boys born.

"This time, at least," José-Maria said with firmness, "they're not going laugh at our misery they way they did all our lives. My father's now the owner of a decent house and he's got two sons and a daughter-in-law to take care of him in his old age."

The old man's hands trembled all the more. He tried to stop sweating, but he could feel it running down his spine in a thread and his mouth was as dry and his gums as stiff as cork.

"My son, my son!" he implored. "Maybe I no longer have any enemies. People are in the habit of imagining hate in others and when they come to their senses everything around them is dead and they've died, too."

"In that case we're not of the same opinion. Papa's going to see them come here and ask his forgiveness. He knows exactly who they are: the ones who stole his land, who killed Mama, all those who wouldn't give him work and left us to eat horseshit all our lives. They're going to pay for all the bad they've done to us and they're going to suffer the revenge of the parish."

João-Maria agreed and then dragged himself off to the attic, even though he knew he wouldn't sleep a single more night of his life. He listened to his heart galloping along at full speed in the furious haste of getting to even he didn't know where and pounding like the works of a crazed clock. Then it flowed through his arteries with a whistle and flew inside his breathing. It was a motor with the cadence of bees lost forever in the illusory honeycomb of his lungs. When he tried to call for help he noticed something strange in the silence of the night where other different sounds abounded and always, always, the frequent and afflicted death of a people with its rats and spiders. His deserted voice had ceased to function. Or maybe the sound of the infinite and the eternal had already left that body in some breath of air, blending into a night of stone, with no pain, no glory, no jubilation, not even the shadow of any use.

234

17

UNTIL HER DEATH AT THE HANDS OF HER HUSBAND GORAZ, THE WOMAN HADN'T BEEN SEEN BY HER NEIGHBORS MORE THAN A HANDFUL OF TIMES, GENERALLY IN THE BACKYARD HANGING OUT CLOTHES OR DRESSING PIGS AND CHICKENS. IT'S said that on the night he strangled her the mastodon screwed her six uninterrupted times, roaring for her to give him a son, and that during the seventh try, when he was bellowing, "Just a son, you worthless woman," he became filled with an inexplicable rage and clasped his hands around her neck. When he saw he had a still warm corpse beneath his body, he got up, wiped the sweat from his neck and face, and hanged her to make it look like a suicide.

She was a very thin woman, sucked dry by the jaws of rats, and her body was swaying softly with the lightness of a breeze when the mayor studied the pores of her skin for a moment and shouted, as if asking for help from the many gods of the night, arousing the whole parish.

"His roars were like some underground howling, the howling of ships lost in a storm," José Guilherme the rat catcher related, his voice still congealed with the white sounds heard in the dark, the white noise of the solitude of a man used to darkness, that is.

"They were distant groans, those of a whale, lost at intervals in the sea wind and in the flight of the dead and sleepless birds. The beginning and the end of all nocturnal places fit perfectly into that whale cry, and then I was filled with an affliction similar to the fear that flies inside those faceless birds when they come upon death."

The old blind woman on the Rua Direita who in times past had said, "Our Lord has died," wept again this time and said, trembling with cold, "My time has come," and she made ready to die, to which the faceless man, her husband perhaps, replied, "That, woman, is the voice of the people, your time hasn't come at all." People were already running in the direction of the mayor's shouts and the old woman said between sobs again, "I hope they won't be about killing at my time." And her husband said, "I'd just as soon have death kill them all, and you and me, too, woman."

José Guilherme the rat catcher was the first to arrive and he felt a kind of physical distress as his eyes followed the way his sister-in-law's ever so thin legs were swaying, abandoned in the air.

"Her legs were hitting each other and there was the clink of dry bones done in by weariness," he told João-Lázaro later.

It had been easy for him to conclude there was nothing left in the woman's eyes, not even the hate of someone who hadn't forgotten the crime. Nothing except that bony and vertical weariness, light and heavy at the same time, coming from her soul and her body.

"They were deserted eyes, burned out by fatigue, not the fatigue of death, but the fatigue of life. That's why her death was looking the world up and down, out of the corner of her eyes, and was jeering at all of us. She'd found liberation in a certain way, while we were left in life without enjoying it."

The ratcatcher immediately began to check all the marks on his sister-in-law's body and right away thought he saw on her neck, beneath her look of triumph over the world, the proof of his suspicions.

"He went along killing her a little every day. Sometimes he'd beat her until she passed out, other times he'd stick himself inside her bones and fuck and fuck: it was a fucking that went on all through the night! My sister-in-law's pussy must have been all torn up, like a fig when it's ripe and dribbles out a stinking drool. Her stomach was soft and slippery like mud and then she was no longer a woman but a plot of ground plowed many times over and always without seed. And in the same way that substances will combine to make another new substance, so my brother's green fingers, the smell of his sperm and sweat impregnated that body with his own."

How long had it been since he'd been taken with such a rage? The tiny, noisy patience of rats had divided his spirit in two: on one side was the strength of the former cow abuser, on the other side the gentle habits, the suspicion and the fear of those small and inoffensive animals who spend their existence hidden almost innocently in their nests. José Guilherme had never been in the presence of a murderer and when he saw his brother sitting on the floor there facing the wall, all the nerves in his body broke out in hate.

"He was crying like a drowned man, a castaway, a repentant sinner. I'd never seen Guilherme José cry. Not even as a child had he ever shed a single tear as far as I could see: he was a bull of a man, carved in stone. But that time he was crying and I was a bit surprised to see a river growing and thickening under his mouth there."

Without moving his head he looked for a good club, because, he said, a terrible impulse to kill had been born in his muscles. He tried to find an iron bar, an axle, a blacksmith's sledgehammer, very heavy and capable of splitting his brother in two, something like that was in his soul, a fever, and the power of stone and knives at the same time, to kill him quickly and avenge the poor unhappy skinny woman sucked dry by the jaws of grandmother-rats—but no damned club was within reach, and his brother had dropped into a corner of the house, curled up among the shavings and still weeping like a child.

"It wasn't exactly human crying, more like the bellowing of an ox, as if they were gelding him in cold blood and he was resisting, resisting to prove that he was strong," José Guilherme corrected himself to João-Lázaro later as he told the tale of that exceptional night.

He finally found the almost loose sill of a door, a kind of sash or board or something like that, unattached to the cement, he said, and he pulled it out with a tug, and when he was about to lower it with all his might and with the anger of his vengeance onto the curled-up animal squatting there howling, a whale or an ox or even a stone god, his brother leapt up and fled into the yard. José Guilherme ran after him and struck the first blow blindly. He swore there was glow in the air and then on the ground. His aim was to hit him on the skull and bash his brains out, the way it's done to a pumpkin before giving it to the pigs. Nevertheless, Guilherme José dodged the blow and flew over the walls, gates and hedges and took off at a run through the back lots toward the sea. As for him, he took a long time getting over the wall dividing those plots of lupine. His body cooled off with the prohibitions of God and the Devil. Since he couldn't penetrate the stalks of the hedge, he shouldered his way through, and that way he dragged everything after him, knocking down reeds and reed-mace tangles. So he was caught up in the lupine, looking like one of Christ's unfortunates, his arms, his face and his shoulders all bloody, and his brother was running far off toward the woods, always in the direction of the sea.

"He was falling down and getting up and falling down again. Like an animal running away from fire, he was pushing away trees with his body and opening up an impossible path through the underbrush and brambles."

He wasn't a man, no, he was a beast caught up by the fear of dying under the claws of another beast. The way they say a gazelle runs from a leopard or a mouse from a cat or a cat from a dog or a dog from a panther, that was how his brother was running ahead of him, unarmed, firmly believing that the woods would end up ensuring him his last opportunity to remain alive. José Guilherme began to pant then. His lungs and liver were already aching. His intestines had awakened and were filling up with unexpected convulsions. He had an urge to crap, and his chest was a bellows whose breathing burned in the dampness of the night, and when he reached the woods a chill attacked his soul and froze all his blood, because the trees were the shadows of the Devil in agony. He'd never liked trees at night because they lived, trees did, according to what they'd taught him when he was child, in places where the dead without any rest or burial had passed. As solemn as bishops, the dead were feverish creatures, and he'd never liked priests or bishops because, he said, how could you like their eyes of death, that fraternity of owls, the sour smell of vomit and sacristy wax or even their pale look of a woman without a pussy?

"It couldn't have been the wind howling in the branches of those trees in the woods darker than the night itself; it was the dead with their mouths open, without eyes or noses, the white gleam of their teeth purple like fava beans soaked by the rain."

In spite of everything he was determined to confront the wandering souls and fight them, certain his brother was to die in that or some other spot, but only by his hands and no others. Afterwards he would leave his body forgotten there so the kites, the sea birds, and the dead of this world would quickly devour it. He'd only gone thirty feet in the woods when he was surrounded by a chorus of moans and the sound of feet and the noise of birds taking flight among the branches. Do you people know what panic is? he asked. The iron hand of a dead man wraps itself around our neck and squeezes, squeezes; we cry out again and our shouts frighten us, and then the echo is the mirror of those cries that never have an end. You shout and the iron hand relaxes the pressure of its fingers and nails a little, that's what panic is like. We never know when that hand will tighten its grip forever and not let up its pressure on our neck. So the dead were frightened by the way in which I shouted at them. They fled and I saw them fly off, hunched over, skinny old men with bird noses and bat arms. They flew with their nests on their backs and I sent all my nightmares after them in one last cry, hoping the murderer would give his hiding place away:

"Son of a she-goat," I roared. "Son of a deaf priest and a dead mare, son of three priests, a thousand priests, a million priests!"

Suddenly the woods repeated those cries with the same fidelity with which rusty mirrors give back the ugliness of monsters and José Guilherme received the echo riddled with terror: "dead mare, son of three priests, a thousand priests, a million priests-priests-priests!"

"Right there I thought, Feet, do your duty!" he narrated emotionally, facing João-Lázaro's complete passivity as he listened to him. He ran away over those slopes, stumbling across vines and lupine trunks, and he leapt over a barrier as high as a big wave when the sea is fat and white. Then he fell and his mouth struck the ground; he'd never experienced the taste of earth, that's a fact, but he could swear that it might have tasted like wheat bran, the kind used to heal mumps and minor swellings like bubo of the groin, for example, according to Cadete the healer's inscriptions. He slipped into the backyard immediately, broke through the hedge of reeds and brambles, got his legs entangled in the thorns. Then he bumped into the henhouse and its critters, blind as a bat, friend João-Lázaro, because even the grill on the gate gave way under the weight of my body. Then he was in his brother's house, which was full of people, a crowd of people, the poor and innocent of this lawless world who'd taken down the body of his sister-in-law from that sadness of death and still hadn't understood the impossible things in this world of dogs.

While the women were giving the body its first care I noticed the woman's extreme thinness and I thought, "She never was a figure that had any reality but maybe she was only the soul of the objects in whose midst she moved," and I remember now that my sister-in-law must have lost her voice, her look, her breathing, a simple and miserable animal clarity, because all she had was her enormous pussy, half-open like a fig and everything in her had been transformed into that coagulation between her legs that were so thin that a breath of air would make them sway with the sound of seared bones.

Then he saw the tumultuous force of the diggers who were pillaging the house and had identified the numerous objects stolen by the mayor from their work in the fields. A group of drovers was freeing goats, sheep and donkeys. Some fat women with bountiful breasts like loaves of still warm wheat bread were running behind the stolen chickens, and the diggers with sandpaper beards and big muscles were filling sacks with corn, beans, and lupine from the piles that had been lying there for years in the unchanging little bedroom in the center of the house.

"And then I found myself with the rats of all my life again. I saw that some of those animals still recognized me from the time when I'd lived with them in the thatched sheds of the parish. I knew they'd devoured the things inside because their fatness gleamed before it was squashed by the diggers' galoshes. So they died looking at me from far off, their guts showing, kicking, but always with their lively gray eyes following me to protect them from death. Then the diggers attacked the oil press and the corncrib and once more began to decimate my rat friends, who were lying about in hellish agony by the hundreds. And I thought, "I'm not going to stand for this, I'll pick up a cart pole and start hitting right and left, because rats, friend João-Lázaro, can be a civilization, whatever priests want to think, but they're certainly animal angels, they make love among themselves by devouring each other, prolonging the species and preserving it from extinction, and when a man like me has lost everything in life except the right to his solitude with animals, the rats respect that feeling. They always forgave me for hunting them the way I used to so I wouldn't starve to death. And you should know, friend João-Lázaro, they're terrifying animals: they could have eaten me alive easily whenever they pleased, because I always saw them in such numbers that maybe it would've been enough for one of them to have given me the first bite and I'd have been greedily sucked down to my skeleton. Right after that Rozário would be devoured, and then the Island, and then the world, who knows. And that night the diggers went off carrying great sacks on their backs while others, always just as many, would arrive, coming in packs as if they too were rats, and they filled sacks with fruit and potatoes, and others still filled their demijohns with wine from the cellars of the mayor's house and the Parish Council.

"Suddenly looking around, I saw the house deserted, with nothing left. The women had abandoned the corpse on the bed in her best gray taffeta dress. The men ended up carrying off everything that belonged to the people, and I looked at myself, first at my hands, then at my stomach, and I felt the pride of being one among many, a man just like all of them. I'd spent years and years sleeping in mangers, it's true. I'd given up my trade as a rat catcher many years ago, however, without any fuss and had changed into a digger, too. Of course I ate the little animals. But I'd always been the last and only friend they had in this world, as I think, too, that my sister-in-law had also begun to believe in me when she'd secretly bring me food behind my brother's back and remain sitting endlessly watching how I put an end to my hunger. I used to look upon that silent woman the way I did upon dawn, I don't know if I ever heard her say a single word, but I always found out that she was on my side and against the elephant-man of her nights of a rotting slug between the sheets. I admired her silence and, one day, looking into those foggy eyes of hers, I thought to myself, 'Run away, sister-in-law, get far away from here; while you got a piece of earth in front of your legs, run toward it and never look back again.' But Glória fixed me with the cold and motionless eyes of a person who can't see, shrugged her shoulders, and broke into sobs. Right then and there I was sure that she was going to die on a night like that."

He finally felt himself equal to the diggers because, like them, he was dripping with sweat and his face was bloodied from knocking about in the woods and among the sharp edges of the reeds. The needles of the lupine had left scratches all over his body, and José Guilherme was burning with fever: his soul shivered with cold, still not recovered from the terror of the trees at night, while the echo of the woods, friend João-Lázaro, continued rolling around in my ears like the sound of a conch: "…a thousand priests, a million priests, priests, priests." They say that living on an Island like this is like holding a conch shell to your ear and being able to hear what no one else can. But people don't know that's how it is: somebody who's never left the Island can't hear it breathing in the distance either, isn't that so? Here people look around and only get an oceanic feeling in that slanted way of listening to our sea. People live and work and die here, but they know that another pair of eyes is peeking out from inside, deep inside us.

He thought about sitting down on the floor in a corner of the kitchen while the mob sacked the house and meditating on what might have been meant for him to do in such circumstances. Throwing all those people out into the street so the memory of his sister-in-law would get some respect made no sense. Glória must have imagined a night like that for her death, no? José Guilherme quickly felt sure that if men can forgive everything that had once been an insult for them, the people can't. The people would finish their work by the time night fell and his brother's house would be stripped of everything that belonged to the people. His only fear was that the sacking would turn into the profanation of his sister-in-law's personal effects or that her corpse would also end up facing the vengeance of the diggers or the women. As for his brother, it was written, his time had come. As soon as dawn broke, the people would beat the bushes around Rozário da Achadinha, corner him in some hole and not hesitate to hang him in cold blood. He himself, José Guilherme, would head up the search, armed with an ax, and do everything possible to split open his head with the first blow.

Right at dawn he would have to get the old priest and ask him to come and administer his sister-in-law last rites. Then he would go find João-Lázaro, whose clear head would tell him what direction to follow regarding the criminal.

"You don't have to do anything," João-Lázaro said after listening to him. "Let the people do it by themselves. If the mayor is to die at the hands of the people it's because that's the just thing. What other form of justice could be truer?"

As he went down toward the priest's house he passed people loaded down with sacks and wicker baskets. Women were running in his direction and the night was so full of the sounds of doors and footsteps that he sensed the possibility that half the parish was already aware of what had happened at his brother's house. Shapes were moving in the shadows and José Guilherme was surprised they weren't speaking but only making noise with their feet. And he thought, "They must still be asleep. They're only dreaming about these events, they're dreaming about what they've been imagining for many years and they're surprised by their capacity to dream."

He was almost there when he saw a crowd of people standing by the door of the priest's house and he heard the three bells simultaneously tolling the death knell. He stood leaning on a wall and once more felt the terror of the trees at night.

"That's certainly the voice of death," he thought, quickly taking off the hat that covered his head and ears and part of his face.

His sister-in-law's fate was finally being announced to the people and it wouldn't be long before they all came out into the street in order to finish sacking the mayor's house and the Council's wine cellar. So, he thought, death was being proclaimed and the people would organize, just as João-Lázaro would attest later, to give chase to the criminal. Moments later the bells fell silent and a vibration of ringing metal remained hovering in the night. An instantaneous deafness took over José Guilherme's ears: the buzzing of a bee lost in a labyrinth or the sound of needles hanging and swaying from a tightly-drawn cord. The cord was vibrating and the needles began to tinkle. It was getting easy to imagine that the world had disappeared from the middle of his senses to the sound of that vibration when the voice of a man, the voice of Calheta the sexton, flew down from the belfry and came to light in his ears like an insect. It had the same pitch as when he made the Sunday announcements from the steps of the church, the swap of a bridle for a bit of change or a handful of seed corn, or even as charity for the souls of those present and for the love of God may they forgive his poverty or misfortune. This time, however, he was all worked up with a ragged and vaguely afflicted shout; astonished by its novelty perhaps, José Guilherme didn't receive it in his ears but in his mouth, thinking that a long-awaited god must have arrived in that parish, evident by so many indications:

"Our priest is dead!"

OUR PRIEST IS DEAD, OUR PRIEST IS DEAD, OUR
PRIEST IS DEAD,
OUR PRIEST IS DEAD, OUR PRIEST IS DEAD, OUR
PRIEST IS DEAD...

José Guilherme began to run to the end of the street and elbowed his way through the crowd there. It wasn't possible, it wasn't possible that he was living through a night like that. The women were weeping softly, because women, when they don't feel like crying, do so softly, close to the hearts of men, and the latter were striking their broad-brimmed everyday hats against their chests. No one could hear them murmur a single word, but José Guilherme sensed they were praying silently. It wasn't true they were only doing it for the soul of Father Governo, but rather for the fact they'd been waiting over sixty years for his death and it had finally happened, even after such a long delay.

People ceaselessly went in and out. Some were crossing themselves because they'd seen a saint, others because they'd seen that the Devil certainly couldn't have been any uglier or more frightful than the body of a priest. He decided to go in, too, to pay his last respects. What impressed him most, however, was him lying like that: all dressed up with his nostrils wide open and his stomach swollen tight as a bass drum, a sack of sand, or maybe only a fermenting vat of wine, while his ears, still and always devoid of sound, had grown until they were the size of a donkey's. He had, as well, a very high and ashen forehead, while the skin of his face had a bilious and dull appearance, like the wax images sleeping for centuries over an altar. Unlike all other dead people, Father Governo wasn't smiling, because he held his teeth ready to bite his soul at the moment of flight; it could be seen, furthermore, that the separation must have been difficult because his face kept the tight expression of a refusal or even a revolt against that kind of passion that had come to snuff out his last candle, the final moon of his spirit.

"He was as ugly," José Guilherme said later to João-Lázaro, "as the ugliest animal in creation. He had something like the ugliness of a cross between a bear and a camel, or even worse. The ugliness of a skull squashed by the hoof of a buffalo that had wandered off from the herd."

He stood by the corpse only for an instant, since that was all the time he would manage to see it. He ended up running off in a hurry all upset, thinking the smell was driving him mad and would cling to his skin like sealing wax for the rest of his life, because it was a combination of the characteristic odor of all priests and the intestinal smell of a dead and already decomposing priest. He began running up the street in search of João-Lázaro, to whom he would give the long tale of that night, promised a long time ago, like all the nights that will happen someday to some people on some Island, with its white sea, its snakes and knives, the despair of the gentle whales passing the chariots of the gods and their pale invisible horses running in the direction of the wind. He found out then he wasn't going along alone in those parts; going along ahead of him were the silent men of the soil, the same as always with the only difference that they were no longer the downcast creatures of days gone by, nor had their lungs been hardened by breathing rock-strewn sand wet with tears. They were

THE DIGGERS

and they had finally lost the listless movements of someone who'd learned to walk all by himself without the protection of a mother, or even the habit of walking eternally weighted down with possibly imaginary burdens. They were the Diggers and they were flying along a little ahead of him and they were going silent, sure, and serious, but not tense, because, it's said, on that night they were traveling inside other unknown nameless birds—and it's well known that birds sail over the whole world like that as they fly. And when they alight, they alight easily, joyfully…

18

THE BIRDS ALIGHT, IT'S SAID, EASILY, JOYFULLY. THEY ALSO TRAVEL IN GREAT NUMBERS, TINY AND USELESS PERHAPS IN THEIR AFFLICTION AND, LIKE RATS, THEY HAVE THE PERPLEXED VOICE OF THE GROUND WHERE THEY SOMETIMES ROOST BEFORE THEY KNOW HOW TO FLY. THEY'RE BIRDS WITH SOMBER NIGHTTIME EYES AND, IT'S SAID, THEY ALIGHT AT NIGHT, SEEING CLEARLY AND NEATLY AND SOLIDLY IN THE DARK ALL AROUND. THE WHOLE EARTH IS SMALL. AND AN INFINITE SEA, AN INFINITE SEA OF REMAINING AND DYING. AN ARRIVAL SEA THAT DOESN'T GO OFF BUT ALWAYS PROMISES, ENDS UP DRINKING IN ALL THE BIRDS' LOOKS AND WETTING WITH SALIVA THE MOUTH THAT REMAINS THIRSTY AT THE WATER'S EDGE AND DOESN'T SLEEP. THEY'RE THE BIRDS, THE NAMELESS, NUMBERLESS AZORES-BIRDS OF A WORLD WITHOUT A KINGDOM, AND I SEE THEM FLYING AS THEY ALIGHT IN THAT JOY. I KNOW I WAS BORN LIKE THAT, TOO, OUT OF THE EXTREME NAKEDNESS OF THEIR NEST, AND ONE DAY I ALIT WITH THEM ON MY BARE FEET ON THE LITTLE LAND WITH ITS VAST INFINITE DESERT OF WATER ALL AROUND.

NOTHING HAD YET BEEN WRITTEN ABOUT THESE MATCHLESS BIRDS WHOSE EXISTENCE BEGINS HERE IN THAT SO VERY SOBER BREATHING OF THEIR VOYAGE THROUGH ME. THEY ALREADY POSSESSED SWEAT, OBVIOUSLY, AND WITHIN THAT SWEAT THE INITIAL PLACE WITH A BREATHING AS SIMPLE TO UNDERSTAND AND LOVE AS THE SMILE OF AN ANGEL.

YOU DON'T KNOW WHAT PLACE?

YOU DON'T KNOW, DON'T KNOW, DON'T KNOW. BECAUSE YOU WERE NEVER ABLE TO LEARN THE WAY IN WHICH SALT FORMS, REFORMS, DEFORMS, AND THEN DEVOURS THE BONES AND LOOKS OF THESE AZORES-BIRDS. THEY MAY BE LIGHT AND HOLLOW AND CERTAINLY THICK. YOU CAN MOST CERTAINLY LIFT THEM UP, THE BONES, TO THE HEIGHT OF YOUR SUN WITH ITS IMMENSE GAZE: BUT THE BONES, THE BONES OF THE BIRDS IN THE AZORES IN THE END ARE THE PRODUCTS, THE (WHITE) SUN, THE SIGNS, THE SOUNDS THEMSELVES, AND, IT'S SAID, EVEN THE COUNTLESS PLACES WHERE EARLY AND TO STAY MANY, ALMOST ALL, OF THEIR MASTERS ARRIVED.

Acknowledgements

Thanks first of all to João de Melo for trusting his work with Aliform Publishing, and to Gregory Rabassa, from whom I long ago learned about the human quality of literature and whose generosity of spirit made this book possible. My great friend Marco Lamoyi offered his painting as cover art. Katherine Vaz provided a luminous contextual introduction; much appreciation to Prof. Onésimo Almeida of Brown University for putting us in touch with Ms. Vaz, and for his help with vocabulary questions. Julie Popkin first facilitated contact between Aliform and Dr. Ray-Güde Mertin, Literarische Agentur; gratitude as well to Julie for her insight and advice about publishing in general. Tamara Sellman saw the import of this work long before any other literary critic in the country. Maria Paula Lacerda and João Carlos Cordeiro da Ponte tracked down vocabulary and regionalisms of the Azores. Carolyn Fox was as ever a most patient graphic designer. Finally, to *la flaca, con ojos que sin palabras hablan*: my everything for always assuring me that dreams can become reality.

J. Miskowiec, City of Lakes, 2003